Praise for Cassandra Dean

I fell in love with this book from the first bewildering, smoldering scene, and was captivated until the last page.
– The Romance Reviews

With just a whisper, a caress, or a simple kiss, Ms. Dean takes the reader on an adventure full of hedonistic pleasure as well as bittersweet moments.
– Coffee Time Romance

Be prepared to experience a wide range of emotions. I found myself laughing, crying, blushing and even yelling at times.
– Romancing the Book

CASSANDRA DEAN

DEAN

Teach Me

By Cassandra Dean

Enslaved
Teach Me
Scandalous
Rough Diamond
Fool's Gold
Emerald Sea
Silk & Scandal
Silk & Scorn
Silk & Scars
Silk & Scholar
Silk & Scarlet
Slumber
Awaken
Finding Lord Farlisle
Rescuing Lord Roxwaithe
Stealing Lord Stephen

To the back of those grey heads on a bus in Scotland.
If I'd found you remotely interesting, none of us would be here.

CASSANDRA DEAN

Teach Me

Chapter One

SHE WAS INSANE. SHE had to be.

Elizabeth balled her hands in her lap, training her eyes forward even as she was dying to explore the whole establishment. The brief glimpse she'd had as she'd been led to this rather benign sitting room a half hour before would inspire curiosity in even the most sedate of women.

All had been red—red walls, red hangings, red floors—and yet somehow the décor still seemed mundane. Surprisingly, the walls sported portraits of the queen, rather tastefully framed. It was probably meant to be ironic, and there was no doubt if Her Majesty knew of the portrait's placement, she would be ill amused. However, it was not as if she would ever know. Really, who would tell a queen, especially one as obsessed with propriety as Victoria, her portrait graced the wall of this place?

Oh, but such inconsistencies were maddening. With the décor and the portraits, the hallway would not have appeared out of place in her mother's home.

This only made her want to investigate further.

After all, it wasn't every day one found oneself in a brothel.

Elizabeth tightened her hands in her lap. Surely there must be some evidence of the purpose of the establishment, apart from the obvious. Paintings of nude women? Gentlemen walking the halls, without reason and ill at ease? Numerous doors had lined the walls, opening to what had to be bedrooms. How were the bedrooms decorated? Was there an illusion of gentility or were they decorated with an eye for sin? The few women she had seen on this and her previous visit could quite comfortably have attended any societal assembly. Was this then what men desired, the facsimile of propriety?

Why was this place called—? Sod it, she'd always had trouble with French. What on earth was it? Oh, *La Belle Jeune Fille Pieuse* which meant…. It meant…the beautiful, remorseful maiden. No, not remorseful, pious. Yes, the beautiful, pious maiden.

She frowned. Was it meant as irony?

Taking a breath, she looked down at her hands. Enough. Her curiosity had gotten her into trouble any number of times. If she didn't curb herself, no doubt she would leap to her feet to investigate. It had happened before and, more than like would happen again, but even she conceded one shouldn't go wandering alone in a brothel.

Absently, she rubbed her thumb and middle finger together. The kid leather of her gloves was still supple, though the seams were beginning to show their age. How long could she continue to wear the gloves before they fell apart? Rocksley had given her this pair on the occasion of their engagement, and while their marriage had not turned out to be all she had dreamt, they reminded her of a happier time, when her life was before her and so very exciting.

A smile tugged at her as she thought of those days anew. The balls, the dancing, the stolen kisses Rocksley had pressed upon her. Remembered excitement bubbled through her as memory touched his lips to hers once more, the brush of his mouth as sweet as the champagne she had so daringly enticed him to consume.

Her smile dimmed. Rocksley was gone now, these three years past.

The door opened. Immediately Elizabeth stood, a little too fast if truth be told, pulling the panels of her cloak together as she did so. The ensemble was too dramatic, but really what does one wear to a brothel, at least, if one was not going to employ their services? Well, maybe she *was* going to employ their services, but not in the usual way. Then again, what did she know of the usual way? It could be women sought their services daily. The name of *La Belle* had easily been obtained, and perhaps Lady Wright's knowledge of the place had a more intimate acquaintance than she supposed—

Stop it, Elizabeth.

Taking a steadying breath, she looked toward the door, pasting on what must undoubtedly appear a false smile. She knew why she prattled silently. Nerves were besting her, and she always blathered on when she was nervous.

A man entered instead of the madam she expected. Surprise rid her of nerves. His cold gaze raked over her and, from his lack of expression, very little about her impressed him. Unfortunately, the same could not be said for him.

He wasn't beautiful. He was too haughty for

that, but something about his bold features, his strong jaw, his jet-black hair, and ice blue eyes combined to make him absolutely compelling. Dark hair curled gently from a centre part, shorter than most men would wear. Even his sideburns were shorter, stopping just as his cheekbones began. Did this display a concession to fashion, or a flaunting of it?

His garb, however, caused no such doubt. Dressed in the height of fashion, an exquisitely tailored coat hugged his form, outlining broad shoulders and a slim waist. Pale grey trousers contrasted with the unrelieved black of his coat, exhibiting his form to perfection. How very disappointing if he wore padding, but such a form could not be natural, could it?

He could not be an employee, not with those clothes and that demeanour. Who had the madam of this establishment sent in her stead? He had to be a member of the aristocracy, nothing else would explain his appearance. Good Lord, what was Mrs. Morcom about with this?

While she was low enough in society to pass almost unnoticed no matter what her discretion, Elizabeth still had some reputation to maintain. However, she had placed her trust in the madam. She would believe Mrs. Morcom would not steer her wrong.

She refused to think anything but the best.

Unaccustomed sensations ran through her, hot, sudden and impossible to discern for their contradiction. Excitement? Trepidation? Something about him spoke to her, and she couldn't for the life of her understand why. For all his seriousness, Rocksley had been quick to smile. Even Farindon, her one descent into wickedness, had been affable, though he insisted on the façade of an unrepentant rake.

This man now before her, he was cold. Hard.

Unable to swallow past the sudden constriction of her throat, she wondered, quite insanely, what it would take to thaw him.

"You are here to see Mrs. Morcom?"

His voice rushed through her, rich and decadent, and the clipped precision of his words confirmed him as an aristocrat. How would it sound lowered and husky, whispering over her bare skin as he detailed all he would do to her?

Elizabeth blinked. What on earth had come over her? She never thought such things, and never about a stranger. In a brothel.

A brothel.

For all she had planned, the pursuit that had seemed so perfect only moments ago abruptly appeared unwise.

"Well?" Though the word implied impatience, the man himself displayed no irritation, instead continuing to regard her in that cold, hard manner.

Affecting a smile to disguise her imbecilic turn, she held out her hand to shake as a man might, attempting a sophistication she most certainly didn't feel. "Yes, I am here to see Mrs. Morcom. I take it she is on her way?"

He glanced at her hand, then back at her.

Smile faltering, she dropped it back to her side. Humiliation began a slow burn, his disdainful gaze intimating clearer than any words how foolish she was to offer her hand.

She squared her shoulders. No one would make her feel a fool. She was bold and brave, and no one else of her acquaintance had the stomach to pursue what they wanted the way she had. Lifting her chin, she dared him to comment.

He, however, appeared to have already forgotten his slight. "Mrs. Morcom told me of your desire. I am here to fulfil your request."

She could not have heard him correct. "I beg your pardon?"

"I assure you, I am more than qualified. If you require references, I can provide excellent recommendations."

"No, no, I believe you." She had the distinct feeling he was mocking her, but no matter if he was. Placing a hand over her heart, she tried to calm the racing organ. "I was under the impression my education would be verbal, conducted by Mrs. Morcom."

His expression remained unchanged as he offered neither reassurance nor comment. Damnation, would her stomach never cease its nervous churning! She refused to feel nerves and indecision. After the obscene amount of effort she'd expended to convince herself to pursue this goal, no one—not even herself— would sway her from her course. Nothing in life was as expected. Why had she thought this to be any different?

The silence in the room was deafening. Why couldn't she hear outside the room? Was it soundproofed? Anything could be going on, even in the harsh light of day, and no one would be the wiser—

Taking breath, she forced a stillness to her thoughts.

They stood, staring at one another.

"Remove your cloak." His words sounded abnormally loud in the hush.

A moment passed. What should she make of such a command? She didn't know whether to snap to obey, or be offended he expected her to comply.

Her chin lifted. No matter. She had come this far. She would not let a small thing like this man's arrogance stand in her way. And so she complied with his command.

With narrowed eyes, he raked her from head to toe, his face ever expressionless. She felt naked without her cloak, which was patently ridiculous as she was wearing at least four layers of cloth between her flesh and his gaze, so there was no cause for these nerves.

She *would* conquer this anxiety.

"I believe it should be no hardship to educate you," he said.

Inwardly, she heaved a sigh of relief. Thank the Lord, his assessment of her had finished. "That is, if you are amenable?"

"Oh. Well, I suppose…." Why was she balking when what she had sought was offered? "Yes. Yes, I am amenable."

At her words, a curious release rushed through her. Good Lord, she was really going to do this.

"Excellent." He stepped forward, close enough to touch her.

She almost took a step back. He was tall, at least half a foot taller than she. His hand snaked around her neck, cupping her nape with cool fingers. Casually, he took the liberty, and she allowed it though she should object, but this too familiar touch made her breathless…expectant.

"What is it, exactly, you are hoping to learn?" His thumb gently rubbed her skin, toying with the loose strands escaping her upswept hair.

A shiver ran through her, leaving goose flesh in its wake. Should she stop him? Did she want to?

"I...well, I was hoping—" Nerves would not prevent her. Not when she had come this far. Straightening her spine, she looked him in the eye. "I wish to know carnal pleasure. Both to receive and to give."

That cold, almost beautiful face remained impassive. She didn't know why she was surprised. "To what end?"

She frowned. "End?"

"No matter." He took a step away from her, as if he needed the distance to catalogue something about her only he perceived. With the move, his hand dropped from her skin. She couldn't tell if what she felt was relief or a longing for more.

Moments passed, that impassive gaze weighing heavy upon her. An overwhelming urge to twist her fingers assaulted her, but what if her fidgeting made him refuse?

He seemed to make some decision. "I shall show you carnal pleasure, madam. As you say, both to receive and to give. However, pregnancy should be avoided at all costs." His eyes flickered, the first sign of something resembling emotion crossing his face. "I will not marry you, no matter the circumstance."

Well, of course he wouldn't. She wouldn't wed him either. In any event, conception was not a concern for her, not after a marriage that had never yielded—

Good Lord. He spoke of practical application. He spoke of touching and kissing and— Was it warmer in here of a sudden?

He continued with barely a pause. "Actual penetration will be avoided. While many people extol the virtues of withdrawal, I remain unconvinced. We will discuss methods of contraception during your education, but the most effective method is always avoidance. You are in agreement?"

Still confused but now with cheeks aflame, Elizabeth nodded. In all her life, no one had ever spoken so frankly. This, combined with his matter-of-fact manner and lack of emotion, banished any lingering apprehension and left only the excitement. Glorious, thrilling excitement.

"Excellent." Stepping close to her once more, he brushed his hand from her neck to her shoulder, the back of his fingers now warm against her skin. "Shall we begin?"

"Begin?" Blood beat a furious tattoo, the pounding of her heart frantic.

"Mayhap a demonstration?" The words sent shivers down her spine, gathering low in her belly. Her flesh prickled and heated, his voice a whisper against her skin. Never could she remember feeling like this, though she'd some notion of its cause. During her marriage, and of course on those pitiful forays into wickedness, she had felt something similar, but never this intense, this needful. What strange quirk of nature allowed her to want this man she had barely met?

His hand slid from her shoulder to her waist. Resting there a moment, the warmth of his touch lulled her, his fingers splayed wide against the small of her back. A slight nudge, and then he pulled her into him, his hold strong where before it had been lax.

Balance gone, she could only grip his shoulders and hope she didn't fall, but then his tongue traced her ear and with it, all thought dissolved. She bit her lip, barely noticing the sharp pain. Instead, she registered the hardness of his body through the cushioning of her clothing, the feel of his legs between hers. Uneven breath dragged through her lungs, her breasts pressing against him with every draw.

With a mouth suddenly gone dry, she stared at his lips. Would his kiss be the sweet giddiness of champagne bubbles? Or the rich headiness of blood-red wine?

"Would you like a demonstration?" he reiterated, his voice wrapping around her, just as she had known it would. Deep. Husky. Mesmerising. "Tell me." His lips traced the cord in her neck.

"Y-yes." The word stumbled out, made hoarse by a tone she almost didn't recognise as her own. His hand still rested on the small of her back, heavy and warm through layers of clothing. What would it feel like if those layers were removed? If his naked flesh were against hers?

"As your expectations were for a verbal tutorial, we shall begin with such." His lips brushed over her ear. "First, we must determine if my touch is something you desire. Do you want my hand on your skin, my lips tracing its path?" One hand cupped her shoulder, its twin gently trailing up her back and then down, up and down, up.... "How will you react? Will you shrink from me or will you drag me against your skin, writhing as I leave no part of you in want of my flesh against yours?"

As he formed the sentences, she couldn't look away from his lips, their shape, the movement as he enunciated. Something tugged at her deep inside.

"Will you arch against me as I kiss you? Gasp as my tongue traces your nipple? Will your breasts be so sensitive I can make you come just from caressing them, my fingers plucking at your nipples, the pleasure almost exquisitely painful?"

The world narrowed, containing only him and his words. His rich voice seduced her even as his hands stayed motionless on her body, burning through the layers of her clothing. She wanted to beg him to touch her, caress her, anything to force a distraction from the images he painted.

"I'd trace the line of your collarbone with my tongue, burying my face in your neck to nip and bite. Then I'd explore the delights between your thighs, my hand, my fingers circling closer, ever closer to where you were desperate for them to be. My thumb would trace over you and you'd drench me, telling me you want me, my cock inside you, deep and hard, and I'd make you come like that, with my thumb against your clitoris as I thrust my fingers inside you, knowing you want my cock but tormenting you with the substitute."

Elizabeth's imagination ran rife and almost she felt him there, between her thighs. Some of his words were foreign, but he left her in no doubt of their meaning. This was what he'd show her? This was what he'd teach?

"I'd bury my face between your thighs, tasting what my fingers had explored. I'd make you come that way. Then I'd make you take my cock in your mouth, watching as you gave me pleasure as I had given you. And then…." He roughly cupped her chin. Ice blue eyes burned into hers. "I'd do it all over again."

It was too much. Every part of her ached. She was wet, swollen, her nipples tight, her mouth dry, her breath catching. She wanted him closer, touching her. She wanted it so badly and with nothing more than words he had done this, created this *need* inside her.

And then, with no warning, he was no longer near.

She almost stumbled. A chill rushed through her as the warmth of his body disappeared. Taking a shuddering breath, she wrapped her arms about herself, still dazed from his verbal seduction.

That had been…. It was indescribable.

A stupid grin pulled at her. Well, that cemented it. Decidedly, she had chosen well to pursue this course. Regaining a semblance of control, she turned to face him.

Her smile died.

His expression was still dispassionate. His breathing still even. His words, those beautiful words that had conjured such desire in her, had not disturbed his cold beauty.

They had meant absolutely nothing to him.

Embarrassment suffused her, the contrast between her reaction and his too great. Of course they had meant nothing. They were a demonstration of his skill, nothing more. What must he think of her?

"That is what I can expect?" she said, hoping for dispassion yet knowing she'd failed miserably.

"Somewhat." Good Lord, his voice was as unaffected as when they had begun. "It is, of course, more titillating in practice."

Smiling weakly, she attempted to ignore her traitorous body. Lord, let it not be something she had to repeat any time soon. Even swallowing reminded her of the heat still coursing through her, of breasts too sensitive against her bodice, at the ache between her thighs.

"We will begin three days hence, after the

dinner hour. A carriage will be sent for you. I presume the madam knows of your address?"

Dumbly, she nodded. His hands were clasped behind his back, his stance indolent. He appeared bored. Was he bored? Why had he even agreed?

He continued without pause. "As I'm sure you are cognizant of your reputation, we will not continue our lessons at *La Belle*. My town house is far enough away from prying eyes to keep your reputation relatively intact." He raised a brow, as if daring her to disagree.

Like a fool, Elizabeth nodded again. There seemed little more to say.

Having obtained her acquiescence, he bowed sharply and departed.

Left alone, the import of what she'd just experienced hit her. Legs shaking, she lowered herself to the chaise. She had been seduced. In a brothel. By a man she had only just met. Dear God, she didn't even know his name. Only now, when he had left, did she realise she knew nothing about him. What did that make her?

She stood, fairly vaulting from the chaise. It made her exactly as she was before. She refused to feel ashamed. Gathering her cloak about her, she pulled the hood sharply over her head to conceal her face. Pleasure for pleasure's sake was not a crime and this man—this beautiful, cold man—was the means to discovering that pleasure.

And, when they were done, she would thank him prettily and never have to see him again.

***

MALVERN MADE HIS WAY through *La Belle*

Jeune Fille Pieuse, ignoring the curious glances of the whores employed there. *La Belle* opened its doors to patrons only after night had fallen and his very presence at this early hour appeared to have whipped frenzy in *La Belle*'s inhabitants.

He entered the madam's chamber without announcement and headed for the brandy. Pouring a glass, he took his time with the first draught, admiring the quality of the alcohol, appreciating the sweet burn of it down his throat.

Finally, he turned to face the woman lounging on the settee.

Lydia Morcom fanned herself, a faint smile playing about her lips. That smile never left her features, calculated as it was to fire a man's curiosity and stir his lust. She trained that look on him now, even as her artifice was wasted on him. He took a second draw, hardly noticing the taste as he was, instead, entertained by the faint signs of annoyance tugging at her. What would Lydia do if he drained the glass of its contents and turned on his heel? Her curiosity unassuaged, what then would she offer to sate it?

More to the point, did he particularly care? He knew enough of Lydia to know she had not offered such a diversion without some gain on her part. While it would be amusing to discover she had a vested interest, the potential for a titillating reaction was negligible.

However, he'd never let the slightness of such sway him before. He remained quiet, allowing the silence between them to deepen.

A frown lightly touched Lydia's brow. Without fanfare, she gave up her pretence, acknowledging her curiosity outweighed her false complacency. Closing her fan with a snap, she asked, "Did you enjoy my present?"

Her action highlighted the tasteful glitter of diamonds draped about her wrist, the move surely a hint for something new to adorn such a pretty appendage.

He swirled his brandy. "She seems adequate."

"Adequate. How perfectly apt. She is much like a little blonde mouse, is she not?" Lydia trailed the fan across her collarbone.

Cynical amusement wound through Malvern at her seemingly artless move, and he noted, as intended, the perfection of her skin.

"A blonde mouse with a most interesting request." Swirling the liquid inside the glass once more, Malvern contemplated this mouse who'd had the courage to enter such a bargain.

He was incognizant as to her game, but figuring her purpose was for better minds than his. She seemed so ordinary, in her serviceable clothing six months out of date. The blonde hair had curled tolerably about her face, but the sheer mass of it had made her fine features appear smaller than they were, turning a reasonably attractive woman into a plain girl. The eyes, though, they had been startling, a clear green under improbably dark brows.

"Why did she come to you?" How surprising. He genuinely wanted to know.

Lydia raised a delicate shoulder. "I have no notion. I do not even know how she became aware of this establishment. Yet, business is business, is it not?" A wicked smile curved her painted lips. "And there was the added titillation of offering something to you, my dear. Come now, it is a most splendid gift, is it not?"

"It is certainly unexpected." He tilted the glass, watching as the liquid followed the move. Would the mouse be susceptible to brandy? Maybe he could get her drunk, fuck her blind, and send her on her way.

Tilting the glass again, he abandoned the plan before it truly formed. Alas, there was no challenge in that. Surely, this brave mouse warranted some finesse, a small display of the skills she desired. "She gave no indication of what drew her here?"

A slight crease appeared on Lydia's brow before it was smoothed away with another wicked smile. Ah, so she *was* annoyed with him. No matter. It would add bite to any sexual encounter and, judging by her repeated insistence on payment for her "gift," it seemed Lydia was determined to have him fuck her.

"None whatsoever. She simply appeared, announced her desire, and looked at me most earnestly to fill it." Lydia shuddered. "Such directness is so common, no matter that she was married to a viscount. I could not help but think of you, as she stammered out her request."

For a brief moment, he saw the cunning that had enabled Lydia to rise from gutter whore to mistress of this place, a grand little corner in the elegant playground reserved for the rich and the bored. Just as quickly, her gaze shuttered.

They were much alike, he and Lydia. Always performing for an audience.

She smiled at him, that Lydia smile. "Come now, you must reward me for my generosity."

"Must I?" He examined his nails. They were a fraction longer than he liked. "Why me, and not Barton? Or Sandhurst? Or Connaught? Why not some other fool you could ensnare in your game with this woman?"

Lydia shrugged, somehow making the move appear sensual. "Look upon her as the gift I intended. Mayhap this widow will provide some diversion. She does have the makings of something out of the ordinary." The fan trailed across her scarlet lips. No doubt she was alluding to other, more pleasurable pursuits she undertook with her mouth. "I imagine she will be positively virginal. Surely that should appeal to your degenerate soul."

"I doubt I am that far gone, Lydia," he murmured, although the thought of the mousy widow debauched and sprawled across his bed held some intrigue. Mild arousal ran through him at the thought of that hair unbound and wrapped around her pale body, her fingers combing the strands that lay across her stomach only to trail below.

"My dear, I, as always, adhere to your opinion in all matters." Even he could not disguise disbelief at such an incongruous statement. Lydia adhering to his will in all things? He had yet to see that day.

"As for the widow...." She shrugged again. "I never could resist a patron who pays well."

"Ah." He finished his brandy, images of the naked widow still lurking. "The true reason will out."

"And as for you...." Glancing at him from under lowered lashes, she traced the line of her bodice, her fingers trailing delicately along her skin. "We have always dealt well in the past. Our business transactions have been mutually beneficial."

"Indeed." Curiously, Lydia's display interested him less than his imagined image of the widow. He wondered at himself. In the past, Lydia had managed without fail to pique his interest, no matter that it had been with wilder and wilder sexual peccadilloes.

However, the simple image of an unfashionable widow playing with herself held more appeal than the certainty of Lydia's well-practiced charms.

Abruptly, he felt tired. He must be getting old.

"Now." Her smile turned provocative as her eyes darkened with the stirrings of lust. "Where's my reward?" She trailed a hand up her thigh, bringing the fabric of her gown with it.

Ah. He had been correct. The coin of his body held appeal for more than one female.

He went to her, pulling her roughly against him. Lydia's eyes flashed her desire, as he'd known they would.

"I am never one to disappoint a lady," he murmured, and lowered his lips to hers.

Chapter Two

ALTHOUGH SHE WAITED AS was proper in the centre of the room, hands layered correctly before her, one over the other, and her shoulders as straight as she could manage, apprehension jerked through Elizabeth's stomach. The pretence of calm did much to soothe her, though, even as her ears were attuned to the smallest nuance of sound. No doubt she appeared the very picture of demure femininity.

A wild laugh built inside her. Oh yes. That was certainly she.

To distract herself, she studied the room. The velvet wallpaper begged to be touched, and she had to grip her hands behind her back to stop herself from doing so. Never before had she seen such an intricate pattern. Even her sister Anne, with her unhealthy obsession for refurbishing her home on a quarterly basis, had never employed so extravagant a wall covering.

A heavy wooden desk dominated, but of more interest was the enormous chair paired with it. The well-worn leather appeared buttery soft, and it was a struggle not to discover if the chair was as comfortable as it looked. Years of lessons in behaviour and deportment forbade such an action, no matter how much she wished otherwise, and the very proper-looking butler who'd ushered her into the room would no doubt be offended if he returned to catch her examining various items around the room. The man possessed more hauteur than any person she had met. Well, maybe not as much as his employer, but then, there wasn't a person alive who could match him.

Exhaling, she looked at her hands, picked at her nails. Why this anxiety? She'd been excited in the carriage. The expensive coach had arrived at her home just as the clock struck the hour and she'd hastened inside, eager to begin. Only after the carriage had reached its destination, when she had disembarked and was staring up at the stately townhouse, had her excitement abandoned her. Now here she stood, in the middle of the study of a man she barely knew. The man who was to teach her of pleasure.

Indistinct voices murmured outside the door. Abruptly, her stomach relocated somewhere around the vicinity of her knees. Refusing to let them wobble, she patted her hair, smoothed her dress, made sure all was in place.

He was here. Would he still be willing to tutor her? Would he still be as indifferent?

The door opened, and there he stood. Her tutor.

Her stomach twisted, her heart beating as if it would burst from her chest. He strode past her with no greeting, seating himself behind his desk. She watched his progress, unable to speak. Remembered sensation bombarded her, and heat flushed her cheeks. Never had she been more grateful for the layers of cloth shielding her nakedness.

To perpetuate the lie she remained undisturbed, she smiled widely and, ignoring his disdainful lift of a brow, she curtsied. She was rather proud of her curtsy. Hardly a wobble at all. "Good evening, sir. You are well, I trust?"

Amusement wound through her. Always she found herself in precarious situations. One would assume with age came wisdom or, at least, caution. Apparently, not so for her.

The beginnings of a frown crossed his face. "You should not be so open with your emotions." Opening a cigarillo case, he delicately took one of the thin cigars from its housing. "Much can be discerned from an unguarded expression. You would do well to remember that." He lit the cigarillo, his gaze level upon her as he inhaled the smoke.

Her smile faltered. Was he criticising her just because he could? Determined to maintain civility, she kept her tone even. "I shall take that under advisement, but you did not answer my question. How fare you?"

He drew on the cigarillo. "Is it really of any importance?"

With some other man, the question could have been attributed to genuine curiosity. With this one, however, it was impossible to guess his intent. Did he think the dictates of polite conversation could be contravened? Well, he would not be treating her in such a manner. She deserved respect, even if it was only a very little. "Of course it is, sir."

He exhaled. "I fare well, then."

The cloud of acrid smoke surrounded her,

burning her lungs. *Civil, Elizabeth. Remain civil.* She would not sink to his level, though it was difficult to maintain such calm as moments ticked by without an invitation for her to sit. Cigarillo smoke twined through the air as he watched her, his expression impassive.

Well, if he wouldn't say anything she would just seat herself. Perching herself awkwardly on the chair, a sudden memory arose of sneaking into her father's study as a child. Consumed with curiosity about what it was he did all day, she'd managed to disrupt every pile of correspondence, though she *had* tried to repair her error, haphazardly reassembling them in no semblance of order. The tongue-lashing she'd received when her father had caught her still had the power to make her wince.

Shifting uncomfortably, she tried to ignore the feeling she was applying like a supplicant before him. No doubt these seats were hard and unyielding to discourage one from lingering.

That infernal eyebrow rose once more. "Shall we begin?"

His tone grated her. *Calm, Elizabeth.* "How should we proceed?" she asked, ignoring her ire. "Mayhap we should establish guidelines, modes of behaviour, that type of thing."

"Indeed. Guidelines." More smoke encircled her, but she refused to react. "And what do you envision these guidelines to be?"

She snapped. "First, I should like for you not to talk to me as if I were an imbecile. I may not be as knowledgeable as you in these matters, but I possess some degree of intelligence, and I will thank you to treat me as such."

A faint smile touched his lips, and his eyes

warmed for a fraction of a second. "I shall endeavour to remember that. Anything else?"

"Yes." She lifted her chin. "I would like for this to remain solely between us. If our association were to become public knowledge, I would not like to think of the effect it would have on my family. I have taken precautions and should like it if you would also."

Her precautions included making sure her family would not question her absence. Living alone in the small townhouse she'd purchased after Rocksley's death certainly helped, but she would not bring scandal upon her family.

He inclined his head, still wearing that small smile. With the lightening of his features, he almost achieved beauty. How, then, would he look if the expression was true mirth? The image was so incongruous, she couldn't reconcile such a thing. "I should also like to know what you envision for our sessions. Is there anything you require from me?"

His smile vanished. "At this stage, nothing more is required from you. We will meet twice weekly at these premises. With the days shorter, five of the clock will suffice, both for convenience and to settle any matters of propriety. No one will question an unmarked carriage arriving at this house, and I assume none will question such an arrival at yours?"

She shook her head. "Not under the cover of dark."

He inclined his head. "We will begin, then, with the basics and move along as I determine is warranted. Is this agreeable to you?"

As she nodded, excitement bubbled within her. Good Lord, this was actually happening.

"Now, first we must establish what you know. Describe your sexual history."

Elizabeth blinked. She opened her mouth but could not think of anything to say. Indeed, her brain refused to work. It had stuttered on his words: *describe your sexual history*. He was waiting for her answer, she knew, but how could she answer? No one—*no one*—had ever said such a blatant thing to her before. "I beg your pardon?"

"I cannot help you if I am ignorant of what you know. Proceed." With the cigarillo held loosely in his fingers, he betrayed no hint he was cognizant of the impropriety of his demand—and it had been a demand.

Heat flushed her cheeks. "How do I know you are qualified? Maybe you should detail for me *your* sexual history."

Not even a flicker of reaction crossed his face. "Very well." He stubbed out the cigarillo. "My first physical encounter was with a prostitute my father engaged for me at the age of twelve. She instructed me on the basics, at which I became quite well versed in our time together. I took a second lover at fourteen, a third at fifteen, and further extended my knowledge. As a side, I found it amusing to play them off against each other."

He'd had more than one lover at the same time? Before he'd reached his majority? He must have been able to keep them all satisfied—what did he mean he'd played them off against each other? Did they compete for his affections? Well, not his affections, the man appeared to be made of stone, but, well, *what did he mean?*

"By the time I left Oxford, I had become quite versed in carnal pleasures, and embarked upon a career exclusively devoted to catering to my whims. There is little I have not undertaken."

She couldn't help but stare. He was so very different from anyone she had ever encountered. He just said things—things that were inappropriate and lewd, and not fit for a lady's ears. She loved it. "Like what?"

His brow rose. "What variations upon the basics?"

Almost afraid to breathe lest he stop, she nodded.

"I have experimented with numerous positions, with cunnilingus and fellatio. I have had two mistresses pleasure me at the same time on numerous occasions, and have had the reverse occur as well. I have attended orgies, tied my lovers up, spanked them, dominated them, been dominated, watched others as they performed, been watched, fucked men, women, anything in the course of obtaining pleasure."

"Fucked?" The unfamiliar word sounded delicious on her tongue.

"Had sexual relations, intercourse." All said so factually, so calmly, as if his words weren't of infinite fascination. "Language will also be part of your tutelage. Are my qualifications suitable?"

Men? He'd had intercourse—no, he had *fucked* men? Did men do that to each other? Don't be so naïve, you ninny. Of course they did. He'd just said so.

She couldn't decide how the information made her feel. Was she horrified? Shocked? Both those things, and undeniably fascinated. How did it even work? Had he undertaken it often? Would he expect her to somehow participate? To watch?

Finally, she was able to produce a coherent statement. "You seem more than qualified. I suppose I should start with my husband?"

"It seems logical."

"Yes." A smile tugged at her as she remembered Rocksley, the lock of too-long hair that had perpetually fallen over his brow, the feel of the silky blond strands beneath her fingers as she had swept it from his brow. "He was my first lover. He used to kiss me when we were courting, light brushes against my lips." Raising her fingers to her mouth, she could almost feel again those airy caresses, though the turn of his features was indistinct.

Her hand dropped. He'd not even been gone three years and already she had forgotten. However, her tutor could not possibly be interested in those memories. "We consummated our marriage in the usual fashion, I suppose."

"You do not know for sure?"

"It is not the type of thing one usually discusses with others." Not that it had ever stopped her from trying. "I did ask, but those I asked said my curiosity was getting the better of me, and I should be pleased it was not tedious." Her sister, Bella, had been quite emphatic on that point.

"Not tedious? Is that the extent of it?" His gaze narrowed. "Describe what your husband used to do."

Elizabeth shifted uncomfortably in her seat. "Is it really necessary? My husband *is* dead, you know."

Her tutor exhaled. "Are you interested in tutelage or not?"

"Yes."

"Then describe what he used to do."

Certain her cheeks were bright red, Elizabeth averted her gaze. Relating the intimate details of her marriage bed would be much easier if she couldn't see that cold face. "My husband, well, he would tell me he planned to visit me that evening, and I, well, I would prepare. He'd arrive in my bedchamber and he would kiss me gently, raise the hem of my night-rail and…." She swallowed, beyond uncomfortable. "Well, you know," she finished lamely.

"No, I don't. Describe."

"Must I?" Her fingers tapped a nervous beat against her thigh. "This is very difficult for me."

"If you are truly committed to this process, you must know we will be dealing with things more intimate than this. This is nothing. Tell me."

Closing her eyes, she forced herself to continue. "He would put himself inside me, move back and forth until he was finished and then he'd kiss me on the forehead, say goodnight and leave. I would then rise, bathe myself, and go to sleep." Opening them, she found him considering her.

Finally, he spoke. "That was all he would do?"

She regarded him uncertainly. His tone gave no indication how she should answer. "Well, yes. Isn't that what most husbands do?"

"Some." He rubbed his finger against his lip. "Is that the extent of your experience?"

"Um…." Should she tell him? Damnation, she was determined to learn what she could about pleasure, and he was right. As he'd intimated, if she couldn't speak frankly, there was no point to any of this. "I took a lover about a year after my husband's death." She didn't look at him. "He was very kind and made me feel lovely. We only met three times. He kissed me more than my husband did, and differently. His, well, his tongue was involved." Was it possible for one to expire of embarrassment? "Also, there was no bed available, so he would, um, he would…."

She could do this. She could.

"He would take me from behind, which I didn't

know was actually possible, but, well, of course it is, and it felt quite good actually, and he would caress my, um, my bosom and…." *Finish it, Elizabeth.* "We never undressed. They were fleeting encounters, at social gatherings. Three social gatherings. Balls, actually."

His brows had drawn together into something not quite a frown. What did he think of her? Surely he had done worse, and there was no censure on his face. The biggest secret she had, the one she was afraid would forever tar her depraved to the person she revealed it to, and he had no reaction. Nothing but that drawing together of brows, which could be interpreted in a hundred different ways.

She hadn't told *anyone* about Farindon. It had, however, been surprisingly easy to tell *him*, maybe because of his lack of reaction. She had no idea if she had shocked him, or disappointed him, or even interested him with her revelations. Only imagine what the reaction if she had told her sisters. Or, worse, her *mother*.

She felt free. Unencumbered. So free, in fact, that she felt another revelation was in order. "Neither of them made me feel as you did the other day."

"Indeed."

Mayhap no reaction wasn't always a blessing.

"You have given me much to contemplate," he said, as if she had revealed nothing earth shattering at all. Maybe she hadn't. After all, an almost-affair could not possibly be the most lascivious secret he had ever heard.

Determined to act as nonchalant as he, Elizabeth adopted his impassive expression. "So, what curriculum will we undertake? If it's all the same to you, I would appreciate an ordered approach.

I find I respond well to a structured course. Should I bring a notebook?" Lord, she sounded the ninny.

"A notebook will not be necessary." His fingers began a rhythmic drum against the blotter. His hands held beauty, comprised of long, lean fingers that moved gracefully as they tapped out a strangely compelling beat.

So focused was she on his hands, she almost didn't notice when he continued. "I will show you an aspect of carnality each time we meet, explaining it and answering any questions you may have. Practical demonstration will occur when necessary."

"Oh." A thought occurred. "There is more to carnal expression than intercourse and its derivatives, yes?" How could she explain? "I have heard tell of people watching others. Is that stimulating?"

"It can be. One might also masturbate when undertaking a voyeuristic pleasure."

Her brow creased. "Masturbate?"

"Yes. Have you never pleasured yourself?"

At his words, something uncurled inside her, sending out ghosts of sensation. The drum of his fingers replicated in her blood, her pulse pounding in time with the rhythmic sound.

No. Her fascination was solely intellectual. It had to be, or she would end as she had their first encounter—desperately aroused and uncomfortably aware he was not.

The drum of his fingers ceased. "Perhaps I should rephrase. Have you ever caressed yourself between your thighs?"

"N-no." *Intellectual, Elizabeth, intellectual.* "Well, I sometimes felt after my husband's visits a certain pressure. I tried to relieve it by, um, rubbing, but all that did was make it worse."

"Indeed." He was silent for a moment and, probably just to torture her, rubbed his lip. "And with your lover? Did he make you come?"

"Come?"

"Make you orgasm." His brow rose. "Do I need to explain further?"

A dim memory struggled through embarrassment, a conversation with her sister not long after Elizabeth had wed. Curious about others' experiences in the marriage bed, she had asked her sisters, each separately, about their own wedding nights. Bella had looked at her as if she were insane, claimed it was a knowledge resolved solely for husband and wife and from then on refused to speak. Catherine and Anne had simply pretended Elizabeth had never asked the question. Henrietta, however, had blushed and stammered her way through a brief description of her own experience. She had mentioned something about a release, a pleasure that came at the end of lovemaking. The description had made Henrietta blush beet red, but it had also made her look…the look had been indescribable. Happy and smug and blissful and…well. And.

During those moments with Farindon, there had been heat and swiftness and some sort of release. The feelings had grown more intense with each encounter and could have possibly reached the heights described—albeit badly—by Henrietta. Elizabeth remembered quite clearly looking forward to the next time they would meet. However, Farindon had called a premature end to their barely-begun affair, and she had lacked the courage to venture again into wickedness. Until now.

Her tutor stared at her. Oh. He was still waiting for an answer. "Um, I believe he may have."

"Indeed. You do realise that if you are not sure then he probably didn't?"

How could a man with such impassive features convey condescension with such aplomb? Yet, for all of that, it didn't seem malicious.

He was so very odd.

"I want you to pleasure yourself tonight. A curriculum shall be created for you before we next see each other, but to begin, I want you to make yourself come." He paused. "Do you need for me to detail what you should do?"

"T-tonight?" Was this what her mother had meant when she had warned Elizabeth about her curiosity?

"Or when you feel most comfortable." Standing, he moved around the table to pull her from her chair. There was that strength again, just as when he had held her at *La Belle*. Exhilaration ran through her, stealing her breath. It was indecent she should find it so very attractive.

"When you are in your bed, part your legs and caress yourself here." He placed his hand over the juncture of her thighs.

She forced herself to relax. No doubt they would get more intimate than this. Besides, there were layers upon layers of clothing between them. Layers upon layers.

He was so close. Too close. His lips brushed her ear and sensation shivered along her skin. "You will want to concentrate on your clitoris." He exerted a slight pressure, parting her thighs as his fingers delved deeper. Even through the layers of fabric, she felt the caress.

"It's here, buried between your labia." His longest finger pressed against her. "It is best if you discover what gives you most pleasure, but pay particular attention to that area. If you combine that attention with penetrating yourself, most likely with your fingers, you should be able to make yourself come."

Her mind stuttered on the phrase. "Most likely with my fingers?"

"Yes." He released her and settled once more into the soft leather of his chair. She sank back into her own uncomfortable one, unaccountably bereft at the loss of those warm hands. "This has turned into an impromptu lesson. That was not my intention. However, there are many devices to stimulate sexual desire and some to assist in masturbation. One such item is an artificial penis. It can be made out of many materials—leather, ivory, jade. I have seen a few made of wood."

"Oh." All this information was too much. It was insane, and titillating, and, beyond all, marvellous.

She could still feel his hand between her thighs.

He rose to his feet. "I believe we shall deal quite well together. Shall we say three days hence?"

She rose as well, fairly exhausted from the interview. "Three days." A sudden thought pierced her dazed mind. "I'm terribly sorry, but I don't know your name."

"Malvern."

"Malvern?" He didn't elaborate. Was it his last name? His title?

"Yes."

She could really grow to hate that impassive stare. "Well, I'm Elizabeth. I mean, Lady Rocksley." Good Lord, was she a twit for giving him her true name? Well, too late now. Taking a breath, she said, "My name is Elizabeth. Thank you for doing this."

He inclined his head and the next thing she knew, she had been ushered out of the house and was resting comfortably once more in his expensive carriage.

She leaned back against the plush seat, the velvet cool against her fingers. Was she truly going to continue with this?

Plucking at the pile, she grinned. How could she resist?

Chapter Three

DRUM, DOUBLE BEAT. DRUM, double beat.

The sound of Malvern's fingers against his desk slowly drove Elizabeth insane. He pounded out the beat absently, his gaze locked upon her as if he were contemplating some great mystery—what, she didn't know. At least, she hoped she didn't. Oh God, he wasn't contemplating severing their association, was he?

Drum, double beat. Drum, double beat.

Upon her arrival, Malvern had greeted her with a curt nod and an instruction to sit in the chair placed before his desk which, thankfully, was of greater comfort than the last. And then, the lecture had begun. The whole of his speech thus far had been tedious and dry, about anatomy of all things, and it had taken all her restraint to refrain from insisting he skip to something vaguely interesting. Apparently, though, he had a plan, even if it was a plan that invoked extreme boredom.

Now, though, he simply sat and stared.

Chewing her lip, she watched as he drummed. Why weren't they progressing to the practical side of their sessions? Surely, she should once again feel his hands upon her, his lips brushing her ear as he whispered erotic delights. Heart racing, blind eyes staring at nothing, heat and tension and breath caught.

His fingers beat out that rhythm. Drum, double beat. Drum, double beat.

She had been glad he'd asked nothing of her upon her arrival as she'd not had the courage to undertake the directive he'd issued at their previous meet. She just couldn't bring herself to do it. Of what import was it anyway? None, obviously, or he would have ascertained if she had…. *Good Lord, Elizabeth, just say it.* If she had masturbated.

Drum, double beat. Drum, double beat.

Miserably, she watched him, almost seeing him form the words in his mind to end their lessons. She'd be back where she'd begun, lacking knowledge and tutor and having to apply to Mrs. Morcom once more. Dear God, she didn't want that to happen. What she'd gone through to get to this stage she couldn't go through again. She just couldn't. Besides, she wanted *him* to teach her.

Much of her thoughts these past three days had been devoted to him. Their last meeting had fired all manner of curiosity in her, and a thousand questions she'd wished she'd asked had tormented her.

Her eldest sister had commented on her distraction earlier this week, Henrietta's words showing her concern even as she'd extracted her youngest son's hand from a flower pot. Only yesterday, her middle sister had taken her to task for her lack of focus at their book discussion. Elizabeth couldn't even remember what book it was they were supposed to have read. When she'd asked for the hundredth time, Bella had glared. Bella was very good at glaring. How, though, could Elizabeth be expected to concentrate on a novel when there was the much more interesting puzzle of her tutor to solve?

With all the discretion she could muster, she had inquired about him. She had learned Malvern was his title. He was, in fact, the Earl of Malvern, a rather lofty personage to be her tutor. She'd known he was high-born but the revelation of his status, so far above her, had set her to concern, and she'd been certain intimidation would seize her at their next meet. So far, she'd yet to succumb.

He was still drumming. Still staring. Drum, double beat.

Apparently, Malvern had quite the reputation, one not fit for a young widow's ears, or so Bella's husband had told her. When a frown had begun on Burfield's too-handsome face, Elizabeth had turned the attention to other things even as she'd wondered what could possibly have been so dreadful she was too delicate to hear it. Malvern himself had told her of his history. It had seemed no worse than the exploits of which her brothers-in-law had boasted, when it was late and they were drunk and they had no notion she was listening in on them.

The drumming ceased. "This does not appear to be working."

Her heart stopped. Simply stopped in her chest. "What doesn't appear to be working?"

Malvern rose and made his way to stand before her. From his greater height, his gaze swept her from head to toe. She averted her gaze. The man could unsettle a statue with such a gaze.

"I have gone about this all wrong. I have been lecturing on things that are better demonstrated. I apologise for my mistake." Pulling her to her feet, his hand settled on her shoulder. "Allow me to rectify it."

Tremulous hope rose. "You are continuing with my lessons?"

"Of course, my dear. I am simply changing the means of delivery."

Closing her eyes briefly, she exhaled. Thanks be to all that was holy and decent. She really couldn't have gone through the process of finding a tutor all over again.

His hands drifted to the line of buttons marching down the front of her dress and, without leave or warning, flicked open the button at the hollow of her neck. Then, he opened the next. And the next.

"Does the change require my dress to become undone?" Her words sounded light, playful, and at complete odds with the anxiety inside her.

"To begin with." His gaze settled on her. "Shall I continue?"

She wet her lips. Hands still, he waited, his expression giving no hint as to his thoughts.

In for a penny, in for a pound. Tilting her head, she allowed him access to her buttons. "Please do."

Bending once more to his task, he flicked the tiny buttons open, the number and size of them making his progress slow. Each torturous second robbed her a little more of breath.

"Why do you wear such ugly gowns?" Another button flicked open. "The colours ill suit you, and you appear to have a pleasing shape. Why do you not take advantage of it?"

"I don't know." The sight of his fingers working the buttons mesmerised her. Men's hands had always been her weakness. Gloves usually disguised them, but his were bare, the fingers long and elegant, firm muscles shifting as he opened her to his gaze.

"We will do something about your wardrobe." He muttered a curse at a particularly stubborn button. "You are to wear less cumbersome garments in the future. I do not want to fight a plethora of buttons each time you come to me."

A thrill went through her at his words, at the implication of more to come.

Finally reaching her waist, he parted the fabric of her gown. His beautiful, elegant fingers ran over the edge of her corset and tangled in the delicate lace of her chemise.

"You will also ensure your corset is loose." His eyes followed the path of his fingers. "I will not fight undergarments either."

Her flesh rose and fell beneath his hand, the fabric of the chemise a negligible barrier. Eyes wide, she watched him. He gave no sign he noticed her stare, instead dipping his fingers below the fabric of her chemise to brush the top of her breasts.

The bodice of the gown fell easily from her shoulders when pushed, and she felt his fingers trace lightly over her collarbone. An oddness filled her, a kind of emptiness and, unable to breathe, she stood almost frozen as his fingers traced the line of the chemise.

His hand continued down her body, resting at her stomach, letting the weight and warmth seep through her clothing but a moment before lazily retracing the path. The corset had loosened enough so her breasts were no longer contained by the starched fabric and, cupping her, he swept a thumb over the upper curve. "Do you know the proper name?"

"My breast." She couldn't help but to arch her back.

"And this?" His thumb circled her nipple, making the taut flesh ache.

Dear God, it was difficult to talk. "My nipple."

"Good." Somehow, without her notice, he had taken advantage of her lowered corset, arranging her on the edge. The boning of the corset thrust her breasts toward him, and the feel of cool air washing over her exposed flesh made her gasp.

He took a step back. She swallowed a protest, wanting his hands on her, not resting uselessly at his sides. Now that he was no longer touching her, now that the heat of his hands had been replaced by the cool air of the room, she became aware she was half-naked and, good Lord, he was fully clothed. A dull flush heated her flesh, dimming the arousal he had stirred so easily.

His eyes swept over her, his perusal intensifying the flush marking her skin. "How do you like to be touched?"

"I don't know." She shook her head in an attempt to clear it. "It's why I came to you."

"You do know." Lord, his *voice*. "Show me."

Arousal flared again, embroiling her once more in sensation. Biting her lip, she raised her hands to her breasts. Uncertain, she let them rest there, his impassive gaze giving no hint of how to proceed. "I don't know what to do."

Silence weighed heavy, as heavy as his gaze.

Finally, he spoke. "Circle your nipple with your fingers."

Hesitantly, she undertook his direction. As she traced the puckered flesh, flutters of sensation streaked through her. Blood pulsed, beating a demanding rhythm, and she took her bottom lip between her teeth, the slight pain giving her some much needed clarity.

"Trap your nipple between your fingers, pulling outward. Gently."

Following his direction, she gasped as pleasure arrowed through her. Overcome by boldness, she closed her eyes, cupping her breasts as her thumb feathered over her nipple, her nail scraping the tip. The pleasure intensified, grew until it couldn't be contained, her knuckles worrying and pinching the puckered flesh of her nipples, the delicate underside of her breast.

The sensation plateaued. Frantic, she tried to force it higher but her hands weren't enough. Something was missing.

Frustrated, she opened her eyes. He was staring at her breasts, his stance unnaturally still.

"I need more." When had her voice become so hoarse?

At her words, he lifted his gaze and she shuddered at the heat banked behind ice. He took a step toward her, then another, looming closer, his body blocking the room, until all she could see was him.

And then he replaced her hands with his mouth.

She moaned at the sensation, at the hot wetness of his mouth covering her, his tongue flicking her nipple. His teeth gently worried her as his hand shaped her breast, mimicking the movements she had discovered only moments before. Tangling her fingers in his hair, she held him to her and pushed herself further into his touch.

Abruptly, he gathered her in his arms. She gripped his shoulders as he lifted her, arousal melting through her at the ease of his handling. He laid them both on the chaise lounge, her leg falling to the floor so that he was cradled between her thighs. Before she could gain her bearings, he bent his head, enveloping her nipple once more and all thought vanished. Clutching at the material covering his shoulders, her head fell back as a moan gathered in her throat.

He pushed his hands under her skirts, raising the material so her legs were exposed. She should protest, but what she was feeling, what he was making her feel…. Skin tight, breath trapped, she couldn't—

His fingers trailed over her drawers and then slipped inside, whispering over her damp flesh as his mouth pulled at her breasts. Over and over his fingers played and she wanted him closer, deeper. Then he parted her, pressing against something that made pleasure streak through her like wildfire. A shriek ripped from her, and she didn't care she sounded like an idiot, she didn't care as long as he kept doing what he was doing, his fingers gently pinching, his thumb gently rubbing.

"This is your clitoris." His eyes glittered as he spoke. "It enables a woman to feel sexual pleasure. A good lover will know where and how to manipulate it for the woman to come."

She barely heard his words, distracted by the feel of him between her thighs, on the stunning pleasure he was wringing from her.

"I could make you come from doing this, from my fingers against your flesh." He flicked.

She moaned. He could do whatever he wanted,

if he would just do *that*.

His lips quirked. "However, I believe something else is warranted."

His body slid down hers. The muscles in her neck gave out, and her head dropped back. She wasn't sure what he was about, but no doubt it would be—

She sat bolt upright, shock dispelling her arousal. "What are you doing?"

His shoulders had pushed her knees wide, and he was between them, his breath warm on her core. Squirming, she tried to push him away, battling to close her legs.

Grasping her thighs, he forced her to remain open. "Teaching you."

And then he put his mouth on her.

She gasped, her hands braced against the lounge. This was…it was…she abandoned the thought as his tongue traced her, flicked her, sent waves of pleasure through her until she was certain she would explode. It kept building and building and building, all centred on him, on what he was doing.

He played with her, explored her, his clever tongue showing her things she could never have imagined, and she pushed herself against him, her legs falling open of their own accord. His hands free now, he used them, his fingers tracing her and then thrusting into her. It felt so good, he felt so good, and she loved what he was doing to her. She loved it, and she was a bloody genius for finding this, for pursuing it and oh God, what did he just do?

She screamed, her eyes flying open, panic and something else building in her, something dark and wonderful, and then everything inside her seized, pleasure holding her captive as waves of startling intensity broke over her.

Reality returned slowly. Harsh breath forced air back into her lungs, and the coolness of the room dried the perspiration on her skin. At some stage, she had collapsed, her legs spread wantonly before her.

Dear Lord. That had been…. She had no words to describe it. A stupid grin split her face. A bloody miracle, is what it was.

It could have been minutes or it could have been hours when finally she found the strength to sit up. Malvern was sitting on his haunches before her, his forearms balanced on his thighs. This time, he did not appear as unaffected. Perverse pride battered her at the proof outlined by his trousers.

His brow quirked in query. "I take it you enjoyed that?"

"Whatever gave you that idea?" More than like he could read her emotion in the stupid grin stretching her mouth, the one that just wouldn't go away.

His demeanour never softened. She didn't care, though. She felt wonderful, absolutely wonderful. And he had made her feel that way.

"Thank you." Elation bubbled inside her. "Thank you so much."

"My dear," he said. "That was only the beginning."

Chapter Four

BOOK LYING FORGOTTEN IN her lap, Elizabeth could no longer maintain the pretence that she was even slightly interested in reading the story detailed within its pages. Instead, she saw her tutor, his gaze on her as he undid each button of her dress, his hands steady as he opened her to his gaze. Once again, she felt the soft strands of his dark hair slipping through her fingers, the silkiness of the skin at his temples. Again his lips nudged her, encompassing her in wet and warmth. His hands firm at her back, pushing her into the slide of his mouth as he nipped and licked and sucked.

A moan escaped her.

The drawing room came back in a rush. Good Lord, had anyone heard? Horrified, she looked about. Dear Lord, please, do not let anyone have heard her. None stared, so she must have escaped notice. Thank goodness.

Her heart slowing to a normal rhythm, she scowled down at the book sitting so innocuously in her lap. The silly thing was responsible for her current woes. It was supposed to be interesting. Exciting. Something to distract her from thoughts about her first lesson.

She couldn't even remember what the book was about.

Sighing, she glanced around her, hoping observation of her fellow guests would distract her more successfully. To her right, Henrietta and Anne were conversing with Lady Cartwright, an old friend of their mother's. Both sat straight-backed on the chaise lounge, rapt expressions on their faces.

Lady Cartwright's face was hidden, but Elizabeth could well imagine her expression. Her ladyship excelled at quiet disappointment, a look Elizabeth had engendered repeatedly. Many a time that look had quelled Elizabeth to the point where she'd dread a visit with Lady Cartwright, as she knew at some point that look would make an appearance. Her mother, conscienceless brute that she was, had allowed her friend free reign to dispense the look as she saw fit, claiming it was more effective at curbing Elizabeth's wilder impulses than anything else she knew.

Imagine the look if Lady Cartwright knew of Elizabeth's latest adventure?

Not even the threat of the look, however, could keep her from her lessons. Actually, there didn't seem much that would keep her from returning to her tutor's door, ready and eager for further enlightenment. Lord, one lesson and she was a fiend, but how could she think of anything else?

Her tutor. The caress of his voice. The whisper of his breath. The feel of him against her skin, her flesh, her core.

Henrietta laughed.

Elizabeth started, her heart tripping erratically. Oh Lord, she had done it again. She *had* to stop thinking of him. Tucking one hand tightly in the other, she undertook a concentration on her sisters. And—because she was desperate—Lady Cartwright.

Anne was displaying her version of grinning, that sedate half-smile she insisted was an appropriate display of mirth. Lady Cartwright's back was, well, Lady Cartwright's back. It could be her shoulders were a fraction less stiff.

Elizabeth's brows drew together. Surely, they had exhausted all gossip at the dining table? The three of them had huddled together through the courses, their conversation confined to each other. However, did she really have care for what they discussed? If they wished to limit their conversation to each other, it was of no concern to her.

After the meal, the ladies had left the men in favour of this drawing room. No doubt the dining room now saw an orgy of port swilling, cigar smoke, and tall tales that couldn't be uttered in the presence of ladies. A time or two, her curiosity had compelled her to eavesdrop on these allegedly lurid conversations, but each and every time she'd been overwhelmingly disappointed. The anecdotes she heard had been of little note, with nothing racier than the purchase of a mistress discussed. Maybe the best tales were saved for a gentlemen's club, a venue she'd unfortunately never found a way to infiltrate.

Tonight, well, she had no need to seek out wild tales. Tonight, she would simply recall her own adventure.

Catherine was playing cards with Viscountess Patton and Lady Amelia. Mother and daughter currently trounced Catherine while Catherine's partner, a lady whose name Elizabeth could never remember, valiantly tried to save her. Lady Amelia and Catherine had been fast friends from infancy, and the third lady—what was her name?—appeared to be some sort of relation to Lady Amelia. Oh wonderful, she couldn't remember her name, but she remembered the familial relationships. *Well done, Elizabeth*.

The meal, though, that had been sublime, Viscountess Patton surpassing all previous efforts yet again. Elizabeth had been particularly enamoured of a creamy pasta dish, some Italian fare the Viscountess had declared her new Italian chef had created. Conversation around the table had flowed easily, apart from Henrietta, Anne, and Lady Cartwright. Elizabeth had remained quiet for most of the meal, for how could she speak when she had thoughts of her tutor to so pleasantly distract her?

No point pretending interest where there was none. Closing the book, she plastered as innocuous an expression as she could muster on her features.

What would it be like if *he* were here? Again and again he would draw her gaze, to the exclusion of all else. In minutia she would examine him, the way he moved, the flawlessness of his dress, the lack of interest in his gaze. Perfection such as his screamed to be mussed and the desire to do so would overwhelm her.

In the presence of others, distance must be maintained and so she would make him notice her in recompense for her notice of him. He would level that cold gaze on her, his features expressionless, and his very coldness would stoke a fire inside her, flames licking her belly, her flesh, between her thighs. An arched brow would communicate her wishes and he would come to her, take her out of the room, take her somewhere deserted and—

"What are you smiling about?" Bella's frown was ferocious, suspicion lending her face an unattractive cast.

"Oh, nothing of any great consequence." Elizabeth fought to contain her smile, but the wicked shape of it refused to be cowed.

Bella's scowl grew fiercer. "That I refuse to believe. You have sat there with a smug look on your face all evening. I demand to know what put it there."

Elizabeth drawled, "Demand?" Lord, she sounded just like him. A shiver went through her as she remembered that husky voice, lowered and rough against her ear.

Bella's breath exploded. "You are so very annoying, Elizabeth. Why did Mama and Papa have to burden me with a younger sister?"

"Divine justice? By all accounts, you plagued our elder sisters."

"I was two when you were born, you idiot. Are you claiming I was so prodigious a child, I was an annoyance to our sisters at such a young age?"

That was exactly what Elizabeth was implying, and according to the stories their elder sisters told, she wasn't far wrong.

Bella crossed her arms, apparently deciding that particular argument settled. Elizabeth didn't have the heart to dissuade her of that notion. "Are you going to tell me what has put such a look on your face?"

If Bella knew, if she'd known a virtual stranger had touched her sister, had caressed her, put his mouth and his hands on her, had made her body come so gloriously alive and taught her things she had only ever imagined…if Bella knew, that imperious look would be wiped from her face.

Two more days. She'd only had to wait two more days.

Bella made a sound of disgust. "You are not going to tell me, are you?"

Elizabeth smiled the most annoyingly bright smile she could manage. Bella's lips twitched, though she tried to maintain her ire.

They had ever behaved thus. Bella was adversarial by nature, so the only way to hold one's own against her was to be as stubborn as she. Besides, Elizabeth didn't want to tell Bella about her lessons. They were hers and hers alone, not to mention if Bella *did* know, it would shock the life out of her.

Next time, would he let her touch him? Would he let her put her palm against his chest and feel the beat of his heart against her skin? His muscles would twitch beneath her fingers and she'd watch her progress, watch her pale hand against his skin. Her mouth would dry and her chest would ache and she would want so intensely for him to touch *her*—

"What are Henrietta and Anne discussing so intensely with Lady Cartwright?"

Damnation, she'd descended into distraction again. Wrenching herself away from those too-alluring thoughts, she looked over at their sisters. A crease formed between her brows. They really did seem fascinated by Lady Cartwright. What could the woman possibly be saying to them that warranted such attention? "I don't know. It must be thrilling, though."

"Well, go find out."

"I? Why do I have to find out?"

Bella sighed, probably in exasperation. Bella

was nothing if not predictable. "Isn't that what you do? You find out things. So go. Find out."

"What do you mean, I find out things?"

Bella appeared as though she were trying to force Elizabeth to move through sheer will. Simply raising a brow disabused Bella of that notion. Concealing a grin at her sister's scowl, she could see why Malvern found such an action so effective.

With a huff, Bella finally answered. "Elizabeth, you have always pushed things too far. You ask inappropriate questions, do inappropriate things, and care nothing for the disorder you cause. So," Bella sat back, crossing her arms over her chest, "Find out."

Well. Maybe Bella wasn't so predictable after all.

Averting her gaze, she considered her tightly clasped hands. Bella couldn't mean that. Look at her. She couldn't. She couldn't just say that and blithely continue with her perusal of Henrietta and Anne and mean it.

Elizabeth pressed her hand against her stomach in an effort to quell the sudden sickness. She wasn't thoughtless. Her curiosity compelled her to do certain things, ask certain questions, but she didn't have a wanton disregard for others. Did she? "Do you truly think that?"

"Think what?" Bella still stared at their sisters, a frown between her brows.

"Nothing." And it was. It was nothing.

Bella turned to face her. "Are you going to find out or not?"

Elizabeth painted a smile on her face, though it felt horrendously false. "Not, I think. You can do your own discovery, Bella."

"Hmph." Bella gave a slight shrug. "It's

probably of no interest, anyway. We are speaking of Henrietta and Anne, after all."

"True." Still shaken, Elizabeth sought to change the topic. "The boys are home from visiting Mama and Papa at Aylesbury soon, are they not?"

At the mention of her sons, Bella forgot about their sisters. "Yes, in a week. I am hoping to take them to the country, maybe even out to Cornwall."

Grateful Bella had succumbed, Elizabeth hurried to comment. "Oh?" *Well done, Elizabeth, most scintillating.*

"I thought to spend some time with them before Henry starts at Harrow. Cornwall is a delightful place, is it not?"

"Oh yes. All those bogs and moors and rocky outcrops. Delightful indeed."

Bella shot her a sour look, but then an unholy gleam lit her eyes. Elizabeth regarded her sister warily. That look never boded well.

"I say, Elizabeth, do you want to come along? I should dearly like your company."

Horror suffused her, seizing her lungs, freezing her limbs. Leave London now? When she had found a tutor and discovered the delights he had to offer? As mildly as she could manage, she said, "I don't think I can, actually,"

Bella's smile fell. "Why? You don't have anything to do here."

Frantic, Elizabeth tried to think of an excuse to placate Bella, cursing the heat that suddenly flushed her cheeks. "I just don't want to leave town. Not for a while anyway."

"Why not? You pestered me ceaselessly to take you with us to the Lakes. I would have thought you would leap to join us."

"Yes, well…." What could she say? "I am expecting a delivery." She winced. Good Lord, that was pathetic.

"A delivery." Bella's flat tone more than adequately displayed her disbelief. "You are giving up a holiday with my boys and I for a delivery."

"It's a very important delivery," Elizabeth defended. Really, Bella had no call to be looking at her like that.

"What are you up to?" Bella said finally.

"What do you mean?" Elizabeth widened her eyes, trying for the very picture of innocence. "I have a delivery. It is important. Ergo, I cannot go with you. Besides, wouldn't you prefer time alone with your sons? You know I will just get in the way. They will want to spend all their time with me, and it will be "Aunt Lizzie did this" and "Aunt Lizzie did that" and you know how you hate that. You will be better off without me."

Bella, thankfully, let the delivery nonsense die. "Yes, they will want to talk to you, won't they?" She sighed. "Seriously, Elizabeth, why did you not have your own blasted children?"

Elizabeth shrugged. "It's not something I could control, Bella." And that casual rejoinder was the product of years of convincing herself the truth of the statement. "Besides, you should have a family outing. No doubt Burfield will enjoy showing the boys his estate there." Why was Bella looking at her so oddly?

"Burfield isn't coming."

"Oh." Elizabeth had no idea what to say.

"Maybe it is best you don't come," Bella continued. "The boys and I will do well together. You stay in London for your—" Bella's lips twitched "—your delivery."

"I shall," she said loftily.

Bella laughed, and Elizabeth smiled with her, and they both pretended all was well.

Though God forfend should Bella ever discover what truly kept Elizabeth in London.

***

LYDIA TAPPED HER CHEEK with her fan, her gaze trained on him.

Ignoring her, Malvern instead watched the flow of the brandy as he rolled the glass, the pattern cut into the crystal refracting the candlelight. He had come to *La Belle* to attempt diversion. Lydia, however, seemed determined to destroy such a simple goal.

He exhaled. The day had been barely passable, and an effort to alleviate that state with one of his mistresses had failed miserably. Monique had pleaded indisposition, which had only increased his ire. She was paid a fair and equitable sum to be available to him at all times and she thought to contravene that simple edict? He had informed the butler Monique no longer lived there and went on his way. The servants would organise her removal from the house. They had done it for her predecessor and would do it again.

He had thought to visit another, but by that stage, the inclination for a female had left him and he'd settled for an hour or so at his club. When that, too, had lost all interest, he'd made his way to *La Belle*.

The brothel, however, held even less appeal than his club. Thus, he had not objected when Lydia had appeared at his side in a cloud of delicate perfume and greasepaint. She had smiled, that mysterious smile, and he'd allowed himself led away from the masses. Unfortunately, he could not stir himself to initiate anything remotely sexual.

With a delicate flick of her wrist, Lydia opened her fan, her eyes shadowed and mysterious in the candlelight. Was the placement of her chair deliberate? More than like the whole scene was designed to show her in the most favourable of lights. He applauded her showmanship.

"What tickles your fancy, my lord?" Lydia shifted, her breasts plumping above her neckline. The sight of her pale flesh aroused, to a degree. A very small degree. "Are you after dalliance? I have a new treat, one I am willing to share. Fresh from the country, skin like a pearl, breasts to make your mouth water." She licked her lips, a deep red shine glittering in the candlelight. "I shall give you first crack at her, or we could share her. I must admit, I *have* wanted to partake of her assets."

Malvern remained silent. Lydia did amuse him. She'd been his favourite whore before she'd managed to claw her way to her present position. Now, she took customers only when she desired and, for some reason she had never explained, she desired him.

"She has a brother. A twin, I believe. Would that be preferable?" Now there was annoyance in her voice, faint though it was.

Looking back at his glass, he ignored her, effectively ending her attempt to cajole him into debauchery. Staring into the crystal, he saw not the whiskey Lydia had pressed upon him. Instead he saw blonde hair and green eyes and a smile that persisted no matter the provocation.

Lydia snapped her fan shut. "Why are you here?"

Ah. Outright annoyance. It always entertained him when he could force a natural reaction from her. He smiled, though it was faint. "You question me?"

Face paling, she faltered, but stoically she continued. Was there any wonder why he returned to her, time and again? "You haven't fucked, haven't watched, haven't partaken of any of *La Belle*'s offerings." Her expression once again smooth, a small smile flitted around her mouth. "Is something the matter, my dear?"

Her tone arch, she appeared to have regained some measure of control. Pity.

"How long have we known each other?"

Lydia appeared startled by his sudden change of topic. Another natural reaction. It seemed the night for them. "I don't know. Five years, perhaps?"

Five years. Five years he had known her. Five years he had been back in England. And for five years, the earl had been dead.

His father's death was the only thing that could have compelled him to return to the country of his birth. His mother had greeted him with proffered cold cheek at the funeral and, her duty fulfilled, had promptly retired once more to the convent that had been her home since shortly after his birth. For reasons unknown, his father had been more than happy with his wife's production of a single heir and the whole of his childhood he'd not seen his mother above four times.

Malvern had occasionally thought to pursue such a curious satisfaction on his father's behalf. Never, though, could he find the right way to phrase the question. Besides, his father had, to all appearances, been more than pleased with the issue his wife had provided. It was a rare day when

Malvern had not trailed along behind his father, following him to the houses of friends and acquaintances, cooed over by the painted ladies whom he had later realised were the earl's mistresses, jostled with hearty male enthusiasm by the men in his father's club. When asked if it was appropriate for the boy to be present, the earl had laughed and claimed the boy had to learn sometime. Malvern supposed he should be grateful for such an early start to his education.

At twenty-one, Malvern had bid farewell to his father and his country and embarked upon a grand tour, from which he had neglected to return. Italy had been too tempting, with its sun-drenched shores and grand palazzos, with artefacts of Rome strewn carelessly on common streets amongst the debris from the Empire's descendants. He had found society when he required it, and something approaching contentment had settled upon him. The chance discovery of the cliffside village of Positano, where houses clung precariously to rock to loom over the Mediterranean in haphazard splendour, had only added to the strange satisfaction. The quiet and the calm of the small village had soothed him, and he'd given thanks each day that he'd set out from Naples for a brief sea voyage.

He would have been content to remain forever in that place, but the death of his father had brought the responsibility of the earldom, and there was nothing but to return to England. Easily he had fallen into old habits, and he found himself now ignoring an annoyed madam as he contemplated the intricacies of the house of Malvern.

He knew it should hurt to think of his father as dead.

Others seemed to grieve for the death of relatives. The mousey widow had appeared affected by the mention of her husband, and surely, he had been dead a similar amount of time. She was undoubtedly the sort to adhere to convention, and the conventions for mourning would put the event as occurring at least two years ago. What was it about the memory of her husband that inspired such an expression of wistfulness?

He took a draw of brandy and wondered what it would be like to be the focus of a mouse's affection, so strong that even now it lingered.

"Did you really tell Lady Mouse you wouldn't marry her?"

Lydia's words rose unexpected in the still of the room. Before he could prevent it, a shred of panic sliced through him. Was he so easy to read?

Ruthlessly, he forced the emotion away. "And you know this how?"

Her smile grew, though her eyes remained watchful. Lydia could conceal much, but always her eyes betrayed her. "Do you honestly believe I do not monitor everything that occurs between these walls?"

"You have never mentioned it before."

Ignoring him, she continued. "You are not going to fuck her? Really? I agree, pregnancy is a risk, but she is so very…." The fan rested at the corner of her mouth. "Delectable."

He said nothing. Lydia did not appear to require his agreement.

"There are a myriad of ways to protect against pregnancy. Surely you know them, my lord. If not, I would be happy to educate you."

Almost Lydia appeared spiteful. What an interesting turn of affairs.

She carried on, her smile now almost feline in aspect. "The widow, though, she does seem a tiresome choice for bedsport. I do not blame you for avoiding her cunny. No doubt she would weep and wail if ever she did feel your cock inside her. Imagine how dry and tight she'd be, but then, that would not be a deterrent to you, would it, my lord?" Lydia's smile widened.

"You will cease, madam." The widow was so different from what Lydia had described it seemed a sacrilege.

"Tell me, what liberties has she allowed you? Have you caressed her breasts? Did she blanch? Scream? Was she shocked, my lord?" Her hand trailed over her own breast.

"I do not see how my interaction with the widow is any business of yours."

Lydia froze. "My lord, I did not mean offense. It is simply— She came to me and I-I—"

Malvern kept his face impassive as he took a swallow of brandy. Lydia's demeanour held confusion tinged with fear, though she appeared to be desperately trying to conceal any reaction. She had miscalculated, and her livelihood depended on providing what her patron desired.

He should have found her efforts amusing. Instead, he did not.

"Nonetheless, you have caused offense." Malvern finished his brandy in one swallow and stood. "I bid you farewell."

He left her there, sprawled on the lounge, her bewilderment plain for all to see. And still, he was restless.

***

THE BALLROOM OF MALVERN House brought back old memories, ones he'd not had cause to think on in years. Malvern leaned a shoulder against the door jamb, observing the room as he raised the glass of whiskey. The alcohol had long since lost the power to burn, a pleasant numbness blurring the edges of his vision.

Throngs of young bucks clamoured for entrance to *La Belle* as he had departed earlier that night for home, their warbling voices pleading for admittance. He had left them to pursue the dubious pleasures contained within, instead striding through the streets of Seven Dials, his cane and his attitude keeping the worse of the footpads at bay. Gaslight had lent the streets an eerie luminosity, reflecting in the wet cobblestones and throwing back meagre light to limit the shadows with a weak glow. Mist had clung heavy to his clothes as the damp of the approaching winter seeped into his bones.

Now, here he was, staring into the ballroom he had seen a thousand times before. Dust cloths covered the fixtures, and the dim light from the windows hit the white sheets at odd angles, refracting around the room weakly while his shadow stretched long over the polished floor.

He saw none of it.

Instead, he saw the room as it had been, an oak table set in the centre and the ruins of the meal lay abandoned across the floor, plates and goblets strewn with careless abandon.

Amidst the wreckage, the earl's dinner guests lounged. Women lay draped over the table, breasts bare as they moaned at the attentions of their partners. Others rutted amongst the overturned plates, a tangle of limbs and flesh frantically thrusting at each other. Some did not confine themselves to one partner, or even two, writhing together in a parody of sexual congress. Some straddled chairs, others bent over them, and there were men fucking women, women fucking men, men buggering each other, women licking cunt, sucking cock, anything in the pursuit of pleasure.

And his father at the centre of it all, a goblet in one hand and the other tangled in the hair of the woman fellating him. A king surveying his depraved kingdom.

Malvern would have liked to have said it was an isolated incident. Instead, it had been one of many and he had been an unwilling observer until his father had deemed him old enough to join the fray. He may have been thirteen, but the memories blurred together. It was possible he had been younger.

He took another swallow of brandy. Its warmth, and that of the house, should have banished the chill and yet, stubbornly, it lingered within him, etched almost into his bones.

Abruptly, he turned from the ballroom, long strides taking him down the hall to his study.

None of the other rooms held any peace for him. In this strange mood, he found no quarter from old memories, each room offering something of his father's debauchery and, later, his own. Only his study brought respite, something about the room banishing thoughts of the past and bringing blessed silence in its wake.

The chair behind the desk beckoned. He sank into it, the scent of leather and old cigars winding about him as he settled into its comfort. It had been his father's, this chair, and his father's before him.

Generation upon generation of Malverns had enjoyed its embrace, just as generations had worked upon the surface of the desk before him.

He looked toward the centre of the room and could see nothing but the widow before him.

The widow. Again he thought upon her. She occupied his thoughts too much, though it was understandable why it should be so tonight. Lydia had been determined to talk of her, for all that he'd not wanted it. Every word she had uttered wound him tighter, and yet he was unsure as to why it had bothered him so. She had spoken of nothing but the truth or, at least, the truth she perceived. The widow was of no consequence, a blonde mouse who had requested the services of a debaucher to teach her something she could have easily found at any social gathering.

A faint smile quirked his lips. The widow had known that and had attempted to seek it out. How was it possible her lover had botched the job so badly?

He drank his whiskey, lost in thoughts of her. So lost was he, he didn't notice the coldness, the restlessness, had disappeared.

Chapter Five

ALWAYS SHE WAITED FOR him. A good half hour had passed since her arrival with no sign from her tutor. The excitement she'd felt when she had first walked through his door, her cheeks stinging with the cold while her body heated in anticipation, had died in the face of boredom.

Elizabeth glanced about the room, twisting her fingers idly around a loose thread from her skirt, again and again. His desk dominated the space, a heavy oak structure looming over all, the set of drawers on either side lending a certain sort of monstrosity. The leather blotter, so precisely centred, left little room for the forlorn, empty inkwell at its head.

The surface was neat, precise and completely devoid of personality. How did he work in such a Spartan area? There was nothing to indicate he did indeed work, no ink stains, no scraps of paper, nothing. Maybe the desk was for show, solely to intimidate those unwary enough to enter his study.

She blanched. And wasn't that just a dramatic and overwrought thought?

It did beg the question, though. What *did* Malvern do with all of the bits and pieces that inevitably littered one's desk? Her own was a mess of correspondence, invitations and scribbled notes she always meant to one day file. Did he keep his papers in the drawers? If she were to look, would she find her schedule, the one he insisted he had written?

The potentially intriguing drawers were out of her line of sight and she fought the impulse to investigate, telling herself it would be extremely rude to invade her tutor's privacy, but really it would be his own fault. All who knew her were aware she couldn't be trusted to keep her distance when her imagination fired. To be fair, Malvern had known her for all of a week and a half, and he couldn't be held at fault for not yet realizing how far she would go to slake the niggling compulsion to *know*.

Oh, sod it all to hell and back. She hurried around his desk, her fingers itching. The first drawer was locked. And the next. And the next.

Damnation. Folding her arms across her chest, she stared at the drawers, contemplating stratagems for forcing the things open.

"I lock all my drawers, as you have no doubt discovered."

Malvern's voice cracked through the room, abnormally loud and utterly unexpected. Heat rushed to her cheeks. Good Lord, she had been caught at his desk like an unruly child with her hand in the biscuit tin.

He offered no rebuke, however, and remained framed in the doorway, his arms crossed over casual attire of shirtsleeves, robe and trousers. "Was there anything in particular you were hoping to discover?"

She shrugged, attempting nonchalance, as if she were caught trying to rifle through men's desks daily. "I thought to find my schedule. To facilitate your tutelage, of course."

"Ah." Not a raise of his brow to convey his indifference, nor a twitch of a lip to show his amusement. Nothing. "So you weren't planning to steal my millions?"

Her gaze flew to his. Had he just made a joke? But no, his face betrayed no trace of humour, was set in its usual disinterested lines. The first sign of insanity, imagining things. Well, that and snooping in people's desks. She was terrible. She truly was. "I should not have attempted to invade your privacy. It is *such* a bad habit of mine. No one is safe from me, I fear. I shall endeavour, though, to remain on that side of your desk." She gestured to the side away from all those interesting drawers.

"It is of no consequence." He came to stand beside her, close enough to touch. Unfortunately, he did not take advantage of their proximity. "Today, we shall discuss the male form. Have you seen a man fully disrobed?"

Surprised by the change of subject, it took her a moment or two before she could remember if she had seen Rocksley naked at any time in their marriage. On occasion, she'd pressed Rocksley that they might undertake their martial relations fully unclothed, out of curiosity's sake if nothing else. However, he had consistently looked so horrified at the notion she hadn't the heart to pursue it further. Thus, their marital relations had continued as ever they had, the lights doused and their night clothes raised only so the necessary could occur.

"Never." The denial was stark. Embarrassing. "I have examined an anatomy book, though." As if the examination of a book could negate the embarrassing truth. Twenty eight years of age and never had she seen a naked male. She would wager even *Anne* had seen her husband unclothed and there could be no one more aware of the bounds of propriety than Anne.

"The anatomy book will make this easier, then." He shed his robe, coming to stand before her. His face, as always, betrayed nothing of his thoughts. "First, our discussion shall encompass what makes us desire. It can be a small thing—a turn of a wrist, a flash of skin—or it can be more obvious. Breasts swelling above a corset, skin tight breeches outlining a perfect thigh."

Her mind skittered where he had surely intended, to her own surreptitious studies of male groins, so perfectly outlined by formal wear. She had known she should not have looked, but she had, and having looked, she had wanted.

"Desire is a personal experience, at the discretion of the one experiencing it. There is no way for me to teach you this. You will discover what attracts you. Arousal, though, is another matter. The signs are similar in all. For a man, arousal is more obvious. The penis will become engorged, rising from its flaccid state to become hard, ready to be stimulated until semen is released. This process, of course, can be achieved in many ways."

She pressed her hand to her chest. Where was he going with this? A few possibilities occurred to her, and each set her heart to racing.

"I will demonstrate how a male can be stimulated for ejaculation to occur." He began to unbutton his shirt and her mind went blank as his chest was revealed.

Pale golden skin glowed softly in the candlelight, lovingly caressed by shadow and flame. Her eyes ran greedily over his wide shoulders, his strong back. Sleek muscles flexed, strong biceps curling and releasing, as he removed the shirt from his person, the long muscles on his side standing in relief as he twisted to place the garment on his desk.

She barely noticed the slight pain as her tongue slid over the ridges of her teeth. Good Lord, the man was stunning. She wanted to touch him. To trace her fingers over him, to find out if that pale gold skin was as warm as it looked, to discover for herself its texture, the resilience of his flesh. She wanted to *taste* him. She could do so, could she not?

He lectured, something about the various muscles on his body, though who could care what he said when such a bounty was before her? She needed to place her lips on his skin, above his nipple, and rub them back and forth until they became sensitised. Then, with her flesh stinging from the feel of his, then she would savour his salt on her tongue.

His voice wrapped around her, his body filling her vision, her fingers aching for him beneath them, sense of his words drowned by the pounding of her heart. If this was lust, it was absolutely insane she'd not pursued the experience years earlier.

If she had been listening to him, it probably wouldn't have shocked the life out of her when he opened his trousers. As she choked, he pushed the fabric down his thighs, gracefully stepping out of them. She tried to maintain some sort of dignity, but really, where was dignity when a man so very calmly revealed himself?

Her gaze skittered to his face and that infernal

brow raised, no doubt in amusement at her reaction. Well, she had no defence. He was the first man she had seen naked. He was lucky she was too overwhelmed to ask questions.

Patiently, he waited until she had fully recovered. "As you can see, the penis is already starting to lengthen. Further stimulation will result in full tumescence. I shall demonstrate." He encircled himself, his strong hand unashamedly stroking his flesh.

She couldn't tear herself away from the sight. He was displayed for her, like one of those anatomy books, but gloriously alive, gloriously touchable. Her palms itched to feel his flesh, to measure the strength of his erection for herself. Desire cut through her, a steady litany of *I want... I need...*

"They are many names for the penis." His hand continued stroking his length. "Some are clinical, some are base. Many are meant for amusement. Penis, cock, dick, phallus. I prefer the term cock." His flesh grew before her gaze, the head becoming flushed as he worked himself.

He was saying something about stimulation and strength, but it was merely noise. She followed the slide and pull of his hand on his flesh, lip caught between her teeth, barely remembering to breathe. "Can I—would you mind if I…touch it?"

No response. Her gaze flew to his. She awaited his answer, apprehensive she had said something wrong, exhilarated that maybe she hadn't. How could he still seem imperious while unclothed? His gaze locked with hers and they remained thus, his breathing even for all his apparent arousal.

Finally, *finally*, he reached for her hand and placed it on his…his cock.

The weight was heavy in her palm. She bit her lip as she traced the flesh, learning the shape, the feel of it. The skin should have been rough, but instead it was silky soft, sliding sinuously over the hardness it contained. Satisfaction filled her as the flesh hardened further, blood staining its skin as she stroked from root to tip.

His small groan tore her captivated gaze from his groin. Ruddy colour flushed the skin along his cheekbones; his teeth gritted against the pleasure. Shamefully, she remembered there was a person attached to that fascinating bit of flesh, a person who appeared wholly taken with her touch.

"Am I doing this right?" Strange, the throatiness of her words. Only now her attention had been broken did she realise her own susceptibility. Shallow breaths pushed her breasts against her corset, scraping her sensitised flesh against the stiff material.

"Too well." He hissed as she ran her thumb over the indentation at the tip of his cock. The harshness of his tone made her skin tighten. "Do you wish to continue with this or—?" His voice broke as she increased her grip.

"Or?" The muscles of his abdomen leaped in time to her strokes, his hips rolling against her as he pushed himself into her hand.

Her grip tightened again and he swore under his breath, that deliciously foreign word she found so titillating. Catching her wrist, he lifted her hand from him. The index finger of his other hand trailed down her cheek, along her jaw to under her chin, tipping her gaze to his. Perspiration gleamed on his skin. Fire burned behind blue ice, and a shiver rushed through her at the sight.

He traced her upper lip, then the lower, her

flesh stinging in his wake. Then, he pushed inside her mouth. Her lips automatically closed over him and slight panic filled her, her hand grasping his wrist to prevent him from intruding further.

His eyes locked on hers. For an endless moment she stared at him, his finger motionless in her mouth, her mind racing.

"Suck me," he said.

Never taking her eyes from his, she drew on his finger, the suction gentle but firm, her hand cradling his wrist. The taste of him was salty on her tongue, the flesh resilient as she gently scraped her teeth against him. Each pull found companion with the pulsing inside her, heat and wetness gathering between her thighs as she recognised the rhythm. She swept her tongue over him, triumph washing through her as he fought to contain his reaction.

Gently, he drew his finger from her mouth, her lips closing over the tip before allowing him to leave. He caressed her cheek with his knuckles as he sat in the chair she usually occupied, tugging her down to kneel between his spread legs.

"Now." His tone was low, beguiling. "Suck me. There."

Eager, she lowered her gaze to his lap. His erection was proud, strong, and her mouth watered as she imagined that flesh in her mouth. Her tongue darted out, touching the corner of her lip as she considered possibilities, stratagems.

Malvern, conscientious tutor that he was, offered assistance. "Take my cock in your hand." His voice strained, his own hand covered hers, directing her to hold him just under the head. Again a wash of pride, that her touch had done that to him. "Take it in your mouth, as far as you can manage."

Somewhat apprehensive about the matter but raging with desire, she moved to undertake his directive.

"Wait."

She froze.

He closed his eyes, and when he opened them, some of the fire had dimmed. "It would be better to build up to that. I apologise. My only excuse is I became carried away. Pleasure is about anticipation, driving your partner wild with lust. Sudden and direct has its uses, but in a situation such as this, taking one's time is preferable." His fingers gently cupped her chin, and his eyes burned. "You should make me desperate for your mouth."

Her pulse beat loudly in her ears. "What should I do?"

"Play with me, pet me, drive me insane with small, quick touches. Deny me, and then give me everything. Keep me off balance. But most of all, do what you will." A small tick started in his jaw, though his gaze was steady, as if he weren't exposed and naked before her. "Nothing is wrong, indulge your whims, your desires. Surprise me."

Whatever she wanted? Aroused by the possibilities, she gently traced his shape with her hands and, feeling suddenly brave, she placed a small kiss on the tip. Her breath brushed along him as her fingers played delicately, cupping him, stroking him, and she feathered kisses along his length, revelling in the freedom to do whatever she wanted.

The feel of him was astounding, becoming more so with each passing moment. Her tongue darted, licking up his length, the taste of him salty and sweet. He made a slight noise, small enough she only glanced up at him, and he gently pushed her towards the head of his cock. Licking delicately at the plum-shaped head, she experimented with the flat of her tongue, the tip, circling around and around as she played with her tutor.

She must have been doing something right as he cursed, his hand clenching in her hair. Pride and arousal danced inside her, and then she took him in her mouth.

A moan escaped at the way he filled her, strong and straight, and she went down on him as far as she could, enveloping him in the warmth of her mouth. A gentle tug at her hair made her retreat, helped her learn the rhythm, the push and pull as she took him inside her.

He whispered harsh commands as she learned him, his shape, his texture, his taste. He whispered how to hold him, when she should caress him, and a slight stroke on her jaw encouraged her to lick here, suck there. Lost in sensation, lost in him, she learned how to read his moans, his curses, the flow and ebb of his body.

Her body responded to his, her breasts aching, her core molten and a fierce pulse beating between her thighs. She wanted to touch herself. No, she wanted *his* hand, his lips, his tongue. But first, she wanted to make him scream.

"Stop." Gravel ground his voice as he issued the command. She barely heard him, her attention solely on the thick flesh in her mouth. Her hands dug into his thighs, clenching and releasing as she sucked at him.

The pressure between her legs was unbearable. She ground herself against her heels, wishing she could touch herself but there were too many clothes. There were always too many clothes. Not on him, though. He was gloriously bare, his skin glistening with sweat, his hips thrusting his cock into her mouth as his hands gripped her hair, tangled almost painfully amongst the strands.

"You have to stop. Now. I'm going to—" He groaned as she almost let go of him, her tongue curling under the head of his cock, her hand cradling his taut flesh as she tortured him.

He swore, pushing her away from him. She landed with a heavy thud, her hands braced behind her, the taste of him on her tongue. Grasping his cock, he pulled hard at the flesh, his hips moving frantically in time with his hand. He cursed harshly and shuddered as climax overtook him, but then he covered himself with a handkerchief she'd not before noticed, obscuring her view.

However, any disappointment remained brief as he was so very beautiful in his pleasure. His throat arched, his eyes closed as the orgasm she had given washed over him. Her tongue touched the corner of her mouth, tasting him still, and she didn't realise she was stroking her stomach, her hips undulating against the floor, not until she felt the heat of her palm through the layers of clothing. Empty, she was empty, her core throbbing, demanding that she do something about this ache.

Slowly, he recovered, the rise of his chest slowing as his breathing eased. By contrast, her heart raced madly, her skin hot, and oh, she so desperately wanted to touch him.

He opened his eyes and his gaze ran over her, her wanton sprawl, the desire she couldn't hide. "Come here."

His voice rushed through her, a shiver against her nerves, sending sensation down her spine, over her skin. She moved closer, but not enough to satisfy him, and he grasped her beneath the arms, lifting her to her feet. His hands slid down, heavy on her hips, burning through the layers of cloth even as, logically, she knew she shouldn't be able to feel his heat. Turning her, he tugged her to his lap, her back settling into his chest, the threadbare material of her oldest gown a thin barrier between her skin and his. One arm across her hips pulled her further into him, while the other braced between her breasts.

"You did a good job." His arm tightened against her breastbone. She arched her back and a helpless moan rose from her, her skin on fire as she felt his hardness cradling her.

"Such a good job," he crooned, his hand sliding over her tortuously. He cupped her breast through the fabric of her gown, using the rough slide of fabric to abrade her tender skin. "You should have a reward."

A gasp escaped her when he licked the cord of her neck, her hands digging into the arm of the chair as he traced a line to the curve of her shoulder. His hand slipped beneath her bodice, and he made a sound of approval at the looseness of her corset.

"You made yourself ready for me, didn't you? Like I told you." His breath whispered against her ear, stirring loose strands of hair.

"Yes." There were no undergarments to impede him either. She pushed herself into his palm, his skin hot and rough against hers. The scent of him teased her, the soap from his bath, the tang of his cigarillo, the hint of alcohol on his breath. It wound about her, drove her mad, and she imagined drowning in it, enveloping her in him completely.

Lost in the sensations he aroused, in the desires his touch engendered, she wanted to feel him beneath her fingers, to trace his chest, to measure him, feel his cock leap beneath her touch once more. But she couldn't. She was helpless before him, her body at his disposal, displayed for his pleasure.

Arousal roared through her.

He squeezed her breast, lifting it from the confines of her bodice. Cool air rushed across her fevered skin, and she moaned at the contrast. Her nipple beaded tight, the cradle of his hand rubbing against her, making the bud firmer, tighter, pain and pleasure combined.

"Put your legs on either side of mine."

In a daze, she complied, her head nestled in the gap between his neck and shoulder. His hand continued to play with her breast, moulding and shaping, pinching her nipple, tracing the tight flesh. Grasping the arms of the chair, she pushed back into him, her legs loose on either side of his as she tried to ease her ache.

"Calm, my dear." His other hand trailed over her stomach to rest lightly on her mons. "I shall take care of you." Slowly, achingly slowly, he gathered the fabric of her dress.

Cool air caressed her calves, her knees, her thighs, and then the outside of his knee was against the inside of hers, his flesh resilient and warm. He abandoned the fabric of her gown and rested his hand on her thigh, making little circles against her skin. Breath frozen in her chest, she waited in agony for what he would do next.

Deliberately, he widened his legs. Draped over his, her own legs followed, until she was open, spread, cool air licking at her heat. She couldn't think, couldn't speak, could do nothing but wait for him to touch her. His lips whispered about her ear, playing over her flesh as one hand caressed her breast while the other—good Lord, the other—trailed up her thigh and then back, a little higher and then back, and all the while she ached, she wanted, her core weeping for him, a wicked pulse demanding him inside her.

She almost screamed when he put his hand on her, his fingers delicately tracing her folds. Stubbornly, he avoided the spot she most wanted him to touch. He avoided it, and she called him a bastard, she cried and his hand tightened on her breast, his legs opening wider, opening her wider to him. He crooned words to her, about heat and wetness and what he was going to do to her. And then, finally, he touched her.

It was almost too much, his fingers on her, gently flicking against her, driving her out of her mind. The precipice was coming, it was racing toward her and she thrust against him, her fingers digging like talons into the arms of the chair. He pushed a finger inside her, his thumb still massaging as he hooked somewhere inside, somewhere that made sensation storm through her and that was enough.

She exploded.

Dimly, she heard herself cry out, felt him hold her firmly, restraining her writhing body as climax rushed through her. The feelings were uncontrollable, too intense, too brilliant, storming through her like electricity, like lightening.

And then it was over.

Slowly, she came back to herself, her chest rising and falling harshly, her head lolling against his shoulder. His hand covered her breast, holding her gently, his other hand stroking her stomach through her gown. Moisture clung to her lashes, dampened her hair, and she realised at some point, she had wept.

His body beneath hers offered comfort and warmth and, strangely, the man who had caused the maelstrom now offered respite from it. She placed her hand over his on her stomach.

His hand jerked as she did so, and for an endless moment, she was certain he would pull away. He did nothing, however, remaining motionless beneath her palm. Tentatively, she linked their fingers.

And he let her.

Chapter Six

MALVERN STARED AT THE wall as he awaited his pupil, one finger tapping against his temple. After numerous attempts he'd found a comfortable sprawl. Bloody chair. One would think gaining comfort would not be difficult, especially as the chair provided rest for the wealthy benefactors of the women patronizing the store. Instead, the chair seemed a torturous device designed in the farthest depths of Hell.

The owner of the device, and consequently the shop, a female with the unfortunate name of Madame la Belette, had been persuaded to open her doors late at night with a ridiculously small amount of coin, and her discretion had been purchased for even less. However, what could one expect of a woman who didn't take the time to research her *nom de plume* before assuming it? No doubt her true name was Bucket or Shovel or something equally as common, never realizing her new moniker translated to weasel.

Still, the woman could sew and his long association with her establishment had been of benefit to them both.

Now, though, he waited.

He shifted his seat. Buffed his fingernails. Examined the ovals. Picked a piece of lint off his trousers.

And then he wondered what the hell he was doing.

At the time, the idea had mustered long-absent interest—tutor some clueless widow in matters of sex and desire, maybe even amuse himself with corrupting her totally. Or, conversely, he could scare her with the depths of depravity people could, and frequently did, sink to. A myriad of possibilities the endeavour had held, each more salacious than the last, but never had he thought the woman would actually embrace it. After all, what little nobody widow would really desire actual tutelage on sex? The use of a few graphic words and he had imagined she would balk, horrified, before she ran screaming from the room. He had amused himself with images of a grim-faced matron, shocked to the bone by his use of the word *fuck*.

The widow, however, was far from a grim matron. Instead of reluctance, she displayed an abundance of curiosity, and a genuine desire to learn all she could about pleasure. She had taken to his instruction with enthusiasm, and where he thought he would have to coax and compel, instead she had taken the lead. All that had been required from him was a willing body and a general push in the right direction.

Reluctant amusement tugged him. Never could he have foreseen such a fortuitous circumstance when first Lydia had suggested the widow's tutelage to him. What man wouldn't desire to be the focus of a curious woman's experiments?

A small rap at the door and the object of his thoughts poked her head through. He straightened, all trace of his amusement wiped from his features.

His pupil appeared vastly troubled, which could only bode well for the design of the gown. "I am unsure about this."

"That's the point. Your garments are supposed to be alluring. It's a mystery how you managed to attract a lover in that sack you were wearing."

"Well, I wasn't wearing that. I do have *some* nice clothes."

He raised a brow. If she had, he had never seen them. "Show me what you are wearing."

Worry lurked in the depths of her green eyes as she bit her lip, the flesh red raw. "All right, but know I will kill you if you laugh."

Amusement tugged again. Most surprising, this mouse.

She emerged from behind the door. A good portion of her corset showed above the low scoop neckline, but the colour and fit were a vast improvement on her previous garments. At least Madam Weasel had the sense to expose her skin, even if the intent was currently compromised by the ill-fitting corset.

Red flattered the mouse, the vibrancy of the fabric putting him to mind of the roses bordering his mother's garden, those that had been planted before he was born and had been maintained even after her decampment to the convent. Her blonde hair gained lustre from the combination of bold and pale, her skin fairly glowing against the fabric. In fact, everything about her was enhanced by the pairing.

The corset, however, would have to be replaced. As it stood, one could not discern she even possessed a pair of breasts, let alone they were of a pleasing shape. He shifted in his chair, ignoring the hardening of his body at the thought of those breasts beneath his hands. His mouth.

She appeared as if she expected him to comment. Should he make her wait? A valuable tool, anticipation heightened any pleasure, and she would do well to learn it. Enjoying the faint flush on her skin, he entertained a brief fantasy where her agitation was caused by the delights wrought by his hands. Rubbing his thumb over his lip, he imagined beneath the digit instead was the flesh plumping so temptingly above her corset. Then she'd straddle him, the scarlet fabric rucked up around her hips as she moaned and moved upon him.

Her eyes darkened, as if she knew the direction of his thoughts. Her gaze drifted to his mouth and he teased her, rubbing his thumb languidly over his lips, over and over.

Lips parted, eyes slumberous, her face held the window to her desire. Such a responsive mouse.

Satisfaction flowing through him, he turned his attention to her gown. His brows drew together. "This is what Madame thinks you should wear?"

Though obviously fighting for composure, his pupil attempted nonchalance. "Apparently it will look different once I have the correct underwear."

"Yes, it will." At his words, a frown creased her brow. Ah, ire at the simplicity of his statement. She was so easy to read, this widow. He leaned back in his chair. "Shouldn't you don the correct underwear, then?"

Clearly, she did not want to obey. She looked

instead as if she wished to reprimand him for his high-handed command, obviously under the impression her words could sway his intent. As if she realised the folly, she pressed her lips together and left the room, grumbling to herself as she did so. He permitted himself a small smile at her display.

After the door had closed, Malvern waited a moment. Then another. An appropriate period passed and he got to his feet, making his way to the concealed peephole opposite the chair. Another of Madame's specialties.

His protégé stood in her undergarments and yet she remained completely immersed in white cotton. Of true amazement, the ugliness of the clothes with which she covered her form. Seeing them, he could well understand why she had to actively seek out physicality, though she had somehow managed to obtain a lover.

He frowned. The existence of this unknown man was somewhat disconcerting, though he had no notion as to why.

"My lady, you would like help undressing, yes?" For the first time, he noticed the presence of Madame, who appeared to be fawning all over her newest client. Of course, it helped that Malvern had spent a small fortune at this establishment in the past. No doubt Madame was attempted to further line her coffers with Malvern coin.

"If you wouldn't mind, Madame." His pupil sighed. "I don't think he approved of the gown."

"Nonsense." Madame worked quickly to unlace the corset. "He did not see it with the correct undergarments. This thing—" Her distaste coloured her words. "This thing would make anyone appear unattractive in any gown. We must find you the correct support, a garment that will lift your bosom to best advantage, while allowing for the line of the gown to flow, uninterrupted, down your body. *Voila*." She pulled the corset from his student's body. "See, already it is better. You have a good shape, my lady, and we will find the right garment to show this. Now, you will remove your chemise."

"Pardon?" The mouse raised her arms to cover her breasts.

"For my corsets, you will not need a chemise. And this one, this one is an ugly thing. We will take it from you." Madame clicked her fingers. "Off."

Clearly uncertain, his pupil stared at Madame, as if that alone would change the decree. Madame, however, was not paid to be deterred. With a sigh, the mouse uncrossed her arms and pulled the garment over her head.

Malvern's breath hitched at the sight of her unbound breasts. Her nipples had contracted in the coolness of the room, the dark pink buds standing erect. She covered them with her palms as soon as she handed Madame her chemise, leaving her standing only in thin drawers as the dressmaker fussed about her.

"Now, you will wait while I fetch the garments for you." Madame ignored her protests at being left half-naked. The dressmaker gathered the garments and left, but not before shooting a smug smile in the direction of the peephole.

Malvern ignored the woman. A small smile touched his lips as he watched Elizabeth. Madame's game was nothing new to him, but never had he played with someone who did not know the rules.

Madame was known for allowing gentlemen to watch as their current mistress modelled the clothes he purchased, with all involved devoted to making the experience as decadent as possible. Never one to let an opportunity for profit to pass her by, Madame kept a stable of girls to add to the spectacle—for a small fee, of course. Malvern had spent many a dissolute hour watching as this mistress or that performed for his pleasure.

He returned his attention to the woman standing so uncertainly in front of the mirror. He'd honestly not thought of Madame's extra service when he had brought his pupil here, but who was he to deny himself such a show?

All of her was on display to him, from the lip caught between her teeth to the tense set of her shoulders as her hands plumped the soft flesh of her breasts in a vain effort to cover herself. Her gaze darted about the room, returning time and again to the door as she waited for Madame. Little did she know how very long she would wait.

Bracing one hand against the wall, he leaned closer to the peephole, enjoying her disconcertment.

Her brow set in worried lines, she used the mirror to examine the wall behind her, trailing her gaze over the pretentious wallpaper, the too-fulsome gilding. A small quirk danced about her lips at the portrait of the queen, and her brow cleared a little as her gaze came closer to the peephole.

Then, suddenly, it was as if she were regarding him directly.

He stepped back, the move instinctive, before telling himself there was no possible way she could know. Madame would have ensured it. He told himself that, and yet still her gaze was upon him.

The crease between her brows deepened. Her gaze flicked away, and he breathed again. Just as quickly, he berated himself. What care had he if she had discovered the game?

Her gaze returned to her image in the mirror. She appeared to be thinking on something. He cared not for her thoughts, instead drawn to her pale back. She had beautiful skin, a heady mix of cream and velvet, stained with an intriguingly dark freckle below her left shoulder blade. How had he missed such a thing? He would have to explore that patch of skin when next he had her naked and before him.

Arousal began a slow burn through his veins as he thought of situations, entanglements, to facilitate the examination of her skin.

She still looked at herself in the mirror, lip once again caught between teeth. Whatever she thought must be worthy of intense study. Slowly, her teeth worried her bottom lip, reddening the flesh before she soothed the abrasion with her tongue, and then beginning the process over again. She bit her lip often, when she was thinking. One day soon, he would replace her tongue with his, soothing that flesh himself as he drew her inside him, his hands in place of hers on her breasts.

Disgusted with his lack of control, he braced both hands against the wall. Good God, he *knew* Madame had deliberately placed her so in front of the mirror. He refused to disgrace himself like a boy over nothing more stimulating than a mouse's image in a reflective surface.

Though still he stared.

Her head tilted to the side and a smile crossed her face. That smile hardened him instantly. Jesus, what had she just thought?

The hands so tightly clasped on her breasts loosened, her thumbs stroking the upper curves. He watched as she watched herself in the mirror, that small smile a siren's call. Now each hand cupped the corresponding breast, her tongue touching her upper lip as she examined herself. A flush began on her cheeks as she pushed her breasts up and together, turning on her side to admire her form from a different angle. His breathing thickened as she allowed her breasts to fall to their natural shape and then pushed them up again, her smile becoming feline as she stared at herself, her gaze caressing her form in a way he suddenly wished he could.

Slight amusement stretched his mouth, the expression fighting through tendrils of arousal. Even though she had said nothing, she appeared to have undertaken his directive to pleasure herself. He smothered a groan as he imagined what she would do if he strode into the room and replaced her hands with his own.

She widened her stance, her hands moulding her breasts, her breath quickening as she touched herself. She hadn't exposed her nipples, her palms rubbing against the small nubs. The need to see them consumed him, his arousal shocking in its depth. How was it such an untutored woman could rouse this level of desire?

Finally, a nipple peaked through, caught between her fingers. She squeezed gently, and the bud of flesh elongated beneath her touch, her nipple a dark pink, almost angry in its distension. On a gasp, she released one breast and brought her hand up to her mouth, licking her palm before returning it, a moan coming from her as she started her caress again. He stifled his own groan, imagining her licking him, her tongue playing with his cock as she pulled at her nipples before him, her knees spread wide as she took him deep into her mouth. He started to stroke himself, one hand braced against the wall as the other travelled his length, his eyes trained on her and what she would show him next.

She gave another moan as she arched her back, her breasts thrust forward and her hands moving upon them. Her hips started to undulate, her breathing harsh in the still room. His own was just as ragged. God, could she come from caressing her breasts alone? His cock hardened further at the thought, blood thickening as he watched her.

She looked at herself once more in the mirror, the muscles of her back working as she palmed herself, her shoulders blades rising and falling with the motion. Her left hand kept at the motion on her breast as her right abandoned its flesh, her breast fully exposed to his gaze, displaying white flesh and cherry pink nipple.

He exhaled harshly.

Her right hand snaked across the bare flesh of her belly, hesitating slightly before disappearing beneath her drawers. Her eyes closed as she played with herself, her lip gripped tightly between her teeth.

A curse tore from his throat as he conjured images of what she was doing. Her hand reaching into her drawers, her fingers tangling in the curls before reaching lower. Slowly, delicately, her fingers stroking at the lips of her sex, tormenting herself with the wetness coating her outer lips before she dipped inside, only an inch, only to tease.

She whimpered, adding credence to his fantasy, one hand moving rhythmically between her thighs, her other pinching her nipple.

Shoving his trousers open, he took his cock in hand, executing harsh strokes as blood pounded through him. He stroked in tandem with her, breath strangled as he watched, unable to look away.

Now she found the bundle of nerves hard, as hard as his cock and so sensitive she had to touch it gently, a mere whisper of movement, or she would come immediately. Her thumb would caress the hard bud as her finger thrust inside, finding she was wet and empty. Another finger, reaching deep inside, stroking the walls of her core, and now she could push hard at her clitoris, could circle the flesh as she was circling her nipple, pinching and pulling, her head thrown back, her hand moving frantically. Then she came, her hand stilling on her breast, her mouth open on a silent moan, beautiful in her pleasure.

Blood pounded through him, boiling in his veins, and he could feel it begin, gathering low in his belly. He pulled at his cock, his hand stroking fast, his grip strong, almost painful, but God, he needed it, needed it hard. His balls drew up tight, he wasn't far and then he came, releasing his semen over his hand, the orgasm crashing over him.

His senses returned slowly, his climax affecting more than any he'd had of late. Breathing harshly, he dismissed the ridiculous notion. Surely the sight of her hadn't affected him as greatly as he supposed. A few deep breaths, that's all he needed to recover.

Finally, he calmed. He tidied himself, glancing through the peephole.

His blood turned cold.

She looked directly at him in the mirror. And her smile was smug.

**

ELIZABETH KNEW HE WAS there, watching her.

She had to admit, a large part of her pleasure had been the thought he watched, separated only by plaster and brick. It had spurned her on, making her climax more intense than any she had given herself before.

When he had suggested this trip to the dressmaker's, she had been hesitant, uncertain how she was to afford such finery. The last half hour or so, however, had been so enjoyable, it was well worth however much Madame charged her.

It had been Madame, actually, who had given the game away. The woman had kept glancing behind them, as if she were seeking approval from the wall. Elizabeth had wondered what on earth could be so very fascinating. From somewhere had come the memory of spying on her parents as a child through the peephole Bella had shown her in their parents' private sitting room. She knew then Malvern was in the room behind that wall and it had all fallen into place. She had wondered why he had brought her here, to this hardly respectable dressmaker who so obviously clothed the demimonde. She had wondered why Madame was so eager to get Elizabeth half naked, leaving her alone in the room.

Now, she knew.

Her mind, so recently turned to the possibility for carnal pleasure, had taken it a step further and she reasoned this room must be some sort of display area; only instead of gowns, *she* was on display. A tiny thrill had shuddered through her. It was embarrassing, and nigh on degrading, but she couldn't deny it had been strangely exciting.

A small smile crossed her lips. He truly was debauching her, one small act at a time.

Elizabeth had finally found the courage to

undertake his directive to seek her own pleasure—
Good Lord, had that been nearly a month ago? With
some trepidation after she had retired for the night,
she'd cupped her breasts, her fingers alien against her
flesh. She had remembered him doing those
wonderful things to her, and her fingers had started
stroking her flesh lightly, her breath quickening as
she had replayed their encounters in her head. Before
she'd known what she was doing, her hand was
between her legs and she'd felt it building, that
glorious release she'd experienced with him, and then
she had broken, the same lovely feeling washing over
her.

She had lain in her bed, panting, surprised she'd
managed to do that to herself and that it had felt so
good. Then, in the interest of exploration, she had
done it again—and as often as she could manage ever
since.

So when she had discovered he could see her,
she'd thought, why not show him what she had
learned? And so, she'd pleasured herself and
somehow it had been better, knowing he was
watching. In the midst of it, she had been reminded of
those few times with her lover, in the library of Lady
Markham's town house, Farindon's chest against her
back as he had thrust inside her. Somehow, it had all
gotten tangled up and she had imagined it was
Malvern behind her that night at Lady Markham's,
his cock inside her, his voice husky in her ear. That
had been what had finished her in the end.

The door opened and Madame entered the
room, her arms full of a variety of riotously coloured
corsets. Certain a blush stained her cheeks, Elizabeth
hastily covered her breasts, trying to act as if she
hadn't just been pleasuring herself.

The dressmaker paid little attention to her, however. A smug expression twisted her features, as if she were imagining the extra pounds she would be paid for the use of such an exclusive room.

All embarrassment left Elizabeth at the woman's impertinence. Imitating Malvern's superior demeanour, she levelled a stare on the dressmaker. "Is something amusing, Madame?"

Madame's expression hastily took on a more deferential cast. "No, my lady." She indicated the corsets still in her arms. "I have brought some garments for your perusal. If you would be so kind?"

Elizabeth suddenly wondered how much Malvern could see from his vantage point. Would the mirror display all of her to him? An imp of mischief raised its head. Let's find out, shall we?

She dropped her hands from her breasts, spreading her arms wide as Madame came forward with one of the corsets, all cares about being half naked in front of the woman disappearing. She fancied she heard a groan.

Smiling to herself, she was quiet as Madame fastened the corset around her. She'd never gone without a chemise before. The sensation of the silk against her naked breasts was both cooling and arousing, something she could easily get used to.

"You see, my lady." Madame ran her hands over the corset, smoothing the fabric against Elizabeth's waist. The corset barely covered her nipples, pushing her breasts up, the rounded flesh looking much fuller than her previous corset had ever made them. "This undergarment will allow for a more daring design of dress. The front—" she swept her finger along the edge of the corset "—provides for a deep décolleté and the low back—" Madame's hand was now sweeping her back, measuring the space from Elizabeth's neck to the edge of the corset. "*Et alors, vous serez très à la mode.*"

Elizabeth couldn't look away from her reflection in the mirror. She looked *wicked*. Her waist curved in dramatically, impossibly tiny beneath full breasts that swelled with promise above the corset. Add to that the faint blush left on her cheeks from her pleasure, and she appeared as if she were of the demimonde. All she needed were ruby red lips and a fan, and the picture would be complete.

She loved it.

She licked her lips, wishing Madame would leave the room so she could explore this new shape of hers. "And you have the gown with you?"

Madame inclined her head, producing the gown and pulling it over Elizabeth's head. Good Lord, underwear really did make a difference! The gown was perfect now.

"Will you show my lord?" Madame asked.

Elizabeth nodded slowly, her gaze still on her figure as she smoothed her hands over her waist. Unbelievable, that it was she in the mirror. Still distracted, she allowed Madame to lead her to the connecting door between the rooms.

Oh, he did well pretending he had not seen her. Sprawled in that chair, his elbow resting on the arm as his finger tapped at his temple, one would never believe he had moved from his seat. But she knew better. She *knew* he had watched her, and judging from the faint colour still staining his skin, he had enjoyed what he saw.

He ignored her knowing smile, however, instead focusing on her gown. This time, he appeared pleased by her couture.

"Leave us."

Madame hastened to comply with his order, shutting the door quietly behind her.

Malvern stared at her in silence, his finger rubbing at his temple. Did he mean to disconcert her with such intense scrutiny? Or to distract her from what she knew had happened?

She couldn't contain an impish smile. "Did you like what you saw?"

His finger still at his temple, he said nothing.

"Oh, please don't pretend you don't know what I'm talking about." Her smile stretched wide now as exhilaration flooded through her, lending bounce to her step as she came before him. "Wasn't it glorious? I'm so glad you brought me here. I had no idea such places existed. And to think, I thought such places were solely for the purchase of garments!"

Finally, he deigned to speak. "You are amused, are you?"

The wonder of discovery burned within her, and she knew she was grinning like a fool. "How could I not be? This is all working out extremely well. Really, I must thank you. This is much more than I ever expected, and we've only touched the tip of the iceberg." She stopped. "Haven't we?"

He nodded, the fingers of his hand swaying close to her shoulder. "You have started well." His fingers brushed against her skin, goose flesh rising in its wake. "Your progress is much further along than I anticipated. I shall have to reassess your curriculum."

She settled into her seat, enjoying the unfamiliar feel of exposed flesh and the way her breasts moved with the new corset. "Do you really have a curriculum for me? Or are you just being facetious?" Wickedness bubbled within her. "Because if you do, could I have a copy for my records?"

His finger stopped its relentless rub against his temple, and she had the strangest feeling he wanted to smile at her comment. Nothing crossed his face, however. "Do you really feel it would be beneficial for you to have access to your curriculum?"

Well now, how was she to not tease him at that? Affecting a winning smile, she could have sworn she saw an answering flicker in his eyes.

He got to his feet and, just like that, he was cold imperiousness once more. "We will be on our way. Tell Madame to meet me out front."

"Yes, sir." She almost saluted at his request.

He paused, and she couldn't tell if he was fighting laughter or scorn. He settled for neither, instead quitting the room.

She sat where she was for a moment. Then, with a little smile, she got to her feet, asking for Madame as she left the room.

***

MALVERN TRIED TO IGNORE his hand, but the damn thing wouldn't stop shaking. It was ridiculous to have such a reaction to a woman so much his inferior, both in knowledge and in rank, but there it was, his bloody shaking hand. He trapped it with his other, concealing them behind his back as Madame came to greet him.

"You were well pleased by your visit, my lord?" The woman's impertinence would have to be dealt with, standing there with an arch look on her face as if she could pass comment on his activities. Maybe it was he had patronised her store too often and too well.

"Tolerably." His hand still tap-danced behind his back. "You will send the bill to my man."

"Yes, my lord." She curtsied deeply. "Will this include my lady's clothing?"

"Of course it would. Do not make me take my business elsewhere."

She blanched, her smug smile becoming uncertain. Good. Finally, the woman remembered her place.

"My lady, she insisted she would pay for her garments." Madame's voice faltered, a hint of Manchester bleeding through the French. "Maybe there has been a misunderstanding of your intentions?"

"It is none of your concern." The statement had come out more forcefully than he had intended. And still his hand shook. "Add her clothing to my bill."

"Yes, my lord." Her voice somewhat steadier, she curtsied again and left.

Dismissing the dressmaker from his mind, he instead contemplated her revelation. So his student thought to pay for her garments? For all intents and purposes, the woman was acting the role of his mistress, and he would assume responsibility for her as such. Besides, he was the one who had to look at her. If such a small sum guaranteed the end of the eyesore that was her clothing, he would pay twice Madame's asking price with nary a blink.

His pupil entered the room dressed in her old clothing, her eyes sparkling. He forced his hands still as she took his arm, disguising the tremor as they left the shop for Malvern House.

The shaking, though, did not leave until long after she had.

Chapter Seven

THE DESCRIPTION OF WHAT had been one of the standout events of his life seemed to fall upon deaf ears. Malvern studied his protégé, noting that while she nodded in a facsimile of rapt attention, her mind was elsewhere.

The evocative description of the most memorable erotic performance he had ever attended had not piqued her interest. The burlesque show had featured a woman who had charged an obscene amount for the mere privilege of gazing upon her clothed form as she'd shimmied and swayed. A subsequent attendance, including a significant hike in price, had encompassed the woman's transition from clothed to unclothed. It had been well worth the extra coin. Just thinking about it had him half hard.

His pupil, however, had evidently decided there were more scintillating things to ponder than that long-ago performance. Her preoccupation had been obvious upon her arrival, her brief greeting at odds with her usual enthusiasm. Now that he thought on it, the distinct lack of questions, those that so often interrupted their lessons, should have immediately raised his concern. On a few occasions, she had fairly looked as if she would burst if she didn't impart what she was thinking, but somehow she had managed to contain herself.

He was beginning to wonder if he would have need to question her directly.

Mayhap the lack of physicality of their encounters had distressed her. They had been meeting now for over a month, and he had decided on a series of less demonstrative routes to pleasure. It had seemed prudent to begin such a course, in the wake of the disturbing incident in the dressmaker's. She was his pupil, not his mistress, and a lack of control could only be detrimental to her education. Such lapses could lead to others, and he would not engage in penetrative sex.

So, he'd endeavoured to introduce her to the art of seduction from afar. With the assistance of a fan, he had shown Elizabeth how with a flash of eye, a trace of lip or a frame of cheek, she could enslave a man from across a ballroom. He'd then proceeded to instruct her on a far more decadent version of fan language, and the intrigue of enthralling a man with little more than thin slivers of wood and cloth had seemed to strike a chord. Surprisingly, she was quick to memorise all, and with a seriousness he had not thought her capable. Also of surprise how quickly she'd turned the tables on him. With a flick of her wrist, she'd lured and seduced, his heart racing as shadowed eyes enthralled him.

Then, just because she could, she'd proceeded to make up her own gestures and combinations. His heart had slowed to normal rhythm as each became sillier than the last. Her laughter, light and frequent, had even coaxed amusement in him as she'd exchanged seduction for burlesque.

Last week, they'd discussed erotic poetry. Unfortunately, the discussion had destroyed his resolve and they'd ended up enacting the scenarios described in a most satisfactory manner. The scenarios barring coitus, of course. A few days ago, she had surprised him by sending her own erotic poem, an effort which had aroused him to the point where he'd had to seek relief like a schoolboy before he'd been fit to leave the house. The poem was currently locked in his drawer, along with the schedule she was convinced didn't exist.

Now she sat before him, her gaze focused on something only she could see. Her distraction, however, allowed him to indulge himself. He settled back, permitting himself the pleasure of examining her.

She wore one of her new gowns, this one in a dark green. It looked well on her, the rich shade suiting her colouring, the shape displaying hers.

He shifted in his seat. Maybe the shape suited her too well. Her breasts swelled above the neckline in a way they'd not in her previous wear, putting him to mind of the corset she must be wearing beneath, and of how she'd looked without the corset, how she'd stood in front of the mirror, her hands caressing her breasts as he'd watched….

He shook himself. Damnation, again that lapse.

The new clothing, though, had been a source of dissension between them. His pupil, upon finding he had settled the bill, had been adamant to reimburse him, though she was far his inferior in fiduciary matters. Beyond ridiculous, that she should insist upon such an action. Almost he had told her this but something had stayed him. She had been so determined, so resolute, it had become plain his usual methods to ensure compliance would be of no use. And so, he had done the only thing he could think of. He'd lied.

Claiming the money for the attire had been taken from the payment she had made to Lydia, he had run roughshod over her objections and ignored her sceptical look at such a patently false statement. Her attempts to insist had been met with his refusal to engage in argument and eventually she had seen the futility of pursuit. She had not seemed wholly comfortable with the outcome, but seeing no other recourse, she had demurred with quiet, and strangely intense, thanks.

He had no notion why he had been so obstinate. All he knew was a strange sense of triumph had suffused him at the knowledge that clothing *he* had bought for her lay against her skin, that each morning she donned garments *he* provided. Even now, seeing her in the clothing he'd purchased for her, that same sense surged through him.

Abruptly, he grew tired of her distraction. Though it lacked subtly, directness had its benefits. "Is there something you wished to discuss?"

Her gaze rose and for the first time that evening, her attention was solely on him. "Discuss? No, nothing."

"Nothing." Did she truly think him so dense as to not observe her preoccupation? "That is why you have not listened to a word I've said tonight?"

"Of course I've listened, you were saying—" She paused. "I'm almost certain there was dancing involved." Sheepishness crept into her smile. "I am sorry, Malvern. You are right. I wasn't listening."

"So I say again, was there something you wished to discuss?"

She hesitated, her every thought crossing her face. What was it like, to be so exposed? One of his father's mistresses had impressed upon him at a young age one must always be on guard, and the truth of that had been demonstrated time and again over the years. He still remembered her voice, her face, as she had said it, the incident of greater importance to him than she'd probably intended. It was seared into his memory, a strange affinity forever binding him with this woman whom his father had discarded without care less than a fortnight later. When given her conge, true to her word, no expression had crossed her porcelain features.

His pupil appeared to have finally reached a decision. "Well, there is something. I have a question. Well, not a question. It's really more of a request."

"A request?" A request could be interesting. His gaze wandered over her face, her throat, lingering on the swell of her breasts. Mayhap her request would have him removing her dress, bearing her breasts to his gaze, his touch, his tongue….

Oblivious to the direction his thoughts had turned, she twisted her hands. "Last night, well, last night was the Swannson's ball, the one for Pippa Swannson's debut. Lady Swannson had quite outdone herself, and could one have really expected that after Sophia's debut last year? Now that was quite the spectacle."

Concealing his interest, he noted the colour in her cheeks, her rapid breath. This request, it must be of a truly depraved nature to warrant this level of distress. Arousal ran through him, stirring his blood, thickening his cock. What could a mind such as hers possibly have conjured?

"Anyway, I was at the debut, and it was really quite lovely. Lots of people I knew in attendance, loads of gossip and we all were having a very merry time. I—Were you there?"

With a nervous laugh, she answered her own question. "Of course you weren't there, as if you would be. I don't know what I was thinking. But anyway, I was chaperoning for my niece, my eldest niece—Lord, it's hard to believe she is seventeen—and I had just popped out of the ballroom for a moment. I needed a spot of air. It was so stuffy in the ballroom and so I wandered into the garden and, well, I happened upon a couple." She spoke as if in a race, stumbling and tripping with all haste to a finish he could only guess at.

"And what were they doing?" he asked, though he already knew. His own experiences at debuts surfaced, quick fucks against walls, fellatio performed behind curtains. The gardens were particularly rich fodder, the seclusion and the lack of light concealing some of the more depraved encounters.

"They were kissing. Soft. Light. Like they were courting." A soft smile lit her features as she lost herself in some memory. Suddenly, she looked young, innocent, not more than a girl herself. "Rocksley used to kiss me like that."

"They were kissing? That is all?" A naïve couple were kissing, no doubt badly, and she was on the point of swooning?

Or was it the memory of her husband?

Annoyance inundated Malvern. Nothing he'd done had resulted in the look she had on her face now, halfway between wistful and luminous. He had shown her pleasure, true pleasure, but that look was reserved for her dead husband, a man so idiotic he couldn't even *recognise* how easy his wife's passion ignited.

Pain flared, distracting him. He glanced down. Bloody hell, his hands were clenched so hard his nails would leave marks in the fleshy part of his palm. Disturbed this had somehow happened without his knowledge, he released the tension, flexing the tight muscles surreptitiously.

Thankfully, she had remained unaware of his lapse. "Their kissing was enough. They were so sweet standing there, absorbed in one another, their whole lives ahead of them." Her eyes lost their dreaminess and that fleeting glimpse of how she must have been before her marriage was gone. "Do you realise we've never kissed?"

"Of course we have." Their lesson needed to be guided back to more familiar footing. It was unnecessary to wonder what she was like upon her debut. To wonder if she would have regarded him with that innocent desire, allowed him to kiss her as she'd described.

Ridiculous notion. Never had he wanted to be that innocent, to court a maid like a fool.

A rueful smile pulled at the corner of her mouth. "No, we haven't. Strange, isn't it? We've done so much, and yet we haven't done that."

Bloody hell, she was right. How could it be that he'd never kissed her? His mouth had traced her body, he'd learned her contours with his tongue, and yet never had he touched his lips to hers. Never explored the shape of her mouth, never traced her lips with his tongue, never taken her bottom lip between his teeth.

He shifted in his seat, uncomfortably hard. She wasn't helping matters, with her new gown displaying her breasts so prominently, the flesh plump and ripe for his touch. It also didn't help that he knew exactly how she would feel beneath his fingers. Soft, hot, her skin silky smooth.

And still she spoke. "I haven't actually kissed that many men, so I was wondering if we could experiment. With kissing." She looked at him, all that was expectant and eager. "What do you think?"

Malvern didn't hasten to reply, much needed clarity arriving with her request. She wanted to kiss? Innocently kiss when he could instead pull down that thrice-damned bodice and encase her nipple with the wet heat of his mouth? Kissing was the appetiser to a meal, not the main course. But how was she to learn if he didn't show her the error of her ways? "If you feel it will benefit your education, by all means, we should undertake it."

Her brow creased, and he knew she wondered at his words. And then, she smiled.

Such a smile should not be so radiant. His heart, disturbingly, started to pound.

"Excellent." She came toward him and, with little more than a soft touch, coaxed him to his feet. "So, how should we proceed?" Her gaze wandered to his mouth.

He ignored the rush in his ears. "Start, and if you require any instruction, I shall provide it."

She nodded, her gaze still on his mouth. Her hand curled around the back of his neck and, lifting herself onto her toes, she touched her lips to his.

He restrained the shudder that threatened at her touch. Bloody hell, such a reaction was absurd. Slowly, she brushed her soft mouth against his, her lips parted, her breath whispering over him. His already labouring heart grew worse, setting his blood to thrum through his veins.

The response was incommensurate to such a pedestrian embrace. Remaining still, he fought to give lie to his reaction, to pretend she had not just reduced him to a green boy with nothing more than her lips upon his.

With a final soft touch, her mouth lifted from his. Judging by the worry in her eyes, she had felt nothing of his response. "Am I doing something wrong?"

"Do you always kiss with such timidity?" With his words, he tried for indolence, and he must have succeeded. Damnation, she looked hurt. He hadn't meant to hurt her.

"That was a courting kiss."

"A what?"

"A courting kiss." A blonde curl rested on her forehead. His fingers itched. "The kind you give when you are courting. Rocksley used to kiss me like that."

"No wonder he never made you come," he muttered.

She looked at him sharply. "What?"

"A courting kiss. Interesting." She still looked at him askance, as if deciding whether to make an issue of his remark or not. Evidently, she decided not. Crossing his arms, one part of his mind was pleased to note his hands had stopped shaking. "It seems the kiss you give a virgin."

"Well, I was a virgin." Pink stained her cheeks even as she attempted to appear nonchalant. Damn her for looking so attractive with that tinge of colour.

Her chin lifted and a smile crossed her features,

one that made him slightly apprehensive. "Before I was wed, my suitors used to do this." Her hands cradled his face as her lips whispered over his brows, kissed his temples.

His heart, that damned unruly organ that was not heeding his mind, picked up pace.

"And this." She traced a light path down his cheek before her mouth returned to his, pressing lightly against his lips.

Unwillingly seduced by her chaste kisses and light touches, he attempted in vain to dispel her effect on him. "And this is what swept you off your feet?" he said harshly. "This play?"

She smiled, her thumbs tracing his cheekbones. "Of course. What can be more romantic to a young virgin than a man gently introducing her to pleasure?" She arched a brow, the expression he used to such effect appearing playful upon her. "But, of course, after innocent play, they always tried the passionate kiss."

Malvern was disgusted to find he was holding his breath. She smiled suddenly, wickedly, and then she stepped forward to demonstrate once more.

His brows rose as she mashed her lips against his. Her kiss was…interesting. His heart steadied as she continued her…he hesitated to call it a kiss. She was trying her best, though. It shouldn't cheer him that it appeared she had had some very poor tutors.

Gently, he set her from him, relieved they were back on familiar footing. "That was passionate kissing?"

A frown creased her brow. "Was I doing it wrong?"

He effected an elegant rising of the shoulder, the distraction of a moment ago forgotten. "It was not the best kiss I've ever received."

"Oh." The light in her eyes dimmed.

"'Tis easily remedied." Taking a step toward her, he fairly crowded her with his body. She didn't retreat, curious mouse that she was. Her scent wound about him, that scent that was hers alone, flowers and musk and her.

"How?" Her eyes fairly drowned him with innocence.

Suspicion rose at her guileless tone. "Are you being facetious?"

"Now, why would you say that?" Wickedness danced behind the innocence.

His lips quirked and, before amusement could find expression, he covered her mouth with his. His kiss destroyed the shape of her smile.

Concentrating on overwhelming her, he demanded entrance to her mouth. A hand placed at the small of her back pulled her against him, and with her body aligned with his, he brought his considerable experience to the fore. She was sweet, tasting of the tea she had consumed, her tongue eagerly following his as he tutored her in the art of kissing.

His hands clenched against her back, he tried to maintain a ruthless control on his body, to keep this about their lips and mouths and tongues. She learned too well, though. She took control of the kiss, her lips slanted against his, her arms twining about his neck as she rose to afford a better position. His hand clutched the back of her head, keeping her still for him as she bit and licked at his mouth, his body hardening yet again. He forgot this was about teaching her, forgot he was to remain dispassionate and removed.

Trailing small kisses down her neck, he nuzzled her skin, licking at the flesh behind her ear. Arching her neck, she gave him greater access and her hands roamed his back, always pulling him closer to her, trapping him in her. Her breasts pushed against his chest, the flesh bared by her gown burning through the fine lawn of his shirt, making him wish there was nothing between them, that he was deep inside her, that this kiss was prelude to something more.

Forcing himself away from those thoughts, he instead returned to her lips, her tongue, the wet warmth of her mouth. He would not think of how it would feel to be inside her, fucking her until she screamed, until he was the only lover she remembered.

She tore her mouth away from his, sucking air into her lungs in great gasps. Her eyes were wide, this time with shock instead of feigned innocence. "That was…I don't…."

He, too, felt the effects of the kiss, arousal running wild through his veins. "A passionate kiss." The words came out fairly even.

A sudden smile brightened her face, fairly dazzling him with its brilliance. "It certainly was. We should do it again."

He wanted to say no. He wanted to order her home, to bring the lesson to an end. He *should* send her home. "I am at your disposal."

Again, that smile. "You are, aren't you?" She launched herself at him, covering his face with kisses. Some light, some hard, but all with the same effect as the first.

Bloody hell, again that absurdly incommensurate response. She was seducing him with her soft touches and her mouth on his. Pleasure rolled through him, and it was impossible to separate it from the woman in his arms.

Rubbing his thumb against her cheek, he traced her features, her name suddenly crystallizing in his mind. "Elizabeth."

"Yes?" She placed a kiss against his jaw.

"That is your name, isn't it? Elizabeth?"

She stilled. She pulled back, and in her face he read the shock, the hurt, the disbelief that he was unsure of her name. Letting her go without protest, Malvern quashed the desire to reassure her, to tell her that he was just teasing, because it would be a lie.

He had made certain not to think of her as Elizabeth until this moment. Even now, he had little notion as to why her name should be so important, to either her or himself. He just knew that now she was Elizabeth, no longer a mouse, more than his student.

Still, she was uncertain, her eyes troubled. She was too free with her emotions. Did she not know the power an observer gained if one's every thought was displayed?

"Yes," Elizabeth finally said. "Elizabeth Marie. My mother claimed a lack of imagination in the choice of my name." Her lips quirked. "I'm actually glad for it. Can you imagine being named Iphigenia? Or Eunice?"

He stared at her. She had just brushed the insult aside. Wholly. With no recriminations. He was not so unfeeling as to not realise what his unthinking comment had meant. She had to have known he did not think of her as a person, simply his student. And yet, she made no ruckus about it. After what they had shared, he would have thought she would be devastated. Women were known to prescribe feeling where there was little, and she had scant experience to buffer her. In truth, he had not thought of that. It had just seemed right to call her by her name, to think of her by such.

"I feel silly asking this now, but would you tell me your given name?" A rueful look crossed Elizabeth's face, as if she knew the irony of her question. "I know you are known as Malvern, but—"

"James," he said. "My given name is James."

"James." His name sounded beautiful when she spoke it. "It seems your mother possessed a lack of imagination as well."

He shrugged. "I wouldn't know."

"Oh." Compassion softened her features. "I'm sorry."

She believed his mother was dead. Most did. He considered letting her continue to believe it. "Don't be. My mother probably does lack imagination."

Elizabeth paused and then, softly, "Do you not know?"

He raised a brow at the pity in her voice. He didn't much care one way or the other if he knew his mother's mind. On occasion he had seen her, each encounter as if with a stranger. There was nothing wrong in that. It was much the same as any other child's life.

As his hand began to tap against his side, he glanced away. "I cannot say it ranks highly on the things I must discover in life." He forced himself to still, to turn back to Elizabeth. "Do you wish to continue with your lesson?"

"The kissing, you mean? No, I should go home." She made a face. "My sister is making me attend a dinner tonight. It always takes a good hour or so to get me in the right frame of mind to see her."

"Oh?" He cursed himself for his curiosity. What did he care what she did?

"Yes, she must always insist on trying to fix my

life. I swear, one of these days...." Elizabeth regarded him ruefully. "But you don't wish to know this. I do apologise, James." A smile lifted the corner of her mouth. "I must say, I like calling you that."

He hated to admit it, and he didn't let himself until after she had left, but he liked hearing Elizabeth call him by name as well.

Chapter Eight

JAMES GESTURED AT THE book propped before him as he explained the sexual positions depicted within its pages. Elizabeth hadn't the heart to tell him she had already examined this book most thoroughly, when she had come across it in her father's study as a girl.

Besides, she enjoyed watching him.

His chair had been dragged from behind his desk, and hers had been turned so they faced each other, a new state of affairs. Up until tonight, the verbal part of their interaction had always taken place with the barrier of his desk between them. She had no notion as to why tonight was different. It was affording her much pleasure, though, being able to observe his whole form as he lectured.

James offered anecdotes to further illustrate both the purpose and the pleasure behind each picture. Elegant fingers drifted over the page as they had drifted over her skin, careful and delicate upon the parchment as he was of her flesh. Though his brow was clear, his lips precise as he spoke, she fancied she could see the faint hint of concentration and cursed herself as a fool for imagining it.

It drove her insane, his inscrutability. Never could she read him. He was an enigma to her, a puzzle she wanted desperately to solve. She wanted to know of the events that had shaped him into the man he had become. She wanted to ask of his family, his childhood, his life up until she had met him. How did he spend his day? What did he have for breakfast? Did he go to societal gatherings and if he did, why had she not seen him?

What did he think of her?

Rubbing her hands against her thighs, she looked away. Good Lord, there it was. She had tried so very hard to conceal her desire from herself, but all it took was one errant thought to shatter the illusion that she didn't care.

Did he think her facile and stupid for her lack of knowledge? Did he find her observations annoying? Was he truly enjoying their meetings or was it merely something to pass the time?

Did he like her?

Elizabeth told herself it didn't matter. He wasn't required to think well of her, just as she wasn't required to like him, but for all that she pretended, she knew she did. She liked him. She liked that he made her think, made her question her own abilities and boundaries. She liked talking with him, and she most assuredly liked playing with him. More than that, he fascinated her, beyond the erotic instruction, beyond how he made her feel. He could be sitting there as he was now, his beautiful voice espousing some tutorial, and there was no place she would rather be.

She exhaled. All of this conjecture was

pointless. She should know better than to torment herself with an endless litany of unanswerable questions. Although, he *had* answered every query she had ever posed. For almost two months, never had he dissuaded her. He had simply answered, and when she had asked the next question, he had answered that as well.

Two months, and still their association was a secret. None had questioned her movements, her sisters easily believing her tale of regular appointments, and she didn't think James *had* any family. The new clothes she wore only around him, or at least she would until she could think of a plausible excuse.

Thank God no one had discovered her true purpose. She should not yet like to give him up.

Warmth suffused her as she traced his features with her gaze. The slant of his cheekbones. The slope of his brow. The strong jaw. His features were becoming so well known to her, so much so that when she closed her eyes she could picture him perfectly.

An elegant hand turned the page.

Suddenly, she wanted to push him, to see what he wouldn't answer. "Have you noticed Lady Barronn and Mr. Sykes don't speak? They stand on opposite sides of the room, pointedly not looking at each other." The question wasn't the most provoking she'd ever concocted, but it would do to begin.

He fell silent and then his gaze rose to meet hers, revealing nothing. "Do you not find this interesting?"

Was he annoyed at her interruption? Unsure, she smiled, more than like too brightly. "No, I do. It's only they do tend to ignore each other, a little too much, in my opinion."

He returned his attention to the book. "That's because she had an affair with his brother while she was his mistress." He pointed to the page. "This picture has the man—"

"And Lord Walters always disappears from the ballroom two hours into the ball. I've been tempted to follow him a time or two."

"If you had, a part of your education would not need explanation."

She waited.

Clearly annoyed now, he exhaled before continuing. "He meets his lover there."

How was that a revelation?

"His lover. Who is a man."

"What? Oh." She frowned. "How does that work?"

"There are many ways. They could masturbate each other, or they could perform fellatio, or undertake anal sex."

"Anal sex? As in, up the bum?" Feeling the burn of a blush, she lowered her voice. "And men say that as a toast when drinking. It puts a whole new slant on the phrase."

His lips quirked. "Yes, it does, doesn't it?"

"You have undertaken this?" She still couldn't believe it. Whoever would have thought such an action would even be possible? Well, of course it was possible, after all sexual engagement was all about slots and—Good Lord, she was stopping right there.

"Once or twice. Buggery is not to my taste, but there are many who enjoy it." He raised a brow, which she had decided must be his primary form of communication. "Women, even."

Elizabeth sat back in her chair. Well. Women

found it enjoyable? Really? The thought of taking someone *there* was disturbing to say the least. "If it's all the same to you, I am happy to leave that out of my, um, education."

"It is listed on your curriculum for Thursday next. Are you sure you do not wish to partake? By all accounts, it can be quite pleasurable for the woman."

"Can it?" Dread curled low in her belly. She should not doubt him. He was her tutor. Surely he knew what was best. "Well, if you think…."

No expression crossed his features, his face impassive as ever, and yet she was certain he was amused. Another man might have been grinning.

Relief flooded through her. "You are teasing me."

A faint smile curved his lips. "Elizabeth, if there is something you do not wish to do, you must tell me. Pleasure is about what is right for you, and what is right for some is not right for others. If you don't wish to do something, then we shan't." His smile disappeared but his gaze, intensely serious, captured her own. "By the same token, if there is something you wish, we shall explore it to its furthest reaches. This is about you, and what you want. No one else can tell you what that is."

At his words, something inside her shifted. Never had someone given control to her. No, not given. He had not given her control at all. He had simply told her it had always been hers. Strange thought. And strangely liberating.

"Thank you." Too much was churning inside her. Looking down at her hands, she tried to sort her emotions. "I *should* thank you, for what you've done for me. For everything."

"There is no need."

She looked up. That ice-blue gaze was still upon her. It was odd, but she didn't feel cold. A peculiar sensation gripped her chest, warm and breathless, similar to excitement but different somehow. The silence between them was heavy with something, she knew not what, but it made her feel....

She blinked, and the moment disappeared as if it had never been. James looked down at the book, his index finger tapping against the page, a faint frown creasing his brow.

Endeavouring to return to a more familiar mood, Elizabeth grinned, uncaring that it felt somehow false. "So, anyway, I was wondering about the figures in paintings, you know, the ones that are nude?"

He glanced at her, and she could swear gratitude crossed his face. She continued, forcing a brightness she didn't feel into her words. "Are they anatomically correct? Are all men made as they, and I suppose, you?"

"I would venture to say they are as correct as the sculptor could make them."

What else she could ask? "Why have you moved your chair from around the de—?"

"Elizabeth," he interrupted. "Is there a point to this?"

She shrugged. "I was curious."

A sudden smile quirked his lips. She drew in a breath, her heart suddenly racing.

"You are curious?" Good Lord, but his voice was almost criminal.

She nodded, her gaze trained on his as arousal hardened his features, making his eyes burn. He leaned over, trapping her hand with his, his thumb rubbing over her skin. The small caress raised goose bumps and she shivered, her stomach tightening as she became lost in him.

"What are you curious about?" His words wound about her, seducing her. The movement of his thumb, the slight push and pull against her skin, drove her insane. Such a small caress, so innocent, and yet she could feel her response deep inside her.

"Do you truly want to know?" Even her voice had become affected, husky and low.

His eyes dark, wickedness lurking in their depths, he nodded.

"What did you do today?"

Face blank, he dropped her hand. This time, this one time, it wasn't because he didn't want to show what he was thinking. It was because she truly had shocked him. So much so he couldn't disguise that second of disconcertment, allowing her a brief glimpse at true emotion. Pleasure suffused her that she could affect him so.

"You wish to know about my day?" Incredulity stole the seduction from his tone. "What, pray tell, do you wish to know?"

"Only what you did."

"What I did? You mean sexually?"

"No." Ridiculous heat burnt her cheeks. Really, she had nothing to blush about, after all they'd— "You have done things today? Sexually? What—" Did she really want to know? "Um, no, I was wondering about what you did. Did you do estate work, or did you take a walk? Did you go to your club? Did you enjoy your breakfast, if so, what did you enjoy the most? Did anything amuse you today? Shock you? Bore you?"

"You don't want to know much, do you?" He studied her, his forefinger rubbing his lip. She waited for his response, wondering if she had overstepped a boundary.

"I enjoyed my coffee," he finally said. "And the new footman has an annoying way of greeting one in the morning. All chirpy and awake." Disgust punctuated his words at the last.

"Really?" She tucked a hand under her chin. "What else?"

His gaze became distant. "I don't know. I went to my club. Nothing much of interest there." Eyes clearing, he shrugged. "My day was fairly uneventful. What of yours?" The corner of his mouth lifted. "I suppose you are a morning person and would have been charmed by an energetic greeting."

Elizabeth gave an exaggerated shudder. "Heavens, no, I can't stand the mornings. Some days, I have to be dragged forcibly from my bed— especially now that it is colder." She thought back. "My sister decided to visit me this morning, bringing her horde of children with her. She has five of the little monsters, all of them under ten years of age. Have you ever faced five children first thing in the morning? Not the best of endeavours to begin the day."

Her nieces and nephews had rampaged through her town house, tracking mud over the cold marble floors, leaving marks on the pristine walls. Their rambunctious behaviour had resulted in her home appearing well-used and lived in, a state that was all too often absent. Catherine had the harried look Elizabeth had often seen on the faces of her sisters, the mingling of exasperation, exhaustion, and love as she looked at her children, though still she'd called them wild little beasts as they'd trampled past her.

Belatedly, she realised that somehow the

conversation had turned to her. "But we were speaking of you and your day. What else did you do?"

He shrugged. "Nothing."

"Oh please. Of course you didn't do *nothing*. You had to have done *something*—"

She squeaked as he covered her mouth with his, stopping her questions most effectively. His lips moved slowly against hers, teasing her mouth open, his tongue darting inside. She promptly forgot what she had been saying as her arms crept around his neck, her body arching into his as she returned his kiss enthusiastically. Mumbling something encouraging, he deepened the kiss, his hands wandering over her body fervently.

Her last thought was why no one had ever thought of this most pleasurable method of silencing her before.

Chapter Nine

WHERE, EXACTLY, WOULD ONE go for a demonstration of stripping?

Elizabeth chewed her lip, staring at James as he gave yet another lecture. She didn't see him, though. No, instead she saw the whirl of silk and the flash of limbs, golden skin teasingly revealed and then concealed in the next breath. Hard muscles, soft thighs, a decadent version of hide and seek, men and women enticing with the revelation or denial of their flesh, stoking the lust of any who watched to fever pitch.

The attraction of such a display was palpable. Ever since James had described it, she'd wanted to see such a thing for herself. No doubt there were performances in London, but the continent would surely hold more decadent pleasures and, for her first, she should have the best. A trip to Paris, to see the woman James had told her about, or was that in Vienna? No matter, she would visit both, and James could show her all his iniquitous haunts. They would punt the Seine, enjoy the vistas of Florence and dance the nights away in the music halls of Vienna.

She sighed. It was a pleasant fantasy. One day, maybe, she would travel, but never with James. Sadness threatened, though she quickly pushed it away and instead returned to the slow reveal of flesh and skin.

James had said it was an art, but she couldn't see how the removal of one's clothes was anything but titillating—especially as, when describing it, he'd had a glint in his eye she knew well. The thought of people removing their clothing, layer by layer, driving the viewer wild with the slow reveal, teasing them, stoking desire and want higher and higher until the atmosphere seethed with its frenzied presence could do nothing but stoke desire.

Elizabeth swallowed, phantoms of these imagined performers turning her blood to flame.

How would it be if, rather than a public performance, it were just they two? Her mind raced, half-formed images tumbling over one another. What if James slowly revealed himself for her pleasure? Her mouth went dry as she pictured his golden flesh slowly unveiled, his throat bared, the muscles on his chest flexing, his hands on the buttons of his trousers and then, lower.

Oh God, what if it were *her* disrobing for *him*?

Her mouth closed with an audible snap. James, however, was so occupied with his recitation he'd not noticed.

Descending into fantasy, she imagined James's eyes hot on her as she removed her gloves, her skin prickling under his intense gaze. Each flick of a button an agony, each tug of cloth a tease. Her fingers trembled as she undid and untucked and untied, as she both hid and revealed her body. She teased and provoked until desire was a heavy presence between them, given life by heated looks and implied promises. Nothing would stop her, not until *he* stopped her, by kissing her, caressing her. Taking her.

Touching her tongue to the corner of her mouth, she watched as James expounded upon his lecture. How would he react if she did as she wanted, if she removed her clothing piece by piece?

The more she watched him, lecturing steadily with little notice of her, the more she wanted to find out. Her clothing rasped against her skin. She itched to remove it, to watch the dispassion on his face disappear as she rid herself of her gown, her corset, her drawers.

She stood. James paused in his recitation with a slight raise of his brow. With a small smile to placate him, she luxuriated in feeling naughty and knowing and, yes, a little bit wicked. True to his order, she'd worn clothing that was easily removed, and she was about to take advantage of his demand.

Slowly, she undid the buttons at the back of her gown, her gaze wandering around the room as if the action were extremely tedious. Thanking whatever prompted her to wear a low backed gown that evening, she performed a little twist of her torso, the move helping unhook those buttons at the top. Her breasts pushed against the bodice of her gown, swelling temptingly above the neckline. She bit her lip, her flesh suddenly too tight.

James had resumed his lecture, but she could feel his gaze upon her. He was attempting to conceal his interest, but his steady gaze couldn't quite hide the intensity. She studiously avoided looking at him, pretending she wasn't desirous of his attention, as if she were undertaking this solely for her own benefit and had absolutely no thought of him.

With a sigh, the panels of her gown parted, the low neckline gaping at the lack of tension. The move displayed her new corset, the creamy silk blending into her skin, the boning pushing her breasts into prominence. She shrugged out of the sleeves and the dress pooled about her feet as it slipped from her body. Every breath she took dragged her nipples against the fabric of the corset, and the feel of her sensitised skin exposed to the room, to his eyes, had desire coursing through her hard and sharp.

Quickly, before she lost focus, she untied her petticoats, let the cloth slither to the floor. Gracefully, she stepped out of the mass of fabric, dressed now only in corset, drawers, and stockings. Bending to pick her garments from the ground, she paused when she heard a smothered groan. Wickedness suffused her, and she remained bent over, taking her time to gather her clothing.

Slowly rising, she turned to the chaise, presenting him with her back as she draped the garments over the arm. Arranging them this way and that, she made sure to bend and twist often, counting her success in the slight intakes of breath, the faint stumble of his words.

Deeming she had tormented him enough, she turned and finally met his gaze. Face impassive, he stared at her as if he were unaffected. The clenched fist resting on his desk, however, made mockery of his expression.

Stepping out of her shoes, she sauntered over to him, hips swaying. Lord, she felt all that was power and female. A wicked grin flitted about her mouth as she placed her foot on the chair between his spread thighs.

He was hard. He could hide many things, but he couldn't hide that.

Eyes locked on his, she untied her garter, languorously rolling her stocking down her leg, enjoying the feel of her skin beneath her hands. He didn't touch her, but merely watched as she repeated the action with her other stocking.

"What are you about?" His tone was cool, even. A lie.

"Merely getting a head start on the evening." Placing her foot back on the floor, she turned, presenting her back. "Loosen me?"

He remained still, and for a moment she thought he wouldn't respond. He said not a word as he stood, looming over her, so close she could feel his breath stirring the hair at the crown of her head. The backs of his fingers brushed the skin above her corset and she shivered, her throat moving convulsively as the response he always engendered streaked through her. Gently, he loosened the laces of her corset, his knuckles bumping against her skin as he worked silently. Containing her reaction, she pretended an indifference she most certainly didn't feel.

Once the corset slackened he moved away, taking his place in his chair once more. All was silence now as she turned to face him.

Never taking her eyes from his, she unhooked the busk, holding the corset to her body as she did so. Barely breathing now, she was completely caught by his gaze upon her. She could not falter now. Draping an arm across her breasts, she covered her nipples and then pulled the corset free, letting it dangle, watching as the silk caught the light.

His gaze upon her was like a caress, tracing the

line of her neck, the length of her arm, the curve of her breast. Power rushed through her, that she could capture his attention so completely.

Untying the waist of her drawers, she let them drop to the floor. Of a sudden, the reality of the situation hit her. Good Lord, she was completely naked. Taking a deep breath, she fought apprehension. Many times she'd been naked before him, and most like would again.

Ignoring her anxiety, she covered her breasts and mons in false modesty, determined to play this out. Seating herself on the chaise, she dropped her arm from her breasts and clasped her hands demurely in her lap. And then she looked directly at him.

A muscle ticked in his jaw as he stared at her. Staring back, she ignored the thump of her heart, the tightness of her nipples, the emptiness of her core.

Then, as if he were unaffected, he began his lecture again.

She had no notion of what he said and less care. The only care she had was that he had not taken his eyes from her, that his voice broke every now and then, and that his hands were still white-knuckled on the desk.

Taking an expansive sigh, she idly played with her left nipple.

Within seconds, he was on her, his mouth crushing hers, his hand jerking hers aside to cup her breast. His attack forced the breath from her lungs, and his body pushed her against the chaise, his hips forcing between her thighs. Recovering her breath, she gave a delighted gasp and surrendered to him, her head falling back as his mouth ravaged hers. He grabbed her thigh, bringing it against his hip, opening her to him.

As she moaned against his mouth, his tongue took advantage and darted inside to play with hers, to fill her with him. Raising her other leg, she cradled him, the cloth of his breeches chaffing her deliciously. She tore frantically at his shirt, wanting his bare flesh under her hands, needing it, and finally, *finally*, she felt him, his skin hot against her palms.

His grip tightened on her thighs and he forced her further open, his hand between her legs, his knuckles flicking an impatient caress against her. God, he was working at his trousers, pulling them open, the fabric loosening as the closures gave beneath his fingers. She slid her hands over the firm flesh of his buttocks, beneath his trousers and she hauled him against her, her breath escaping on a sharp gasp at the feel of him. He was thick, and he was hard, and he was sliding against her, back and forth, back and forth. Lips brushed her ear as he spoke, the words too guttural to make any sense. There was a scream building inside her, higher and higher and soon it would burst from her and she couldn't stop it, couldn't contain it. His cock notched against her, demanding entrance, and she dropped her head back on a silent moan, angling her hips, wanting him inside her, wanting him.

And then, he was gone.

Dazed, she lay where he left her. Harsh breath forced air into her lungs. Unappeased lust shrieked along her body. Her brain refused to work.

Painfully, she struggled to a sitting position. Control. She had to establish control. She focused on breathing. One breath. Two. Instituting a fairly even rhythm, she then focused on her surroundings.

James was on the other side of the room. Why was he over there? He had been here, with her, and then he…wasn't. Chest heaving, he raised a shaking hand, ploughing through his hair with little care for the style his valet had no doubt carefully arranged.

"James?" She hated the waver in her voice. Clearing her throat, she started again. "James?"

Still he wouldn't look at her. Cold whispered across her, and suddenly she was all too aware that he was clothed—and she was not. Feeling horribly exposed, she hunched her shoulders and pulled at the garments still hanging on the chaise, draping the cloth to conceal her nakedness as much as she could. "James?"

All was silence and then, "Elizabeth."

She licked her lips. "What happened?"

Moving suddenly, with precision, he sat himself in his chair, his dishevelled appearance causing him no concern, as if a disordered shirt and rumpled clothes were the height of fashion. "We were discussing the outcome of a voyeuristic interlude during an orgy, I believe. Shall I repeat what has already been stated?"

She pulled the edges of the gown tighter. "James, don't be obtuse. What just happened? Why did you stop?"

Moments ticked by and still he didn't answer. The fine hairs on her neck stood on end, but she refused to be intimidated by him. She absolutely refused.

Finally, he spoke. "Do you realise how close we were to penetration?"

She blinked. And again. "Pardon?"

"I was almost inside you, my dear. Ruination was only a moment away."

"But I don't understand." Why couldn't he just say what he meant? "Why is that bad?"

Ice could not be smoother than his face and would, at the very least, offer a distorted reflection of her own emotion. "Because you are unmarried. Because a child could result. Because coitus was never part of our curriculum. A hundred reasons of which those are but a few. You should thank me, my dear, for remembering myself in time."

Damnation, she *hated* feeling stupid, and she hated him for making her feel so. "Do you not achieve penetration with other women?" Only now did she realise it was strange they had not completed the sexual act. Vaguely she remembered him saying something about abstinence at the beginning of their agreement, but it had never been a consideration for her. She had no concern for pregnancy, not with her history, and she had been so caught up in everything else that the lack of penetration had meant nothing. And yet only now it was denied did she realise how much she wanted it. Wanted him.

"Don't be obtuse."

She had never understood the appeal of counting to ten, but he was demonstrating most ably why her sisters undertook it with regularity. "Do you have any children?"

"No."

"So you undertake preventative measures?"

He nodded sharply.

"Then why not me?"

A muscle ticked in his jaw, the only indication he felt a degree of agitation. "Why not you? You would do well not to question me. You have placed yourself and your education in my hands, and I will not be second-guessed. You will simply agree to my methods and count yourself lucky I deign to educate you at all. Furthermore, you shall not undertake any activity that deviates from my outline for the evening." His hands on the arms of his chair were clenched, so tight he had to have done himself an injury. "Your impromptu disrobing has disrupted my plan, and I will not have my curriculum disturbed in such a manner."

"I have disturbed you." Calm. How could she be calm when she was so very angry?

He took no notice of her words. "Your lack of respect for my methods is troubling, madam. Should it become necessary, steps will be taken to ensure your compliance."

Something inside her broke. Anger flared, at him, at the situation, but mostly at *him*. "You will not talk to me in such a manner. I will suffer much, James, but I will not suffer that."

That muscle ticked in his jaw.

Refusing to look away, she held firm, her shoulders thrown back even as the gown barely concealed her nakedness. She would not allow him to cow her. He had no call to treat her in such a manner. None.

Stiffly, he inclined his head. "You are correct, madam. I apologise." Abruptly, he got to his feet. "It would be best if we desist for this evening. I shall leave you to dress."

Why was he acting so? He seemed of a sudden to place great care in a curriculum she was not fully convinced existed. To go from sublime pleasure to this….

Oh God. Did he wish to end their arrangement?

Panic ran through her. What if she never saw him again? This couldn't be the last time they would see one another. It couldn't. "We will see each other Tuesday?"

He paused at the door. Shoulders tense, he nodded.

"And…you will say goodbye?" Heart in her throat, she awaited his answer.

Forever passed before he spoke. "Yes."

With that muffled reply, he left the room, closing the door quietly behind him.

Pulling the garment tighter around her, Elizabeth saw only the door, the shape of the panels burned into her mind. Goose flesh rose on her skin as the chill in the air invaded her.

She couldn't exactly say why she started to cry.

***

MALVERN'S STOMACH CHURNED, AT odds with the leaden feeling in his gut. Stumbling into the sitting room, he collapsed into the chaise, and then shot up again, unable to sit on a seat so similar to the one *she* had sat on. He chose another chair, but the feelings inside him wouldn't let him still, and he vaulted to his feet to pace and pace and pace.

What the fuck had happened back there? What had he been thinking? Goddamn it, he *hadn't* been thinking. He had let his goddamn cock rule him and he'd almost…they'd almost…fuck, he could not come inside her.

Never had he felt thus. He didn't even know what he felt. It was beyond comprehension. There had to be a reason for it. All of it.

This desperate need to escape—from her, from what they had almost done—never had he felt it so intensely. Previously, he had no restriction for sexual play. The acts he had undertaken, he could not recall them in their entirety. His one restriction, the only thing he'd ever ascertained was should his seed be spilled, no child would result.

Procreation. That had to be it. Calm descended at the thought, some of his usual dispassion returning. Already he'd determined his usual methods would not be employed with the widow. None were failsafe, and it would be best for them to completely avoid that which resulted in pregnancy. If the widow became pregnant, there would be none other who could claim her child. A compromising situation could be explained away, bribes exchanged, threats uttered—a child could not so easily be forgotten. For all his transgressions, he would not leave a child of his unclaimed. To his knowledge, he'd never impregnated a paramour, and he would not start with the mouse—the widow—

Damnation. Exhaling, he rubbed at his temples.

He would not start with Elizabeth.

It had to be that, this apprehension he felt. He did not want to have his hand forced. Breathing easier, tension eased. Yes, that was it. He did not want to burden himself with a child.

One day he knew he would have to produce an heir for the great Malvern line. That day, however, was far in the future, and it would arrive by purchasing some young chit barely out of the schoolroom. It would not arrive with a widow not five years younger than himself, who looked at him with curiosity and mischief and a host of things best left undefined.

For all his justifications, the explanation did nothing to ease the feeling in his gut.

His stomach twisted again and he remembered Elizabeth beneath him, her thighs hugging his hips, her heat luring him and, God, he had wanted inside her so fucking badly.

Raking his hands through his hair, he forced thoughts of her away. No, it was best to remain separate from her. Apart.

Decision made, he re-entered the study. Elizabeth was properly attired once more, every taper tied, every button fastened. Upon seeing him, she pulled her cloak tighter. Regret, an emotion he had little experience with, suffused him. She had been glorious in her nakedness. Now, he had made her feel shame. He knew it, even as she attempted a smile. Bile rose in his throat, and he cursed himself for the bastard he was.

"Good-bye, then." He would rid himself of this unwarranted emotion. He would.

"Good-bye." She hesitated. A moment passed, and then she came forward, placing dry lips against his cheek.

Malvern closed his eyes at the touch of her mouth, and his gut twisted again. Fuck. When she would have moved away, he gripped her waist, holding her to him for the briefest of moments. Putting his cheek to her hair, he breathed her in, the scent that was hers alone. With his touch, his embrace, he tried to say all he could not verbalise, could not explain.

She stayed still, allowing him the embrace and then, with a gentle push, she prompted him to release her.

He watched her as she left, and he did not think, let no thoughts cross his mind. None.

Chapter Ten

THE COLD FOLLOWED MALVERN into the hall, clinging to him tenaciously as he handed his gloves to his butler. The weather was always brutal this time of year, but this night it was particularly vicious. Hail and sleet had attacked him as soon as he had set foot outside the house, the wind easily cutting through the layers of clothing he'd thought adequate protection. The glut of carriages on the roads had slowed the traffic's progress to a limping crawl and he'd spent most of the night ensconced within his carriage, cursing the need that had driven him out into such damnable weather.

Cartwright took the proffered items with no comment, though the butler must have been curious as to why his master had returned at such an early hour. Malvern questioned it himself. He'd had every intention of attending his club until the wee hours of the morning, to imbibe an obscene amount of alcohol and maybe amuse himself by antagonizing some twit possessed more of bluff than brains. As *La Belle* was conveniently located not five minutes from his club, he'd even toyed with the idea of visiting Lydia's establishment. However, such a transitory desire had left him when confronted by the prospect of venturing once more into the harsh December night.

All of this had nothing to do with Elizabeth.

His club had not improved in his absence. As he'd wandered aimlessly, he'd been reminded rather forcibly of why he had quit the place. Still the same patrons with the same stories. Still the same posers attempting notoriety, the same lackeys snivelling for attention. The younglings may have changed face, but they were still the same in their callowness. The play at the tables was tiresome, the conversation dull, and he'd left it all behind rather than suffer through such a miserly entertainment.

An unrelenting feeling of restlessness had dogged him. It couldn't be appeased by his club, by Lydia, by anything that usually diverted him. All he knew was he was waiting for something, but as for what, he had no bloody clue.

And none of it had anything to do with Elizabeth.

Leaving Cartwright to dispose of his outerwear as warranted, Malvern entered his study. At the very least, he would become as inebriated as his brandy stocks would allow. Malvern settled into his chair, pouring himself a generous helping. He raised the glass to his lips and his gaze lit upon the chair opposite his desk.

Her chair.

Damnation.

Draining the brandy in one swallow, his gaze remained firmly locked on the chair. He couldn't stop thinking about Elizabeth. Everywhere she haunted him. Her features animated as she explained the difference between a courting kiss and a passionate kiss. The wicked glint in her eyes as she trailed her hand down his bare chest. The look of wonder when he made her come.

Bloody hell. His hand tightened around the glass. Mere thoughts of her hardened him, arousal an unassuaged burn in his blood. Pouring another glass, he downed it in the vain hope the heat of the alcohol would burn stronger than his arousal.

Of course it didn't bloody work.

It had been a week since he'd seen her, a damnably long week in which she'd had to attend her family's Christmas gathering. After the shocking lack of control that should have sent her running, they had settled back into their routine, so much so he had been thrown when she'd mentioned the holiday and the decampment to her parents' estate. With her absence, their lessons were of course temporarily suspended.

For his part, he'd not noticed the build-up to the holiday, had not even thought about the season until Elizabeth had mentioned it a little over two weeks ago. Once made aware, he'd entertained vague notions of a private celebration, the two of them together, but fate and her familial commitments had prevented the thought from solidifying. It was for the best. What use had he of Christmas? He'd never celebrated it before and, more than like, wouldn't again.

He scrubbed a hand over his face, the brandy starting to do its work. For at least another week she would be gone, not returned until well after the new year had begun. She had told him about her family's tradition, about celebrating at their country home, where she had grown up and her mother had confiscated the Christmas tree as punishment one year because Elizabeth and her next eldest sister Bella had broken a prized ornament. They would sing carols and drink eggnog, and her father would become a bit too merry on mulled wine and tell ribald tales of how he had courted Elizabeth's mother.

Good God. He downed another glass, the burn now reduced to a tickle. He should not ruminate on Elizabeth in her absence. Lydia had offered the widow as a gift, not an obsession. It did not matter that Elizabeth's green eyes sparkled when she looked at him, as if inviting him to share in a joke only they two knew. It did not matter that she made him want to hold her next to him, his skin against hers as they absorbed each other's warmth. None of that mattered. She was merely a mouse of widow of little sophistication, and was never meant to be more than temporary.

As the justifications flowed, he knew them to be false, the platitudes of a man unwilling to admit—

Malvern stood, pulling at his cravat as he began to pace. When had the measure of the room become constricting? Never before had he noticed its smallness. In the past, it had always adequately suited his purposes but tonight…tonight it was a veritable closet. A man was barely able to take two steps before he had to turn in the opposite direction, and whose idea was it to put so much damned furniture in here?

He swore as he narrowly avoided the chaise lounge where Elizabeth had perched, a wicked smile on her face after she had unhooked her corset, after she had bared herself for him. She had been naked but still she'd sat there so properly, her knees together and her hands in her lap as she'd tormented him.

Fucking merciful god, why had he thought it a good idea to think on *that*? Now, all he could see were her breasts, her legs, her smile, Elizabeth watching him from her perch, knowing she was driving him crazy and yet he had persisted with his lesson, determined to show her—Jesus, he had no idea what he had been going to show her.

Then he had behaved like an idiot. He still had no notion what he had been thinking. It was all a blur, those frantic moments on the lounge. He'd put it all from his mind and Elizabeth seemed to have as well. That state of affairs—total denial—suited him well.

Stopping in the middle of a stride, he rubbed his eyes, cursing the beginnings of a headache. No matter what he did, his thoughts returned to her. Every single bloody time. Memories of her saturated the study, but he knew if he entered another she would follow him, the ghost of her laughter brightening the room, the memory of her touch a shiver on his skin.

Christ. Mayhap this was the first sign of insanity.

A gentle knock drew his attention. His butler entered the room, bringing with him a modicum of distraction.

"What is it, Cartwright?" Malvern was glad for the coolness of his voice, though it was belied by the heat bubbling in his veins.

"I beg your pardon, sir, but you are needed in the ballroom." The butler's unemotional voice was oddly soothing, and showed no sign if he had noticed his master's uncharacteristic display of emotion.

Malvern schooled his features into their usual lines, the impassiveness of his servant's response reminding him of his own. "The ballroom?"

"The request was insistent, sir."

"Insistent," Malvern repeated.

"Yes, sir."

"And whom is so crass as to insist, Cartwright?"

"I beg your pardon, my lord, but I am not at liberty to say."

"Indeed."

The butler quailed infinitesimally at Malvern's level gaze but he resolutely remained silent.

He rubbed his lip, considering his butler before saying, "I shall be there momentarily."

The butler nodded, shutting the door quietly behind him.

Malvern waited an appropriate amount of time before rising to make his way to the ballroom. Demands. His staff issued demands now. It appeared he was too lenient. If nothing else, he would go to the ballroom to disengage the impertinent fool.

The door was ajar, soft light spilling from the gap. Candles had been left burning in the room, highlighting yet another reason to dismiss this servant. He exhaled. It was so tiresome to discipline his employees. Not for the first time, he contemplated downsizing his household, be damned to society and their expectations.

Pushing open the door, he prepared to rebuke the inept servant. He stopped, dumbfounded.

Elizabeth stood in the middle of the room. Candlelight fell softly upon her, her hair by turns gold and shadow, the soft illumination lending a honeyed hue to her skin. The bottom lip caught between her teeth did nothing to mar the wide smile lighting her face, and the soft light did not hide the laughter in her eyes.

He wanted to take her face between his hands. He wanted to kiss her, hard, soft—it didn't matter. He took half a step forward before he controlled himself, linking his hands behind his back, interlaced fingers digging into each other with the force of his restraint.

Making himself look from her smile, he instead swept his gaze down her body. Bloody hell, what a stupid idea. She was wearing one of her new gowns, this one of blue silk that clung to her rounded hips and small waist, her breasts barely contained by the fabric.

Arousal ran through him, thick and hot. Ruthlessly, he forced his response aside. He would not react to her so slavishly. A degree of distance must be maintained.

All of this happened in the blink of an eye, and went unnoticed by her.

"Surprise!" Her brow quirked, as if she knew his shock and, what's more, was amused by it.

"Indeed." Gesturing to the blanket and basket at her feet, he raised a brow in imitation of her. "What is all this?"

A cheeky grin lit her face. "It is my thank you. I would wager you never expected a picnic."

"You would wager correctly." He paused, giving himself time. There was something…warm settled in his chest, something that had begun at her appearance. Curious. "Are you sure this is a picnic?"

"Of course it is. We have a blanket and food. How can it not be a picnic?" She knelt on the floor, her skirts gathered beneath her as she peered into the basket.

Lowering himself to the floor, he stated the obvious. "We are inside."

She huffed in exasperation. "Fine, then, pretend

we're in a field, under a tree."

"We're in a ballroom, Elizabeth."

"You're not trying hard enough, James. Here." She walked on her knees over to him, cursing as her skirt got tangled beneath her. An unwilling smile tugged at his mouth as he watched her pull her skirt out of the way, curses falling from her lips all the while. She really was adorable sometimes—bloody hell, had he just used the word adorable?

She managed to get the skirt out of her way and cross the distance between them. Warm hands covered his eyes as she leaned close, her lips flirting with his ear. "Now, imagine we are in a field. The grass moves gently with the breeze, the summer sun warming the air. We're shaded by a copse of trees, the branches reaching for the clear sky."

He snorted at that. A harsh exhalation of breath exploded from her, and he could hear her counting to ten under her breath before, gamely, she continued.

"Imagine we had strolled, searching for a place for our picnic, and we saw the trees and thought it would make good shelter. You spread out the blanket and we lounged across it, enjoying the shade the tree provided from the midday sun. It is summer, and we had thought to take advantage of the warmer weather, of the sunshine and the heat. We can hear the wind gently pushing at the leaves in the tree, and the smell of sun-warmed grass is in the air, earthy and deep. Can you picture it now?"

He took her hands from his eyes, holding them in his own. She was smiling. Something inside him shifted, something that had been cold and dark, that feeling of warmth expanding. Bringing her hands to his mouth, he pressed a kiss against her fingers. "No. But thank you for trying."

A mock frown couldn't quite contain her amusement. "Well, pretend then we are in your ballroom in the middle of winter about to eat delicious food. How's that?"

"Perfect."

She made a face before turning to the basket, unpacking a variety of foodstuffs and grouping them together in some order, which only made sense to her.

He watched her, enjoying the opportunity just to observe her. Who grouped a tangy lemon tart with a hunk of roast beef? Eventually, curiosity, an unfamiliar emotion, pushed him. "Why are you here, Elizabeth? Should you not be with your family?"

She paused in the setting of the cutlery, and then deliberately, she completed their arrangement. "I was with them."

"Yes, but you said you wouldn't be back until after Twelfth Night. Surely you are missing out on, what was it, apple bobbing?"

She looked up. "Apple bobbing?"

He shrugged.

"Apple bobbing." Ridiculous warmth spread through him at her rueful grin. "Yes. Well. I opened presents with them. We laughed, we cried, Papa became insanely drunk. It seemed prudent to return to London." Lowering her gaze, she started fidgeting with the edge of a napkin. "There are a million people in my family. I'm sure they won't miss me. And, I thought…well, you were here on your own with no one to help you celebrate, and I wanted to…." Her chin lifted. "I just wanted to be here. In London. So, I came."

She had come to London for him? A swirl of some emotion he refused to name tossed low in his gut at the thought. He pushed it away, as he always did with an unknown feeling, and deemed it unimportant. Because it was.

"So, do you like your present?" she asked, a teasing glint lighting her eyes.

"I don't hate it." She thwacked him with the napkin. Capturing her hand and disarming her, he traced the delicate bones with his thumb. "I'm glad you're here."

***

AGONY SHOT THROUGH HIS back. Malvern clawed out of sleep, his spine protesting violently, the stiffness in his lower back an unwelcome companion to the pain.

Bloody hell, had he slept on an anonymous floor once again? He had not done such a thing since his youth, preferring to sleep in his own bed no matter what manner of debauch he had undertaken. Still half asleep, he pried open an eye. There seemed to be a blanket between his body and the floor, but the covering had done little to cushion the hard surface. He noted the presence of a female body lying curled around him, her head buried in his neck, her breath light and warm against his skin. Cautiously lifting his head, he braced himself for the remnants of a night of excess.

Instead, he saw Elizabeth.

A curious feeling of relief swept through him. No remnants of a licentious night, but instead the remains of a picnic.

Gradually, the events of the previous evening came back to him. His surprise when he had discovered Elizabeth. The wide smile on her face as she had detailed the reason behind the inclusion of each dish. Watching her tear her bread roll into thin strips before eating them. She had defended her strange eating habit immediately, as if she were often rebuked for it. He cared not how she ate and he had told her so, affecting his most imperious manner. She had laughed. He remembered her laughing often.

He looked down at Elizabeth. She was dead to the world, her mouth slightly open, and, good god, was she snoring? It was a delicate snore, but she would no doubt be mortified if she knew. When she awoke, he would tell her, and watch as her pale skin reddened and she spluttered and insisted she didn't, even though she was in no position to argue. And then she would berate him for telling her.

He couldn't wait.

Lifting a finger to her cheek, he traced the bone, memorizing her soft skin. He remembered pouring champagne, her conversation becoming sillier the more she drank, until her animated re-enactment of an embarrassing incident at her first ball had startled a laugh out of him. He remembered pulling her into the crook of his arm, lying back with her as she whispered how tired she was. He remembered saying she should rest for a moment.

Dropping his hand from her cheek, he glanced at his pocket watch. His eyebrows rose. A moment had become four hours. Weak light streamed through the window, the sky beginning to lighten with the new day. Bloody hell, what if someone saw her?

"Elizabeth." He touched her shoulder gently. "Elizabeth, wake up."

With a soft murmur, she buried herself deeper into him.

"Elizabeth," he said again, a bit louder this time.

No response.

"Elizabeth!" He pushed her shoulder sharply.

She sat bolt upright, her expression startled. "What? What?"

He smiled mildly. "Wake up."

"Oh." Yawning hugely, she rubbed her eyes. "You scared me to death. Why did you have to yell?"

"Because you sleep like the dead." Folding his arms did nothing to quell the urge to smooth back her disordered hair. "By the way, it's almost dawn."

"Is it?" Seeming unconcerned, she rubbed the small of her back. "Good Lord, but my back is sore. Did we fall asleep?"

"Yes." Did she always look so in the morning? So mussed and touchable? "Aren't you worried about the time?"

She shrugged, yawning. "Not particularly. No one is going to remark upon a veiled woman leaving your house, and all my family are in the country." The sleepiness disappeared. "Why? Are you worried?"

"Only for you."

Her breath hitched audibly. "Only for me?"

Scowling, he looked away. Damnation, did she have to look so? For God's sake, he was only worried about her reputation. Preparing to inform her of such, he turned to her.

She still had that same expression on her face, as if he had hung the moon. He started to speak, but she leaned forward, her lips stealing his words. The kiss she gave him spoke of all that had been in her face, all the thoughts and emotions he refused to name.

Her hand resting against his cheek, she leaned back from him. "I should go."

"Yes." A lump had formed in his throat and his mouth was dry. It must be that he was parched. They had drunk little water last night.

Dark green pools of warmth and humour held him captive. Her hand was still warm against his cheek. Then it fell away.

Sudden panic filled him at the loss of her touch. "You'll be here Thursday?"

"Yes, of course."

Relief swamped him, and he shook his head in disgust. *She meets you every Thursday, you fool*. She was back from the country now and had no plans to return. Thus, their lessons would continue as usual, and he refused to acknowledge the lightness of heart that accompanied that fact.

Elizabeth was searching around them, lifting up the mussed blanket, her skirt, his jacket. "Have you seen my shoes?"

He shook his head, still combating the lingering remains of unaccustomed emotions. Her picnic had been the least lascivious action he had undertaken for as long as he could remember, but never had he enjoyed himself more. It made little sense, and yet he would not examine it too closely, instead simply take it as she had meant it. As thanks. Simply, only, that.

In the end, she didn't need his help, finding her shoes and pulling them on before standing and smoothing her dress into a semblance of order. Draping her cloak about herself, she leaned down to kiss the top of his head. "I'll see you soon."

Long after she had left, his gaze remained trained on the door, the ghost of her now inextricably imprinted in the ballroom. Instead of his father's debauchery, he would think of Elizabeth, her smile bright as she knelt amongst the makings of a picnic.

He got to his feet, leaving the night behind as he made his way to his bedchamber. Memories of Elizabeth's laughing eyes followed him all the way, through the hall, into the washroom, while he was dressing.

He had been right. It didn't matter what room he was in. Elizabeth followed him through all.

He couldn't decide if he were grateful or resentful.

Chapter Eleven

DEEP SCRATCH DOWN the left side of his blotter marred the perfection of the *Firenze* leather. Malvern couldn't remember when it had happened, but it looked to be an old injury. He'd not used the study for the purpose intended for so long, it could very well have been there from his father's time. Better men than he took care of the business of the earldom, and, after spending the day wading through said business in a misguided attempt at distraction, he was more than happy to leave them to it in the future.

The scar before him blurred. With measured breath, he attempted calm, devoting himself to the expansion and deflation of his chest. The leather bled into the polished surface of the desk as he focused on the rhythm, the pace, on the slowness of his deliberate breathing.

The process should have soothed him.

The rise and fall of his chest did nothing to slow his racing heart, or rid him of the tightness in his chest. Doubling his efforts, he slowed his breathing further, his brow creasing in concentration. He refused to succumb to this whatever-it-was. He would not allow his body to betray him, to completely disregard the dictates of his mind and wishes. He wouldn't allow it life.

But, for all that he tried to combat it, the truth could not be denied. Tonight, Elizabeth would come.

Exhaling in disgust, Malvern gave up trying to establish calm. Never had he felt this level of anticipation before Elizabeth's arrival, and he could see no cause why he should do so now. Maybe last time they'd organised a meet he'd somewhat looked forward to her arrival, but this was ludicrous.

Since early morning, Malvern had been ensconced in his study, ostensibly actioning the stack of letters his man of business had handed over upon his order. In actuality, the ploy had done little to distract him. As he'd stared at the letters, he had pictured her face, and once her image was evoked, he could not stop the flood that followed. Elizabeth, animated and lively as she asked question after question. The feel of her hands as she explored his back, her fingers tracing his musculature under his shirt. The mole under her shoulder blade he'd now had ample time to catalogue and explore. Her head thrown back as she moaned her pleasure, the pleasure *he* gave her.

Pulling at his shirt cuffs, he aligned them perfectly with his wrists. He refused to think about it. About her. Refocusing on the blotter and its scar, he again began the slow breathing that had been so spectacularly unsuccessful to this point.

Bloody hell, it still wasn't working. The picnic. It had to be the picnic. The talking, the laughing, the lack of anything remotely sexual. Clearly, it was not beneficial for his peace of mind. Instead, he found himself recalling the way she had tilted her head, her smile as he'd talked about nothing, *nothing* for God's sake, and she had not asked for anything, she'd simply listened and commented and fallen asleep in his arms.

This upset in their schedule could not happen again, though he knew it would. How could it not, with Elizabeth being who she was? She would suggest some action, something wholly separate to sexual pleasure and he, suffering from this unknown malady, would allow her anything.

The doorbell rang. His heart, unruly organ that it was, leaped. Straining to hear the muted voices outside his study, he managed to glean Cartwright's voice, his words indistinct. Then he heard Elizabeth answer.

She was here.

He smoothed his hair, arranged his robe in casual folds, and contented himself with the knowledge that at least, to the world at large, he appeared unaffected.

Elizabeth rushed into the room, her skirts whirling about her. He rose from his chair in greeting, all polite attention, affecting the pretence that his blood didn't thrum through his veins at the sight of her, that his heart didn't pound when she appeared.

Goddamn it, every fucking time. Her effect on him should lessen, not grow with each meeting.

"In a hurry, my dear?" The excitement had subsided somewhat with her presence, a small hum instead of a roar.

"Don't start." Elizabeth collapsed into her chair. "I've had three of my sisters in my ear all day, and I'm liable to do someone serious and irreparable damage if that someone insists on being smart." She waved a finger at him, her stern expression belied by the grin bubbling beneath the surface.

"Indeed?" Calm, that elusive state he had chased all day, settled upon him. He came around his desk, leaning comfortably against it with Elizabeth less than an arm's length away. Crossing his arms, he frowned as he took in her appearance. Faint shadows darkened the skin beneath her eyes, and a drawn look pinched her features. Concern tightened his hands on his biceps. "What were they belabouring you about?"

"Oh, I don't know." She rubbed the bridge of her nose, her thumb digging into the corner of her eye. "I'm sure it was important, whatever it was."

Hooking his foot beneath the hem of her skirt, he flipped the frothy fabric around. "I really must insist you pay strict and sole attention to me. I dislike this habit you have of becoming distracted by the most inconsequential of things."

She looked at him from under her lashes. "Truly?"

"Of course." He allowed arrogance to colour his words.

A grin sneaked out, her face lighting with her fleeting smile. "Well, then, I do apologise." And then she kicked him.

The kick didn't hurt, hampered as it was by her skirts. "I must insist you do not do that."

"Really?"

She kicked him again.

He assumed his coldest expression, his haughtiest mien. "You will not like the consequences."

"Indeed?" she mimicked, her inflection almost a perfect copy of his and drew back her foot to kick him again.

It never landed.

With a speed he'd not thought himself capable, Malvern lifted Elizabeth from her chair. She shrieked and struggled and pushed against him ineffectually.

"What are you doing?" Laughter coloured her words.

"You thought to defy me."

She snorted at that, a decidedly unladylike sound. Wanting to grin, he instead shifted his hands, concerned he may hurt her with his grip.

Unfortunately, in order to do that he had to set her down. A patent mistake, as she took the opportunity to escape, scrambling across the room and grinning at him as she used the chaise as a barrier.

Suddenly, she dodged to one side and he blocked her escape. Her gaze never leaving his, her chest heaved as her breath came in excited bursts, and he could see her weighing her options, deciding best how she could avoid him. He moved to block her on the right, but she pivoted and dodged left, running around the edge of the lounge to crouch behind the protection of his desk.

Adrenalin rushing through him, he leaped over the desk, unmindful of the items that fell to the floor with a protesting crash. She gasped, more of a splutter really, and ran from him, the material of her skirt threading through his fingers as he came close to catching her.

His heart beating wildly, a crazy laugh built inside him. Never had he had done this. Never had he chased a woman around a room, for no other reason than it was fun. God, he was *playing*.

His arm wrapped around her waist. Unfortunately, his move threw them both off balance and she tripped, her fall triggering his as they both tumbled to the ground. Twisting, he took the brunt of the fall, grunting at the impact. His shoulder burned, and his hip ached, but he didn't care. Elizabeth was unhurt.

Her face alive with laughter, still she struggled, trying to tug her wrists from his grip. A smile crept across his face as he restrained her easily, rolling her to her back and pinning her wrists on either side of her head, trapping her struggling legs with one of his.

Then, with little warning, everything changed. They both stilled. Her wrists felt tiny in his hands, the bones fragile. The realization she was helpless beneath him crashed through him. He could do anything he wanted to her, anything at all, and she would struggle even as they both knew it was but a game, that she would let him do whatever he wanted because it was what she wanted, too.

Dark green eyes watched him, her tongue flicking at her lip, and he wanted it, wanted it on him. Her eyes narrowed, and he knew she was planning something, something that would make both of them burn.

Raising her head, she licked his nose.

Malvern blinked. "Did you just lick my nose?"

Elizabeth nodded, her grin stretching wide.

"My nose?" he repeated, incredulous.

She shrugged. "It was there."

"Really?" He leaned down and licked her chin. "It was there," he mimicked.

She bit his earlobe. "That was there, too." Her grin was infectious.

His gaze focused on her mouth and just like that, playfulness vanished.

"It was there," he said hoarsely, and then he

covered her mouth with his.

God, the taste of her, sweet and spice and salt and a hundred other contradictions that spelt out Elizabeth. She made a little sound, her lips eagerly following his lead as he nibbled, stroked, licked. Trailing kisses over her cheek, he placed one on her nose, measured her brow with his mouth, kissed each eye closed. Returning to her mouth, he plundered her, his hands tight on her wrists as he stole her breath and replaced it with his own.

The encumbrance of her gown prevented him from lying against her as he wanted. Her leg rubbed against his, but it wasn't enough. He needed her wrapped around him, his hips wedged against hers, his cock against her heat.

He pulled up her skirts, bunching the fabric around her thighs, and he thanked God she had not worn undergarments. She immediately wrapped her legs around him, as if she knew his thoughts, as if she wanted this as much as he. Running his hand under her thigh, he cupped the back of her knee, pulling her closer to him as he rocked against her, groaning at the feel of her against his rapidly hardening cock. The removal of the barrier between them allowed him free reign to move against her as he wanted, to tease her with the thrust of his body against hers.

He left her mouth to trail his lips down her neck, over her breastbone, his fingers working frantically at the bodice of her gown to push it aside. Her corset easily went the same way and then she was bared to his gaze.

The sight of her stole his breath. God, she was so beautiful. He ran his hand over her, down her throat, to the mess he had made of her bodice. To her breasts. He cupped her flesh, his thumb sweeping over the pink tip, staring in fascination as her nipple darkened, puckered.

Elizabeth's fingers curled his hair around his ear, and Malvern tore himself away from his fascinated perusal of her breasts to meet her gaze. Her eyes dark with desire and the remnants of laughter, her fingers trailed over his cheek. Turning his head, Malvern pressed a kiss to her palm, his tongue lightly touching her flesh.

"Am I paying attention to you now?" Even with desire darkening her voice, her eyes laughed at him.

"Not enough." And, to really make sure he had her attention, he took her breast in his mouth.

She moaned at the touch of his mouth, her hands tugging painfully on his hair to pull him closer. Triumph surged as he traced the under curve of her breast, curling his hand around her breast to present it for him. Her taste sweet against his tongue, he teased her nipple, grasping her with his teeth. Her moans were music to his ears and he did it again, over and over, just to hear her sing for him.

Pulling back to study his handiwork, he ignored her protest. Her nipple tightened further, becoming harder under his gaze.

"You have such pretty breasts, Elizabeth." His voice a harsh rasp, the words betrayed the depth of his arousal. He didn't even try to hide it. "Look at them, begging for my touch. So full, so ripe, so ready for my tongue." Encasing her nipple in his mouth, he groaned at her taste, her texture, hard and sweet.

With a harsh intake of breath, she arched her back, driving him wild with her abandoned response. He almost didn't notice her hand trailing over his back, didn't really notice her cupping his buttock.

He sure as hell noticed, though, when she

placed her hand on his cock.

Startled, he lifted his head. She smiled sweetly, deceptively, tracing his shape through his trousers as she looked at him so innocently. Blood thundered in his ears and breath strangled in his chest as her hand moved on him, his vision filled with that wickedly innocent smile. Then her hand was cradling his cock, his buttons somehow undone. She stroked his length and he cursed.

"I love how you feel." Her voice, throaty, seductive, found an answering lust in him, and he wanted inside her now, wanted to feel her hot and wet and gloving him, squeezing him as he fucked her until she screamed his name.

Her eyes flared. "I love the way you feel in my hand." Her thumb swirled over the head of his cock. God, she was driving him insane. "I love the way you taste and most of all…." Her breath whispered across his skin. "I love it when you come."

He stared at her, at the look on her face, at the desire in her eyes, at Elizabeth. And something snapped.

He shoved her skirts out of his way, and he put his hand on her, testing her readiness and she was exactly as he imagined, hot and wet and so close to coming. Wanting to give her pleasure, needing to, he thrust his fingers inside her, his thumb circling her clit, and she bit her lip, whimpers coming from her as her hand stilled against him, pleasure flushing her skin. His own response rigidly controlled, he gauged her reaction. She was going to come, he could see it and so…he stopped.

She moaned, her hand grabbing his wrist, trying to force him to move. Nothing she did swayed him, nothing would force him from his intent to tease her, even as his own arousal burned through him. He pulled back, ever the tormentor, but she foiled him.

Grasping his arms, she pulled him forward, his groin solidly wedged against her. Grunting at the unexpected move, he braced himself, his arms falling next to her to protect her from his full weight. She didn't notice, curling her hands around his biceps as she wrapped her legs about his hips, her heels digging into his buttocks. He sucked in air, the feel of his cock against her overwhelming. She moaned, the most glorious sound he had ever heard, and then she shifted, his cock sliding against her. Trying to regain some measure of control, he dug his hands into the floor, but it was near impossible to control the movement, the intoxicating feel of her beneath him beckoning him to thrust, to take, to push inside her. He heard himself muttering, something about how he wouldn't come inside her, how he would tease her, he would restrain himself, he swore it.

She didn't answer, her lip caught between her teeth as her hands ran up his arms, her hips pushing against his. Fuck, he wanted inside her. He clenched his hands against the feel of her hot and wet against the head of his cock, and he told himself he could go inside, just one thrust, what sense was it to deny them? Gritting his teeth, he forced himself still, knowing he was justifying it to himself even as the thought of it terrified him. He couldn't be inside her. He couldn't.

Her eyes opened, and he drowned in their depths. Thrusting against her slowly, he devoted himself to her pleasure, denying himself while he drove her wild with the feel, the shape of his cock. He kissed her, using the play of his mouth against hers to tease and torment, to distract her. Restlessly, her hands moved over his back, clutching the fabric of his shirt, pulling at it, and then her hands were against his skin, hot and hungry, as her mouth mated with his. Fuck, she was so near, so close, wet and hot and open, so open to him and it would take nothing, less than nothing. Mindlessly he thrust against her, control shattered, sliding back and forth, back and forth and she was panting beneath him, telling him yes and yes and yes and then he was inside her.

They both stilled. Her eyes slumberous, she stared up at him, her legs tight around his hips. God. He was buried so deep inside her. Her core gloved him, tight, hot, wet silk surrounding him. He fought the urge to thrust, to pound, to fuck her until he came.

Panic wound with lust, one becoming the other as he realised he was inside her. *He was inside her* and nothing good would come of it. She was beneath him, so beautiful in her passion, and he couldn't be here with her, he couldn't. Things would change, everything would change and fuck, he needed to move. He shook his head, trying to force rational thought into a body that was screaming at him to thrust, to pound, to make her dissolve beneath him. This was happening, God Jesus, it was happening, and he couldn't prevent it. He was weak, and it terrified him.

Her hand cupped his neck, trailing down his chest. Panicked thoughts silenced as, with dazed eyes, he followed the progress of her hand, her fingers light on his skin. Leaning forward, she licked a bead of sweat from his throat, and then she began to move, little circles of her hips. Her other hand beat a rhythm against the small of his back and he followed it, hypnotised by her, rocking in concert with her movements, withdrawing a little, coming back, gentle and slow, finding the right angle so she gasped and moaned, his terror forgotten as she showed him how to make love to her.

He concentrated on her, determined that his pleasure would wait until he had satisfied hers. She tensed, and he could see it was upon her, so close, and he reached down to where they were joined, willing her to come and then she did, breaking over him, her body rigid as she screamed her pleasure.

He did all that he could to prolong it. Then, when she was lying lax in his arms, he grasped her hips and pulled her into him, thrusting heavy and deep, and she was tight and hot and wet and heaven, and he wanted to fuck her harder, deeper. He was close, and she was moving with him now, she was doing something with her muscles, and oh God, she was making it so fucking good and then he came, a strangled groan exploding from deep in his chest as he released inside her.

He collapsed, his chest pushing against hers as he struggled to take in air. Wrapping her arms around him, she murmured in his ear, smoothing his hair, her legs still around his hips and he still inside her.

Eventually, he came back to himself and with the return of his senses came reality. He buried his head in her shoulder, avoiding her gaze and with it, the inevitable. What could he say? What would she say? He had been so damned insistent they avoid penetration and, well, that was shot to hell. He had no notion what he had been so bloody worried about anyway. Looking back, it was patently ridiculous. He had denied both himself and Elizabeth mind-numbing pleasure and for what? Because he had been *apprehensive?*

He'd performed the act countless times and he

knew, *he knew* there was nothing to be apprehensive of. Ever since his father had facilitated his initiation into the erotic arts, he'd had no cause for fear. After the first few times, he had even become good at it. More than good. Sublime. He was a fool. A bloody fool. She would be right to rail at him, to deride him, to call him a fool for his idiotic behaviour. He deserved it. More than deserved it, he *welcomed* it.

The tension was horrible, the silence worse.

"Well, that was certainly unexpected," she finally said.

"Is that all you have to say?"

She flinched, and he cursed himself. What had happened to his finesse, his delicacy? Not half a minute ago, he had been lauding his damned *sublimeness*.

Turning, he lifted her so she sat in his lap, muffling an oath as he slipped from her. Running his hands through her disordered hair, he removed the pins, allowing the mass freedom, using his touch to gentle her, to woo her.

"Are you well?" He kept his gaze trained on the motions of his hand in her hair.

"Yes." She was silent a moment, and he risked a glance at her. A soft smile lit her face, her eyes closed as she tilted her head into his hand. He stilled and her eyes opened, that brilliant green ensnaring him as easily as strands of blonde did. "I do have a question, though."

"Of course you do," he said, attempting levity. "When do you not?"

A wicked grin flashed across her face. "When can we do it again?"

Something inside him lightened, something that had been closed, buried. Protected.

This would change everything. He shook himself but he couldn't rid himself of the fear. And it had nothing to do with sex. Somehow, it had been…more.

So instead, he focused on the feel of her in his arms and on the fact that he wanted to fuck her again, as many times as she would let him.

"You have only to wish it, madam." He thrust lightly against her, half-hard already. "Shall we take this to a more comfortable locale?"

"I shall bow to the greater knowledge of my tutor." The last ended on a moan when he thrust against her again.

As he carried her from the room, as he laid her on his bed, as he brought her screaming to pleasure, as he made sure not to spill inside her again, he told himself over and over—*not afraid…I'm not afraid.*

Chapter Twelve

"HOW ABOUT THIS?" JAMES changed the angle and thrust deeper inside her.

Sensation exploded. Elizabeth gasped, her hands gripping the bed sheets as she absorbed his thrust.

"That's good," she managed. He retreated, and she moaned, pleasure threatening to consume her. His forearms flexed as they supported his weight, his hips pushing her legs wider as he increased his thrusts, testing out the new angle.

"Better?" he asked, his voice hoarse.

She nodded, her own voice stolen. Sensation gathered inside her, a maelstrom of need and heat and lust. Harsh breath rasped from burning lungs as his thrusts grew rougher, pushing her against the bed.

"What would give you more pleasure?" He punctuated each word with a hard thrust. She whimpered, feeling him so deep inside her she couldn't remember a time without him. His body moved in a glorious slide of entry and retreat, and she never wanted it to end. She wanted him inside her always.

"Elizabeth." He stopped moving, pinning her to the bed, his cock a thick intrusion inside her.

Moaning a protest, she grasped at his buttocks, clenching and releasing around him to tempt him to move. He swallowed harshly, yet still he did not move.

Trailing her fingers up his spine, she clenched again, rubbing her thigh against his hip. God, she would do anything to get him to move. The arms braced either side of her shook, but he remained motionless, the heavy presence of him inside her driving her mad.

"Elizabeth." He faltered, his voice full of gravel. Taking a steadying breath, he continued. "Elizabeth, what would give you more pleasure?"

Restlessly arching her neck, she tried to clear her head as she attempted thought. What did she want? She didn't know. She didn't know.

Licking her dry lips, she instead gave the decision to him. "What do you want?"

He was watching the flick of her tongue, his expression dark. She flicked her lip again, and triumph ran through her at the flare of heat in that ice-blue gaze. *Now* he would move.

She didn't count on his self-control. Instead, his attention moved to her breasts, and her flesh prickled at the caress of his gaze. "Touch them."

Bringing her hands up, she cupped the flesh delicately, the feel of her own skin decadent, her nipples hard against her thumbs.

Watching her, he started to move, a little swivel of his hips, not deep, not hard. "Tease them."

Pushing her tongue to her teeth, her gaze locked

with his, she flicked at the sensitive nubs. Face dark, he watched her, his body still ruthlessly controlled. She wanted him to shatter, to break, his control gone as he succumbed to passion. Desperate lust roared through her, and her light touch was no longer enough. Fingers working frantically, she pulled at her nipples, squeezing them, the pleasure of the pain arrowing to where they were joined. Thighs tightening on his hips, she moaned as her hands pushed and moulded her breasts, her nipples unbearably sensitive. He was still motionless inside her, his cock thick and huge and filling her. She needed him to move. She needed *him*.

"James. Move. Please!" Desperation broke her voice, just as it broke him. Exploding into motion on a harshly uttered curse, he thrust into her, deep and hard, just as she wanted him to.

"Harder, James, harder. Deeper, yes, ohgGod, that's it, just there." Fingers still working her breasts, she arched her back, his cock ramming into her and her pleasure tangled between her fingers and his cock. It built and it built and the sensation was overwhelming, so much, too much. "James! Please, James, now!"

He swore, he cursed, he ordered her to come and she did, breaking beneath him, little pieces of herself shattering, spiralling apart only to reform into a woman in thrall to him, to his touch, his body, to how he could make her feel.

Heart slowing, breath evening, she came back to herself. A lazy smile stretched her face, satisfaction taking the place of consuming pleasure. Dear Lord, James was so very good at that.

Gradually, she became aware of her surroundings and aware of James, still thick and hard inside her. Head bowed, he was coated in perspiration, his arms shaking with the effort of holding himself still. For her. He was trying to give her as much pleasure as he could. Dear, dear man.

Wickedness chased away her languor, and she set about returning the favour. She looped her hands around his arms, stroking the straining muscles delicately. Not yet deducing her intent, his head still hung between his shoulders as he held himself motionless. Undulating her hips, she began a slow seduction, her inner muscles caressing him as she moved.

His eyes flew open. A muscle ticked in his jaw as he stared at her, brows drawn. "Elizabeth…." A warning evident in his tone, her name ended on a groan as she flexed her hips suddenly.

He *would* lose control. She would settle for nothing less.

"Yes?" A half-smile playing about her lips, she made her reply all that was innocence, though there was nothing innocent about her actions.

"Don't," he groaned, his hips starting to follow her movements, the muscles in his abdomen contracting and releasing.

"Yes?" Hands drifting down his body to grasp his buttocks, she pulled him into her, wrapping a leg around his back to trap him.

Control broke. Swearing harshly, he dropped his arms, his chest crushing hers, and his face buried in her neck as he drove into her. Gripping him with every thrust, she fought against his withdrawal, making him work for each retreat. Harsh, basic words mixed with pleas and groans as he strove for his release, her pleasure forgotten in the pursuit of his own. She bit his ear, loving that she could do this to him, that she was the cause of his madness. At her bite, he stiffened in her arms, his cock growing impossibly large, and then he wrenched himself from inside her, shuddering as he came.

She stroked his hair as he calmed, his large body trembling from the force of his climax. Smug, content, she stared at the canopy of the bed as her fingers tangled and smoothed. Good Lord, how had they managed to avoid this for so long?

"That was supposed to be about your pleasure." His words were muffled against her skin.

"I know." She continued to stroke his hair. "But isn't this more fun?"

He pulled back. Heavens above, he was beautiful. "You are so very odd."

"Yes, I am," she agreed. Cocking a brow, she continued archly, "What are you going to do about it?"

Passion darkened his features, wickedness chasing the wonder from his face and he became once more the consummate seducer, bent on debauchery and dissolution. Bent on corrupting her.

Desire, so recently satisfied, roared to life.

Intense, deliberate, he bent to her and she shivered at the intent written on his face. "I am going to fuck you until you scream."

Everything inside her stopped. She tried to speak, but his kiss stole her attempt to reply.

***

THE MOST WONDERFUL LANGUIDNESS permeated her body. Elizabeth stared at the canopy, at peace with the world and all in it. In fact, she felt ridiculously blissful and was fairly certain that if anyone asked her anything at this moment, she would reply with charity and goodwill no matter what the provocation. This heavenly lethargy was remarkable, and when it had dissipated she would no doubt examine the feeling in minutia, but, as of here and now, she was content to lie next to James, a silly grin on her face as she allowed herself to wallow.

"Elizabeth? Are you listening?"

Muscles wonderfully loose, she turned her head. James was propped on his side, his gaze intense. Running her gaze over his bare chest, she contemplated the play of candlelight over the warm golden skin she could touch and kiss and lick without barrier. Her gaze wandered down his chest, following the light dusting of dark hair that disappeared under the sheet gathered at his waist. What would he do if she pushed the sheet down and followed that interesting trail of hair?

"Elizabeth?"

"Hmm?" A sharp tug would do it, and he wouldn't complain if she followed her impulse. In fact, she had little doubt she could put a smile on his face in under a minute and then, when she was done, he was bound to reciprocate.

He exhaled. A frown marred the perfection of his brow, and she couldn't help but think her lips would do a fine job of smoothing it away.

"You must listen. We have been lax in preventing conception and, demonstrably, I have no control when it comes to you. Even now, you could be carrying my child." The lines of his frown deepened, and she found herself wanting to taste his irritation. "There is no excuse for my failing, and you should not be made to suffer the consequences."

Listening with half an ear and much more

interested in watching his lips move, she made the appropriate noises and nods. She could take his bottom lip between her teeth and lave it with her tongue.

"We must attempt to prevent such an occurrence, at least from now on. Now that this has occurred, there is no point in refraining from doing so in the future. Thus, we should protect us both from unwanted consequences."

Damnation, she'd just experienced the most pleasurable night of her life, and he was insisting on bringing reality into it. Sighing, she pushed herself to a sitting position. The night wasn't even over yet. Surely they could just enjoy the afterglow for a little while longer?

Languidly, she crossed her arms above her head and stretched, her back loosening with the movement. The motion pushed her breasts free of the sheet covering them, her nipples tightening at the touch of the cool night air. Catching him covertly glancing at her breasts, she concealed a grin as she twisted and sighed, every sense trained on his reaction. James was of much more interest than the negligible release of loosening her muscles.

"There are many ways we could prevent conception. I have already ensured I did not release inside you, apart from the first." His tone distracted, his eyes followed her every move. Lazy arousal wound through her, somewhat startling after the last few hours. They had made love, had sex, *fucked*, so well and so often she was surprised her body could even respond.

He cleared his throat and, with that, broke her hold on him. His expression once again intense, he continued. "A vinegar soaked sponge is probably our best option. I can secure French letters as well, just to be on the safe side. In fact, it was a horrendous oversight I did not have them on hand and I apologise profusely."

Elizabeth dropped her arms. "French letters? What on earth are they? They can't be what they sound like. Can they?"

The slight frown smoothed as amusement lit his eyes. Bloody hell, he was laughing at her. "Don't you dare laugh at me, James. You know I don't know much about all this."

"I would never laugh at you." The solemnity of his words made her roll her eyes and, of course, that increased the amusement in his. "But to answer your question, French letters are sheaths made of animal intestine that prevent me from ejaculating inside you."

"Good Lord. Don't they hurt?"

His brow raised in inquiry. "How do you mean?"

What masochist would come up with such a thing? "Well, how tight must they be to prevent you from, well, you know?"

James stared at her for a moment, his face incredulous, and then an expression that was very close to outright mirth crossed his face.

He may as well have laughed at her.

Elizabeth wrapped the sheet around her and wished the rest of the bed covers hadn't been shoved to the floor. Obviously, she had said something horrendously wrong, and he was kind enough to alert her to the fact by laughing at her. Fine, maybe he hadn't actually laughed, but he may as well have. Setting her jaw, she wished he would wipe that smirk off his face. Or better yet, that she could smack it off.

Crossing her arms, she refused to look at him, feeling like the veriest twit and wishing she could take back the last few minutes.

Placing his hand on her shoulder, his fingers lightly stroked her skin. "I should have explained further."

"Yes, you should have. I don't appreciate feeling the fool, James. I comprehend that I don't know anywhere near what you do about this. That is made clear to me constantly."

His voice, his beautiful wine-dark voice, was of a sudden chill, each syllable precise. "Are you complaining about my teaching technique?"

Cold perfection once more. Even the golden glow of his skin had taken on an icy edge.

"It has nothing to do with your teaching technique." The peevishness in her voice irritated even her.

"Then what, pray tell, madam, do you have to complain about?" A note, a hint of something gave her pause. Had she heard uncertainty? Cold gaze level upon her, he appeared relaxed, and yet she could swear he had braced himself.

Her shoulders slumped. She didn't want to fight with him. He had done so much for her, and she'd repaid him by acting like the fool she didn't want to be. To add insult to injury, it was all over nothing, an offhand comment that held no real censure and thus no real reason. She *was* a fool.

"James, I'm sorry, I just—I have always felt I—" Frustration burned within her. Bloody hell, where were the words when she needed them? "I just hate feeling the fool."

Cold silence greeted her. Her thoughtlessness had caused this tension between them. Even her explanation, pitiful as it was, did little to erase the divide.

She really was a fool.

Finally, he spoke. "You are not regretting what happened between us?"

"What?" Surprise sharpened her tone. "No, of course not."

"Truly? I have broken one of my own stipulations." To her, he still appeared unaffected. Why then did she know he was not? "And after I was so adamantly opposed to it."

True, he had not wanted to…how did he phrase it? Achieve penetration. One only had to recall the events of the other evening to find the truth of that. Now that it had happened, and so spectacularly, surely he had no objections. "Why are you bothered by this?"

He remained silent, but no longer so impassive, a hint of uncertainty bleeding through his unnatural calm.

Finally, he shrugged and looked away. "I have no desire for a child and I assume you are of the same mind. Therefore, abstinence was the better option. Now, however, we will have to rely on preventative measures."

Why did she feel as if that were not the reason? She studied him, trying to glean the answer from his impassive features. An exercise doomed to failure. For some reason, the next part of that long-ago conversation flitted across her mind.

"So, you aren't going to marry me then?"

The look of horror on his face should have been amusing.

Smiling brightly, she ignored that something that flared inside her so fiercely at his expression. She would even neglect to name it. "Besides, we don't need to be concerned about preventing pregnancy anyway."

"Indeed?"

Well, she had started the conversation, she couldn't abandon it now. "I was married to Rocksley for eight years, and I was never with child. I think it's safe to assume I'm barren."

"This is what you base your notion on? Your idiot husband's inability to impregnate you?"

"How can you dismiss it?"

"Easily. How often did you fuck?"

She blinked. Some devil prompted her to answer, "Never."

Incredulity stole the calm from his features. The expression was so foreign that she couldn't help but find it diverting. She tried to conceal a grin but was sure she had failed miserably.

"Never? So you were virgin before tonight?" He was all that was sarcasm and disbelief.

"No, of course not. Remember, I had a lover?" He looked nonplussed. Delight danced through her that she could disconcert him so.

She continued on blithely, as if she hadn't wanted to torment him at all. "Rocksley and I, we had polite marital relations. We never...fucked." A shiver ran through her as she uttered that deliciously wicked word. "And, I suppose, it wasn't that often, especially after the first few years."

"Well, there you go." He folded his arms against his chest. His bare, golden chest that was begging for her tongue. Hmm. "See? Idiot."

"I didn't become pregnant that other time, either," she reminded him.

"You are basing your whole argument on

infrequent bouts of sex with men who clearly didn't take the time to appreciate you. We will take precautions."

He was so very adamant.

Cupping his cheek, she forced his gaze to hers. He resisted, seeming determined not to look at her direct.

"James."

Reluctant, he raised his gaze to hers.

She smiled gently. "If it means so much to you, we will take precautions."

He looked away, swallowed, and when he looked back, he had locked his fear away.

Trailing a finger down her cheek, he said, "How could your husband have left you alone? He really was an idiot."

She scowled. "Don't call Rocksley an idiot. You didn't know him."

"'Tis plain he was an idiot. He obviously didn't know how to pleasure you."

"Still." Now it was her turn to look away, the thought of Rocksley still holding bittersweet memories. "I loved him once."

With the wisdom of hindsight, she could see now that they had been too young and too bound by convention to marry. Stupidly, she had thought the dictates of society's expectations of more importance than her own convictions, and Rocksley had been the same. They had been so very young.

How romantic it had been, to be sixteen and wed, a runaway bride after she had pleaded and pressed and convinced Rocksley to steal away with her. The romance, however, had lasted only a few months before it became terribly obvious how ill-suited they were. Once the wild passion of new love had passed, it had been plain Rocksley did not understand her, nor she him. His calm, sedate nature, which had fired an inappropriate passion in her young breast, had been at odds with her inquisitive soul. In fact, it had become all too clear that all that wild, inappropriate passion had been on her side, that Rocksley had simply allowed himself to be carried away by her enthusiasm. Oh, she knew she hadn't forced him into marriage, but if they'd had a long engagement, had waited until after her debut as he had wanted, they might have discovered long before it became irrevocable that they did not suit.

They had never seen eye to eye. He never understood anything from her perspective, stubbornly clinging to his own standpoint and never conceding that she might have a different opinion to his own. Of course, to be fair, she had never understood his viewpoint either. They had never fought, never yelled, simply because Rocksley refused to. If they disagreed, he had calmly weathered her emotion until she was spent, and then would do what he thought best. Unsurprisingly, the last third of their marriage had been spent apart.

And, well, they never could figure out the intimate part of their lives. She smiled sadly. They had missed out on so much through ignorance. She wasn't even sure Rocksley had found passion with someone else, but she hoped he had. She hoped he had found some pleasure before he died.

His death had been such a stupid accident, such a terrible waste. It hadn't been the horse's fault, of course, and Rocksley had never been reckless. The horse had simply misstepped, fell and Rocksley had been crushed, his bones broken and his life forfeit. That had been three years ago now.

Now she looked at James, studied him. He had shown her so much, introduced her to such a myriad of pleasures. But for all that he'd come to mean so much more to her than a mere tutor, she'd no notion why he'd *become* her tutor.

"Why are you doing this?"

He gave her that look, the one he was so good at, the one that said you were insignificant and why were you bothering him with such trivialities? "Doing what?"

She gestured at the bed. "This. Teaching me. It can't be that interesting for you to train such a novice."

He shrugged. "Boredom will compel a person to do worse things."

"Oh." Strangely hurt, she looked away. She had not expected any sentimentality to his answer, but such an expectation did not prevent his response from cutting deeply.

Silence stretched, unnatural tension weighing heavy upon it. She shouldn't expect more. She *didn't* expect more.

It was that picnic, stupid impulse it had been. The thought of it had occurred to her while in the country. The festivities had done little to excite her, the sense of something missing dogging her every step. In truth, she had been glad of the excuse to return to London, and to him.

He had been so surprised to see her, but also, she thought, glad. The night had been wonderful, and she had enjoyed herself so much. No indication of any deeper feeling had ever been displayed, nothing other than that of passion, lust, and the impersonal nature of a teaching relationship. Not even after the picnic. But she, fool that she was, would insist on seeing something that wasn't there.

"That was the catalyst." His abrupt words cut through her thoughts, startling her. "Nothing could amuse me. And thus, your education was suggested. However, I am finding it…diverting."

Her stupid heart leaped at his words. "Really?" Crawling over to straddle him, she grasped his hands in hers. "I do believe that is the nicest compliment I've ever received. Diverting. I must remember to record it in my journal."

Spread beneath her, he looked a veritable feast for her senses. "Please ensure you record the proper inflection and delivery. I would hate for the moment to be lost to the ages through poor description." And yet, his fingers tightened on hers.

She laughed, her heart buoyed. She even felt the ghost of a smile on his lips when she kissed him.

∗∗∗

"ARE YOU TUTORING ANYONE else?"

James kept his gaze trained on her hand. Tracing the lines on her palm, he made a little pattern only he could discern. Holding her breath, Elizabeth could only hope he would answer soon and wish she didn't care quite so much.

Dawn was approaching. It had been the most glorious night, exceeding by far her wildest expectations, and somehow an intimacy beyond the lovemaking had risen between them. So much so that she'd felt brave enough to ask the question that had been tormenting her for months.

Finally, he spoke. "Yes."

She flinched. James's grip on her fingers

tightened infinitesimally, as if to stop her from jerking her hand from his.

"I see." That had not been the answer she'd been hoping for. Which was stupid. She knew what he was. It was why he had been chosen. Her throat closed on the torrent of words she wanted to unleash on him and yet, she didn't. She didn't want to know who, how often, where.

Forcing herself to relax, she reminded herself, again, that he had no ties to her.

All was silence between them, with not even the tick of a clock to mark the passing moments. The night was waning, and soon there would be the cry of market men, peddling their wares to servants as they made their daily rounds. Soon she would have to leave. Soon, there would be no reason, no excuse for her to stay. It would be for the best. They were tutor and pupil only.

"That is, I was." The sudden words startled her, making her jump. His tone, though, was steady, his gaze still trained on her hand. "I found it was growing stale, and the trysts had dwindled in recent times anyway. I hadn't attended for weeks." He traced that pattern again. "And there were our lessons to consider."

"Oh?" she said carefully.

Tension grew as he stared at her hand, his thumb following the same path over and over. Tracing her knuckles, he explored every bump and groove before pulling her hand to his mouth, placing a hot kiss in the centre of her palm. She shivered as his tongue tasted her flesh, his eyes gleaming over the top of her hand. A willing thrall to his seduction, she swayed toward him and he leaned closer, his mouth inches from hers.

"Care to be diverted?" he asked, wickedness a husky companion to his wine-dark voice.

She allowed him to distract her, to gloss over his revelation as if it meant nothing. Truth to tell, she didn't want to think on it. Besides, when he was kissing her as he was now, his lips and tongue rousing her desire so very easily, she couldn't think.

Tonight he was hers. Only hers. She pulled him into her, hooking her leg around his and gave herself up to him.

That was really all that mattered.

Chapter Thirteen

GOOD LORD, SHE WAS going to an orgy.

Elizabeth bit her nail, apprehension twisting low in her stomach. Oblivious to her state, James sat opposite, all that was ease and unconcern as he stared out the window of the carriage. Willing him to turn, she wished he would give her some reassurance. A smile. An imperious raise of a brow. *Anything*. He, however, remained fixed on the scenery outside the carriage, leaving her with no recourse but to look out her own window.

She balled her hands in her lap. Why, *why* had she agreed to this? When James had made the suggestion, it had seemed wild and forbidden and so blasted exciting she couldn't wait. But now that they were sitting in the carriage and they would arrive any minute, the reality of it gripped her tight.

The churning in her belly became impossible to ignore. What happened at an orgy? She couldn't even begin to imagine. What if as soon as she cleared the door something occurred to shock the living daylights out of her, and she fainted and hit her head and bled all over the place and—?

Elizabeth, get a hold of yourself. What could possibly happen that would be that shocking? Obligingly, her brain provided such scenarios, and she cursed herself. Honestly, what she had just pictured was ridiculous. She didn't even know if that *were* possible.

James had told her very little about the parameters of the event. While she wore a mask, who knew what strictures governed the anonymity of others? What if she recognised someone? She had no desire to learn the depravities of which her contemporaries were capable. Or, dear Lord, what if it were someone like Lady Cartwright?

A shudder racked her as she imagined the prudish woman in the throes of passion, on display to all and sundry. Ugh. And with that thought, a little piece of her just died.

What if she were expected to participate? Blood drained from her face, leaving her lightheaded and slightly nauseous. No, no, she couldn't, besides, James wouldn't allow it, not unless she wanted it— what if she wanted it?

Damnation, she should have asked James more questions. What was she thinking, going into something so unprepared? She always planned to a ridiculous degree. Even her brothel folly had been undertaken only after she'd conducted a rigorous examination of the merits of such a plan. She always had to know everything. Why then did she not know *everything* about this?

Raising a shaking hand to her forehead, she closed her eyes. She knew why. Of course she did. She could not bring herself to tell James of her qualms. Questioning him would highlight her fear and thus she had remained mute, foolishly entering the fray uninformed. James wouldn't understand. How could he? No doubt he had done this a million times, and she could just picture the look on his face as he excused her from attendance at tonight's endeavour.

Lowering her hand, she traced a pattern on the window. How unfair was she, to paint James with the same brush? Never had he reacted as her father always had, avoiding her questions or meeting them with a bewildered frown, as if wondering how he had fathered such an inquisitive child. James had never made her feel foolish for questioning even the most mundane of details, and she was wrong to think he would.

Why, then? Why now did she feel such apprehension? Long ago, she had resolved to be bold and daring. When had that resolve disappeared?

A distraction, that's what she needed. A small smile began as she ran her gaze over James, still staring out the window. He was so delicious. His hair fell in a riotous tumble, no doubt ruthlessly disordered by his valet as the strands did not naturally fall in such wanton splendour. In fact, if left alone, his hair had a tendency to flop about his face, in direct contrast to the mien of a dissolute roué. At such moments, one could almost term his appearance boyish. That was, until he fixed his gaze upon you, and then, well, then there could be no mistaking him for a boy.

The slope of his brow flowed gracefully into a strong nose, and one would barely notice the faint scar on his cheekbone. He still wouldn't tell her how he'd acquired it. One would never imagine the wickedness his mouth could engender, or the pleasure afforded when tracing the strong line of his jaw with lips and tongue.

The last few weeks they'd spent almost every night together. Of course, in consideration of gossips, much of that time had been after nightfall, and what glorious nights they had been.

As she'd known they would, her courses had arrived as usual, negating James's unnecessary worry. Even though a child would have been disastrous, still she'd felt the familiar twinge at the proof she wasn't pregnant. Stupid, really, but she couldn't help it.

In any event, James had taken the news she wasn't with child with the same degree of emotion he seemed to take everything else—that is to say, he had ostensibly reacted not at all. She had, however, seen the twitch of his hand at the news, and at his one small tell she had smiled to herself. It was rather sweet, really. The dear idiot thought he was protecting them both when clearly there was no need, even if he refused to believe it. Nevertheless, it cost her little to accede to his wish and the reward was him, however she wanted him.

More than the physical, though, she found she simply wanted to be with him, so much so that her day felt incomplete if spent without him. It did not matter if they acted upon their passion, or if they did nothing more than converse. She simply needed to be near him, and she thought he might need to be near her.

The carriage shuddered to a halt and breath deserted her. Lungs screaming, she took great gulps of air, each more erratic than the last. *Good lord, Elizabeth, stop it.* She was bold and brave and daring. What could an orgy possibly contain to combat that?

James had already exited the carriage, holding

out his hand to help her down. A strange paralysis froze her as she stared at the proffered appendage. His hand. It represented so much more than a steady grip.

"Elizabeth." Still fighting to breathe, she met his gaze. A slight frown creased his brow. "Are you well?"

Breath finally coming easily, she nodded, her body strangely numb. His eyes never left hers. Gathering her courage, she took his hand in hers.

Cold air slapped her as she exited the carriage. Drawing her cloak about her, Elizabeth watched the carriage drive off and with it, her only means of escape. Turning her attention from the disappearing conveyance, she was surprised to recognise the district. The streets of Mayfair were different at night, the shadows lending a sinister air that was absent during daylight. An unassuming townhouse stood before them, far removed from the den of iniquity it supposedly was.

She pulled her cloak tighter as the wind tried to slip beneath her skin. "Orgies are held here?"

"Where did you think they were held?" James tucked her into his body and guided them up the front steps of the townhouse.

Tugging at the mask covering her features, she clutched James's forearm, hoping her claw-like grip wasn't doing him too much damage. "I don't know. I just didn't expect them in London."

He shook his head, a small, rueful smile on his face as they were admitted into the town house. No mask disguised James's features, as there was little point. The dissolute Earl of Malvern was almost a fixture at these events. Elizabeth shifted, a sliver of discomfort at the thought dampening her excitement.

The foyer appeared the same as any other. The

faint strains of music and laughter drifted down the stairs at the head of the entrance hall, and weak light beckoned one to ascend. James led her past rooms with doors closed, past rooms with doors wide open, past—had that man been tied up? With that woman flogging him?

Dragging her heels, Elizabeth craned her neck to get a better look, but James never let go of her hand, never paused in his tread to accommodate the fascinating sights flashing by.

Apprehension was forgotten as curiosity consumed her. An orgy. She was at an actual orgy. Why had she been so apprehensive when there was so much to observe—What on earth was that couple *doing?*

"Is that two women over there?" They kissed passionately, absorbed in each other and seemingly oblivious to those observing them. How did they give each other pleasure? Was it with tongue and fingers, or did they employ those false penises James had described to her?

"Yes," James said impatiently before ushering her on, his grip firm on her elbow. Why was he forcing her past each fascinating room? Surely the purpose of this was for her to experience what occurred at an orgy. The way he was pulling her along, they would be through the house and out the other side with nary an examination of anything at all.

But he couldn't force her past this. James tried to move her along but she slipped free of his grasp, pushing the door wide.

The chandelier cleverly illuminated only the middle of the room. There was movement in the ring of shadow, but the darkness concealed detail, lending anonymity to those watching the performance before them.

As if on a stage made of light, three people writhed on a dais of midnight-blue silk, the luxurious fabric sliding with their bodies as they moved against each other. A woman moaned as one man suckled her breast, her hand in the hair of another, his face buried between her thighs. All three wore little, the woman solely clothed in a corset the same midnight-blue as the silk beneath her, the garment thrusting her breasts into prominence. One man wore the remnants of a shirt, also midnight-blue, while the other was completely naked, his skin pale and gleaming with sweat beneath the candlelight.

The woman arched her back, giving the man at her breast greater access even as she lifted her leg over the second man's shoulder, exposing herself more fully to him. Her hand snaked between the first man's thighs, grasping his cock and stroking it in time with his pulls at her breast. The man grunted his approval, his buttocks clenching in rhythm.

There was a screaming in Elizabeth's chest, a lack of air. Breathe. She had to breathe, so as to keep watching the sight before her.

"Do you like this scene?" James's voice stoked her desire, built her lust. "Do you see what they are doing, how she is moaning as they lick at her?" His arm stole across her to pull her into him, his chest against her back. Delicately, his hand stroked her stomach, his touch burning through her clothing. "Do you imagine it's you, Elizabeth, with two men servicing you, devoted to your pleasure, to making you come?"

Her teeth dug into the soft flesh of her lip as his words painted images of faceless men serving her, licking her, four hands, two mouths running over her body.

"Do you think you could keep them entertained, both of them?" Hand flat, he wedged her against his hips, his cock thick and hard against her. Growing heated, growing wet, she pushed back into him, her bottom rubbing his groin as she watched. As she wanted.

The man between the woman's thighs abandoned his place, lying back on the silk and pulling the woman over him. His erection was massive, the head rosy and exposed. A gasp escaped Elizabeth at the sight of his cock, her tongue darting out to wet the centre of her upper lip. The rasp of teeth against tongue sent sensation rushing through her, pooling between her thighs.

James pushed inside her corset to cup her soft flesh, the hand on her abdomen pushing her into the rhythm of his hips. Push and retreat. Push and retreat. Lips skimmed her ear and sent shivers along her skin. Head lolling on his shoulder, will stolen, she waited for what he would do next.

"Watch as she takes him, as his cock disappears inside her. He's too big for her, do you see? She grits her teeth, forcing herself down, but it's not a grimace of displeasure, is it, Elizabeth? No, she's imagining how deep he can reach inside her, how far he can go."

Strong thighs braced either side of hers as James maintained that rhythm. Push, retreat. Push, retreat. The hand on her breast tightened. Heat swirled inside her, skin too tight and breath trapped as she watched the scene before her and imagined the one described by his words, until the two became inextricably entwined.

Before them, the man was now fully inside the woman. The second man, not content on the sidelines, moved before the woman, stroking her jaw as he presented his cock for her perusal. The woman smiled wickedly up at him, then took him deep into her mouth.

Oh God, in her mind it was she in the woman's place, stuffed full to bursting, both her core and her mouth filled, being taken even as she took. It was she who was making them moan, making them sweat and James was with her, encouraging her, and he was both of them—no, it was just him, him and her and he was inside her, making her moan like that woman, and they lost themselves in each other.

The men, in tandem, thrust into the woman. Moans erupted from all three, gasps and pleas and they looked so desperate, as desperate as she. Shuddering, she tried to contain her reaction, to ignore her lust.

She couldn't. She couldn't block what James was doing to her, with his touch, his words, his body next to hers. Couldn't take her eyes from the sight before her, from the writhing of three beautiful bodies. From the sight of their lust.

"Shall I take you somewhere, Elizabeth?" James's voice raked through her, making her flush, making her tight, making her wet. "Shall I bend you over and fuck you, take you hard so you can imagine it's you in there? Do you want to suck me, make me come in your mouth?"

His hand ground into her breast. Undulating against him, she wished their clothes vanished, nothing to stop the slide of their naked flesh. Nothing to stop him from being inside her.

"What do you want, Elizabeth?"

Desperate, she turned in his arms, pulling his head down to hers, kissing him hungrily, the image of the three burned into her mind. Strong hands gripped the small of her back, dragging her into him as close as they could get. He kissed her back as if he were as desperate as she, his lips and teeth and tongue biting her, laving her, loving her.

Tearing his mouth from hers, he searched the hall wildly. "Where's a bloody room?" The voice that had been so seductive was now savage, violent. It meant little to her as she attacked his neck, savouring the slight taste of salt beneath her tongue.

"Malvern?"

James froze, his hand digging into her back. Elizabeth belatedly realised his tension, dragging her attention from his neck to blink at the man blocking the hallway.

A faint smile on his handsome face, the man stood indolently, as if he were greeting them in a drawing room and not with an orgy surrounding them. Like James, his features were not obscured by mask, his hazel eyes amused.

"Barton." The coldness in James's voice startled her. Taking a shuddering breath, Elizabeth swallowed her arousal, trying to make sense of the change in James.

The man—Barton—swept his gaze over her. The admiration lit in his eyes sent a tiny thrill of pleasure through her dazed senses. "And who is your lovely companion?"

"No one you know." As if in protection, James's arm tightened around her.

"What a shame." Barton grinned, his open face and easy demeanour at odds with James's lack of both.

Elizabeth smiled in return, ignoring the clamours of her body. Strange that this man knew

James. Blond, mobile of feature, he seemed James's opposite.

"Perhaps you could introduce me?" Barton's gaze drifted over her and, of a sudden, the uncomplicated charm slid away.

Her smile died. Maybe this man wasn't so different from James after all.

James had not taken his gaze from Barton's. The faint smile on the other man's face never wavered, but the intensity of challenge radiated from Barton all the same. What was between these two? That they knew one another was clear. Were they partners in iniquity? Was it only fate, or the whims of Mrs. Morcom, that had given her tutelage to James instead of this man?

Visceral reaction gripped her and, involuntarily, her hand tightened on James's. He looked down at her, and she stifled a gasp at his stormy gaze. For a moment, it appeared as if he would refuse Barton's request, but then his eyes shuttered and he released her from his embrace.

Not knowing what to make of James's reaction, she tried to glean something from that impassive gaze. Nothing, no indication of how she should act, how she should proceed. He only stood there, silent and still.

Barton seemed to have no qualms with how to act, capturing her hand and bringing it to his lips. "It is a pleasure, my dear," he murmured, his eyes on hers as he placed a delicate kiss on her palm.

His lips were soft against her skin. It was all she could register. Her thoughts tumbled over and around, so jumbled she couldn't catch hold of them.

Barton pulled her toward him, raising one hand to cup her cheek, looming large in her vision as the muscles in her stomach seized. He was going to kiss her. He was going to kiss her and she didn't know if she should stop him.

James wasn't helping, standing with arms crossed and eyes blank. He stood there and offered no suggestion, nothing, and she didn't know what she should do. How could he just stand there and allow Barton to touch her? Was it part of her tutelage? Was he making a point?

And still Barton loomed ever closer.

An errant thought occurred, over and above those of James and his non-reaction. What if her feelings for James were not anomalous? What if all she wanted was a man, any man? So when Barton placed his mouth gently against hers, she allowed it. To be sure.

His lips pressed lightly, asking for entrance rather than demanding. Opening her mouth to his, a pleasant tingle ran through her at his kiss, though he tasted strange. Mint and lemon and something she couldn't place. All she knew was he was different.

His tongue toyed with hers as his hands curled around her ribcage. Warm, firm, his touch employed the right amount of pressure. As he ran his mouth down her neck, she noted the slight touch of his tongue at odd moments as he progressed to her chest, erratic enough that she couldn't predict when it would fall. The move was most ingenious and was no doubt designed to stir lust effectively. His lips then feathered over the skin revealed by her bodice, his thumbs lazily sweeping the curve of her breast.

Barton's touch *was* skilful, and if given further opportunity, she was sure he could arouse a warm passion, leading to an undoubtedly satisfactory pleasure, but he wasn't James. Barton would never make her burn.

Tugging his head up, she set her mouth against his, to make certain. Again, Barton's kiss was pleasant, and his delicate exploration of her mouth should stoke her arousal. Barton was just as delicate in ending the kiss. The taste of mint sat upon her tongue, the flavour of it discordant as Barton pressed a kiss to her collarbone, his hand plumping the flesh of her breast.

And she felt nothing.

Relief ran bright and sharp. Confirmation had never felt so sweet. About to push Barton from her, she glanced at James.

And froze.

James stood, his hands biting into his biceps as his cold glare bore into them.

Barton chose that moment to nestle deeper into her cleavage. James's stare became colder, until it appeared he was made of ice. Brow creased, she placed her hands on Barton's shoulders, intending to push him from her.

James's glare became, if possible, colder.

Suddenly, she realised what her move must have looked like. It must have looked...he must have thought she meant to pull Barton closer. He must think that she was enjoying Barton's kiss.

Elation ran through her. Could it be...was James jealous?

Immediately she set about to prove her theory correct. Cupping the back of Barton's head, she ran her fingers through his hair, surreptitiously watching James. His expression darkened.

Directing Barton to her nipple, she waited for James's reaction with bated breath, heady with the knowledge that he might be possessive of her. Barton cooperated delightfully, his hands plumping her breasts for the touch of his mouth. Affecting a facsimile of passion, she watched James through her lashes, stoking his ire by pressing herself into Barton's caress.

Dear Lord. Menace emanated from James, his body braced as if violence was barely controlled. Excitement shivered through her as she goaded him further, arching herself into Barton, her heart quickening as James's eyes glittered, as he grew more and more agitated, more *jealous*. Blood beat loudly in her ears and still she provoked him, pushed him, did all she could to incite him to break.

And break he did. With a harsh curse, James tore her from Barton, his hand tight about her wrist as he dragged her away. Stumbling along behind him, she struggled to keep pace, excitement flooding her veins, lust making her clumsy.

James shoved her inside an unoccupied room, locking it behind them. She turned to face him, her breath coming in great heaves as she watched the coldness in him become fire. He stalked toward her, forcing her back, and she couldn't contain her excitement, the heady emotion welling inside her uncontrollably as she felt the edge of a desk bite into her thighs.

"Did you enjoy that?" His words almost soundless, he crowded her so she was forced to sit, his arms braced on either side.

Lord, he loomed over her, so much bigger than she. For all his menace, though, she didn't feel fear. Oh no, what she felt was so very far from fear. Cocking her head, she considered her options. She could defuse the situation. Calm him. Reassure him. All she had to do was say no.

Slowly, deliberately, she nodded.

He growled. He actually growled. "Enjoyed it, did you?" Shoving her skirts up, he wrenched her legs open, wedging himself against her. "Would you have enjoyed fucking him?"

She knew she shouldn't push him further. His eyes glittered down at her, feral and out of control. She knew, and yet she couldn't stop the wicked smile, the false confirmation of every accusation.

Roughly, he pushed her against the desk. The wood hard at her back, she lay spread before him, her breasts cutting into her corset with every ragged breath.

"I wouldn't have allowed it." Pulling her legs around him, he shoved his hips against her. "I wouldn't have allowed him to have you." He tore at his trousers, wrenching them open. She groaned at the feel of him, hard and heavy with wanting. "I wouldn't have allowed it, Elizabeth," he ground out as he drove himself inside her.

She screamed, the wetness of her arousal making his entry easy. Books thudded to the floor as he pounded into her and her hands scrambled along the surface, seeking purchase as he jostled her against the desk, as he shoved deep inside her, again and again and again.

"You're mine," he grunted, his heavy thrusts punctuating his words. "Mine, do you hear me?"

She tried to nod, her voice stolen otherwise she would scream her assent, confirm it again and again. She was his. She was his, just as he was hers.

Arching, she pushed herself into each thrust, the violence of his possession intoxicating. He wanted her so badly he wasn't bothering with preliminaries, he was just slamming into her, *fucking* her, hard and deep and with such raw power she could feel it building. It was rushing toward her, coming so close and then it broke, violent and shattering and beautiful. She heard him curse as he released inside her, his hips jammed against her, his hands biting into her hips as he held her in place for his pleasure.

Finally, he moved, pulling away from her and smoothing her skirts into place with care. Reaction still hammered at her, her breath still out of control. She lifted a hand to him, but he slipped away and her hand fell to her chest, any movement too much. A silly smile flirting over her lips, she could do nothing but lie there, stupid and happy. Good Lord, and she had been worried about tonight? They should attend an orgy every night, and twice on Sundays.

After much debate to convince herself she did have the energy, she struggled upright, her bones languid and uncooperative in the face of such stunning pleasure. Bracing herself, she looked about for James.

Far on the other side of the room he sat with his head in his hands, his posture tense. He looked…wrong. Unease wound through her and she hopped off the desk, her legs wobbling as she crossed to him.

"James?" Kneeling, she took his hands in her own. His hands were so cold.

He raised his head and he said nothing. Concern for him chased away any lingering pleasure.

"James, what is it?" Her voice wavered as fear grew. Dear Lord, what was wrong?

"Did I hurt you?" Face impossibly still, his words implied a lack of care that their content decried.

"What? No, of course you didn't." Panic welled

inside her. "Lord Malvern," she stated formally, hiding her fear behind his title and a firm voice. "You will tell me what is wrong."

His eyes flickered. "I'm sorry." The words pushed past his clenched jaw, abrupt and cold.

"Sorry? What for?" Panic blossomed, consumed.

Muscle ticking in his jaw, he stared past her. "That."

She followed his gaze, her brow creasing when she realised he was staring at the desk. "For what?"

"For—" His voice broke and his throat moved convulsively. "For behaving the animal. I apologise."

The desk. Their lovemaking. "That is what has upset you?"

He inclined his head. And still he refused to look at her.

Reassurance. This she knew. "James." Linking her fingers with his, she gave a gentle tug. "James, that was the most incredible experience of my life."

Finally he looked at her. "What?"

"Believe me, James." Remembered pleasure thickened her blood, finding expression in a deepened voice. "You have nothing to apologise for."

His fingers slipped beneath the edge of her mask. She remained still, allowing him to remove the cloth. Gently, his fingers read the truth of her words through the arch of her brow, the slope of her cheek.

She kept her gaze level upon him. Reassurance. This she knew.

The icy calm cracked. "Did you come?"

"Yes."

His hand cupped her cheek, his thumb caressing the line of her jaw. Still she kept her gaze upon him. Gathering her to him, he held her, his legs hugging her body as his arms tightened. Warm lips hesitantly touched hers and the kiss felt like relief, like thanks.

Moments passed. She didn't know how many. Finally, he pulled back and retied her mask about her face, that delicious half-smile that always made her want to trace his lips with her tongue playing about his mouth. "Is there anything more you wish to see, or shall we discover what depraved delights I can offer you at home?"

Leaping to her feet, she bowed with flourish, laughing as he hurried her through the door. Following James through the house, her hand held tight in his, she ignored all save him. Now, his determination to rush held purpose. Now, nothing the rooms may have held could come close to what James offered. She picked up her pace, anticipation thrumming steadily through her veins.

"You bitch."

At first, Elizabeth didn't realise the words were directed at her. She was disabused of this notion rather quickly when the woman who had uttered them with such venom drew back her hand and struck Elizabeth across the face.

Confusion painted the room in garish colour. Her cheek stung as if separate from her as she registered a swirl of skirts, an angry face. She dropped James's hand. Raising her palm, she encountered the edge of her mask. Oh, yes, that's right. She was wearing a mask. The fabric, though, that had done little to protect her from the woman's wrath. She fingered her burning cheek, the echo of the slap reverberating on her flesh.

The woman stood boldly in front of her, her brow arched imperially. All were gazing upon her, upon her and Elizabeth, a throng of half-dressed people eagerly observing this new display of scandal.

Nothing made sense. It felt as if a nightmare, humiliation and debasement in a too public forum, a sea of unknown faces gaping at her. It must be a nightmare. This couldn't be happening.

"Madam." James's voice, cold and brutal. Yes, James was here, wasn't he? He stood before her now, between her and the woman. His coat was wrinkled. Had she done that?

A spark of triumph burned in the woman's eyes. "Why, Malvern, I had no notion you would be in attendance this evening. Come, my dear, are you enjoying yourself?"

So they knew each other, James and this woman. A dull pain started in Elizabeth's chest, burning in concert with the burn in her cheek.

"What do you think you are about?" Simultaneously, his voice demanded and derided. She wondered vaguely how he did it. "You do yourself no credit with this vulgar display."

The woman smiled thinly. "I do myself no credit? I? I think not, my love. No, you will be the one they will speak of on the morrow." Bitterness coated her words. "None shall remember me."

"Why should they remember the histrionics of a woman with no sense?" James's cold voice was cruel. Had she ever heard James be cruel? "You have accosted a lady with malice and no cause."

"A lady? This chit? Do not make me laugh, Malvern." The woman's gaze raked Elizabeth. "See how he treats us, sister. He will leave you with nothing as well."

A nightmare. It had to be.

Abruptly, the woman paled. Elizabeth couldn't understand why. The woman, she looked afraid.

Then James spoke, and the reason for the woman's fear was apparent. "You, madam, will not address her in such a fashion. Apologise and remove yourself. You will regret it otherwise."

The woman no longer looked so confident. Indeed, she looked as if she could not speak, her mouth gaping unattractively. And still the lurid fascination from the crowd.

No longer could she stay here.

The realization forced a reaction, and so Elizabeth turned and walked away. She pretended this sort of thing happened to her daily and really, there was nothing of interest about it, nothing at all.

The crowd parted before her. She kept her head high. She even managed to smile.

The fiction lasted as long as it took her to find an unoccupied room. Somehow, James had quit of the woman, shutting the door quietly behind them. He stood with his back to it, stood in his perfection and his impassivity, and she could only stare at him, lost in a nightmare that could not be.

"She hit me," she said.

He leaned against the door. "I'm sorry."

"But she hit me," she repeated. How strange, the sound of her voice.

James had found something of extreme interest on the floor. He said nothing.

"Why would she hit me?" Elizabeth lifted her hand to her cheek. Why did it still burn so? It had not been a hard slap. The sensation should have faded.

He pushed away from the door with what could be termed agitation. "It seems she believes you have replaced her."

"Oh." So she had been correct. James did know that woman. She rubbed her cheek, her fingers encountering the mask yet again. She was glad for it now. "Have I?"

Again, he wouldn't meet her gaze. "She seems to have taken umbrage to the severing of our…ties." He seemed disconcerted by her lack of response, clearing his throat before continuing. "I would not be surprised if that had all been for show. Of a certainty, her reputation would have to be maintained in some manner."

"By hitting me? In front of those all those people?" She was not going to cry. She was not going to—

Tears spilled, despite all her objections. And still her cheek burned. "Why didn't she hit *you*? You were the one she was *fucking*."

His damnable calm remained in place. "It appears you are upset."

"Really? What gave you that idea?" She dashed at her eyes. Breathe…she needed to breathe. Slow, measured. *Calm, Elizabeth.* "So…can I expect to get slapped again?"

Wariness etched deeply into his face. The display of emotion would have been astounding under other circumstances. "Maybe."

Incredulity rose at his response, screaming to escape. She could expect to again face down a roomful of gleeful watchers, each eagerly observing the humiliation taking place. And all because of James, who stood there with no defence and no apology.

Then reality hit her, with force stronger than that unknown woman's slap. This was the exact reason he had been chosen for her. For his prowess, for his knowledge…how did she think he had obtained that knowledge?

A hole yawned inside her. She could expect to encounter a paramour of his wherever she turned, and she had no one to blame for it but herself. She knew what he was, but never before had it been real.

With great care, she said, "Please tell any others who you might sport with to keep away from me. I would not appreciate a recurrence of this."

How remote and untouchable he appeared now. "I cannot control the actions of others."

"You will do your best to do so."

Silence fell. Distant reveals sounded, muffled by the walls. Someone shrieked and laughter trailed, but there was only silence in this room.

"Elizabeth." Why did James have to say her name like that? As if he loved every syllable. He came to her, placed warm hands on her shoulders and her will, damnably weak thing that it was, crumbled. "I would take back these last few moments if I could. More than like, it will happen again, but know that none shall ever be allowed to offend you."

The words vibrated intent. It might be attempted by another, at another time, another place, but he would not allow what had occurred tonight to happen again. He would stop it. His eyes, steel and promise, never wavered.

Suddenly, the nightmare was real. Horribly, overwhelmingly real. She ripped the mask from her face. "In front of all those people, James." Broken. Her voice was so broken.

"I know." He pulled her into his embrace. "I'm sorry."

Lips whispered over her temple, formed soft words to offer comfort. Emotion stormed within her and he held her throughout, his mouth smoothing away her tears.

Finally, it had to end. Taking a shuddering breath, she pulled the mantle of strength about her and managed a watery smile. "You were saying something about taking me home?"

Wiping her cheek with his thumb, he erased the last of the moisture from her skin. "You are amazing."

"Am I?" His gaze, fierce and admiring, made her believe in things she should not. "Do you want to show me how amazing I am?"

He smiled, that half-smile of his. "Always."

Chapter Fourteen

THE DAY HAD DAWNED bright and clear, the sun shining fiercely in the cloudless sky. Many had been lured from the protection of their homes by the false promise of warmth, only to dash back inside when confronted with frigid stillness. The lack of cloud, so pleasing in the warmer months, precipitated a particular cold, and while the sun shone brightly, the light could not combat its frozen grip.

The waning days of January had ushered a bitter chill through London. Ever enterprising, the chill found its way through cracks and gaps, insinuating itself beneath the skin, chilling the bone. This night, only a breath from February, the sun had set to be replaced by the barest sliver of moon, the air turning glacial as a thin film of ice covered all, lending a strangely ethereal beauty to a city that glistened with silvery brilliance.

Earlier that day as Elizabeth had sat in Bella's parlour, she'd hoped the bright sun would herald the beginning of spring. Though the chill had brought with it the pleasures of ice-skating and whimsical ice sculptures, she would not be sorry to see the end of winter. Even Bella, who'd always had a passion for the colder months, had complained heartily about the weather. Of course, she'd been influenced by the harebrained dinner gathering she was determined to hold, even though most of society had decamped to the country for the winter months. Bella, though, insisted she'd still manage to assemble a decent guest list.

Elizabeth dreaded the gathering. She never enjoyed such affairs, especially those organised by Bella. Elizabeth's attendance, however, had been secured under penalty of death, and though she would much rather spend the evening with James, she rather liked her limbs intact. Therefore, she would attend Bella's dinner party ten days hence.

Ugh. It would probably be freezing that night, too.

Now, in the entrance hall of James's townhouse, and with her feet undertaking a fair impression of blocks of ice, she lingered on removing her gloves, loath to lose their warmth. Strangely, Cartwright had not been there to greet her, a footman opening the door and then absenting himself as soon as she'd entered. Unsure what to do, she'd decided to remove her coat and gloves before going in search of James.

Scrunching her toes in an attempt to force blood into the nerveless appendages, she cursed the short trip from carriage to door. Such a brief exposure to the elements, and yet somehow she'd managed to douse her feet, bringing them to their current icy status and staining her slippers beyond recognition. Idiotic to have donned slippers in the first place, but they'd matched her gown and so she'd worn the flimsy things. She'd wanted to look pretty—nay, *beautiful*—for James and, obviously, slippers were the path to beauty. So, dunderhead that she was, she now had blocks of ice for feet, even though he'd never noticed her footwear before. Besides, the point would be moot once he saw the gown she was wear—

Strong arms hauled her against a warm body, trapping her in an embrace. Letting out a small yelp, she was disoriented before comprehension dawned. With a sigh, she settled against him, and his arms tightened about her as she relaxed into his embrace.

"You're here," James murmured. Soft lips brushed beneath her ear and finally the cold dissipated. Finally, she was warm.

They stayed so but a moment before he pulled away. Cold rushed to replace his heat and she wrapped her arms about herself as she turned to face him. She frowned. Why on earth would he be wearing such a heavy coat and gloves in his own home?

"How warm is your cloak?"

She blinked. "My cloak?"

Impatient for an answer, he took a hank of fabric between thumb and forefinger. The heaviness seemed to satisfy him. Changing tack, his hands delved inside the cloak to sweep it open. At the sight of her gown, he visibly lost composure, his throat moving convulsively as his eyes ran over her. "Jesus, Elizabeth."

"You said to wear something alluring."

Her grin widened as he muttered a curse under his breath. Brusquely, he pulled the cloak back in place, his hands lingering just a little too long. "You would cause a riot in that dress."

Smiling, she flipped the cloak behind her

shoulders once more, exalting in his groan. His was exactly the reaction she had hoped for when she had donned the gown that evening. The garment was new, only delivered two days ago. A deep blue, so deep it appeared black at times, it made her flesh appear creamier than it actually was. The gown fit like second skin, so much so that she wore no corset, the bodice cleverly designed to hold all that needed to be held. The low neckline displayed her breasts almost to the nipple, only saved from true exposure by a tight band of dark blue lace that hid and concealed depending on the light. The skirt was less full than fashion dictated, moulding more to her hips and thighs than was deemed seemly, but then, she would never wear such a garment in view of society. This gown was for James alone.

Throwing her shoulders back, which had the delightful side effect of thrusting her breasts forward, she swept past him.

"Not that way." He stopped her, taking her hand and instead leading her through the hall and into a portion of the house she'd never before seen.

Stealing a glance at him, she raised her brows at his expression, a strange mix of anticipation, fear and a sort of grimness. "Where are we going?"

"You'll see."

He led her through the corridor, proceeding at an unwholesomely brisk pace. The corridor led to a room, which led to another, and yet another, and then they were traversing another hallway, narrower than the hall leading to his study.

The corridor wound up and around, a set of stairs appearing out of nowhere to lead them to the upper levels of the house. Paintings of what she could only presume were Malvern ancestors lined the walls, the monotony of the empty hall broken by the odd forlorn table.

"Where are we going, James? Are you leading me into something depraved? You are, aren't you? Debauchery lies in wait for my poor, innocent self."

He provided no answer, but the ghost of a smile flitted across his face.

"What do you have in mind?" She tapped her finger against her lip. "Oh, but I shouldn't even try to imagine, should I? The mire of dissolution that is your mind could never be fathomed by one such as I." Flinging her hand against her forehead, she continued in grandiose fashion. "For one such as I couldn't even begin to traverse its dark and twisted...hmm." She mused as if a thought had just occurred to her. "Are you going to strip naked and have me do wicked things to you?"

No matter that he tried to disguise it with impatience, he couldn't quite conceal his amusement. "Can you not wait and see?"

She thought about it for a moment. "No. So, what is it? Where are we going? What do yo—?"

James stopped, so suddenly she crashed into him. Before she'd gained her bearings, he'd turned and pushed her against the wall, his larger body crowding hers. Fleeting unease filled her as he stared down at her, his hands cupping her face. Then he slanted his mouth over hers.

All thought fled. Wrapping her arms around his neck, she opened to him, accepting his tongue, giving him hers in return. He played and teased and tormented, murmuring approval. Her brain turned to mush. Burying her hands in his hair, she returned his kiss, lost in his taste. His texture. James.

Slowly, he pulled back, his hips still pressing

hers to the wall, his hands still cupping her face. Dazed, she stared into his eyes, a hint of the wicked dancing in their depths.

"Elizabeth." His tongue flicked her upper lip. "Be a good girl, and you'll find out where we're going."

Breath and thought returned only once he stepped from her, and they had begun again their progress through the house. The ghost of his kiss on her lips, she had not the wit to recommence her teasing.

When he chose to enter the lushest conservatory she'd ever seen, astonishment instead stole her tongue. Never would she have imagined James caring for a conservatory, and caring for such an unusual one.

A delightful warmth lingered in the air, what little heat the day had to offer trapped by glass tiles. The lush greenery swayed gently, as if entreating one to lose oneself amongst their dense foliage. The second story locale was both whimsical and insane, but it was obvious from the abundantly healthy condition of the plants that a great deal of effort had been expended to maintain their wellbeing. "Do you have a green thumb?"

"Pardon?"

"The plants." A smile touched her lips as she glanced around them. "They're beautiful."

He shrugged. "They were here long before I was. My mother may have had something to do with it." No glance was spared for the plants, no sense of pride in his voice. Curious. "Stop dawdling, Elizabeth."

Taking her gaze off a particularly fulsome rhododendron she smiled winningly, just to be annoying. Laughter threatened as his frown deepened into a scowl. Really, the man could be so very endearing. "Why do you have a conservatory on the second floor? And why do you maintain it so?"

He exhaled. "You're not moving until I tell you, are you?" Raking his hand through his hair, he gave in. "My mother. I think she was responsible. Back in the days when my father would have done anything to secure an heir." His lips twisted, a hard glint entering his eye. "Even building such an impractical thing as this."

"And why is it still here?"

He shrugged. "I don't know. The order to maintain must never have been rescinded. I really don't care. I'm never up here."

She searched his face, his posture, something to show he may have been hiding his true reaction.

He stared right back at her. Hmm.

Elizabeth grinned. "Anyway, why must we rush? Do you know I've never been in this part of your home before? Surely I can take the time to enjoy it a little. Or is there something we absolutely, positively, must attend this second, dash it all?"

An unwilling smile twisted his lips. "No, nothing, it's—" Exhaling, he ran a hand through his hair, disrupting the carefully disordered curls. "You'll see."

"What will I see?"

He raised a brow, his fingers tapping against his thigh. "Do you really think to pry this out of me? It's not much further. Come. We can look at the conservatory later."

He ushered her through the conservatory, and she allowed herself to be dragged along but not, of course, without doing her best to protest each step, simply for the delight of seeing him become frustrated. So focused was she on antagonizing him that at first she didn't realise he wanted her to step through the glass-panelled French doors. The glass-panelled French doors that led to the balcony. The fully-exposed-to-the-elements balcony.

"Outside? We are to go outside?" It was freezing out there. Well, it was official. She had finally driven him insane.

"Elizabeth, would you just go through? Your cloak is warm enough." He sounded so very frustrated, the poor dear. And, unaccountably nervous. Still, it was no excuse to send her out into the elements.

Shooting him a look that quite clearly intimated she would kill him if she froze to death, she pushed open the doors. A blast of iced air raced to steal the warmth from the conservatory. Pulling her cloak about her chin, she stepped out onto the balcony and braced for the worst.

It was indeed freezing, this night surely the coldest yet. Frigid air battered her, cutting to the bone and frosting her breath. None of this she noticed, for if it weren't so very cold, the ice sculptures on the balcony would never have existed.

Carved into florets and leaves and vines, ice skipped across stone, meandering lazily from the ceiling to join in delicate congress with the balustrade. Dozens and dozens of candles surrounded the ice, throwing light and flame as swans and waterfowl chased the other ever upward in a grand sculpture reaching almost to the roof, impossibly ringed by carvings of birds frozen mid-flight. Perched on a frigid branch, an icy bird peeked out from a delicate flourish of frosted leaves, each detail rendered perfectly.

The contrast should not work. Neither flame nor ice existed with the other present, and yet somehow they'd been coaxed to co-exist, to create the dichotomy before her.

The beauty of it stole her breath.

James wrapped his arms around her, his body encasing her in warmth. "You said you liked ice sculptures."

"Did I?" Each intricately carved shard was more dazzling than the last.

"Last week. You said you had been to the display along the Serpentine. You said you liked it."

"Oh." He had done all of this. For her. This magnificent display was all for her.

The man could be so very endearing.

"Are you—do you like it?"

Nodding dumbly, she couldn't tear her eyes from the sight before her.

His chest pressed against her as he let out his breath. Until then, she'd not realised he'd been holding it. Still distracted by ice and flame, she made no protest when he led her to a bench, piled high with cushions and furs. "Are you warm enough?"

She nodded again, still unable to look from the scene. Oh, there was a rabbit, hiding in the foliage on the floor! "When did you organise this, James?"

He shrugged. "On and off for the past few days."

"James, I...." She gave a helpless laugh. Gratitude, affection swirled inside her, tangled together in a mess no words could ever explain.

Gently, she pressed her cold lips against his. This. He had done all this for her.

He was so very dear.

Resting her head on his shoulder, Elizabeth watched as an icicle twinkled in the candlelight. "Do you like winter?"

James's lips moved against her temple, a soft exhalation of warm breath washing over her cold skin. "Not particularly."

"Oh? Why?"

"I've never liked the cold. It's one of the reasons I chose to stay in Italy for all those years."

Surprised, she lifted her head. "You lived in Italy?"

He looked as if he wished he had bitten his tongue. "Yes. For some time."

Before she could ask, as he must have known she would, he continued. "I found a *casa* in a small village on the Amalfi coast. Positano. It was amusing, so I deigned to stay. It was of no consequence."

No consequence? For the son of an earl to live in another country, and one so very far from society? Not bloody likely. This town, Positano, was unknown to her, but then, she'd not travelled further than London, and none in society would talk of a small Italian village. Florence was all the rage and many had waxed lyrical about Venice and Rome, but beyond those cities she knew nothing. Never could she have imagined him staying in such a place, let alone living there for a time. Vienna, yes. Paris, definitely. But a small village on the coast of Italy? "What was it like?"

Affecting that look, the one she had seen so often, the one that said you were a fool for asking such a question, he shrugged. "It was hot and green and the food was tolerable."

She hid a smile. What a fine attempt at nonchalance. Dear man. Thinking he could get away with so little when it was obvious it had meant so much.

He exhaled. "You want more? Fine. It was magnificent, with dramatic plunges of coastline, a sea that went forever and a sky that raced to meet it." His words began as mockery, but soon he lost himself in memory. "An acquaintance in Naples pressed me into a cruise along the Amalfi coast and, when I saw Positano, something about it…." He exhaled. "There it was, this village scoured deep into the mountainside, houses clinging precariously. The people were gregarious and always welcoming. Every Sunday, the woman would cook for all in the *villaggio*. The smells were intoxicating—exotic herbs, ripe tomatoes, and huge slabs of meat, and we would gather together at a communal table to enjoy the bounty. Every week it seemed there was a religious festival, celebrating this saint or that. The procession through the *villaggio* would see all the people on the streets—" A peculiar expression came over his face and he stopped abruptly.

"Yes. I can see you hated it." At her words, he found something of extreme interest in the curve of her shoulder. Hiding a smile, she prodded further. "Say something for me. In Italian."

Ah, there was that look again. That imperial, highhanded look. Why did he persist when it so obviously did not sway her?

"What makes you believe I can speak Italian? No other would learn such a pedestrian tongue."

None other than him. Now the surprise of his revelation had passed, it wasn't so very strange James had lived in a small village. The man everyone thought of as Malvern would have lived in Paris, Vienna, but James would have relished the village life. He would have gone to those village festivals every week. He would have sat at the tables and observed the festivities around him. He would have revelled in it.

And so, she waited.

Exhaling, he muttered something under his breath. Though she barely heard the words, she was fairly certain they were English. So still she waited.

Finally, with rather an intense scowl, he said, "*Siete la donna piu fastidiosa.*"

Her breath caught. "What did you say?"

The scowl melted away and…oh God, he had such a wicked expression. He had said something terrible, she was sure of it.

Gleefully, he translated. "You are the most annoying woman."

"I am annoying?" Throwing a good-natured swat at him, she mock-scowled. "I'm not the one insisting I don't speak Italian. Which is patently false, you big liar."

He grinned, the sight of which took her breath though she tried to act as if it were an everyday occurrence. Capturing her wrists to avoid her half-hearted blows, he placed a kiss against her palm. "*Mi dispiace, il mio topo. Sono gravi.*"

Cradling her hand against his cheek, he laced his fingers through the other, his eyes darkening as his gaze burned into hers. "*Gli amo il tatto sotto mi. Intorno a mi.*"

The words flowed through her, holding her captive. She had no notion of what he was saying, but the way he said it, the wickedness in his expression as he formed the words….

"*Voglio farvi gemito. Urlo. Voglio fare tanto cosi con te...*" The soulful words trailed away, and he turned to brush his lips against her palm. He rubbed his cheek against her nerveless hand, his lips brushing against her fingers with every pass. A faint smile touched his mouth, affording her some sanity.

"What—" Swallowing harshly, she started again. "What did you say?"

His lips quirked. "I love the feel of you beneath me. Around me." His fingers trailed sensation up the skin of her thigh under cloak and covers. "I want to make you moan, make you scream. I want—"

Unable to bear any more, she stopped his words with one hand against his mouth while the other halted his hand on her thigh. Undeterred, his tongue flicked against her palm, his eyes wicked.

"That's quite enough, sir." Good lord, but her voice was husky. She cleared her throat and ignored his sudden grin at her all-too-obvious reaction. "Why did you leave Italy?"

His grin froze and then disappeared as if it had never been. Smooth, emotionless, his face revealed nothing, all playfulness bled from him with her question. "It was time."

"That's it? It was time?" She ignored the niggle of foreboding at his reaction.

"Leave it alone, Elizabeth."

"No, really, why did you return to England?"

"It is of no consequence." He shifted, his hands grasping her upper arms.

Refusing to let him set her from him, she persisted. "There must have been a reason, James. You wouldn't have just left."

A muscle ticked in his jaw, his lips pressed tight. Doubt unfurled inside her. He wasn't going to respond, he was just going to stare at her like that and make her feel horrible for asking. But it was obvious something had forced him from Italy, something over which he'd had no control. Only…why was she pressing him? 'Twas obvious he didn't want to talk about it. Damn her and her insatiable need to *know*. Was she really going to make James answer because of her stupid, relentless desire—?

"My father died." The abrupt words tore through the silence between them. "He was dead, and I was now Malvern, and I had to return."

"Oh." She had no idea what to say. He'd only mentioned his father in passing, and never more than a handful of words at a time. "I'm sorry," she said lamely.

He shrugged.

All the closeness of the evening had disappeared. Always this happened, always she took her questions to a ridiculous degree. She didn't know what to say, how to put right what she had rent apart.

So she avoided it entirely. "So you came home and entered into a life of debauchery."

His whole bearing relaxed. "More like re-entered. Besides, it was a little more subtle than that."

"And then you met me."

"Yes," he said. "That is exactly how it happened. Amazing how my life can be boiled down to two sentences."

"Hmm." Tracing the lines of his palm, she kept her gaze trained on his hand. "So why did you?"

"Why did I what?

"Why did you enter—re-enter—the life of debauchery?"

His hand went lax in hers. She said nothing when he pulled his hand from hers. "It is what one does. My father, and before him his father, and his before him."

"Indeed?" His face was so cold, so flawlessly impassive. She shouldn't push. "How do you know?"

Impatience flashed across his features. Then, just as quickly, a sultry glint lit his eye and, hands grasping her hips, he leaned in to kiss her.

To distract her, of course. He was so very obvious. Avoiding his mouth, she placed a hand on his chest. "No, how do you know?"

Exhaling in frustration, he leaned back, his arms crossed and hands gripping his biceps. "I don't know. My father told me. It's our family history. My grandfather decreed it in his will. Pick one."

"Oh." Annoyance fairly vibrated from him, and she knew she should cease. "Do you enjoy it?"

His hands bit into his biceps. Finally, he shrugged again.

"Then why did you do it? The whoring, the drinking, any of it?"

A kind of frustrated impotence came into his eyes. "Does it really matter why? It is who I am. Who I was raised to be. I cannot think why we need to discuss it."

"Yes, but James—"

This time she couldn't avoid his kiss. His lips moved over hers, his tongue seeking entrance, and she let him distract her, her arms creeping around him as she returned his kiss. Clearly he did not wish to speak further. Well, she could take a hint. Eventually.

Blood thrumming through her, she pulled back. "Oh, so the ice sculptures are not a present? You expect payment, do you, my lord?"

Brows drawn, he stared at her, then languid sensuality painted his features as he seemed to realise she wasn't going to ask any further questions. "Of course not, my dear. I operate purely from an altruistic standpoint, as always." His hand drifted over the soft flesh presented by her indecent bodice. "If, however, you wanted to show your appreciation, I would not object."

"Indeed?" Rolling her hips against him, she bit back a smile at his groan. "And how may I do that?"

"Lean closer, my dear, and I shall tell you." Face schooled to impassivity, only his eyes displayed any emotion. Wickedness twined with lust and approval as she suited action to his words. "Ah, no, it is not close enough. If you will allow?"

Heart pounding erratically, she nodded. A half-smile wreathed his lips as he arranged her so she straddled his lap, running his hands over her, all ostensibly in an effort to keep her warm.

"Ah. Now this is workable." His lips brushed against her ear. "See? We are close."

A tremble ran through her. Yes. They were close.

"Are you warm?" His breath, chilled by the air, shivered along her neck.

Nodding slowly, she shifted closer, unaccountably drunk on him. All it took was a touch, a glance, and he brought fire to burn inside her.

"Good." He dragged his hands up her back. Then down. Then up. Then down. "So what should I ask of you, Elizabeth? There are so many things that would afford me pleasure."

His fingers feathered over her lips. The light touch against her sensitive flesh was a kind of agony, a barely there caress. "Should I ask for your mouth? Your lips moving against mine, the slide and retreat of your tongue."

Cold pushed against them and though her cheeks stung with it, the rest of her was aflame.

"Should I ask for your touch? Your fingers, light, delicate, tripping over my skin." His eyes, wreathed in ice and fire, mesmerised in their intensity. His words beguiled her, conjuring images out of the ether, half-formed fancies that shimmered and swayed, dancing in the ice and the flame. Wetting suddenly dry lips, she couldn't tear her gaze from his as he seduced her with his words, with light touches, with himself.

"Or should I do this, Elizabeth?" Hand sliding down her chest, he pushed the thin barrier of lace from her breasts. Cold wormed its way between them and she gasped, her nipples tightening in reaction. He cupped her flesh, and the contrast between the cold of the air and the heat of his hand echoed sharply on her skin.

"Shall I circle your nipples? Shall I stroke you?" Clever fingers traced the puckered flesh, streaks of sensation radiating from his touch. His lips quirked, and everything inside her froze at the wickedness in that small expression. "Elizabeth, shall I make you scream?"

Grabbing his wrist, she tried to direct his movement, but he resisted with a faint smile. As punishment, his fingers stilled, resting lightly against her and not at all what she needed. No, she needed him to trace her, to tease her, but no matter how she pleaded, how she moved, he resisted, that faint smile still flirting with his lips.

Finally, *finally*, he relented, trapping her nipple between his fingers and pulling gently at the distended flesh. Pleasure, mixed with a touch of pain, streaked through her.

"Elizabeth. You're not screaming." That damned smile on his face, he waited a moment, maybe two.

Then he bent his head, encasing her nipple in wet warmth.

How could she scream, when he stole her very breath? Clenching the soft strands of his hair, she held him to her as his teeth gently grasped her nipple, his hand covering her breast, pushing and pulling as he suckled. Her world was him, this world of ice and fire that contained only they two and the magic he plied with lips and tongue.

With a final lick he released her breast, trailing kisses up her neck as he pulled the lace back to cover her, only to have his fingers worry the lace against her tender nipples. Her hands knotted in his hair.

Eyes glittering with controlled desire, he leaned from her, his hands still on her breasts. "Or maybe my wants are too lascivious for such a simple thing as gratitude. Maybe we should sit together, like this, and nothing further." And with those words, his hands abandoned her completely.

No, no, what was he doing? Frantically, she tried to force him back to her, but his only response was a languid smile.

"We could count the beat of your heart against my chest, the steady rhythm lulling us into peace. You could rest your head on my shoulder, and I could play my hands down your back and we could simply exist together, you and I. We wouldn't feel the whip of the cold around us, not when we had the other, and we'd stay as we were, locked together with your breath mingling with mine and the frost in the air."

Mesmerised, she was barely aware of anything but him. All she could do was drown in his words.

Abruptly, his eyes darkened. "Or I could just do this."

Urgent hands tugged at her drawers, opening her to him. An impatient stroke, another, and then he pushed inside her. Gasping, she ground on his hand as he thrust, her fingers digging into his shoulders. His thumb grazed her clitoris and she did scream, burning as she moved against him, her hands clenching.

With a low growl, he removed his hand and she wanted to hit him, pummel him, how dare he do this to her…but then he was against her, hard and hot, and then he was inside her.

Time froze. Deep, he was so deep inside her, and she loved the feel of him, the feel of them. The bare skin of her thighs against the rasp of his trousers. Her barely clothed breasts against the fine material of his shirt. His fingers digging into her hips, her hands clutched in his hair. The moment lasted forever, and a second, and she wanted always to be like this. With him.

"Elizabeth." His lips whispered along her cheek. "Ride me."

Fire raced through her at his words, at the sensation they created. Tentatively, she lifted and slid back down. Hand steady on the small of her back, he guided her, muttering a curse when she caught the rhythm. Rising, falling, rising, falling. Soon it wasn't enough. Soon, she needed more.

"James?" His name was faint, barely a breath.

His answer a strangled groan, he covered her mouth with his and then his fingers brushed where they were joined. She screamed into him, the touch enough to send her over the edge, to drown her in rapture. Climax raced through her and blindness fell, all dark except the brightness of the pleasure inside her, pleasure wreathed in ice and flame.

The last tendrils of sensation held her captive as

she slumped against him. Gentle hands stroked her back. As reality returned, so did the world around them…and the fact he was still hard within her.

Trailing her lips across his cheek, she lifted herself only to return in a slow caress, giving him what he needed. He stifled a groan, his eyes closing and then he was thrusting inside her, striving for his own pleasure. Hard fingers dug into her hips as he held her captive and she revelled in it. A groan, a curse and then he stiffened, spilling inside her, his hand tightening in her hair.

All was silence between them, broken only by the harsh sound of their breath. His. Hers. Slowly they regained breath. Slowly the cold returned and the beat of their hearts synchronised to one.

Later, after they had left the balcony, after they had settled in his bed, Elizabeth replayed their conversation as James slept. She thought of his reaction, of hers. She thought on his father, his legacy, and James's obvious love of another country. She thought of all that could have been said, and hadn't.

But this time…this time she wouldn't question. Just this once, she wouldn't push.

Chapter Fifteen

BELLA'S CEILING WASN'T THAT interesting. Perfectly ordinary really, decorated as it was with subtle mouldings barely more than a suggestion of form against the unending stretch of white. Shadow threw strange patterns against the ceiling, but even the light of the flickering gas could not create interest when none was to be had. The chandelier itself held some attraction, with forty-two large tear-drop crystals and a further fifty-eight smaller ones spaced between them, and she couldn't believe she was so bored she had counted the drops from a light fixture.

With an almost imperceptible sigh, Elizabeth switched her attention to the dinner table. Maybe the silverware had gained some excitement in the minute and a half it had been since last she'd perused it.

It hadn't.

The other guests conversed easily with each other, obviously none battling boredom. There was, of course, Bella, who appeared wholly impressed with her own consequence. Burfield sat opposite her, the whole length of the table and several decorations between them. They each studiously ignored the other.

The guests were a veritable hodgepodge, some obvious choices, others perplexing in their strangeness. The Earl of Maddox was a contemporary of Burfield's, a large, brash man with a shock of blond hair and a surprisingly exquisite social delicacy. His Countess sat opposite him, a pallid woman who always seemed to have one hand wrapped around a wineglass.

Captain Duddely, however, seemed an odd choice. Elizabeth had no notion why her sister had invited the captain but he did seem great fun, with his bluster and his decided lack of tact and, judging by the raucous behaviour from that end of the table, Burfield and Maddox agreed.

A particularly loud guffaw emitted from the three and Elizabeth could not contain a smile. Lady Caldicott, however, did not share her amusement. A more sour look Elizabeth had yet to observe and as she watched, Lady Caldicott nodded to herself, as if their behaviour confirmed something she had known all along.

Lord Caldicott was engaged in conversation with Mr. Sutton, both men apparently finding something of common interest despite the disparity in their stations, even if Lord Caldicott did at times break the conversation to leer at the serving maid. By contrast, Mr. Sutton conversed with the whole of his attention, his open face displaying his enjoyment of the evening.

Of course, if Mr. Sutton were here, it meant that his wife was also. A shudder went through Elizabeth as Regina Sutton chose that moment to laugh, a high, shrill sound that never failed to scrape along every one of her nerves. Something about Regina Sutton rubbed Elizabeth the wrong way, and she could not believe Bella insisted on inviting her to social occasions.

The final member of their party was a small, rather rotund man far more studious in appearance than Elizabeth would have thought Bella would deign to invite. He'd been introduced as a Mr. M. Harlow Brown, but Elizabeth had no notion what his connection to Bella was, or why he'd been invited. He seemed comfortable with the company, however, and appeared to be holding decent conversation.

Which was something she should be doing.

Again she sighed, again covertly. She just couldn't muster any enthusiasm. The evening had been a waste, especially as she could have been employing her time much more agreeably. Any number of things required her attention, and most of them she would much prefer to this tedious dinner.

Besides which, she missed James.

She rubbed a pattern on the tablecloth. Right now, if not for this, she would have been with him. Maybe they would be snuggled beneath blankets, his arms loose about her as they watched the fire crackle. Mayhap even they would be ensconced once again on the conservatory's balcony, the remnants of the ice display creating a wall between them and the world.

It was still unbelievable that he'd done such a thing. The rest of the night they'd stayed in that icy wonderland, watching the play of ice on flame. Well, they'd stayed until James had remarked he could no longer feel his feet and, while he enjoyed the sensation, he would prefer not to develop frostbite. She'd grinned and assured him she had ways of warming him. He'd raised his brow and inquired, in the most dispassionate of tones, what, exactly, she'd had in min—

Regina Sutton brayed again. Grimacing, Elizabeth glanced at the wall clock. It was still early. There were hours and hours of this torture to go. Maybe she could plead illness. Surely she would not need specifics. If she hurried, she would even be able to make her way to Malvern House—

The clink of metal against crystal broke her thoughts. Lord Caldicott held his knife poised before his glass, a smile on his florid features. "My dear Lady Burfield, may I take this opportunity to extend my congratulations on a marvellous dinner? I cannot remember the last time I was so well fed."

Bella inclined her head, a pretty smile wreathing her lips. "Thank you, Lord Caldicott. My guests' comfort is of extreme importance. My chef and I did all we could to ensure a superlative meal, and I am delighted we succeeded."

"Superlative? I would venture to say divine." Lady Caldicott's smile should have been pleasant. "Such a bold move, the fowl course. I cannot remember the last time I had such a simple, uncomplicated dish. The palate, my dear…why, one could almost call it provincial."

Astonishment battered Elizabeth. What did the woman think she was about, to insult Bella so?

Before Bella could reply, Burfield added his voice to the table. "You are quite correct, Lady Caldicott. I find a table can quite frequently be overwhelmed with flavours. Sometimes, all I desire is a single ingredient, prepared well and surrounded by good English food. A turnip, you know, never did anybody any ill." A frown marred the perfection of

Burfield's face. It was criminal, really, how beautiful Bella's husband was. "Except my sister. She once had the oddest notion to excavate the cook's garden, for buried treasure or some such. Unfortunately, all she found were turnips. Oceans of them, by all accounts. She was most distraught. Inconsolable for days, from what I remember. It was extremely taxing on our poor cook, who had been planning a grand feast featuring the turnip. Turnip soup, roasted turnip—I believe there was even mention of turnip gateaux. By turns, Cook took to her bed, and Letitia to hers and there was much wailing and lamenting." Burfield's expression turned mournful. "We never did get that turnip feast."

"Turnip feast?" the earl asked.

Burfield shrugged. "We had an odd cook."

"And why have we not heard mention of this grand turnip feast before? I've never heard your sister speak of it. One might almost think it was some odd fancy of yours, this talk of rescue, Burfield." Was it her imagination or did Maddox emphasise the word 'rescue'?

Elizabeth could have sworn Burfield was silently consigning his friend to the devil. Maddox only grinned.

Finally, Burfield spoke. "It really did not signify. It cannot be said that a feast of the turnip would feature high in one's list of events one must attend before one dies."

"Turnips were Papa's favourite vegetable," Regina Sutton announced. "He always declared it the most noble of all the taproots."

Mr. Sutton smiled warmly at his wife, his eyes alight with affection. Elizabeth could only grit her teeth.

"Never could stand turnips. Always went rotten after a month or so. Used to toss 'em off the side of the ship." Captain Duddely punctuated his statement by downing what remained of his wine.

A bit harried, as if wondering how the conversation had devolved to include turnips, Bella cleared her throat. "While I, like many others, enjoy the particular benefits of turnips, I must direct your attention to other matters." An almost eager glint lit her eye. "We have a very special guest this evening, one who can enlighten us to *darker elements*." Bella turned to the studious man seated opposite Elizabeth. "Mr. Brown, have you had a chance to speak of your studies as yet?"

Elizabeth stared at her sister. Did Bella just emphasise those words?

Mr. Brown delicately wiped his mouth, then folded his napkin precisely. "My dear lady, I'm afraid not. And I must thank you for extending the invitation to me. I am honoured to be in such exalted company."

"It is I who am honoured, Mr. Brown. Your field of study attracts such a limited number of scholars, which is of great shame. Truly, it is something that we all have an interest in." Bella looked as if she could not contain her excitement. Or, at least, she did to Elizabeth. "Mr. Brown studies those arts which are *provocative*."

Elizabeth's brows shot up. Bella couldn't mean....

"Mr. Brown...." Bella lowered her voice. "Studies the *erotic*."

Incredulous, Elizabeth could only stare at her sister. Her staid, sensible, prudish sister. The sister who had never put a foot wrong. The sister who had lectured Elizabeth ad nauseam about her elopement with Rocksley. *That* Bella had invited an expert on the erotic to her dinner?

Elizabeth's shock was mirrored in Bella's guests, who ran the gamut from mildly interested to horrendously aghast. Burfield had raised his brows at the pronouncement, clearly surprised by his wife's choice of guest. The Earl of Maddox seemed more amused than anything else, while his wife displayed little care one way or the other. Lady Caldicott's face was suffused with outrage and indignation, while Lord Caldicott definitely seemed taken aback. The Suttons, though, appeared unaffected. Of course. Bella must have told Regina Sutton what to expect. Damnation, why was Bella so friendly with the woman?

It seemed no one knew what to say. Silence took a stranglehold on the dining room.

Captain Duddely guffawed. "A bit of rumpy pumpy study, hey, Brown? Always did like a bit of the stuff."

A quick raise of her hand covered her smile. If anyone was to break the silence, she was glad it had been Captain Duddely. And in such a magnificent fashion. Truly, she could grow to love the man.

Mr. Brown seemed a bit scandalised by Captain Duddely's comment. "Yes, Captain, it is a fascinating subject." He cleared his throat. "But it is a pleasure and a delight to be asked to speak to you all on my work. I have found that discourse on the sensual arts to be shockingly lax in recent years. We do love our queen, do we not? And as such, we adhere to her sensibilities. But it can be a tad limiting. Don't you agree?"

"I make it a point never to be limited." Burfield smiled blandly. "Except on Tuesdays. For some reasons, I can never do anything to excess on Tuesdays."

Bella glared at Burfield, who responded with a look of perfect innocence.

As for herself, well, Elizabeth could only stare at the man. She'd never heard of him, and James certainly hadn't mentioned him. Surely if he were that conversant on erotica, James would have included him in her curriculum. They had discussed erotic fiction, studied pictograms and lithographs, and James had even procured a tome on lascivious artworks. But never, in any of those studies, had this man been mentioned.

Her lips quirked. Maybe for once she would be able to enlighten James.

"I have found, though, that many a study into the earthy pleasures have not maintained a proper grip on propriety." Mr. Brown shook his head. "Most are crude representations of what should be celebrated as a private congress between husband and wife. Indeed, some of the papers by my contemporaries." Mr. Brown tutted. "My ladies, they are not fit for my eyes, let alone for such luminous personages such as yourself."

"It is right and proper of you to censor your findings, Mr. Brown," Lady Caldicott announced. "Morality has become shockingly lax, and we can only follow the example of our magnificent queen in steering those weaker than ourselves on correct behaviour."

Mr. Brown nodded gravely. "My lady, I could not have put it better myself. You understand perfectly my dilemma. Such studies are of the utmost importance, and yet one must deal delicately with the finer sensibilities. Many would be shocked by my findings. Simply shocked."

"Shocked." Captain Duddely snorted. "Man shouldn't be shocked. Bunch of nambies, land folk. You'd never find this on the waves. The sea is a cruel mistress, but she's not a jealous one." He laughed heartily, and again downed his wine.

As the footman with the pitcher of wine took up residence slightly to Captain Duddely's left, Elizabeth could only gaze in awe at the man. The captain was brash, uncouth, and blessedly unconcerned by those facts. He was, in a word, brilliant.

"Mr. Brown, have you been at your studies for long?" The Countess of Maddox's quiet features offered no clue as to her thoughts.

"Since my university days, my lady. I developed a passion for the classics and the erotic adventures of the ancients has been well documented in several forums. I found myself consumed with a desire to know everything I could about the subject and dedicated my life to studying its finer points."

"So you study ancient erotica?" The words left Elizabeth before she could stop them.

Her bald question apparently shocked Mr. Brown. He appeared flustered, in any event, and not only Mr. Brown seemed so. Several at the table gave her odd looks.

"Um, yes, my lady, I do, although I would not put it quite so boldly. We must always retain a certain delicacy, especially in relation to matters such as these."

Elizabeth smiled weakly in response.

Bella saved her from having to comment further. "My sister, Mr. Brown, sometimes speaks without thinking. Please, do continue."

Mr. Brown appeared as if he didn't know what

to think. Bella, however, seemed to have no trouble and, covertly, shot a glare at Elizabeth.

Elizabeth raised her brow, much as James would have. Bella had no right to chide her in such a manner. Maybe Elizabeth's comment had been on the edge of appropriate, and maybe she should have held her tongue, but she had done nothing irreparable. Bella was overreacting, as usual.

There was an awkward pause, and Lord Caldicott chose to fill it. "Mr. Brown has some of the most interesting theories I have had the fortune to peruse. In fact, his pamphlets are most informative, and very well researched. I myself have all seven." The officious man looked so proud of himself for his diverse reading habits.

"Thank you, my lord. I am always cognizant of the flattery my readers do me by regarding my work in the highest esteem." Mr. Brown looked over the rims of his glasses. "Such studies, of course, are all-consuming. I find my time and my funds are quite often depleted. Patrons such as yourself, sir, help with furthering my studies. But the pursuit of knowledge is worth any sacrifice, and one gains such a sense of satisfaction from pursuing such a thing. However, it is such an expensive exercise, and I find that the publication of my pamphlets do not always cover costs."

Good lord, the man had attended Bella's party to solicit funds. Even now, he had an avaricious gleam in his eye.

The Earl of Maddox was the first to respond. "A contemporary perspective would surely draw more patrons, Mr. Brown. We all delight in learning further about ourselves, do we not?" The earl smiled urbanely at the man, though his eyes were cool.

"You are correct that a, uh, contemporary perspective would be of more interest, my lord. However, there is less grace, less majesty in more recent publications. Just the other day, I acquired a tome published but a year ago, and it is shocking in its depiction of libidinous activity. Simply shocking. It does seem to be popular with the common masses, and many of them cannot contain themselves when asked to discuss it. I would almost deem them frenzied, fiendishly close to salivating. If not for my study, I would have quite steered clear of the rabble, but many of them had interesting views of the publication. Completely uninformed, of course, but interesting."

The man droned on and on. Elizabeth played with the handle of her knife, listening with only half an ear. What she wouldn't give for James's directness right about now. He would have plainly said what was in the book, given a brief precise, and then demonstrated the more pleasurable bits.

Damnation, she had to stop thinking about James. Sighing, she folded her hands in her lap, resolving to at least pretend interest in the conversation.

"It is a necessary assertion that passionate desires, when not tempered by wisdom and restraint, can lead one into the darker areas of the human condition. Indeed, the unfortunate heroine finds herself in such a quandary and rather than applying to her conscience, she instead slides further, ending in lascivious congress with a man not her husband."

"And the book's name, Mr. Brown?" Surprisingly, it was the Countess of Maddox who asked the question. The woman had not said above five words all evening, and now she had spoken twice in ten minutes.

"Ah, the book. Yes. Such an intriguing tome. In my pamphlet, which is much in demand, I flatter myself to think, I discuss the merits of focusing on the heroine's shocking lapse into depravity and the depths to which she sinks."

The Countess of Maddox's expression remained calm. "But the name of it, sir. You've neglected the name."

"Oh, my apologies, my lady. It is simply called *Sophia*, an innocent name for such a book."

Maddox, who had just taken a draught of his wine, choked. His wife regarded him impassively. "*Sophia?*" he managed to say.

"A semi-biographical tome, I believe. The misadventures of a young girl. Quite shocking, really." Mr. Brown shook his head.

Maddox appeared unable to speak. His wife regarded him with that same impassive stare. Elizabeth glanced between the two. Suspicion rose. The book was one James had given her, and a large portion had detailed the title character's affair with a lord. The reason for its notoriety amongst society was because, as Mr. Brown said, it was reputed to be a biography. From Maddox's reaction, could it be the gossips were right for once?

"Maybe you are correct in that this is not proper discussion in mixed company, Brown." Burfield's smile was amiable, but an edge of irritation lurked beneath the genial expression. "Books always get one into trouble, you know. I had a friend once, Rolston, good chap, went to Rugby with us and set up the most amazing betting system I'd ever encountered. Anyway, he once had an ill encounter with a book and, though he'd never tell us the particulars, 'twas obvious it scarred him for life. So mayhap it is better to leave such things undiscussed."

Bella's smile was pleasant. "Burfield, we do not need to hear about your friend Rolston."

"I was under the impression this was my house, my dear," Burfield said mildly. "I can do what I like."

Bella and Burfield stared at each other, his expression open and amused, hers fractious. Well, this was certainly an interesting turn of events. Mostly, Bella would pretend all was well between her and her husband, even when it was so very obvious it was not.

"Please, Mr. Brown." Bella's gaze never left Burfield. "Won't you continue?"

Mr. Brown looked between the two, obviously torn.

Suddenly, Burfield smiled, and looked away from his wife to his guest. "Please, Brown, do continue. Pardon my interruption."

Though he looked troubled, Mr. Brown began a hesitant description of the book. As none gainsaid him, he grew bolder, outlining some of the content and yet none of the licentiousness.

Elizabeth ignored him, instead watching Bella. Though his attention had returned to Mr. Brown, Bella still regarded at Burfield and, in that small glance, wholly unnoticed by the table at large, a story was written. One where Bella, amazingly, harboured some feeling for her husband. For just a moment, less than a second, Bella's face had held frustration, anger and, beyond all else, a strange longing.

Never would Elizabeth have considered Bella entertained tender feelings for Burfield. They'd been married for years, had two children and yet lived completely separate lives. Surely she had imagined the faint longing in Bella's eyes. Surely.

Suddenly, comprehension of what Mr. Brown was expunging hit her. "That's not what happened at all."

Oh lord, her mouth was running away with her again. And now everyone was staring at her.

Mr. Brown smiled condescendingly. "I know this a bit better than you, my dear."

"But sir...." *In for a penny, in for a pound, Elizabeth.* "Do you not think that, while celebrating erotic expression, the story also shows the follies of uninhibited sensuality without thought?"

Mr. Brown pursed his lips. "My lady, you have read this book?"

Deep silence, almost as if every breath was held awaiting her answer.

Right, well, into the fray, such as it were. Raising a brow, she did her best impression of James. "Yes, I have."

Scandalised glances from all at the table, between each other, at her. Bella looked horrified.

There was little to do but continue. "The erotic must always be grounded in sense, not undertaken simply as a whim or a hedonistic pleasure."

Mr. Brown's expression grew florid, almost as if he would have an apoplexy and expire upon the spot. "This book is nothing more than a discourse on the degeneracy of lustful behaviour."

"But surely erotic expression for the sake of it is not a sin." Elizabeth couldn't stop the stream of words now. "Indeed, as Sophia discovers, it is a celebration of pleasure between two consenting adults. The book itself articulates the glory of sexual expression, and the joy one can glean from the opposite sex. By the conclusion, Sophia is happily ensconced with her lover, a man dedicated to ensuring her happiness, both the emotional and the erotic. Do you not think, sir, that the novel shows how women can seize control of their sexuality and become mistresses of their own fate?"

Intense silence had fallen. Around the table, all stared at her, all scandalised. All except Regina Sutton, who wore an expression of gleeful horror.

Oh. Oh, no. She was an idiot. A fool. No lady knew of the erotic, and if she did, she kept it to herself. More so, her words displayed a depth of knowledge no lady should have.

"I am shocked," Lady Caldicott announced.

Regina Sutton nodded, as if she agreed with Lady Caldicott's pronouncement. The countess simply stared, her motionless features displaying no opinion. The earl wore an odd combination of shock and gratitude, and Elizabeth stupidly realised she had drawn the attention from speculation about him. Well, wasn't she the courteous soul.

Disappointment drew the lines of Mr. Sutton's features. Captain Duddely and Lord Caldicott regarded her with a degree of calculation in their glances, and she looked away, unable to bear their scrutiny. She didn't want to know of what they were thinking. Even Burfield, who surely had been subjected to her inappropriate behaviour before, seemed taken aback.

But the worst was Bella. Pale, silent Bella.

God, she wanted James. James would protect her. He would put his hand on her cold one and stare each of them down, daring them to say something, and they would all look away and everything would return to normal. Later, when they were alone, she would lambaste herself for a fool, and he would hold her and comfort her.

But James wasn't here. She would have to face this herself.

The silence was broken by Bella's laugh, the sound tight and high. "Please excuse my sister. She does not know of what she speaks."

No one uttered a word. Finally, Elizabeth ventured a rebuttal. "Bella, I thank you, but I'm perfectly capable—"

"Elizabeth, you will be silent." Bella's smile was pleasant, but her tone....

Elizabeth swallowed, and was silent.

After an agonizingly endless moment, Mr. Brown cleared his throat. "As I was saying, any discourse on erotica needs to have established parameters. A lady should not attempt to things that do not concern her."

Fury burned away some of the shame. How dare he say that? That little man had no right to say such things about her, to judge her and hold her in contempt. She had risked much to gain her knowledge and, by all accounts, had a much better grasp of the erotic than this officious little man with his condescension and his contempt. Opening her mouth, she prepared to lambast the man.

Bella shot to her feet. "If you will excuse us, my sister and I must talk." She turned burning eyes upon Elizabeth. "Come, Elizabeth."

There was no way she could refuse such a command. Placing her napkin with great deliberation on the table, she rose to her feet and, as abruptly as it flared, her fury died.

The men stood haphazardly, as if they suddenly realised she was still a lady and, as such, politeness dictated they stand. Shame suffused her at their hesitation and she executed as perfect a curtsy as she could manage to prove that, despite all evidence to the contrary, she *was* still a lady. As she rose from her curtsy, she hadn't convinced herself, let alone those at the table who stared.

Bella waited for her in the hall and, turning on her heel, clearly expected Elizabeth to follow. Dread churned in her stomach as she did so. She was in for it now. Bella became angry over the most inconsequential of things. How, then, would she react to this?

Elizabeth gnawed at the nail on her thumb as Bella led her to a sitting room not two doors from the dining room, closing the door with a sharp snap. Taking a deep breath, Elizabeth turned to face her sister, bracing herself for Bella's fury.

Her sister rounded on her immediately. "What were you thinking?"

"I—"

"How could you say such things? In front of other people? How could you?"

"Bella, I—"

"You have made this dinner infamous, Elizabeth. Tomorrow, all that shall be talked of is your knowledge on some sordid *book*. And the question will be asked, how did you gain such knowledge? There will be whispers, Elizabeth, and they won't be contained to you alone. How dare you bring this upon my family? How dare you?"

Abruptly defensive, Elizabeth grasped at the few options left to her. "He was a pompous fool, Bella. What else was I to say? Besides which, why did you even invite him? He studies the 'erotic', Bella. Already you had a recipe for scandal. Besides, of what possible interest could the erotic be to y—?"

Bella's expression grew thunderous. "A pompous fool? I care not a whit if he's a pompous fool. I care that you have decided to be decidedly indecent in *my* house. And it is absolutely no concern of yours why I invited him."

A memory pierced through the haze, a memory of Bella at the table, that mix of longing and defiance in her eyes. "Bella, this is not some misguided attempt to garner Burfield's attention, is it?"

Blood rushed to Bella's face and she appeared unable to speak. Finally she ground out, "That is none of your concern."

"But Bella, maybe if you tell me, I can hel—" She snapped her mouth shut. Bella looked as though she wanted to hit her.

"Stop pushing! You always push! Can't you just leave well enough alone?" Bella hit her hand to her forehead, so hard she left a mark. "What am I saying? Of course you can't. Look at tonight. Mr. Brown is an expert on erotica, and yet you had to question him. You had to push. Now, all of society knows my sister possesses intimate knowledge of a scandalous book!"

Though she knew she was wrong, she couldn't stop her mouth from saying the words. "Bella, it's not as bad as that. You are overreacting. Besides, you invited Mr. Brown in the first place. If you were worried about scandal, why did you do so?"

"It is not Mr. Brown's presence here that is scandalous. Elizabeth, you *know* this book, and what's worse, you challenged a renowned expert. You sat there, argued with him, and demonstrated for us all that you know this book. Extremely well!"

"Bella, there is nothing wrong—"

"Of course you don't see what is wrong!" Bella

exploded. "You never do. You blithely go your own way, do whatever you want and nobody ever stops you. Nobody! Meanwhile, the rest of us have to deal with the mess left in your wake."

Elizabeth stared at her sister. No. This time, Bella was wrong. "I don't do whatever I want with no care for others."

"Of course not. That is why, at this very moment, my guests are in shocked disbelief that my *sister* could be so coarse. Your lack of concern for how your bloody *inquisitiveness* affects the rest of us is truly vile. I am ashamed to call you my sister."

Elizabeth wrapped her arms about herself. She did have care for others.

"You've changed, Elizabeth. Don't think I haven't noticed your demeanour these last months. You are up to something, and I will not have whatever it is intrude upon my home." Bella enunciated each word precisely, her eyes burning. "I will not tolerate your smug looks and your stupid little smiles and…and...when did *you* become an expert on the erotic?"

Brief panic flared. Had she slipped? Did Bella know about James?

Just as suddenly, the panic faded. She *had* done what Bella said she had. She'd undertaken a venture that, if discovered, would bring shame to her family. James was proof she had little care of others. Without thought or concern, she had applied to a madam of a brothel, engaged James's tutelage and proceeded to learn things, do things, that would bring shame to her family. No matter the precautions she'd taken against such an event, the care she'd taken to ensure none should discover it, still she'd courted risk.

Once again, she'd acted in service to her

curiosity. Once again, she'd acted without care. All, always, was in service to her bloody desire to *know*.

"You have ruined this dinner party, Elizabeth. God only knows what Burfield thinks of it. Of you. Do you know how long it took to convince him to attend this evening? And now, all is undone. Because of you. You and your questions and your inappropriateness and…and…."

Bella swallowed. "You never think, Elizabeth. You have to know, and nothing stops you. Not even when it will be to the detriment of others."

Elizabeth stared at her sister and offered no excuses. No defences. Because she knew Bella was right. Her sister's words echoed, the weight of truth behind each one. How could Elizabeth defend herself? She'd done the thing Bella accused her of. She'd acted coarse and immodest, and she'd done it with no thought as to how her actions would affect others.

Bella sighed. "I shouldn't expect anything different, should I? Always it has been so. I am sorry, Elizabeth. I never should have invited you."

Absently, Elizabeth noted Bella had calmed, had regained normal colour and temperament. She watched as her sister wiped her face, checked her hair.

"Well, there is nothing for it. We'll have to brazen it out, I expect." Bella smoothed the front panel of her dress, her fingers deliberate on the fabric. "I shall return to the table now. Follow me in a few minutes. We shall get through this night and then, God willing, we shall never have to speak of it again." Bella pasted a wide smile on her face. "Right. I shall see you in there."

Elizabeth stood alone in the room, the silence

deafening. Finally, she managed to make her way to
the dining room. She laughed and she conversed, and
she did all the things a dinner guest was supposed to.

Later, when she was alone, she sat on her bed,
hands grasped tightly in her lap, and stared at the wall
until morning came.

Chapter Sixteen

ANOTHER MINUTE. THE TIME piece had counted thirty-two past the hour. She was thirty-two minutes late.

Malvern drummed his fingers against the desk, his gaze trained on the pocket watch he had propped up seventeen minutes ago. He wasn't worried. Nothing had befallen Elizabeth. A mere delay, that was all. It was entirely possible she had decided not to come, in which case he should get off his arse and out of the study and do something with his evening, rather than sit around obsessing over her absence.

Tearing his gaze from the watch, he instead stared out the window. The glacial late February night pushed against the glass, coating the panes in a frost that obscured view of the dimly lit street. Yet, for all its frigidity, the turning of the season was in the air. Each day was incrementally warmer, daylight clinging to the earth just a little bit longer. After the last few weeks of intense cold, the warming of the air was welcome relief.

The waning of winter brought about new complications. Elizabeth could arrive only after the fall of dark and as the days lengthened, the time she could be absent decreased. Rubbing his chest, he frowned. Already they had too little time together, their evenings reduced to thrice weekly with the return of her family and the resumption of her other obligations. With no family of his own, and precious few obligations, he had little to distract him and thus found his days consumed with battling impatience for her imminent return.

Good Lord, he had not thought what summer would bring. Would Elizabeth retire from London for the warmer weather? With nothing to keep her, the temptation of amusement in the country might prove irresistible. If she so chose, it was entirely possible he'd have to endure an entire turn of a season without her.

Not bloody likely. If she must go somewhere, she could go to Brighton for the sea-bathing, but *he* would take her and they would stay in the best hotel the region could offer. No matter that he did not have the authority, that he could not dictate to her so. It only meant he had to broach the prospect in language that would appeal to her, so she would not leave him alone in London for all those months. What would amuse her in the seaside town?

His gaze strayed to the pocket watch again. Thirty-four minutes past the hour.

Nothing to worry about, but just to be safe he should summon Cartwright to send a footman to Elizabeth's home. Maybe a team of footmen. If she had come to some grief on the way to Malvern House—

No. She was fine. Absolutely fine. She was late,

was all. Just because she'd never been late before did not preclude an instance of it. Any number of things could have occurred, not the least of which was simply a desire not to see him. There'd been no sign she was tiring of their arrangement, but such a possibility could not be discounted. In any event, he would rather that than the other.

Fear shuddered through him, his blood cold and the beat of his fingers against his desk erratic. Potential scenarios rose to torment him, each more gruesome than the last.

Nothing had befallen her. Nothing was wrong. She was simply late. That was all. Late.

Footsteps in the hallway, a quiet murmur of voices. Then, the door opened and Elizabeth walked through.

His heart stuttered, then sped to life once more. He shot to his feet, so fast he nearly stumbled over his chair, and had to forcibly restrain himself from bounding to her side. Fighting the urge to examine every inch of her to ensure she was unharmed, he ran his gaze over her instead of his hands, noting she appeared intact, no obvious distress or wounds about her.

As he became convinced of her well-being, his heart resumed its usual rhythm, the panic that had consumed him abruptly dissipating. Only in its absence did he discover how tense he had been, his muscles screaming their relief.

Determined the affectation of nonchalance would disguise his distinct lack of it, he prepared to chastise her for her lateness. Before he could formulate a coherent phrase devoid of any hint of concern, it finally struck him how quiet she was. Usually, she bounded into the room, covering him with affection as if it had been months instead of hours since last they'd met.

Now she seemed…lost.

Seating herself in her chair, she arranged her skirts about her precisely. And yet, not a word. Not a question, not a greeting, not even his name.

Apprehension built in him. He ignored it though, certain if it was not acknowledged then it could not be.

She was wearing one of her god-awful gowns, the ones he had told her to dispose of. This one was a disgusting shade of brown, the buttons marching right up to her throat. In her new gowns she'd appeared vibrant, alive. This gown, it made one think her…dull.

"My dear, I had no idea we were to dress as dowds this evening. Some sort of warning was warranted, don't you agree?"

His attempt at teasing raised no smile from her. Apprehension could not be ignored now. "Why aren't you wearing one of your new gowns?" Unease made his voice harsh.

"I didn't feel like wearing them." Her voice subdued, she seemed to disappear into the chair. She appeared the mouse he'd first thought her, and the image was now so incongruous he couldn't believe how wrong he'd been.

His fingers were drumming against his thigh. Stilling the rhythm, he clenched his hands to prevent a resumption. "What's wrong?"

"Nothing." With her lashes downcast, hands bundled in her lap, she was the picture of a meek little mouse of a woman.

He hated that she seemed so.

Striding to her chair, he knelt before her.

Bloody hell, he didn't know what to do with his hands. Should he hold hers? "It is not 'nothing'. You haven't asked me one question as yet and you've been here for at least two minutes. What else am I to think?"

A ghost of a smile flitted across her face. "I'm that predictable, am I?" Just as a trickle of relief ran through him, a shadow dimmed her smile. "So I do it to you, too?"

"Do what?" He had no idea what to do, how to proceed. Damnation, usually she was an open book, but now, when it mattered, she was as forthcoming as a clam.

She smiled, though it didn't reach her eyes. "It *is* nothing. You don't want to hear my troubles."

How could she believe that he would not want to hear what was troubling her? Imbecilic woman. Did she not know it tore at him, to see her like this? Elizabeth was happy, cheerful. Whoever was responsible for that look on her face, the clenched hands in her lap, would regret it. Severely.

Swallowing his ire, he forced himself to concentrate. "Truer words have never been spoken, my dear." Keeping his tone light, he even attempted a smile. "However, it appears we are not going to engage in anything remotely sexual until whatever it is that has you worried is out in the open. And you know I am all about sexual gratification."

That startled her enough to raise her eyes to his. Slowly, deliberately, he raised a brow.

She gave a little burst of laughter, a glimpse of his Elizabeth shining through. "Yes, I can see the truth of that."

"So, take pity on me. I can't be deprived. It will disturb the rest of my night."

"We can't have that." Her eyes searched his. "Are you sure I'm not troubling you?"

As if impatient he exhaled, the act designed to disguise his concern. "Remember about the sexual gratification? Get on with it, woman."

A faint smile, barely there before it was gone. "If you are certain?" When he said nothing to dissuade her, she continued. "Last night I went to a dinner Bel—my sister held. It was at her house. Which is why I wasn't here." She picked at a loose thread. "I wish I'd been here instead."

If she had been, she would not look so now. His hands clenched.

"Anyway, it was…well, it was boring. I'm always bored at those things. You know what they're like—people you don't really know talking about things that don't really matter. Bella always invites the dullest people, the ones she thinks can benefit her or Burfield. Or she invites them according to some grand design only she perceives, because Lord knows, she doesn't actually *like* these people."

The turn of the thread turned her finger white. "Anyway, one of the guests. This man. He was there and he was talking about—Bella had invited him to talk about—you know, she just did it because she wanted to be risqué, but when it comes down to it, she doesn't really want to be. She is so *comfortable* in her conservativeness." Bitterness soured her every word.

His nails bit into his palms. He could see the pain beneath the bitterness. Damn it, he should be out destroying these persons responsible for making her hurt.

"This man, he was allegedly an expert on *erotica*. Pleasure. The lascivious arts." She laughed.

"Ridiculous, is it not? But this man…." Her gaze flew to his. "His name was M. Harlow Brown. Have you heard of him?"

He shook his head.

She nodded. "Neither have I. This man, this Mr. Brown, he talked and talked, but he didn't actually say anything. Nothing definitive anyway. Then he talked about *Sophia*, and he was getting it all wrong. He was making such a beautiful story into a horrible discourse on the vagrancies of sin and how if anyone anywhere dared to enjoy the erotic they would burn in the fiery depths of hell…."

She balled her hands in her lap. "Anyway, he had no notion of what he spoke, and yet he somehow maintained credibility by talking in circles and deeming everything too delicate for a lady's ears. Too delicate. Lord, that always infuriates me. And so, I asked him some questions. Stupidly. Like I always do. Bella shouldn't have invited me if she didn't want me to ask. She *knows* what I'm like."

He said nothing though he could see where this was going and, damn it, he should have been there to shield her.

"Of course, I managed to horrify everyone. It should have been amusing, all those gaping faces. You would have been amused." A smile did little to disguise her hurt. "And I couldn't let it go. I had to talk of specifics…I…. Anyway, I won't bore you with the particulars. Suffice it to say, none were appreciative of my comments, and then Bella…."

Christ, she looked so small. So broken. "Bella took me to task. I had ruined her dinner party, made her seem the fool. She was well within her rights to say what she did, to say I've no care for her, for others, but she doesn't understand the need—*I* don't understand."

He said nothing, though he had to fight to remain quiet. He wanted to hold her, to somehow draw her pain so she didn't suffer as she did now. And he wanted to kill her sister, who had made her appear thus.

"I'm driven to *know*. I blunder forward and ask things better left unasked. I have no care for the sensibilities of others, nothing save the satisfaction of my own curiosity. And I don't understand *why* I'm like this." Her hands clenched tighter. "I see my sisters and they don't feel that burning desire to know why things are the way they are. They sit calmly and their husbands love them. Our parents are proud of them. Why do I need to *know*?"

She dashed a hand across her cheek. "One only has to look at us. I went out and found a virtual stranger to teach me things I probably should know nothing of. What does that say about me? What does that make me?"

Tears glistened on her cheeks, her eyes fierce. "What does that make me, James?" Then, her expression crumpled, and she buried her face in her hands. "I just don't understand."

He didn't know what to say. How he could make it better for her. He felt so bloody useless. She seemed so defeated, her shoulders slumped, her expression hidden. She hurt, and he had no idea how to make it better.

Hatred for this unknown woman, for her sister, coursed through him. How dare she make Elizabeth doubt herself? Elizabeth may ask a few more questions than others of his acquaintance, but she was never malicious in her curiosity. It was abhorrent to him, to see her customary grin obliterated by uncertainty and despair. He would do anything to make her smile again, to rid her of her pain.

"Elizabeth."

She glanced at him, tears clinging to her lashes. Damn it all to hell, he couldn't take it when she looked at him like that.

"I admire you." Frustration filled him. Bloody hell, where were the words when he needed them? "I admire that you go after what you want. That you want to know why. Any idiot can sit and let life pass them by, never questioning, never knowing if there's anything more out there. But not you.

"You push and you prod and you have the gumption to pursue what you want. Do you know how rare that is? You make others—you make *me*—want to ensure you get all you desire. You inspire me. You are *brave*. Courageous. And you make me...." He ran a hand through his hair, angry he couldn't articulate all she made him feel. "You are the best person I have known. Fuck them," he said fiercely. "Fuck the lot of them if they can't see that."

Thin tracks of silver wound over her cheeks, her bottom lip bitten raw. He couldn't tear himself from her eyes, great pools of green in which he'd willingly drown. In her, he saw the ignominy of his past transformed, the best of himself reflected through what he could bring her. He saw laughter and pain, joy and desire.

In her, he saw what he could be.

Shoving the apprehension such a thought caused aside, he cupped her face, wiping away all evidence of tears. This wasn't about him. Gently, he placed his lips against hers, a delicate touching of mouths, comfort offered. Her lips clung to his, soft and warm and slightly salty.

When he pulled back, she brought her hands to cover his. "Your view of me is lovely," she said softly. "Grossly inaccurate, but lovely."

His lips quirked. She smiled in return and he held her to him, stroking her back, giving her comfort and whatever else she asked of him. Her hand came up to cup his cheek, her thumb tracing the bone before she placed her lips against his.

He didn't know when it changed, when passion burned through comfort, but she held him as she devoured him, as he devoured her, as passion and desire devoured them both. He wasn't sure how he had removed her gown, or how she had stripped his clothing, but her legs were wrapped around him and he moved inside her. Her hands clenched in his hair, and he buried his face in her neck, his lips against her skin as she stiffened in climax, her breath escaping in a sigh.

Only then did he let himself come, releasing inside her in waves of pleasure that were more intense because he knew it was her.

***

HE HAD NEVER FELT like this.

Malvern stared at the wall, the thought running through his mind, giving him no peace, no quarter.

They had made love. He knew it, just as he knew that all that had gone before had...not been. Even with her, there had been distance, an indelible barrier that kept him separate. But this time, tonight, he couldn't divorce himself from the act. From her. Instead, he couldn't tell where she began and he ended.

How had she managed it? Resting the sleep of

the exhausted, a slight smile on her face, one would never suspect she had the power to destroy a life and remake it into something wholly unknown. Somehow, she had become necessary, so much so he could not think of his day without her in it. It had crept upon him slowly, without fanfare or warning, stealing insidiously into his life, his mind, his hea—

He needed away from her. Now.

Extracting himself, he froze when she mumbled. She did not wake, though, instead turning to make herself comfortable on the bed of their clothing before falling deeper into sleep. Blonde hair twined about her arm, snaked across the pillow made of his jacket, and he remembered awakening with it tangled around him, often a hank of it in his mouth. Then, it had been amusing. Now, it was a damning indictment on her influence in his life.

Leaving her to her rest, Malvern sat himself on the chaise only to stare at her. The events of the evening rushed through his mind, the nights leading up to it, the whole five months of their arrangement. Had it only been five months? There had been a time before her, but it was hazy, indistinct.

The beginnings of panic rose within him. He'd been satisfied with his life as it had been. Always he'd known what to expect. No picnics, no surprises. No Elizabeth. Now, his days were spent in want of her, and when she arrived, he lost who he was, instead becoming a man he no longer recognised.

How could this *mouse* have changed him so completely? Who was this stranger who existed solely for her, whose whole life revolved around seeing her, pleasing her? His calm existence had been disordered by her smile, her laugh, the way she looked at him. The way she made him feel.

She made him think there was more, when he knew there wasn't. His father had few lessons to impart, but on that point he'd been distressingly clear. There was no gold at the end of the rainbow, no silver lining in a cloud. There was only what you saw, what you could measure with your hands. More than that, the Earls of Malvern were who they were and nothing could change that. Just as eventually he'd had to return from Italy, this too would end. Elizabeth would leave, to continue her life without him. It was inevitable.

And he would once again be alone.

Launching to his feet, he paced. And paced. And paced. No answer presented itself, no solution. They could not continue thus. There could be no misunderstandings, no illusions.

Cold filled him, the ice of February finally claiming him. Stopping mid-pace, he stared at the wall, one thought running through his mind, giving him no peace, no quarter.

He had never felt like this.

Chapter Seventeen

CHECKING HER APPEARANCE FOR the hundredth time, Elizabeth beamed into the mirror. The silvered glass threw back her reflection indifferently, not at all impressed that, for the first time, James was coming to *her* home.

The Elizabeth in the mirror puckered her brow. Well, to be fair, he was going to pick her up to take her somewhere, but she was still excited. A change in their routine was always welcome and, well, he would see *her* home.

The modest townhouse stood in a less than fashionable part of town, but it suited her needs. After Rocksley's death, it had been understood the new Viscount, a distant cousin of Rocksley's, would not desire his predecessor's widow to occupy his new estate, and when it had been revealed Rocksley had been more than generous in his settlement to her, Elizabeth had found a new home and promptly decamped. It had been no hardship to leave, truth be told. The enormous Rocksley townhouse had always intimidated her, the opulence of the rooms overwhelming when first she'd arrived as a young bride, and that sense of discomfort had never dissipated.

The Elizabeth-in-the-mirror's frown deepened. Truly strange, then, that she'd grown so comfortable in James's home. Malvern House put her husband's abode to shame, and yet she'd become accustomed to it rather quickly. A sudden grin tugged at her lips. Maybe she was becoming mercenary in her old age.

When she'd been considering her options, vague notions of retiring to the country had lurked in the back of her mind, but in truth she loved London too much. The fast pace of the city suited her and a return to the slower country life was not to her taste. Her parents would have been more than happy for her to return to Aylesbury, to live with them in her childhood home, but she was quite sure she would have murdered them both within a week if she'd accepted their offer. She loved her parents dearly, but they drove her insane. Her mother would poke and prod and attempt to arrange her life while her father would champion what he perceived to be "Lizzie's Cause". The two of them would then squabble, leaving her to sneak off somewhere quiet and wonder what had ever possessed her to return home in the first place.

Pushing a lock of hair behind her ear, Elizabeth gave herself one final grin and turned her attention from the mirror to the door. There was a thrilling air of mystery about this evening. A simple missive had arrived to inform her of the outing, the note tantalizingly brief. Little more than her name and the directive to prepare herself for an evening out had been written in James's strong hand. The brevity of the note, and the fact that he'd signed it Malvern, had brought a smile to her lips, and she'd spent the day in eager anticipation for the fall of dark.

Carriage wheels clattered on the cobblestones outside her door. Excitement flooded her and, in a flash of skirt and petticoat, she rushed out the door. The night swallowed her, black pitch punctured with the weak pinpricks of gas lamps.

Fair stumbling in her haste, she stopped short at the sight of a disinterested hackney driver negligently holding the door open for her. With a polite smile, Elizabeth nodded her thanks to the man as he helped her in to the carriage. Where was James? She would have thought he would greet her, but it could be he was employing caution. Her neighbours had no need to be privy to the particulars of her life, and the relationship between she and James was no one's business but their own.

The door closed behind her with a sharp thud. Perching on the edge of her seat, she searched the darkness for James. Hidden in the corner as he was, he could barely be seen. Only his legs spread before him and a cheroot betrayed his presence, the tip of the cigar glowing as he drew in the aromatic smoke.

Delight filled her as she launched herself, throwing her arms around his shoulders and kissing that delightful bit of skin below his ear, her tongue darting to taste the slight salt of his flesh. The scent of him, dark spice and smoke, wound about her and she grinned, stupidly happy. "James. I'm so glad you're here."

He placed his hands on her upper arms and she prepared to be pulled into his embrace, for the shape of his smile to feather her cheek. Disconcerting then, that he lifted her away, settling her on the seat opposite.

"Are you?" More disconcerting, his indifferent tone.

"Of course." Brows drawn, she tried to catch a glimpse of his face. Hidden in the shadows, the dark kept his counsel.

However, sullen James was better than no James. Settling into her seat, she stretched her leg, the outside of her knee touching his thigh. "Where are we going?"

"To further your education." Still his face was hidden in shadow, that cheroot now glowing almost mockingly.

Ignoring the thread of disquiet winding through her, she exhaled heavily, disguising her apprehension with a grin even as she knew he couldn't see. "That's not an answer. Come now, James, tell me. Where are we going? Please?" She made the last as plaintive as possible, hoping for a smile, an amused note in his voice, something.

"You will know when we get there." No amusement, no warmth. Nothing.

Falling back into her seat, she crossed her arms and looked out the window. Usually, he responded to her teasing. Usually, he became amusingly frustrated, almost over-exaggerated in his irritation.

Fine. If he wanted to be sullen, who was she to change his mind?

They completed the rest of the journey in silence. The carriage shuddered to a halt on a relatively quiet street and, once they stepped from the carriage, she was finally able to see him. A relief in some ways and in others, well, it was not such a relief.

He had donned that icy perfection, that elegant

disdain. His garments were the very height of fashion, the black of his evening jacket contrasting sharply with the pristine white of his shirt. A rare occasion indeed, to see James dressed with such precision, such flair. More often he was casually attired in trousers and shirt. The only time he had dressed so was when.... Her mouth dried as instant lust flooded her. The only time was when they had attended the orgy.

Good Lord, was that what he'd planned tonight? Slow heat uncurled in her belly, and she shivered with the force of the lust growing within her. Oh please, let it be that.

He turned to meet her gaze, his eyes shuttered as they flicked over her before returning to the building before them. All that was politeness and correct, he held out his arm and she took it, squeezing the hard muscle of his forearm.

His gaze remained trained forward.

With a frown at his lack of response, she also turned her attention to the building before them. Surprise made her blink. "You've brought me to *La Belle Jeune Fille Pieuse*?"

No reply, not even a glance as he led her into the building with a deceptively lazy stride. Pulling the hood of her cloak forward to conceal her face, she followed, telling herself nothing was astray. James had brought her to the brothel where they had met. While it was strange—very strange—surely he had a reason. The reason was just...vague at the moment. Any number of times he'd told her nothing of their plans. Any number of times she'd been delighted by what he'd revealed. This would be the same.

James led her into the receiving room. Around them, women in various states of undress plied their trade, tempting prospective customers with wicked smiles, flashes of skin. She tried to linger, the sight rousing her curiosity, but James would not be delayed, leading her from the receiving room and through the twists and turns of the establishment, a tad too conversant with the layout for her peace of mind. Finally, he slowed and then halted.

They stood in front of a door, quite ordinary in appearance, like any other door Elizabeth had ever encountered. She waited for James to open it. To knock. Something. Casting him a glance, surprise hit her as he remained frozen before the inconsequential door, his jaw clenched as his eyes bored into the wood.

"James?" His gaze turned to her. For a moment, something lurked in the depths of his eyes, something hesitant, but it was gone before it could be deciphered.

So she offered a smile and asked flirtatiously, "Are we to enter?"

His demeanour changed, spine straightening, shoulders firming, his features seeming to harden. Opening the door, he stood back to allow her to enter, his face a study in impassivity once more. Throwing him a flirty smile over her shoulder, she walked through the door.

Her smile faltered, then died.

Two men occupied the room. One stood in his shirtsleeves, a smile of anticipation stretching his sensual mouth. The stance of his tall, rangy body tugged at her memory, the licentiousness of his gaze familiar. His palm rubbed absently against his thigh and somehow she knew, *she knew*, he was imagining touching her.

The other man's gaze was trained on the floor

before him. Dressed in full evening regalia, he seemed to know the moment she turned to him and arranged himself to display those attributes most desired in a man. His posture incrementally improved, his chest broadened, his shoulders straightened, but he was strangely subservient, his gaze never rising to meet hers. If it was some other time, some other place, she might have thought him attractive, but tonight…. Tonight she could only think on James and why he'd brought her to this room.

Unease slithered through her as she painted a wide smile on her face and pretended a lack of concern she didn't feel. "James?" The slight tremble in her voice betrayed her. Damnation. Why couldn't she have sounded braver? Stronger. Less terrified.

James ignored her. He stood there, in his pristine, fashionable evening clothes, and he didn't look like James. The man before her was like a facsimile of James, a facsimile who had never held her, never laughed with her, never told her she was brave with conviction burning in his eyes.

Unable to bear this sudden stranger, she looked instead at the room, her gaze settling on inconsequential details. The light sconces on either side of the bed. The rich curtains. The plush carpet. Obviously, this was a room dedicated to pleasure. Draped with luxurious fabrics, the walls glowed red and gold, silver and teal. The bed—the almost obscenely wide bed—dominated, a looming presence that clearly announced the purpose of the room.

Well, at least James had gifted her with the opportunity to observe the brothel more closely. When first she'd come, she'd wanted to explore the establishment, to find what all those intriguing doors had led to, and now, lucky her, she knew. She would thank him. Then, maybe, she could calmly suggest they leave. Yes, that's what she would do. She would laugh and say it was a fine joke and then they would remember their amusement later, when they lay entwined together, maybe even in her bed. Surely....

She was blathering again. She always blathered.

A breath, and then a second, and she could playact at calm, but then she looked at the two men and a horrible knowledge began to dawn. Surely James didn't— He wasn't going to suggest—

No. James wouldn't do that.

Tongue wetting suddenly dry lips, she looked away from the sight of the two men. "James, what's going on?"

Standing with his shoulder propped on the door jamb, he surveyed the room before returning his gaze to her. There was nothing in the depths of his eyes. No humour. No warmth. Just endless pools of cold blue. "I'm furthering your education."

"My education?" Her muddled brain was trying to tell her something, but she stubbornly refused to believe it. He wouldn't do this. He wouldn't.

Gesturing to the men, he said, "They are here to cater to your every whim, my dear. They are here for your pleasure. I would suggest you utilise their particular skills."

"What—" She couldn't finish. She didn't even know what she was going to say.

"What skills, you ask?" His voice contained no emotion, no warmth. "As well you might, my dear. Barton can be quite domineering, in fact he prefers to master his partners, don't you, Barton?"

Barton. The man in his shirtsleeves. The man from the orgy. How could he be the man from the orgy? James had been jealous of him. He'd not wanted Barton to touch her. Did he not remember that?

James continued, his cold gaze levelling on Barton. "Are you imagining bonds on her wrists, Barton? Would silk or metal please you better?" Those cold eyes returned to rake over her, assessing, calculating. "I've always been partial to black leather straps. So versatile."

Barton chuckled. "Now, Malvern, don't scare the girl away. From what I've heard, your pupil may not be quite ready for that." He smiled, and she knew she should think him handsome, but she couldn't understand why he was here, why he was looking at her with such a lustful expression, as if he expected—

No. She refused to think about it. James had brought her here. She was with James. "James, what—"

"And then there is young Thomas." James remained leaning against the door jamb. "He will do whatever you wish of him, as per the terms of his employment." His lip curled as his gaze locked on the silent young man. "You will obey the lady's every command, won't you, Thomas?"

Thomas nodded, his gaze never rising from floor. "Yes, my lord." The youth's soft voice almost disguised the trace of cockney flavouring his words.

James returned to Elizabeth, a faint hint of mockery in his gaze. Strange she couldn't tear her eyes away. She wanted to. She didn't want to see him look at her like that.

"But you didn't want anyone else touching me. Remember?" Confused...she was so confused. She couldn't fit the pieces together, didn't know why they had broken apart. She thought she knew him. She did, didn't she?

"I must apologise. It was remiss of me to limit your education. And thus, our scenario."

"But, James…." Glancing at the two men, she lowered her voice so only he could hear. "I don't want anyone else."

His eyes…. There was nothing there. No emotion, no feeling, nothing. "Why limit yourself, my dear?"

Time stopped. Everything fell away, until only his cold face was in sharp relief. His gaze disdainful, as if she disgusted him.

No. He wasn't looking at her with disgust. He looked at her as if he had no opinion of her one way or the other.

He looked at her as if she meant nothing.

Distantly, she felt the wetness on her cheeks. Those must be tears. "James, I don't understand."

He shuddered delicately. "Please refrain from saying that name. It sounds coarse upon your tongue."

She stared at him. She stared at him and a piece of her died. "I don't understand." Her voice was a whisper, barely audible even to her. "Did I do something wrong? What did I do?"

"You have done nothing. This is merely the next stage in your development, as stated on your curriculum."

Her curriculum? But that was their jest. It was a jest between them. Wasn't it?

Something was shattering inside her. She pushed against her stomach, trying to make it stop.

"Multiple partners can be quite diverting. I believe Barton and his friend will please you to no end." Still that coldness, still that contempt. "But mayhap it's the gender you disagree with? Would you like a woman? Perhaps two? It can be arranged."

"Stop it."

He continued as if he hadn't heard. "Mrs. Morcom can no doubt recommend the perfect accompaniment to Barton. Maybe a woman of similar colouring? The possibilities are limited only by your imagination, my dear."

Pressing hard against her stomach, she shook her head, wondering how it was she could stand, how it was she could hear his words.

"Should I call for her?" He indicated an unnoticed bell pull. "She would no doubt drop what she is doing to accommodate you. She did say it was quite a pretty sum you offered for your education. We must ensure you get the very best service."

"You discussed me? With others?" Barton's comment now made sense. James had discussed her with others.

She didn't know why that hurt. Surely she couldn't feel anything anymore.

"Of course. How else was I to determine the particulars of your education?" His gaze flicked over her. "Originally I'd thought it would be difficult to muster enthusiasm in such a bland widow, but you rallied quite nicely. You appear to be developing well, and I congratulate myself on some measure of success. I must be an excellent teacher."

The blood drained from her face. She wondered if it looked as dramatic as it felt. From his impassive face, she would venture to say it didn't.

"Mrs. Morcom was quite impressed by the swiftness of your tutoring. She was of the opinion extra participants should have been introduced at a much earlier instance into our love play." Somehow, he made the phrase sound sordid. "However, now she can see the wisdom in my restraint, and she concurs the delay of such advanced measures was a stroke of genius on my behalf. Don't you agree?"

Everything had faded, leeched of all colour. Funny, all had been so bright only moments before. Only James remained impervious, every detail perfect, every colour sharp. "Why are you saying these things?"

James exhaled. "Really, my dear, you know what you came to me for. This. Your education."

This was not what she wanted. It had ceased being what she wanted long ago. "But—"

"But what?" The words ground from him, as if he could no longer suffer her company.

Mutely she stared at him. She couldn't answer because there was no answer.

Turning from her, James addressed the man silently watching them. "Barton, I leave it to you. Please ensure you outdo yourself this evening."

Without a glance, with no further acknowledgment of her presence, he left. The door didn't make a sound as he closed it behind him.

Elizabeth stood, her hand pressed hard into her stomach, the tracks of tears stretching her skin as they dried. When had she stopped crying? She remembered trying to control the tears, control herself, but in the end she hadn't cared anymore, the pain inside her too great, and she had stopped caring. Unheeded, the tears had fallen and James had not noticed, he had kept going, his words precise and incontrovertible. She had felt as if each tear was dissolving her, who she had been, until there was nothing but a shell. An empty Elizabeth-shaped shell that stood here now in this unknown room, her hand pressed to her stomach and her eyes staring at nothing.

What had happened to change him? He had been different but three nights ago, caring and loving and he had told her, he had said how she was special, how she was brave, did he not remember that? She hadn't believed him, not at first, but when she had looked into his eyes, his beautiful ice-blue eyes that had burned with his conviction, he had convinced *her*. He'd *convinced* her.

Had she said something? Done something? Her greeting had been too strong tonight, she knew, but she'd been so happy to see him, and how could she restrain herself? Throwing her arms around him had been instinctual but he didn't like emotion, she knew that. Why had she persisted in displaying too much?

Something had changed. Something had changed to make him bring her here, to suggest she "further her education" with strangers. One who now regarded her with pity, who had lost his licentiousness and stood awkwardly as if wondering what to do. And the other who averted his gaze, who had never raised his eyes from the ground, because he had not been paid to do so.

Maybe it was her family. Always she prattled on about them, as if he knew them, as if he cared. No doubt he was bored by her descriptions, her anecdotes, by the constant stream of conversation of people he didn't know.

Or maybe…. She swallowed painfully, her throat burning. Maybe it was her questions. Her endless barrage of questions. Maybe she should have curbed herself, like she should have her emotions. Maybe she should have accepted his tutelage without comment. Without pushing.

At the thought, the strange shape of a smile stretched her mouth. Her curiosity had ever caused her trouble.

"My dear?" The one who'd been staring at her had decided to speak, his expression caught between discomfort and concern.

The smile cracked. Yes, how did one deal with this situation? The man before her clearly didn't know. He floundered, obviously torn between a desire to help and a desire to run. She watched as he debated. After a time, he moved toward her cautiously, his hand raised as if to give comfort. "My dear, are you all right?"

Violently she flinched from him, her arms coming up to cross protectively across her chest. "Don't touch me."

His hand dropped to his side. "No. No, of course not." A sharp exhalation, and then he spoke. "Thomas, you may go. My thanks for your presence tonight."

The one who had spoken, his name was Barton, that's what James—no. Malvern. He was Malvern now, wasn't he. Barton didn't watch the other man leave. Instead, he watched her, and the fact that this man, this stranger, displayed a concern for her well-being when James had not almost broke her.

She heard the door close, Thomas obviously lacking Ja—*Malvern's* delicacy.

All was silence between them, between she and Barton. Though he said nothing, she knew of his concern and she hated him for it, this stranger who had witnessed what Malvern had done.

"He can be a bastard," Barton finally said.

She laughed and even she could hear the hysterical edge. "Oh yes, he surely can."

"But I'm sure he…he most likely had…." Barton looked helpless, as if he knew the placating words for the lie they were.

Her laughter died abruptly, as if it had never occurred at all. Numbness settled through her. Numb was good. Numb was better. "I release you from any obligation. You may go. I am going. You should as well."

"Allow me to escort you." Again he tried to touch her.

"No!" She backed away, so fast she stumbled.

That was an overreaction, wasn't it? Carefully, precisely, she straightened, folded her hands before her, the image of a demure widow.

"No," she said in a more normal tone. "There is no need. I shall see myself home. Good evening." And with that, she left.

The red walls that had inspired such curiosity in her that first day were now dull, lifeless. Time seemed to have no meaning, and she wasn't sure how long she wandered. It felt like forever, and then it felt like a second, and she vacillated between the two, her hand held to her chest, trying to ease the burn that smouldered there, dull now, everything far away. She didn't have to face it if it were far away. That was for later. When she wouldn't fall apart.

She had spoken true to Barton, though. She should go home. Mrs. Morcom would help her. Mrs. Morcom would have a carriage. Elizabeth would pay and the madam would provide a service, as she had so ably done before.

Dully she examined each room as she passed, and finally she guessed which was Mrs. Morcom's. Of some amazement, that her guess proved true. She tried to feel some pain when she opened the door and saw James—no, Malvern—in a state of undress, the madam draped over him, her hands roaming under his shirt. Unfortunately, her emotions, which had made her so abhorrent to him, were strangely absent and she could only observe with detachment the scene before her.

James appeared surprised to see her. The madam surely was, though she recovered quickly.

Elizabeth met James's eyes. "I will be taking your carriage, Ja—Malvern." When had her voice become so hollow? "I will send it back to collect you after it has taken me home."

She thought she heard him say her name as she gently closed the door, but she was sure to be mistaken. She had thought a lot of things. She had thought he cared. That what they had was special. That he thought she was special.

But it was all a lie. Everything.

Chapter Eighteen

ELIZABETH HAD COME. DESPITE all, despite everything, she had come.

Malvern dismissed the footman who had delivered the news of her arrival, turning his attention to the mirror before him. He had been dressing for the evening when the footman had interrupted him, and he saw no reason to cease.

Straightening his waistcoat, he cast a critical gaze over his form. The formal wear he had chosen had been surprisingly easy to don without Gibbons. Preferring to clothe himself, he'd dismissed his valet earlier in the evening and Gibbons had departed without comment on his master's unusual behaviour. Tonight, Malvern could not tolerate Gibbons at his toilette, though the man's expressionless face and inoffensive demeanour were as unobtrusive as one could wish for.

Now that *she'd* arrived, the formal attire was wholly appropriate, much preferable to the plain garb of shirt and trousers he had adopted for their other trysts. Indeed, now that he thought on it, a plainer waistcoat would be of greater apropos, maybe the one without the thread of colour through it. Of utmost importance was an air of formality to their meeting, a severing of any illusion of closeness their unusual acquaintance had produced. In any case, one must always appear perfect before one's public. Memories of other nights being so eager to see her, he'd neglected his all important toilette, he refused to entertain.

Malvern donned the plainer fare, the apparent simplicity of the garments suiting his purpose well. He'd not thought she would show tonight. He'd thought she would plead infirmity or some such and their appointments would dwindle, and then disappear. He had not thought to ever face her again.

The various parts of his life had fallen back into place with shocking ease, almost as if she had never been. He had ignored the voice that whispered three days was no indication of a lifetime spent without her.

Methodically, he buttoned the waistcoat, watching his motions in the mirror. The process was oddly calming, his fingers pushing each button through its hole with practiced ease. Pulling his jacket back on, he examined himself, carefully smoothing his perfectly coiffed hair. The man staring back at him was cool, calm, arrogantly certain of himself.

It was amazing the lie one could perpetuate with the proper dress.

Straightening his waistcoat once more, he ascertained his sleeves extended the proper length from his jacket. His trousers were perfectly pressed, his boots without scuff, his cravat tied to perfection. There was nothing further he could do to delay.

He had to face Elizabeth.

Keeping his gaze trained before him, he left the dressing room, grimly treading the path to the study. Of the walk, he remembered nothing.

Finding himself somehow at the study door, Malvern stared at the wood as he had a thousand times before. His father had often summoned him to the study and as a boy he'd stared at this same door, hands shaking as he gulped in confidence while trying to muster the nerve to open it. A summons from his father had never ended well.

His lips twitched into a parody of a smile. This would not either.

Allowing himself one fortifying breath, he made to turn the door knob. His hand was trembling. Staring at the appendage, at the pale skin against the gleaming brass of the knob, panic blindsided him.

Elizabeth was here. She was *here*.

His heart thundered, setting up a deafening rhythm in his ears. Panic flashed hot through his veins, robbing his breath, stealing his composure.

Abruptly, he forced himself to calm. *Good Lord, man, get a hold of yourself.* She was just a woman. Making a fist, he shoved open the door.

She sat in her chair, gaze trained forward. She'd not moved, her posture indicating she hadn't heard his arrival despite the violence of his entry. Her shoulders were rigid, her hands clasped tightly in her lap, and yet candlelight shone softly on her hair, turning it golden. Her face in profile, he traced the flow of brow to nose to lips with his gaze and tried not to think of the times he had traced that same path with his mouth.

Swallowing harshly, he knew himself for a liar. She wasn't just a woman. She was *Elizabeth*.

A ridiculous sense of dread suffused him. All

last night and through today he had felt ill, his stomach churning as if he were suffering from a hangover or the effects of some illness. But now, studying her, he knew he had not been ill. No, it had been nothing that simple.

The memory of her expression as he'd executed his plan twisted in his gut, as it had every sleepless night in his solitary bed.

He remembered again Elizabeth had exploding out of her house in a burst of exuberance and flying skirts, rushing to greet him with the affection she found so easy to express. It had taken everything in him not to respond, to set her opposite him and keep himself uninvolved and separate.

When finally they'd arrived at *La Belle*, when they'd stood in front of that door, he'd struggled with indecision and almost lost his conviction. He'd almost turned back. Almost. But then she'd spoken and the teasing tone of her voice, the affection behind it, had firmed his resolve. He'd kept himself divorced from her, kept his face impassive as hers had fallen, as pain had replaced disbelief and devastation had replaced pain.

Only the flesh of his palms had displayed the cost of his disaffection. Three days later, the bloody crescents his nails had scored remained visible, though she'd never see them.

After leaving her with Barton and the whore, he'd gone to Lydia, no thought clear in his mind but to get away. Lydia had greeted him with open arms, had even tried to interest him in indulging in her favours. He'd let her, though while Lydia's lips had feathered up his neck, as her hands had tangled in his hair, an insidious voice had whispered to him that this was truly the betrayal. Through it all, he'd forced himself to stay, and the whisper had grown to a shriek. But then, all whispers had silenced when Elizabeth had found him with Lydia in his lap.

From then, the evening had only worsened. Her face unreadable, Lydia had watched without a word as the door had closed. A strange happenstance, when usually he could discern her thoughts with little effort. Silence hung heavy until finally she bestirred herself to speak.

"What did you do to the girl?" Curiously, Lydia's tone had held no inflection, and yet he'd heard condemnation nonetheless.

"I did what had to be done." His own voice had remained unemotional. He still did not know how he had maintained the illusion.

Lydia's gaze settled upon him and he'd shifted under its weight. In her eyes, he had seen the reflection of himself, of a man desperately trying to hide behind detachment. She had seen right through his careful act. How was it he'd become so easily decipherable?

Finally, she spoke. "What had to be done? Of course. It is plain to see the joy necessity has brought you." She'd raised her fingers to his cheek, and he'd fancied he heard the faint stirrings of compassion in her tone.

Pushing her from his lap, he ignored her startled gasp as he'd begun to pace. "Why did you send her to me?"

The wariness in Lydia's eyes should have been amusing. A month ago, it would have been. "There was no real reason. I thought her an interesting diversion."

The laugh her words produced had tasted bitter, unpalatable to his tongue. What reply did he have to such a statement?

He'd left before his laughter had died, and Lydia had done nothing to prevent him. After returning to Malvern House, he'd retired to his solitary bed and proceeded to torment himself with reliving the moment he'd seen Elizabeth's faith in him die.

Now, in the study where they had conducted most of their acquaintance, Malvern saw Elizabeth tense and knew she'd finally sensed his presence. Pushing away from the door, he ignored the shaking of his hands as he strode to his usual place behind his desk.

"Good evening, Elizabeth." His voice did not waver. He seated himself, placing his hands against his desk, the unyielding wood halting that faint tremble. "Shall we begin?"

Eyes dark in a pale face, she looked upon him, unnervingly silent. He kept his gaze trained on her left ear, avoiding the reflection of his guilt in green eyes.

Bloody hell, why had she come? Why did she have to force herself upon him, make him remember what he'd done? "Well, Elizabeth? We have scant time, and must use it to our best advantage."

The clock chimed on the mantle, indicating the turn of the hour and, ostensibly, the beginning of their lesson. Clenching his jaw, he hoped like hell none of what he was feeling was apparent.

Silence remained, and that impassiveness staring back at him as he concentrated fiercely on not looking at her. Somewhere in the house, a servant was calling to another, the purpose of their words muffled by the walls.

Then she spoke. "Why?"

Such a simple question. He should be able to answer it. Pushing violently away from the desk, he strode to the window, staring out into the black February night. He could see her reflection in the window pane, watching him without expression as she awaited his answer.

"Why not?" Ah, some degree of unconcern. Well done him for managing it. "You asked for tutorship. That is exactly what I provided."

"Did you?" She gave a laugh devoid of humour. "I beg to differ."

Staring past her reflection, he saw instead the ghostly outline of carriages and pedestrians, going about their nightly business with ease.

Turning from the window, he stalked the room, his skin suddenly too tight. His jacket tugged at his shoulders and the waistcoat he had donned, the one that had seemed so perfect, pinched under his arms.

She watched him, out of those dead green eyes that followed his every move. Raking a hand through his hair, he destroyed his carefully mussed coiffure, his hand snagging in the disordered curls.

And even yet, she watched him.

He forced himself to stillness, forced himself to look at her, arranged his face into an approximation of calm.

Her eyes were too large in her pale face, her mouth drawn into a faint line. "You see, I think that night had nothing to do with teaching me about pleasure. Nothing at all." In an instant, the reticence broke and her face displayed her emotion. Her eyes burned with it. "Oh no, you were intent on showing me something else. You were trying to convince me you didn't care."

Nails dug into half-healed crescents. "Was I?"

She was correct to ignore him. "You were showing me this image you've cultivated—the hardened seducer who cares for nothing and no one—that was you, the real you. You were trying to put me at a distance." Again, that humourless laugh. "Oh, Malvern, for all your supposed subtlety, you can be so very obvious."

She had called him Malvern. At last, the distance he had desired. Now that it yawned between them, it was like a knife rending a hollow in his flesh.

"You see, I've thought about it. About you. These last three days, I've had plenty of time to think." This time, the laugh ended on a strangled sob. "You thought you could push me away, didn't you? What happened? Did I get too close? Did I make you feel something? You see how very well I know you, James?"

"You are babbling." Making his voice colder, harsher, he coached his features into lines of detachment. "You do not flatter yourself, madam. You should cease such baseless notions."

"Oh, very good, James. That's it. Try to convince me I am wrong. Tell me I am overemotional. Tell me my notions are insane. Tell me—" Her voice broke. "Tell me you don't care."

This time, he couldn't lie. Damn it, when it was so bloody important, he couldn't lie.

"You see, James? You can't do it, can you?" She clenched her hands in her lap, and the illusion of composure she'd wrapped about herself began to break. "For some reason, some time in your past, it was decided that you were a baseless seducer. And you, you allowed everyone to think the worst of you. You foster their assumptions by doing the barest minimum to confirm them."

"I am what I am, madam." His father's words, coached in his voice. He stood firm as she stared at him, as patent disbelief flooded her features. Of course she didn't believe him. She never had. She thought the best of him, when it was obvious to all he was not what she thought him.

He was not good. He was not kind. He couldn't be the man she saw when she looked at him, and he would *not* be present the day she realised that.

It seemed he had rendered her speechless with six words. She stared at him. He returned her stare, incrementally squaring his shoulders.

Finally, she found her words. "You are what you are? Oh please. You do little more than have more than one mistress at a time. When have you ever ruined someone, James? Point him out to me. Have you stolen someone's fortune, left them without means? Have you caused a death, in any manner? Have you destroyed an innocent girl's virtue, her reputation? Show me." Her gaze burned him. "Show me you are the bastard everyone believes you to be."

Mutely, he stared at her, and could provide no proof. His father had done all those things and more, yet somehow he, Malvern—James—never had. He didn't know how it had come to be that he had not, an accident of fate more than like, but he hadn't.

It did not make her right, though. It did not make him good…it did not make him worthy.

"Again you stumble." Her voice grew in volume. "You stumble, and you look at me with nothing on your face and yet I know. Everyone makes you out to be a heartless bastard, but I *know*." Making a fist, she pounded her chest, the dull thud of the contact reverberating through him. Her eyes burned through her tears. "I *know* you're not. You're not,

James. And that's what hurts so much. You're so concerned with protecting yourself that you don't see what you're doing to me. To us." Her voice hardened and she became ice before his eyes. "And that is cruel."

Wild emotion rose within him, though ruthlessly he clamped it down. Again, she displayed why he needed her gone. He would allow himself to feel sorry for her, though. Never had he wanted to see his own expression mirrored on her features. The death of innocence masked by apathy. On Elizabeth's face, it was obscene.

Emotion rose again, and again he suppressed it.

Elizabeth stood. "I came tonight to tell you that you will have what you desire." Features smooth, she had mastered the art of impassivity. It seemed she had learned more from him than pleasure. "Your plan has worked. Mayhap not in the way you envisioned, but one does not care how a thing happens, as long as it does. I will leave you to your devices, Malvern. You can pretend none of this ever happened if you like, even that I don't exist. I will not stop you. I will not force my presence upon you. In fact, after this evening, you need never see me again." She paused, and a trace of the old Elizabeth bled through. Pain, affection and an emotion he dared not name. "Thus, I bid you farewell, Malvern. Thank you for your tutelage. It has been…enlightening."

Finally, he forced himself to speak. "Any time, my dear. Do recommend me to your friends."

She froze and a garish smile stretched her mouth. She nodded jerkily.

Malvern watched her as she made her way across the room. He had done the right thing. Numbness embraced him with her every step. He had done the right thing.

A pace from leaving his life, maybe two, she stopped. Insane hope flared and he cursed himself for a fool.

"You know, I asked my brothers-in-law about you. They told me stories, about how you were malicious and cruel." Her voice slid over him, her final caress.

Tracing the line of her back with his gaze, he knew it would be for the last time. And he wished he could see her face before she was gone.

"Those stories…they aren't true. You aren't any of those things. You're simply scared. Of what you feel. What I feel. But you are an expert at pushing people away. Well, congratulations, Malvern." She turned. He saw her face…and wished he hadn't. "You have succeeded once more."

***

MALVERN STARED AT THE door. She was gone.

The mantle clock chimed, a soft indication it had been two hours since she had left. Mild surprise rippled through him. Had he really been staring at the door for that long?

He could still smell her perfume. That delicate combination of flowers and musk that shouldn't work but did upon her skin. It drifted through the room— diaphanous, delicate and fading with every moment.

Memories of her beckoned him from every corner. Elizabeth quoting poetry in a wickedly ribald tone, all waggling eyebrows and exaggerated winks. The absorption with which she watched him caress her, the absorption with which she'd caressed him. The way she would smile at him and then pull his mouth to hers. That little gasp she made when he was deep inside her. The way they would lie together on the chaise, her fingers trailing across his lips, his cheeks, his brow as they talked of nothing and everything.

Launching to his feet, he strode from the room. What was he about? His life was once again ordered, returned to the state that had served him well for all the years of his life. For all Elizabeth's histrionics, his actions had been the correct ones. They had become too attached to each other. There was only harm and disillusionment if they continued. Her education had been an exercise to alleviate boredom, nothing more, and her overreaction would eventually become gratitude when she realised the escape she had made and make no mistake, it had been an overreaction. He'd done nothing irreparable, and she would forget. She *would* forget.

Malvern tore at the sudden constriction of the cravat strangling his throat. Stalking into his bedchamber, he shed the offending cloth and, for good measure, ripped off the too-severe waistcoat. This clothing no longer suited his purpose. He would change. He would wear different clothing, and then he would go to his club. No, not his club. Barton had mentioned something about an event of a more particular taste somewhere in Chelsea. He would attend that. Those events were always entertaining, and this had an added attraction.

It would also be distracting.

If he applied himself, the trip to Chelsea could also address an element that had been sorely lacking to this point. The appointment of a mistress would go a long way toward soothing his troubles. The house employed for that purpose had stood empty for too long, his focus wholly consumed by Eliz—by other considerations. He would choose a woman who was worldly. Sophisticated. One who might even teach his jaded soul a thing or two.

He paused. Even better, he would delay the search for a mistress. Why should he limit himself? He had been doing just that for too many months now, such he had entirely forgotten himself. It could be what he needed was a different woman every night, and never one who was blonde.

Yes, that was what he would do. He would fuck some woman, or a succession of them, in all the ways he could think of. He would get obscenely drunk and then tomorrow, he would do it all again.

Malvern stared at himself in the mirror, noting the lack of expression on the face, the deep brackets around the mouth, the hardness in the eyes. Coldness was his companion once more, and he welcomed it.

The aberration was over. He was as he had always been. Alone. Calm. In control.

He dressed, turned on his heel and left the house without a backward glance.

Chapter Nineteen

FOUR. TWO. FIFTEEN.

THE numbers changed, but the comfort he found in their repetition remained constant. Turning over, repeating, they burned his mind like a brand and brought him some ease, when nothing else did.

Sprawled in an uncomfortable chair, an almost empty bottle of wine propped against his thigh, the numbers swirled as Malvern stared at the tattered remnants of debauchery strewn about him. Vague memories of the previous night and the ones before it drifted before him, of moans and sighs and flashes of colour amidst bare flesh.

Lifting the bottle, Malvern took a long pull of the liquid. The wine had long since lost its taste, leaving only a trail of sourness in its wake. Grimacing, he wiped his mouth, his gaze locked on the thin stream of light the heavy curtains couldn't quite contain. It had travelled across the floor in the last hour, almost reaching the wall opposite. Mayhap in the next hour it would realise its goal.

And so it was he had attended yet another salacious event in which he'd neglected to participate. Was it four or five gatherings Barton had dragged him to? He'd had little interest in all of them, to the point where he ended each as he had ended this, slouched in a chair with a bottle of wine and far from all hedonistic revels. His reputation, delicate flower that it was, would suffer horrendously at such poor maintenance.

Somewhere, a clock chimed the beginning of a new hour. As he stared at the shard of light on the floor, the numbers in his head shifted, changed form. Now they were four, two, sixteen.

This was what his life had been brought to, this orgy of excess. He'd not seen the inside of Malvern House for over a month, had instead caroused with little concern as to his shelter as long as it was nowhere near the study that held too many memories. He had drunk a river of wine, consumed an ocean of brandy, and he'd even tried the drug Barton claimed would cure him of his ills. The opium had made him maudlin, so much so that he'd said her name. By all accounts, he'd screamed it.

He had not tried the opium again.

This latest event Barton had brought him to was held in some godforsaken country house ensconced somewhere near the town of Maidenhead. A smile devoid of humour twisted his lips. Some lackwit had obviously thought the irony of overwhelming amusement. It had begun promisingly enough, with a bevy of beautiful whores displaying their talents, charming and flirting and being the most entertaining they could possibly be. He was yet man enough to enjoy the view of a beautiful woman.

It had all become unstuck when the orgy had

begun in earnest. Pairs, trios, even quartets had begun their game, some not waiting for the privacy of a bedchamber before engaging in their practices. Putting off all who'd tried to entice with some nonsense about voyeurism, he'd steadily consumed his wine, detachment growing within him as he'd watched those he'd deemed contemporaries cavort.

The next day had begun and ended the same. And the next. And the next. Last night, Barton had attempted to pique his interest with talk of twins and some trick that had to be seen to be believed. Indifference, his companion these last months, spread familiar through him and though he allowed himself to be led down to the stage where the twins would perform, he could not summon the desire to remain through their act. Halfway through, one twin snaked about the other, he'd left and found this room, empty of all but the debris of pleasure.

Now sunlight, weakened by heavy drapes, cast long shadows about the room, the shroud-like gloom suiting his dark mood. He watched as that gash of intense light cut across the floor, illuminating the faded carpet and slicing through a discarded goblet. For now, he held grim thanks no one had disturbed him during the night. The room had been occupied before him, and no doubt would again when he left. None would notice his presence, nor his absence. The thought summoned a laugh from him, humourless though it might be.

And so, all continued as it ever had, these last four months, two days, and sixteen hours.

A raucous shout, a sudden bang, and the door burst open. Barton lurched into the room, a stupid grin plastered on his face.

Malvern swallowed a curse, and with it the bile

that rose to his throat. Every time he saw Barton, he was reminded of the man's part at *La Belle Jeune Fille Pieuse*. Barton's continued company had become his pathetic attempt at punishment for the damage he had wrought. Barton was, of course, wholly unaware of his role in Malvern's self-flagellation and now stumbled across the room, his grin widening as he realised he had found what he sought.

"Malvern!" Barton's boisterous exclamation reverberated around the room, skittering along his spine and setting his hackles to rise. "Here you are. I thought you'd left and missed...." Confusion darkened Barton's brow. Then, as he remembered, his face brightened. "The twins! Did you see them? Hammond, the lucky bastard, scored their services in the end, but not before we all got a bloody good show."

Malvern remained silent.

Barton frowned again, obviously stymied by the lack of response. Not long deterred, with a shrug he cast his gaze about the room, brows raising at its dishevelled nature. "Never say you've stayed here all night."

"Very well." Malvern's grip tightened on the bottle. What business was it of Barton's where he spent the night? If he chose to remain ensconced in a dank room with no more than a bottle for company, that was his own concern.

"Damnation. You did stay here, didn't you? One of the finest house parties in the country and you stayed—alone I might add—in this room. I cannot believe you did not partake of the festivities. Do you know how exclusive this place is, what it took to wrangle these invitations?"

Clearly he'd rattled Barton. He found he didn't much care. "To whom do you think you speak? To gain entry, you merely had to mention my name."

A quick grin flitted across Barton's features. "True, true. You have a marvellously useful reputation, which you are ruining by remaining here. Come. We could rustle up some entertainment, I'm sure of it. I spied a dark-haired lass whom would suit my bonds quite well."

"I'm not in the mood for sport." Surely the bottle should shatter beneath his grip. "Go dally with your whore and leave me be."

Barton's grin dimmed a little. "Come now, don't be like that. We've always had fun, you and I. With that dark-haired girl, we could have it again."

Why was Barton insisting on his company? They'd never been the greatest of companions. On occasion, they'd found themselves engaged in the same debauchery, at the same venue, with the same whore. Barton's proclivities had been amusing for a time, his penchant for bondage and domination games of some interest in an unending sea of vice. But Malvern had grown bored of that too, and their acquaintance had dwindled. Until they'd met again at the orgy he'd taken Eliza—

Barton. Think only of him. Why was he acting so affable? The man had never undertaken anything without the right enticement. Be it money or be it favours, always Barton was paid. When Malvern had arranged the display in *La Belle*, he'd offered him a substantial enticement, which the man had accepted without hesitation. However, to have him now attach himself without obvious merit, to have him playing at being a friend, there had to be an ulterior motive.

Of a sudden, Malvern realised what it had to be.

"How much did Lydia Morcom pay you?"

Barton stilled. All foolishness disappeared and the man beneath the mask emerged, the man who would do anything for the right price.

"Enough," Barton finally said.

"Enough." Anger began a slow burn inside him, so different from the cold that had consumed him for so long. "What, exactly, comprises enough? Tell me, Barton, how much am I worth?"

No answer.

Malvern laughed, the rasp of it harsh in the quiet room. "It is exquisitely ironic, is it not? A whore paying an opportunist on a degenerate's behalf. Come, what does that make we three?"

"Lydia was concerned, Malvern, as was I." Barton's face, so open only moments before, was now as unreadable as Malvern's own. "You have not been yourself."

"Aye, well, we who make our bed must lie in it."

"You have not been yourself," he repeated grimly. "And for what? For some insipid widow who has probably not thought twi—"

Barton choked, his eyes bulging. Malvern watched dispassionately, his grip tightening on the man's throat. "You will not speak of her."

Barton nodded wildly. Malvern released his grip, retreating to the chair he had no recollection of leaving. His hands shook. He'd been ready to kill Barton. Kill him for an insult she'd never hear.

"'Tis obvious you care for her. That little blonde." Voice a harsh rasp, Barton cradled his throat. "Why do you not send for her?"

Malvern stared at his hands, the ones that had gripped Barton with such intent. "You saw. You know why."

"You are right. I did see." Compassion filled Barton's voice. "She would forgive you."

The hands before him blurred, becoming shapeless lumps of flesh and bone.

"Malvern." Barton sighed. "I count you as a friend. Even without the money, I would have done what I could."

Drawing composure like a shroud, Malvern fixed Barton with his stare. Disconcerting to most, and Barton was no different. "Friend? I, your friend? We've never been friends. Acquaintances only, you and I."

All fell to silence as Barton studied him. "Is that what you told her?" he finally said.

Barton's words conjured hers. She had said he pushed people away. She had said that he playacted, that he pretended. But it was only because Malverns didn't have friends. They didn't need them. They—

His father's words, spewing hyperbole in his mind. The man had been dead for years, but his lessons had been learned too well. Too fucking well.

As if any other had never been, Barton's face assumed that bemused, half-drunken expression once more. "Forgive me, Malvern. I speak of things best left unsaid. Never could stomach the opinions of others. Don't know why I'm subjecting you to mine." A grin stretched his mouth, almost foolish after the gravity of a moment ago. "I'm off to find that dark-haired lass, if you're interested." He sketched a bow and wandered out. The ghost of his voice echoed from the hall, a robust ditty to his dark-haired lass.

Malvern gripped the back of the chair, the remnants of Barton's song reverberating through the room. With great care, he picked up the empty wine bottle, turning it carefully in his hands. The glass was cheap, probably made in some workhouse somewhere, imperfections and bubbles frozen into the finish. He balanced the bottle on its side, cushioned it in his hand.

And then, he hurled it against the wall.

The bottle smashed into myriad pieces, the sound of shattering glass discordant in the silence of the room. Gaze arrested by the crimson stain it left, he watched as a lone drop of wine separated from the mess, winding slowly ever down until it bled into nothingness.

Abruptly, he turned on his heel and quit the room.

Four months, two days, sixteen hours. He stalked through the halls, past fellow guests, past the debauchery, past everything he'd ever known.

Anger, regret, they followed him, trailing him as he strode outside, as bright sunlight pierced him, ripping away the pretence.

The pretence he didn't miss Elizabeth.

He closed his eyes, halting in his mad stride to allow the sun to wash over him. Jesus, he felt the lack of her. Every day was a reminder she was not near, that he had pushed her away with lies and half-truths. In the months since their parting, he'd not seen her. He hadn't expected to. Even if he hadn't expended effort to ensure their paths never crossed, they moved in vastly different circles, she in her cosy life of family and friends, where parents cared for their children and drank eggnog at Christmas, embarrassing their offspring with tipsy banter.

He, of course, lived…this.

None of it, though, stopped his heart leaping to his throat when he saw a woman with her build, her hair. The last had been two weeks ago, on Bond Street. The woman had passed him by and it hadn't been her. It never was.

No matter how he told himself it wouldn't be she, he didn't stop looking for her. Even as he did, he called himself a fool. She was gone and wouldn't return. He had succeeded too well.

The sun blazed. Abandoning the open space, he found the shade of a tree, collapsing beneath it. Why had he done it? Why had he pushed her away? At the time, it had seemed right, necessary even. At the time, he had not known months without her, without her easy smile, her open affection, her questions. He'd not imagined the gaping hole inside him, the keen sense of loss nothing could fill.

This life, the life he'd lived before her, had never made him happy. Knowing little different, he'd imagined himself content. It had been life, and he'd gone through it, rising in the morning, retiring at night, the legacy of his father pushing him during the time between.

And thus he'd continued until he'd chanced upon Italy, until he'd succumbed to the seduction of simplicity. But he'd never been comfortable, always aware he was doing something against his father's wishes, that if he'd known, his father would have dragged him back to London so fast his head would have spun. So in the end, not even the lure of simplicity could not keep him from the path his father had set him upon. His father had died and he'd assumed his mantle, as if Italy had never been. He'd fallen back into old habits, and even he couldn't have said why. And so he would have continued but for her.

But for Elizabeth.

These last months, he had gone through the motions, had pretended he was the same. He had attended the debauches, had gambled and drank and pretended lust when he felt none. And all the while, he had wished himself back in his study. With Elizabeth.

Ploughing his hands through his hair, he hung his head, the bark of the tree biting into his back. Why had he allowed fear to rule him? Now, right now, he could have been with her; they could have been together and he would not feel this emptiness. If she were with him.

His head snapped upright. Of a sudden, everything became very clear. The house, the gravel on the ground, everything.

If she were with him. Fuck, he was an imbecile. True, he had pushed her away. True, he'd hurt her but true also—he had been wrong. Idiotically, crackbrained, stupidly wrong.

He wanted her. He wanted her in his bed, in his life. He wanted *her*, to the exclusion of everything else. Probably he had done everything to ensure she would never speak to him again, but that didn't preclude him trying.

All this time he had wasted. All this time, he had bemoaned her loss, and all because he couldn't face what he had done. He had done it. There was nothing for it now. But that didn't mean he couldn't make it up to her. That didn't mean he couldn't beg her forgiveness.

It didn't mean he couldn't try.

Good god, he was moping like a fool. He deserved to lose her if he couldn't get a hold of himself. He was the goddamn Earl of Malvern. He took what he wanted and laughed in the face of regret. Well, maybe not laughed as much as stared it down, but still.

A laugh did bubble at that thought, a proper laugh, a happy one. God, that was pure Elizabeth, that thought. That was her influence, on him.

He leaped to his feet and strode into the house to collect his belongings. Enough of this. He knew who he was. He knew what he wanted.

Now all that was left was to convince her she wanted it, too.

Chapter Twenty

THE HEIGHT OF SUMMER, and yet she could find no joy in it.

Staring out the window, Elizabeth watched the world pass, as she had for all the months since…well, since. A sea of green rolled before her, broken by the small copse of trees where she and Bella had played as children, the gazebo where their older sisters had played at love.

As she always had, she could see smoke from the distant village, the tips of chimney pots just visible over the rise. If she'd care to, a short walk would take her to Maria Everton's house though Maria no longer lived there, long since married and decamped to Bristol.

Aylesbury never changed. All was the same. Only Elizabeth was different.

At first, she'd not noticed. She'd been upset, of course she had, but she'd not thought she'd changed, at least not to any significant degree. She'd not noticed apathy had settled upon her, changing her from a person who found delight in the most mundane of things into one who only pretended it. Once noticed, though, the months had been made bearable by its presence, no highs, no lows, just a steady medium which never varied or changed.

Pretence had protected her during that first month in London. Laughter and mirth had been her disguise, though the facade went little deeper than her skin. Every social occasion to which she'd been invited she'd attended, blurring into a whirl she scarcely remembered now.

For all her laughter, she couldn't fool Bella. She'd been sorry for her sister's worry, but she could only assure Bella all was well—that no, nothing was wrong and shouldn't Bella return to the festivities?

Bella, however, had not been convinced, and so Elizabeth had taken to avoiding her. A fortnight she'd managed to avoid Bella, two weeks where none noticed her strangeness and where she had managed to forget. For a while.

Bella, however, could not be avoided forever and, in true Machiavellian fashion, had recruited their sisters to her cause. One morning, they'd cornered Elizabeth in her own home, making escape impossible. Their combined concern had broken the careful world she'd constructed and, once broken, she could no longer pretend.

No longer could she pretend to be happy. No longer could she stay in London, no longer could she run the risk that she might see him. Malvern.

Her shoulders fell. She couldn't risk that she might see *James*.

She had thought to distract herself, to keep herself busy with dinners and balls, knowing she'd never seen him before, so why should she now? And yet, she remained on edge, every tall man with dark hair sending her heart leaping to her throat.

So, the next day, she had made for Aylesbury.

The familiarity of home had gone a ways to providing comfort. Her parents, though surprised by her arrival, had welcomed her with arms wide open. At the sight of her mother, her dearly loved face twisted with concern, emotion had coursed through Elizabeth for the first time in months. Harsh sobs tearing from her, she'd collapsed into her mother's arms. Through her tears, she'd heard her mother order her father to take her bags upstairs, heard the exasperation in her father's voice as he'd grumbled some response. The gruff exchange had only made her cry harder. Her parents loved each other, *they loved each other*. Her father would *never* hurt her mother, *never* pretend he didn't care.

Eventually, she'd calmed and when she did, she realised her mother had somehow manoeuvred them into the sitting room. Face pale, holding Elizabeth's hand, her mother gently but implacably demanded to know what was wrong. The question and tone, so in keeping with her mother, had chased away the remnants of her outburst of grief, but she'd not provided an answer.

Tracing an absent design on the window pane, Elizabeth stared at that sea of green. No matter how her mother prodded, she could not bring herself to tell her of...things. If she talked of it, apathy would break completely, and she would not be able to call it back.

Invitations had flooded the house, to picnics, dances, musicals, assemblies, and her mother had bullied and wheedled Elizabeth into attending each one. After two months, she'd even started to enjoy them. Each event had become easier to bear, and each had afforded distraction, so much so that she hardly ever thought of...things.

Pressing her hand against the glass, she regarded its shape, the creases at her knuckles, the bone at her wrist. The minutia of detail afforded comfort and, when she was alone with only her thoughts for company, had the added attraction of distracting her. She liked herself better when distracted.

A gentle knock at the door broke her attention from her hand. A maid entered and bobbed a curtsy, the lace on her cap flopping with her movement.

"Sorry to disturb you, milady, but you're wanted downstairs by the missus. If you please." The maid bobbed another curtsy.

"I'll be right down." Even her voice displayed her lack of interest.

The maid bobbed one last time and departed.

Elizabeth smoothed her gown, the garment plain. In the country, there was no need of any gown grander than this one. All others had been relegated to storage, packed away for the time when she could look at them and remember him only with faint sadness.

The passage from her bedchamber was a familiar one, undertaken thousands of times. She spied her mother in the entrance hall, her foot tapping an impatient rhythm against the tiles. Arms folded, expression cross, her mother seemed the very picture of ire.

Elizabeth faltered. She hadn't done anything to irritate her mother, had she? "Mama? What is it?"

Eyes flashing, her mother took no pains to conceal her annoyance. "There is someone to see you, Elizabeth Marie."

It must be bad for her mother to call her by her full name. "Have I done something, Mama? Did I alienate one of Papa's acquaintances with my questions again?"

"What? Of course not." A scowl marring her features, her mother's arms tightened. "An extremely unpleasant man has demanded to see you and, apparently, we are all to jump to his bidding. I've half a mind for you to keep him waiting, Lizzie." Her mother sighed. "But where's the fun in that? You go in and you give him hell, my dear."

She eyed her mother warily. "Mama?"

"Don't you raise a brow at me, Elizabeth Marie." Her mother smoothed Elizabeth's hair, pushing wispy strands behind her ear. "I do believe I shall be losing my daughter once more." Her hand drifted down to cup Elizabeth's cheek. Something sad, but also joyful, lit her gaze. "I am so happy for you, Lizzie."

Elizabeth frowned, her mother's words making no sense. "Mama, have you been drinking the Madeira again?"

"No." Her mother leaned forward and kissed her on the forehead. Taking a step away, she let her hands fall to her sides. "Now, go and see your visitor."

"Are you sure you are all right?"

"Yes, yes." Her mother shooed her in the direction of the drawing room. "Go."

Her mother's perplexing behaviour bothering her, Elizabeth started toward the drawing room— No. This was too strange.

Turning, she said, "Are you sure you—?"

"Lizzie." A smile played about her mother's mouth. "Attend your guest."

Even more confused, Elizabeth pushed open the drawing room door, vaguely curious to see what manner of man had flustered her mother so.

James stood in the drawing room, his back to her as he stared out the window.

She could not move. She could not speak. She could only stand there, frozen, as she stared at the outline of his form against the afternoon sun. The protection of apathy broke and four months of repressed emotion flooded her. Shock, pain, anger, joy. All stormed through her, a deafening roar she could barely contain.

And then, abruptly, the storm vanished.

Something must have alerted him to her presence, as he turned to face her. For a moment, a single moment, his expression lit with determination, with purpose. It must have been a trick of the light, though, because then his face held no expression, and he simply looked upon her, impassiveness schooling his features as it had since first they'd met.

Finally, she found the words to greet him. "Malvern, this is a surprise." She was very, very proud of the evenness of her voice. "Won't you sit?"

No response. He simply stared at her, his eyes shuttered and unreadable. There was something off about him. Bruised flesh darkened his eyes, speaking of sleepless nights, while deep creases bracketed his mouth. Though impeccably attired, there was something not quite right about his garments, as if he had rushed through his dress with little care.

Which was ridiculous. Stupid Elizabeth, with her notions and fancies.

Why was he here? To remind her of what she'd lost, what he'd *taken* from her?

Anger unfurled in her, but she ignored it. She

would be dignified, aloof, and he would never know how much his presence pained her.

Still he looked at her, and still he said nothing. Not allowing his silence to unnerve her, she seated herself, balling her hands tight in her lap. No matter how he appeared, she would not make this easy for him. No doubt he had been carousing to all hours of the morning. That was why he appeared tired.

The silence between them thickened.

"Elizabeth." As abruptly as it started, his speech broke off. She watched as he began to pace, his hands held tightly behind his back.

Grip tightening in her lap, Elizabeth tried not to think on how she had missed him. Each Tuesday and Thursday, she had found herself looking for the carriage that would take her to him, even though she knew it wouldn't come. Worse, she'd found herself noting some odd snippet of conversation she'd heard, or observed a strange happenstance, and thinking she must tell James. Somehow, in such a short period of time, she'd become so enamoured that he was her first thought in the morning, her last at night.

More fool her.

James still hadn't continued his abortive attempt at speech. Well, *she* wouldn't be the one to break the silence. He had sought *her* out—Lord, he had *sought* her out. Why?

Hope, resilient emotion that it was, reared its head. Damnation, how could he do this to her? How could he make her want him, after all this time, after all he'd done?

Grimly, she forced the emotion away, concentrating on her lap as he wore a hole in her father's carpet. So long since she'd felt such intense emotion, and now she'd experienced the gamut in only a few moments.

"I propose we marry."

Shocked. She was shocked. That was what had frozen her muscles. Frozen her mind. Frozen everything inside her. Opening her mouth to respond, she then closed it again, her mind completely blank.

He didn't seem to notice her paralysis, instead continuing. "We deal well together and we already know we are sexually compatible."

She couldn't move.

"As for children, I am not overly concerned if we never conceive. However, there is no reason to assume either of us infertile, no matter what your idiot husband said. While you have little wealth to recommend you, I more than make up for such a lack. We are both of an age, and deal tolerably well together. Therefore, I can see no reason for a marriage not to take place between us."

He stood motionless, as motionless as she, his face never darkening, never lightening, never displaying any emotion at all.

Never, *never*, had she thought he'd propose. What possible reason could he have for it? The ones he had detailed, they may be logical and precise, but he would never convince her such reasons would induce him to wed, and he *must* know his reasons would not convince her.

He must know he'd detailed every reason but the one that mattered.

Holding on to calm, Elizabeth managed to recover her voice, enough to speak anyway. "This is certainly unexpected. Did you just now come to this decision?"

He gave her that look, that imperious look. "Of course not. I have thought on it for some time. It seems the most logical course of affairs."

"And how am I to react to this decision of yours?" Her tone just as calm as his, she kept her features politely inquiring. It cost much, but she would not give up her dignity. "What am I to say? It was more than obvious on our last meeting you required—" Here she faltered. How to describe what had occurred, without using words like *pain, bastard, devastation*. Finally, she found the words. "Distance between us."

Not even the flicker of an eyelid. Why was she so surprised by his lack of reaction? Anger rushed through her, sudden and blistering. What was he doing, coming to her parents' home and demanding *marriage*? Could he not have left her alone, to spin her lies of being unaffected, to continue the difficult process of forgetting him?

Unable to bear the sight of him, she looked away, gripping her hands tighter in her lap. "Well, Malvern?"

"It appears I was mistaken." His voice was as beautiful, as compelling as ever. She wanted to scream, at him for making her feel this way, at herself for allowing him to. "I should not have forced such a scenario on you. It was ill-conceived. I apologise."

"You apologise." She clenched her jaw against the torrent of abuse his words conjured. That's all he had to say for himself? Ill-conceived? He had ripped her heart from her body, and he thought it *ill-conceived?* "Well, I thank you for the condescension of your offer, but I find I must decline."

Silence, and then, "You would refuse me?"

Her gaze flew to him. Though he was all shuttered eyes and immobile mouth, something about the way he said the phrase gave her pause. Had she imagined it? "Perhaps. What do you offer?"

Face impassive, he said, "Did I not just detail such?"

"Yes, and what a fine offer it was." She smiled, though it felt garish. "However, what of love? Affection?"

No expression. No hint of emotion crossed his face. "Love was what wedded you to Rocksley, was it not? But, if you insist, I am...fond of you."

Hope faded. Even such a stubborn emotion could not thrive in the face of such barren fare. He stood before her, the man who'd shown her so much, and this time she would eject him from her life. His hands at his sides, his back ramrod straight, he awaited her answer and—

She blinked, certain she'd imagined it. No, there it was again. Infinitesimal, but there. Hope, so recently extinguished, flared again.

James's hands were trembling.

He realised she was staring at his hands and immediately laced them behind his back, but it was too late. She had seen it. She had seen his hands, and she knew what they meant.

James was nervous.

If James was nervous, it meant he was uncertain about the outcome of his proposal. If he was nervous, it meant he had come here with no guarantee of success, only the determination to see her.

If he was nervous, it could mean he cared.

Hope rushed wild through her. She dampened it down, attempting restraint, guarding against the pain should she be wrong. "You are going to have to give me a reason. A real one."

Ice blue eyes regarded her. However, she fancied she could see him trying to think of something, anything, to make her agree.

Closing her eyes, she severed the illusions she wove about him. This was ever her problem. She always saw things that weren't there. Why had she hoped for something different?

He had to leave. Now. Later would come misery. Later would come pain.

Rising to her feet, she prepared to speak to the words that would send him from her life.

"I am sorry," he said. "You have no concept of how sorry I am. I should never have allowed—I should not—" Jaw clenched, his eyes burned with emotion for a moment. "It was very badly done of me."

"Yes, it was." Refusing to give him quarter, she waited though hope held her in its grip.

"You ask me for a reason?" He had regained some of his inhuman calm. In the midst of it all, she almost smiled. It was so a part of him, this composure. "I find I am...at a loss. It was different when you were—" He muttered a curse. "I will do my best to ensure your happiness, in whatever means you see fit. I would hope that happiness would include me in the capacity of husband."

Keeping a tight clamp on her emotions, she regarded him steadily. "And that is your reason?"

He set his jaw. "Yes."

"I see." She needed to think. These last months, they had been nothing without him. "You hurt me." Remembered pain broke her voice.

A muscle ticked in his jaw. "Yes."

"Badly."

"Yes," he repeated. He gave no excuse, no reason for her to forgive him.

"Is that all you are going to say?" Emotion bled

from her, just a bit, just enough to colour her words with desperation. "It's not enough. You're going to have to give me a reason. A real reason. Please, James. Please." She swallowed. "Just one."

He stared at her, silent, impassive. Dear God, it wouldn't take much. She would grasp at any excuse and yet he stood there, as distant as ever he was.

"Elizabeth…."

He didn't expand on her name. She waited, but he said nothing further, simply standing there with his hands now clenched at his side and his cold gaze upon her.

She couldn't do this. She couldn't take this scrap of affection and make a life. Shoulders slumping, she prepared to send him away.

Something in her expression must have alerted him to her thoughts and just like that, he broke. "I need you. I need you, Elizabeth. Please." He swallowed, and in his motion she could see something of panic. "Please."

His voice died away. Silence. Somewhere, someone was singing off-key. Somewhere, someone was happy.

Silence still. She didn't know what to say. Conflicted, she stared at him and he looked away, his hands white-knuckled.

She had to know. Stepping toward him, she gently took his hands in hers. "James."

He didn't raise his gaze. Instead, he stared down at the mesh of his fingers and hers but she needed to see. Untangling her left hand, she cupped his cheek.

His eyes met hers reluctantly. Even now he kept her from his emotions, even now the mask and then…then it dropped. Just for a moment, she saw every emotion, every feeling he had. For a moment, she saw how he felt about her, and it was dazzling.

Joy filled her, intense and bright. *James. Oh, my love.*

"I have a reason for why we should marry, James." Elizabeth's smile hurt her cheeks, her heart beating so fast she thought it would break through her chest. "I love you."

Tension bled from him. He closed his eyes. "You do?"

Nodding in answer, elation rushed through her, then she realised he couldn't see. "Always."

A small smile teased one corner of his mouth. Taking a shuddering breath, he opened his eyes and just like that, he was James again. Impassive. Unemotional.

The loony shape of a grin stretched her mouth. Her James.

"So you agree, then?"

"To what?" Laughter threatened at the disgruntled expression that briefly crossed his face.

"You are being factitious, aren't you?"

All innocence, she shrugged, certain that now everything was as it should be.

Familiar wickedness dancing in his eyes, he raised a brow. Just like that, they slipped back. Just like that, it was them again.

He cleared his throat. "I shall organise a special license. We can be wed next week."

She blinked "Next week?"

"Did I read you wrong, madam?" His fingers tightened on hers until she winced. "Do you refuse my suit?"

"No!" Startled by her loud protest, she gentled her tone. "No, James, of course not. It's only…."

Frowning, she considered the particulars. "I need at least a month to organise my family. And, of course, you shall have to meet them. They will want to scrutinise the man I am to marry." How on earth was she to get all her family in the same place at the same time?

"Your family, madam?"

"Yes." Maybe they should hold a gathering in London. Everyone lived in the city, well, everyone but her parents. Damnation, and her mother hated to travel—

"As in, your mother and father? Your sisters and brothers-in-law?"

Surprised by his tone, she glanced at him. Once again, he'd cloaked his expression in impassiveness, but even he could not disguise the pallor of his skin.

He cleared his throat. "Your mother was at the door. That surely constitutes a meet. We should marry next week."

Never say that James, her indomitable James, was disturbed by the prospect of meeting her family? Oh, this was too funny for words.

"But James, my father will want to question you, most likely about your intentions for after we are wed. And my sisters will most definitely want to talk with you about wedding preparations and guest lists—I am the youngest, you know." She frowned, hoping it concealed her mirth. Poor dear. You would think he would know better than to give her such ammunition. "They will want to give me a proper send-off, seeing as they couldn't the first time. My brothers-in-law will want to throw you some sort of bachelor gathering and they can't do that if they've never before met you. And my mother—" Elizabeth shuddered delicately. "Well, the less said about her, the better. Although, it is only right to warn you—she will want to organise your life. In detail. There will probably be lists."

James had turned an intriguing shade of pale. "Truly?"

Good lord, he really was sick at the thought of meeting her family. Stepping into his arms, she hugged him, the feel of him hard and warm, beloved and familiar. "Don't worry. I'll be there with you. I love you."

His arms rose about her, and with a gentle squeeze, he returned her embrace. His lips whispered against her temple and Elizabeth smiled, truly happy for the first time in months.

James had come for her, with no guarantee of success. He had proposed, when he had said he would not. Her smile widened as his arms tightened about her. He may not have said it, he may not even have recognized it, but she did.

Her love loved her.

Epilogue

FROM ACROSS THE BALLROOM, Malvern saw her. He had lost sight of her for a good half hour, but when one was dressed as she was, one didn't stay unnoticed for long. The crimson gown made her upswept hair glow like gold, her skin pale and lustrous against the blood-red rubies draped about her neck. From her ears, Murano glass winked, reminding him of *Carnevale* and gondolas and her body dappled by a hot Italian sun.

Only Elizabeth would combine ruby and glass, and only Elizabeth would get away with it.

A couple whirled past, obscuring her. Irritation rose within him. Too long they'd been at this tiresome ball. Upon their return from Italy, Elizabeth had thrown herself into society, dragging him along as she'd attended each function. Thankfully, she'd quickly grown bored of the social whirl, eventually preferring to limit most of her engagements to her close friends and family. Malvern had been glad of her dwindling interest, wanting to spend his time only with her.

He shouldn't complain, he supposed. In Italy, they'd had over a year alone.

Wisps of scarlet taunted him as revellers whirled by. Malvern shifted, impatient to see her, even if from a distance. Three years ago, it had been unheard of for the Earl of Malvern to condescend to attend such an event. Even now, he received disbelieving looks, though most dared not approach him. Often he caught people in a whispered comment, and the amusement afforded when they realised his presence made up for some of the tediousness of the whole affair.

Wicked amusement thrummed through him. How Elizabeth chose to show her appreciation for his attendance made up for the rest.

She caught him observing her and bequeathed a smile. He looked away, feigning disinterest when in reality his heart began a pulsating rhythm, just as it always did.

From the corner of his eye, he saw her smile morph into amusement and she raised a brow in perfect imitation of him. Suppressing his own amusement, he maintained his expression, his demeanour as indifferent as usual.

Only she would read the humour in his stance.

She said something to those around her, mayhap excusing herself. Deliberately, she took the Venetian lace fan he'd purchased for her birthday in her right hand and raised it to obscure her features.

A faint smile touched his lips as he deciphered the message. Foolish woman. He would have followed her anyway. Had he not proven that by his very presence at this tedious ball?

As she departed, her fan rested lightly on her

bare shoulder, and his fingers itched to stroke her ivory skin. His cock hardened as he imagined that skin beneath his palm, the curve of her lips as she glanced over her shoulder. He imagined his hand trailing down to her hips to grasp her tightly as he buried himself inside her. Blood pounding harshly through his veins, he saw her gasp and moan, her shoulders twisting as she braced herself against his thrusts, her hot core milking him until he had no choice but to follow her into release.

Shifting his stance, his expression betrayed nothing as scenarios, entanglements ran through his mind. She was on her knees, her silken hair twined around his fists as she licked at him, laughter in her wicked eyes as she took his cock in her mouth. Her tongue found every ridge and crease and he threw back his head, sweat pouring off him as he came.

Now she was on her back and he was holding her legs apart, his face buried in her core, her scent and taste on him, around him. She clawed at his back, her voice issuing guttural commands as she shattered beneath him.

Perspiration broke on his forehead and his hold on the façade of detachment slipped, his desire for her the only thing that could force such a reaction.

As she passed through the door, she glanced at him one final time. Her look promised all his fevered mind had imagined and more, the fan's handle resting lightly on her lips. Burning with the need to kiss her as she had invited, he cursed himself for ever teaching her that damned fan language.

Slowly, deliberately, she again raised a brow, her tongue licking the corner of her mouth as she trailed the fan across her cheek. Her message delivered, she swept from the room, leaving a slavering wreck of a man behind her.

God. A shudder ran through him as he forced himself to composure. She did it to him, every single time. One would assume after three years he would be used to her seduction, but every damned time he reacted such, so much that he was in danger of showing the world how much she meant to him. Every damned time.

Glancing about, Malvern assessed the damage their exchange had caused. None, if he was reading those around him correctly. In fact, no one even glanced their way, the entirety of their exchange going without notice.

Assured of anonymity, Malvern followed her. As he always did.

A door had conveniently been left ajar, eradicating the need to search each room. As he entered, Elizabeth whirled around, all fluttering hands and shocked eyes. Amused by her patent overacting, a smile touched his lips, the expression natural because he was with her.

"Oh, you startled me!" Feigned agitation made her words breathless. Placing a bewildered hand against her throat, she ruined the effect by trailing her fingers over the flesh exposed by her low bodice, her breasts swelling above the neckline with every breath.

"Did I?" Lips quirking, he did exactly what she intended, imagined his own fingers stroking her flesh, imagined pushing down her bodice and cupping her in his hand. A lazy smile stretched his mouth as he thought of all the things he would do to her.

Her eyes widened and a flush lit her pale skin. The fluttering of her fan increased. "I thought to be alone for a few minutes before my husband arrives. You didn't happen to encounter him, did you, my lord?"

So that was her game. Affecting lazy boredom, Malvern fought with his amusement. She did so love to play these games. "Was he the short, fat, balding man scurrying along the corridor, hissing 'love peanut' into each room?"

"That—" Elizabeth's voice broke on a strangled laugh. Recovering, she said, "That would be him, sir. Pray, do not say he is lost once again."

"I fear that may be so, madam." Amusement and lust ran through him, lightening his heart, thickening his cock. Never would he have imagined the two combined before her. "Is there any way I can be of service?"

Elizabeth's gaze wandered over him. Maintaining his composure was a struggle as she studied him, as she took in the strength of his shoulders behind the black evening wear, the breadth of his chest. Even more of a struggle when she walked toward him, circling him as she trailed a finger over the shoulders she'd just admired, smoothing her hand over the chest she'd scrutinised. Her touch ran down his arm, circled his gloved hand with her own, and then she measured her palm against his. A quick look up captured his gaze and, with a wicked grin, she then glanced at his groin.

Stifling a groan, he forced himself to stillness, determined to play out her game. He would not grab her, would not take her, would not get inside her before he expired of lust. *Calm, Malvern. Control.*

Dropping his hand, she trailed her fingers over his stomach. Clenching his hands against the need coursing through him, he barely maintained his impassive stance, the illusion he was unaffected.

Elizabeth, of course, saw right though him. She

peeked at his hands, a slight smile playing about her lips at the proof of her effect on him. Bloody woman was pleased with herself, was she? Well, just wait until she was under him, and he had her screaming his name.

She lifted her gaze to his, her eyes filled with mischief, desire, lust. A wave of hunger roared through him, and he saw her through the haze, saw that she was affected too, skin flushed, her chest rising and falling with erratic breath.

Blood thrummed heavily and his gaze dropped to her lips, her soft full red lips. Remembering what he had imagined, he saw her taking him deep with those lips stretched around him, her tongue playing with his cock until he came harder than he ever had before. Remembered kissing her, her lips doing wicked things to his, and he had taught her that, all of that. Only he knew the pleasure of kissing her so well that she came, that she made him come, kissing her as he fucked her, his cock slamming into her core, her head thrown back, her breasts covered with sweat as she moaned his name.

Only him.

Satisfaction wound through him as she swallowed harshly, her lips parting as she read his thoughts in his gaze. So now she knew how she affected him. Now, she would bear the consequences.

A slow smile twisted her lips. "Can you be of service…? I don't know. Is there anything you can do?"

Taking a step closer, he raised a hand to cup her neck, his other rising to cover her breast. Wide green eyes became unfocused as his hand shaped the soft flesh, the hardness of her nipple pressing against his palm even through the layers of fabric.

"Let me demonstrate." And then, he claimed her mouth with his own.

**

Heat burned fiercely as James kissed her, his tongue parting her lips to tangle with hers. Closing her eyes, Elizabeth gripped his waist, pulling him into her, relishing the hardness of his body against the softness of hers.

His cock ground into her as his hand shaped her breast, his fingers tracing and teasing her nipple. Breath trapped, she pushed herself into his touch, wanting him inside her, filling her, his hands on her bare breasts as she licked his throat, as they *fucked* each other into oblivion.

From across the ballroom she'd seen him, looking dark and dangerous in his severe evening clothes, his expression set in its usual impassive lines. Concealed by the crush, she'd watched as he'd searched for her, his features smooth though she could see his restlessness as his efforts yielded no result. With a smile she'd hid from him, delighting in being able to observe him just for the pleasure of it.

Her vantage point afforded a view of his profile, the strong line of his jaw, the hint of his throat above his cravat. Of a sudden, she had wanted to lick that small piece of flesh. Lust had overcome her as she'd imagined standing behind him, nuzzling the place between his shoulder and neck. Her hands played over his bare chest, playing down and down to cup him and he shuddered with passion, leashed only by her desire that he allow her to do as she pleased.

With effort, she'd torn herself from her thoughts, telling herself they would be home soon enough. The platitude had placated her, enough that she'd felt up to socializing, though arousal burned deep.

That had been when James had finally found her. His lips had softened, just for a moment, and his eyes had warmed as they'd lit upon her.

There was no way on earth then she could have waited until they were in their own bed.

Desire hit forcefully, and she'd wanted to take his full lower lip between her teeth, wanted to suck on it as she meant to suck on every part of him. She'd wanted to feel the play of his shoulders beneath her palms, his skin bare and warm and resilient. She'd wanted him naked while she was clothed, straddling him and taking him deep, his cock pulsing inside her as she thrust and ground herself on him, harder and harder, until they both came, until they screamed with their lust.

Raising a trembling hand to her forehead, she'd gotten herself under control—as much as was possible—and then set about her seduction.

Thank God it hadn't taken long.

His hand gripped her back as his lips trailed down her neck. Beneath her gown, his other hand cupped her bare flesh, his fingers pulling at her nipple, the pleasure-pain making her gasp, making her blind with need.

Wanting to touch him, needing to feel his skin under her palms, she grasped at his shirt, pulling at the fabric wildly, cursing when the stubborn material wouldn't budge from his trousers.

He chuckled against her neck, the brush of breath and lips caressing her as his thumb swept over her nipple. "Feeling desperate, are we?"

She ignored his laughter. "Just help me."

Capturing her ineffectual hands, he brought them to his lips, pressing a gentle kiss against her fingers. Then, he drew her index finger into his mouth.

His gaze burning into hers, he drew slowly on her finger, his cheeks hollowing with every suck. Enthralled, she watched him, giving no protest when he kept her hands prisoner. Taking one, he led her to trail down his chest, to trace the contours of his musculature through his shirt. She watched as he pushed her hand over his stomach, her lip caught between her teeth as he lowered her over his navel, down his abdomen. Her fingers brushed the closure of his trousers and he halted. His eyes smouldered as he released her finger from his mouth, pressing a kiss to her palm before holding her to his cheek.

Together they ventured behind his waistband, his fingers splayed over hers, her palm absorbing the heat of his skin through the fabric of his shirt. His thumb flicked at the first button on his trousers and then the second, dragging her hand down with his. They undid the third button, and then the fourth. Then he released her.

"Do you think you can handle the rest?" A small smile played about his mouth, more of a lifting of lips than a true expression.

He probably thought he was being impenetrable, but she could see the smugness beneath. Moving closer, her mouth a breath from his, she tapped her fingers lightly. "I think so. Do you want to let me?"

As if daring her to continue, he took his hand from hers and spread his palms wide. Ah, her beloved James, always so certain she would do as he expected.

Hand motionless low on his abdomen, Elizabeth buried her face in the curve between his shoulder and neck, inhaling his scent. Licking the cord of his neck, she noted the tensing of the muscles of his abdomen and smiled to herself. Slowly, she drew her hand up, under his shirt, undoing the buttons of his waistcoat with her other hand. Harsh breath rasped above her as she played the skin behind his ear with lip and teeth and tongue, her thumbs just grazing his nipples.

The muscles of his throat worked beneath her mouth. "Take off your gown."

Rough and full of gravel, his voice demanded and yet she ignored him, continuing to work his skin, her hands wandering his chest, wandering down his stomach, wandering....

He grabbed her arms, spinning her around and pushing her against the door. Her vision went black as a wave of lust hit her, and she gasped at the intensity of her reaction. Arms pulled roughly behind her, breasts crushed to the door, she shuddered as his lips moved against her ear.

"Do you want me to rip your gown from you? Everyone will know then what we've done, Elizabeth. They'll know I fucked you, they'll know that you came for me, that I took you so deep and so hard you screamed my name. Do you want that, Elizabeth?" His voice roughened further, as if he aroused himself with his words. "Do you?"

Overwhelmed, she panted against the wood, the grain smooth against her cheek. She couldn't answer, she could only squirm against him and hope to God he would do something, hope he would just *touch* her.

He ground his cock against her bottom, the hard shape of him seeking out her core through their layers of clothing. She pushed back, wanting him inside her,

her body wet and swollen and oh so ready. Transferring his grip on her to one hand, he trailed the other over her hip, bunching up the fabric of her skirt.

"Maybe you don't want me to take off your gown. Maybe you want me to fuck you where you stand. Here, against the door, your skirt bunched between us, your breasts pressed to the wood. My cock ramming into you, hard, deep, hitting you just right until you come. Would you bite your lip to hold in your cry, hoping that your husband doesn't catch us? Is that what you want?" Pulling up her skirt, his hand slipped under the hem to stroke her inner thigh, so close but not close enough. "Is it, Elizabeth?"

A moan tore from her. "James, just do it."

"But your husband, Elizabeth. He's roaming the halls, searching for you. What if you're caught? What if he sees you with another man, his cock buried inside you? What then?"

Lust pulsated inside her, and she almost cried with her need. "James, please."

"I don't know if I can overcome my scruples." His fingers trailed over her damp flesh, and he found the small bundle of nerves. His thumb brushed over it gently, forcing a strangled scream from her that he didn't press harder, deeper. "The sanctity of marriage should never be violated."

Body on fire, she swallowed a moan as his fingers kept up their play between her legs. "Bloody hell, James, would you just stop talking? If you respect the sanctity of marriage so much, quit talking and do your bloody husbandly duty!"

"No." And with that unequivocal response, he released her.

She almost fell when his support disappeared. Whirling to face him, all her frustrated lust spiralled into anger. Standing in the middle of the room, straightening his cuffs, he appeared the picture of bored elegance. Well, if the picture of bored elegance included rumpled clothes and a raging erection.

Impassively he watched her, his arms crossed as she stalked toward him, only the slight flexing of the fingers on his biceps betraying his need to touch her. Stopping just short of him, she slowly, deliberately, slipped her arms from her gown. Trailing her hands up her sides, she knew he watched, his gaze burning like a caress as she smoothed the fabric of her bodice to her waist. The pretty corset she'd bought in Florence pushed her breasts up and together, her nipples peeking over the edge.

He swallowed harshly at the sight, but maintained his impassive expression, his hands now digging into his biceps, his stance braced as if to prevent himself from launching at her.

Well, now, that would never do.

Lifting her arms above her head, she bent them so she could grasp her elbows and then—she stretched. Her breasts lifted free of the corset and she gasped as the stiff material scraped along her nipples. Tilting her head to the side, she lowered her hands to her breasts, cupping the flesh. Imagining his mouth on her, she closed her eyes, rolling her nipples between thumb and finger. In her mind, his tongue flicked at her, getting her wet, on her skin, between her legs. Increasing the pressure, she moaned at the sensation, licking the corner of her mouth as she opened her eyes.

A muscle ticked in James's jaw as he watched her, ruddy skin pulled tight over his cheekbones. His eyes burned with bridled lust. Tightly satisfied with his response, one hand abandoned her breast to snake down her stomach, gathering her skirts before her. Easing her hand under her skirt, her fingers brushed wetness and heat, a telling indictment of how much she wanted him. Head falling back, her eyes half-closed, she bit her lip as she ran her fingers over herself.

"Fuck." The harsh word ground past his clenched jaw and, in a burst of movement, he grabbed her, falling back onto the lounge behind him, shoving up her skirts. Bringing her over to straddle him, he grasped the back of her thighs, forcing her groin against his as he wrenched at his trousers, cursing the stubborn material. Rubbing her lips over his neck, she moaned at the bump of his knuckles against her aching flesh.

They both groaned when he drove into her, his cock deep inside, filling her, and she was blind to everything but him, his length hard and delicious and hers.

His eyes burned into hers as she lifted herself slowly, biting her lip as his cock caressed her. God, she could feel every inch of him, so strong inside her. His hands gripped hers as she lowered herself just as slowly, watching him as he watched her, for the movement that made him grit his teeth, for the one that made him groan. He changed the angle slightly and with her next thrust he rubbed against her, sending sensation streaking through her. The sound of their breathing harsh in her ears, the scent of their lovemaking around them, she moved faster, heat rising in her, gathering closer, swelling.

Letting go of his hands, she braced herself on his shoulders as she slammed down on him, his hands cupping her hips to help her, gripping her through her clothes, his facade of impassivity gone. Instead his face reflected the harshness of his desire, the intense need he had for her, only her, and he was beautiful, so very precious, her James, her love.

Climax stormed through her and she went over the edge, opening her mouth on a silent scream, fire racing through her blood. James didn't stop. He didn't stop, thrusting into her, his cock reaching deep, and he cursed and swore, his voice hoarse as he pleaded with her, just a little harder, a little deeper. Over and over he said her name and then he came, his hands gripping tight on her hips, his throat arched as he obtained his release.

Shuddering, he swore weakly, his eyes drifting shut as his grip loosened. Leaning forward, her own strength stolen by the force of her climax, she rested her forehead against his and wrapped her arms around him, their breathing harsh in the silence of the room.

As she counted the beats of his still erratic heart, her own fell into step, their breath mingling as they calmed. Outside, the faint strains of a waltz drifted on the night air, conversation and laughter following in its wake.

After a time, James reached up and took her left hand from his shoulder, bringing it to his lips to kiss her wedding ring. "Hello."

"Hello." In possession of her hand, his thumb traced the delicate bones, his eyes warm upon her. An answering warmth swelled inside her, and she gave it expression in a small smile. "Are you enjoying this evening?"

His lips quirked. "I am now."

She laughed. In the three years of their marriage, those rare flashes of humour had become more frequent and he seemed more at ease, even displaying outright mirth on some occasions. Few saw him thus, however. In fact, she would venture to say she alone was allowed to see him as he was now—relaxed, happy, and smiling. At moments like these, her love for him swelled, almost overwhelming in its intensity. Never could she have imagined when they had met that they would be here together now, like this.

In Italy, these moments of unguarded humour had come more often. It had been fascinating to see him like that, almost effusive at times, the Italian penchant for exaggeration slowly bleeding into his every day expression. In truth, while she'd enjoyed their trip, she'd had not understood his overwhelming attraction to the place. Too much she had missed England, missed her family, and found herself at odd times wondering what Bella was doing, or how Henrietta's children were faring. She'd even missed the English weather.

Seeing James so happy, though, had been worth the odd moment of homesickness. Those moments, though, may have contributed to her overreaction at their homecoming, throwing herself into society with abandon. Poor James had followed in her footsteps, no doubt bewildered by the suddenly social wife he seemed to have acquired. Eventually, she'd quieted and been more than happy to relegate their social engagements to the occasional ball.

Smile fading, he trailed his fingers over her belly. His hand came to rest on her abdomen and a faint frown furrowed his brow. "How are you feeling?"

"Surprisingly well." Laying her hand over his, she squeezed gently. "It's definitely called morning sickness for a reason."

"Are you sure?" His frown deepened. "We were

quite…active."

"We were *active* before we knew I was with child. If anything were to have happened, well, it would have already. Besides…." She kissed his neck. "I love how active we are."

He grunted, his brow still furrowed.

It had come as a delightful surprise when she had first suspected that she may have been pregnant. Actually, she would venture to say it erred more into the realm of shock. But as the weeks had passed, it had become glaringly obvious that she was indeed with child, and she'd been consumed with a fierce joy at the prospect of holding their baby in her arms.

Also surprising had been the unexpected relief that, in fact, nothing was wrong with her. She hadn't even realised she'd harboured those fears, had thought she'd long ago accepted that she was barren. Only in their absence had she realised how affected she'd been by her conviction that she would never conceive.

She'd worried about telling James she was pregnant. She could think of no earthly reason why that should be, but not knowing the reason had not rid her of her anxiety. He, however, had taken the news with little comment, only establishing she was well, and re-establishing that state constantly.

They hadn't mentioned children since his proposal, but neither had they taken any precautions. At least, not since they'd married. On their wedding night, Elizabeth had tried to undertake her usual measures, but James had tugged her back into bed, making love to her again and again. Every night had been the same since. And most mornings. Not to mention at random times throughout the day.

Looking at him now, one would never suspect

he was the same remote man who eschewed all company save hers, who deemed himself a failure if seen with one hair out of place. He sat with ruined cravat and disordered hair, a creased shirt and a flush on his cheeks.

Amusement crept over her as she pushed a fallen lock of his hair back into place, though he was almost beyond repair. "You've come askew."

"Have I?" His attention was still on her belly, his hand a warm weight on her abdomen. He looked up sharply. "I have?"

Nodding, she hid her smile at his consternation. So very vital to him, his façade of impenetrability. "Don't worry," she said solemnly. "I won't tell anyone."

At her words, his irritation disappeared and an intense expression she'd seen but a few times replaced it. His hands rose to cup her face. "I love you."

Her heart stopped. Simply stopped.

He had never said the words to her. Never. Each day, he had shown his love in a hundred different ways, and she'd never felt the lack of the words. Of more import was the way he contrived to spend most of his time with her, of how he always found some way to touch her, no matter how small it might be. In the inconsequential gifts he gave, in the way he satisfied her curiosity, to this very day. In the way he let himself simply be himself with her.

Never had she been in doubt of his love…but never had the actual words passed his lips.

"I love you, too." Damnation, she was crying. She hated crying.

Wiping away her tears with his thumb, he followed the movement of the digit. "I should have said it before."

"Yes, you should have." She punched him in the shoulder. "Why didn't you?"

"Ow." Rubbing his shoulder, he raised a brow. "Maybe it's because you hit me."

"A likely excuse." Mirth bubbled inside her, drying her tears. "I love you so much."

A smile lit his face, shocking in its brilliance. "I had an inkling. Mainly from you telling me all the bloody time."

"Yes, well, what can I say? You're irresistible."

He preened at that and she laughed, happiness filling her to bursting. Warm blue eyes traced her features and, slowly, mirth faded. Gently, he pushed her hair behind her ear. "Let's go home."

Nodding, she bit her lip as they separated. They righted their clothing as best they could, his hands gentle as he helped with her dress, hers brisk as she re-tied his cravat. Smoothing the fabric of her gown over her belly, he stilled.

"Thank you." His gaze lingered on his hand, resting protectively over their child. "This...I could not have imagined this was missing from my life. You...our child...." He looked at her, and those bloody tears threatened anew at what she saw in his eyes. "Thank you."

Refusing to succumb, she said, "It has been my pleasure. Is there anything else that I should know?" Tossing her head insouciantly, she pretended not to notice his sudden grin. "After three and a half years of intense tutelage, surely we have come to the end?"

"I don't know." His grin turned wicked. "Shall we consult the curriculum?"

Author's Note

TEACH ME was the first novel I ever completed.

Though it wasn't my first published book (that would be ENSLAVED, which will be re-released soon), TEACH ME was the book that convinced me maybe I could actually do this writing thing.

The idea for this story also arrived a dark point in my life, when I was convinced I wouldn't be able to write another word. As I came out of the dark point, I booked myself a holiday to Europe and made the conscious choice to not take a pen and paper with me because there was no possible way I would feel that creative spark.

Stupid decision, Cassandra. So silly.

A holiday is as good as change, and I was in the middle of a bus tour in Scotland when of a sudden a scene popped into my head. A coldly handsome man watched a woman twirl in a ballroom, her joy warming the depths of his heart. I knew he loved her completely, and, as she glanced at him, I knew she felt the same.

I had just envisioned what would become the epilogue of TEACH ME.

But I had no pen! I was stuck on this bus, with no pen and paper to write down what I had just seen. An hour, two hours, and we stopped at our hotel for the night. Rushing into my room, I dropped my bags and searched the desk frantically, looking for—Success! A tiny pad and a complementary pen! I scribbled the scene on that tiny pad and, the next time we stopped in a town, I hunted down a stationary shop and bought a notebook. I spent the rest of the trip in Europe writing TEACH ME.

Elizabeth and Malvern grabbed hold of me and wouldn't let go. They hold a special place in my heart, and I couldn't be more grateful their tale came to life on that fateful European holiday. I hoped you enjoyed their story, too.

Read the first book in the Lost Lords series

FINDING LORD FARLISLE

The boy she never forgot

Lady Alexandra Torrence knows she's odd. Fascinated by spirits, she sets out to investigate rumours of a ghost at Waithe Hall, the haunt of her childhood. Its shuttered corridors stir her own ghosts: memories of the friend she'd lost. Maxim had been her childhood playmate, her kindred spirit, the boy she was beginning to love …but then he'd abandoned her, only to be lost at sea. She never expected to stumble upon a handsome and rough-hewn man who had made the Hall his home, a man she is shocked to discover is Maxim: alive, older…and with no memory of her.

The girl he finally remembers

Eleven years ago, a shipwreck robbed Lord Maxim Farlisle of his memory. Finally remembering himself, he journeys to his childhood home to find Waithe Hall shut and deserted. Unwilling to face what remains of his family, Maxim makes his home in the abandoned hall only to have a determined beauty invade his uneasy peace. This woman insists he remember her and slowly, he does. Once, he and Alexandra had been inseparable, beloved friends who were growing into something more…but the reasons he left still exist, and how can he offer her a broken man?

As the two rediscover their connection, the promise of young love burns into an overwhelming passion. But the time apart has scarred them both—will they discover a love that binds them together, or will the past tear them apart forever?

Read an Excerpt from
FINDING LORD FARLISLE
Lost Lords, Book One

Chapter One

Northumberland, England, August 1819

Lᴀɢʜᴛɴɪɴɢ ꜱᴛʀᴇᴀᴋᴇᴅ ᴀᴄʀᴏꜱꜱ ᴛʜᴇ darkening sky and thunder followed. Stillness held sway a moment, the air thick, before a torrent of rain battered the earth.

Wrestling against the wind, Lady Alexandra Torrence tucked her portmanteau closer to her person as she pushed determinedly toward the estate looming in the distance. The storm had been but a sun-shower when she'd set out from Bentley Close, her family's estate only a half hour walk. While the light cloak she wore protected her from the worst of it, the wet was beginning to seep into her skin.

She pulled her cloak tighter. It was only a little farther and she'd be at Waithe Hall, though there would be no one to greet her. Waithe Hall had been closed for years, ever since the previous earl had died. The new earl—Viscount Hudson, as he'd once been—resided almost exclusively in London. Her family and his had been close for as long as she could remember, their townhouses bordering each other in London just as their estates did here in Northumberland. The earl was her elder by nine years, and his brother Stephen by five, but Maxim, the youngest, had been but one year her senior and—

She stopped that thought in its tracks.

Before too much longer she stood before the entrance to Waithe Hall, and with it, shelter. The huge wooden doors were shut. She could not recall that she had ever seen them closed and locked. In the past when she'd visited the family had been in residence so she would walk straight in, calling for Maxim before she'd completely cleared the entrance—

Slowly, she exhaled. After a moment, she pulled the key from her pocket, the one Maxim had given to her for safekeeping when he was ten and she nine, so they could always find their way back in should the doors ever be locked—

Shoving the key into the lock, she blinked fiercely as she forced memory aside once more. She could do this. It had been years, the wound so old it should have long since faded. She could investigate Waithe Hall and its ghosts, and she would not think of him.

The key turned easily, the door swinging open. She stepped inside. Cavernous silence greeted her, the din of the rain that had been so deafening now distant. The entrance stretched before her, disappearing into darkness, and the storm had made the late afternoon darker than usual, swallowing any light that peeked through closed doors. Pausing mid-step, she wondered if perhaps she had made a mistake in coming here.

Shaking off doubt, she started through the hall. The rain echoed through the vastness, the hollow sound strange after being caught in its fury. Fumbling through her portmanteau she found a candle and tinder.

The flickering light revealed an entrance corridor that opened into an enclosed court encompassing the first and second floors and an impressive chandelier draped in protective cloth hung at its centre. Memory painted it with crystal and candles, and she remembered sitting on the landing of the second floor, legs dangling through the gaps between balusters as she and Maxim counted the crystals for the hundredth time.

Bowing her head, she cursed herself. She should have known she could not keep the memories at bay.

A roll of thunder reverberated around her, leaving behind quiet and dark. All her memories of Waithe Hall were full of life, the butler directing servants, fresh flowers in the vases lining the court, light spilling through from the mammoth windows. Now the windows were shuttered, and an eerie silence broken only by the sounds of the storm pervaded.

Hitching her bag, she made her way to the sitting room. It was as still as the rest of the estate, the furniture draped in holland covers, the windows also shuttered. Setting her candle down, she placed her cloak over the back of a chair and rested her bag on its seat, glancing nervously about. She caught herself. *Don't be stupid, Alexandra. There's none here.*

Before she could think further, she unbuttoned

her bodice. Her clothes were soaked, uncomfortably damp against her skin, and a chill was beginning to seep through, though it was the tail end of summer and the days were still mostly warm. She'd chosen a simple gown, one she knew she could get into and out of herself.

Heat rose on her cheeks as she shucked out of the bodice. There was none here. She knew there was no one. Cheeks now burning, she untied her skirt and petticoats, left only in her stays and chemise. She would love to remove her stays as well, but they were only slightly damp and she couldn't bring herself to disrobe more than she had.

Opening her bag, she pulled out a spare bodice, skirt, petticoats and, finally, a towel. Thanking her stars she'd had the forethought to bring it, she quickly swiped herself, chanting all the while there was no one watching her, that doing this in an abandoned sitting room was not immodest.

In record time, she'd managed to reclothe herself. Hanging her wet clothes to dry, she pushed her hair out of her face. Once she had explored further, she would choose one of the bedchambers as her base, but for right now the sitting room would suffice.

A thread of guilt wound through her. Technically, the earl did not know she was a guest of Waithe Hall—and by technically, she meant he didn't know at all. She was confident however, he could have no objection. She had been a regular presence at Waithe Hall when she was a girl, and the earl held some affection for her. She was almost positive. Maxim had often said his brother thought her—

Damnation. Bracing herself against a chair, she bowed her head. She had thought more of him in the last hour than she had in the year previous. It was this place. She'd managed to convince herself she no longer felt the sharp bite of grief, but she did. It struck her at odd moments, and she could never predict when. One would think it would have lessened with time, but it hit her fresh and raw, as if she bled all over again. She'd been a fool to think she would remain unaffected returning here—he was everywhere.

She closed her eyes as realisation cut through her. She was going to think of him. It was inevitable. However, she had come here with purpose and she would not allow this preoccupation to deter her.

The ghosts of Waithe Hall beckoned.

A darkening gloom shrouded the drawing room. Night approached, quicker than she'd liked, but she was determined to at least do a preliminary sweep of the estate to refresh her memory before it became too dark to continue. There was much to do before she camped out in the affected room one night soon, not the least of which was determining which room was affected.

From her bag, she pulled a compass, a ball of twine, and her notebook. Bending over the flickering light of her candle, she opened her notebook and dated the page, jotting down her notes on the expedition thus far.

There had always been tales of ghosts at Waithe Hall. On her and Maxim's frequent rides about the estate, she remembered listening wide-eyed as Timmons had told them tales of ghosts and woe. The groom had waxed lyrical on the myths and legends of spiritual activity at Waithe Hall, and she'd been completely fascinated. Maxim had never seemed interested, but he'd always followed when she'd concocted a new adventure to discover ghosts and ghouls. As an adult, she'd turned her fascination into a hobby, researching and cataloguing ghost tales at every manor and estate she'd attended. Her own family's estate held a ghost or two, stories her father had been only too happy to tell. She'd documented his tale and others, and had submitted several articles to the Society for the Research of Psychical Phenomena. They hadn't as yet chosen to publish any of them, but she was convinced if she persisted, eventually they would.

Then, four months ago, reports had crossed the earl's desk in London of strange lights at Waithe Hall. He'd mentioned it in passing to her father, who in turn, knowing her fascination, had mentioned it to her. He'd also issued a stern warning she was not to pursue an investigation but, well, she was twenty-five years old and in possession of an inheritance a great aunt had left her. Her father could suggest, but he could not compel.

The lights could be any number of things, but the report had contained accounts of a weeping woman, and the light had become a search light. Memory reminded her of a tale Timmons had told, the lament of a housekeeper of Waithe Hall who had lost a set of keys and caused a massacre. Her lips quirked. Timmons' tales had ever been grisly.

Determination had firmed and within a week she'd made her way to Northumberland and Waithe Hall. Bentley Close had been shut as well, but unlike Waithe Hall, a skeleton staff kept the estate running. Along with her maid, Alexandra had arrived late last night though she hadn't been in a position to set out for Waithe Hall until late this afternoon. Her plan had always been to spend a few days here, but the rain made it so she now had no choice.

She would rather be here than in London anyway. Besides pretending she was unaffected by those who called her odd, her younger sister had finally made her debut at the grand old age of twenty. Lydia was taking society by storm, determined to wring every ounce of pleasure out of her season, and she had confidently informed their parents she didn't intend to wed until she had at least three seasons behind her. At first horrified, their parents had resigned themselves to neither of their daughters marrying any time soon.

As the eldest of her parents' children and a female besides, she had borne the brunt of their expectations in that respect, but at least Harry had now brought them some joy. He and Madeline Pike were to marry next year, the wedding of the heir to a marquisette and a duke's daughter already touted as the event of the season. George had absconded to the continent, no doubt investigating the most macabre medical reports he could, while Michael was still at Eton.

Upstairs, a door slammed shut. Alexandra jumped, hand flying to her racing heart. It was the wind. It had to be. Even now it howled outside, rain pelting the roof and echoing through the hall as distant thunder rolled.

Hugging the notebook to her chest, she shucked off any concerns. There was no time like the present. She would start with an examination of the ground floor. The kitchens and servants rooms would take an age, so better to examine the family rooms and save the servants for another time.

The portrait gallery was as she remembered, a long stretch of hall that displayed the Farlisles in all their permutations. Quickly, she traversed its length, telling herself the dozens of eyes of previous Farlisles did not follow her, that they did not judge her an unwelcome guest. Cold slid up her spine and she moved faster, especially as she passed the portrait of the old earl and his sons, Maxim staring solemnly from the portrait.

Pretending she felt not a skerrick of unease, she noted the gallery's dimensions in her diary and moved on to the second sitting room. Again, nothing in particular was out of the ordinary.

The library was at the end of the corridor, and the door opened easily under her hand. It really was most obliging of the steward not to have locked any of the doors inside the estate. This room was vastly different to her remembrance. Few books lined the shelves thick with dust, and holland covers draped most of the furniture, although one of the high-backed arm chairs before the fire was lacking the covering. Peculiarly, one of the windows here was unshuttered, the weak light of storm-dampened twilight casting eerie shadows on the wall opposite.

She'd always loved the library and its two storeys containing rows upon rows of books. As children, she'd insisted she and Maxim spend an inordinate amount of time within its walls, happily miring herself in book after book. Maxim had always been bored within seconds, spending his time tossing his ever-present cricket ball higher and higher in the air to see if he could hit the ceiling two floors above. He'd even managed it, a time or two.

Sharp pain lodged beneath her breast. Rubbing at her chest, she took a breath against it, pulling herself to the present. Somehow, night had encroached upon the room. How long had she been stood there, lost in memory?

Moving further into the room, she trailed her fingers over the side table next to the undraped chair. A stack of thick books was piled high, the top one containing a marker. Why was there a stack of books? Had an apparition placed them there?

A prickle rippled along her skin. She'd never seen a ghost. She'd heard hundreds, thousands of stories, but she'd never— Steadying herself, she flipped open the book to the spot marked, noting it was a history of the Roman invasion and settlement of Cumbria. Sections and rows were underlined with pencil, writing filled the margins, and there was something about the hand....

Closing the book, she placed it back on the stack. Why was this here? Every other part of Waithe Hall she'd seen had been closed, shut away. This room held an uncovered chair, a stack of books and.... The fireplace held recent ashes.

Her heart began to pound.

Again, something—a door?—banged. Whirling around, she searched the encroaching dark, her gaze desperate as her chest heaved. What if the lights weren't a ghost? What if it was a vagrant, someone dangerous and unkind? What if...what if it were a *murderer*?

The agitated sound of her breathing filled the room. Getting a hold of herself, she reined in her imaginations. Her thoughts could—and frequently did—run to the extreme. Although these anomalies were curious, there could be a perfectly mundane reason for their presence. There was nothing out of the ordinary, besides the books, and the fireplace, and—

She took a breath. *Calm, Alexandra.* She was

purportedly an investigator. She would investigate.

The fireplace had without doubt been used recently. Newly cut logs placed in a neat pile to the side. Sconces held half-used candles, their wicks blackened and bodies streaked with melted wax. She could see no other signs of occupation—

Something banged for a third time, closer now, and brought with it a howling wind. Alexandra jumped, grabbing at the table for balance as the door to the library flew open, the heavy wood banging against the wall, the books wobbling and threatening to fall. Blood pounding in her ears, she looked to the darkened maw of the library's entrance.

An indistinct white shape filled the door, hovering at least five feet above the floor.

A scream lodged in her throat. She couldn't move, couldn't make a sound. She could only stare as the thing approached.

Lightning crashed, flashing through the room. She gasped, a short staccato sound that did little to unlock her chest.

Lightning crashed again. The shape became distinct in the brief flash of light, revealing a man dressed in shirt sleeves and breeches, his dark hair long about his harsh face. A strong, handsome face that held traces of the boy she'd thought never to see again.

Blood drained from her own face, such she felt faint. "Maxim?"

Chapter Two

"WHAT ARE YOU DOING here?" it—he—
growled.

"Maxim?" she repeated stupidly. The apparition
before her looked so much like Maxim…if Maxim
had grown to a man, developed an abundance of
muscle and four inches of height. It couldn't be
Maxim…but if it were an apparition, why would he
appear grown? When last she'd seen him, he'd been
fifteen and skinny as a reed, not much taller than she.
It couldn't be him.

Lightning lit the room once more. His shirt was
loose about his thighs, the ties undone and the neck
gaping open, his breeches smudged with dirt. All was
well tailored and untattered. Surely, if he were a
ghost, his raiments should be tattered?

The same chestnut hair fell over his brow, too
long and ragged, while his face had broadened and
hardened, his eyes were the same, chocolate brown
under dark brows. He'd grown to a man, broad
shoulders and ropy muscle apparent behind the scant
clothes he wore, his breeches stretched over powerful

thighs and strong calves, his large feet shod in well-worn leather boots.

He was supposed to be dead. Eleven years ago, he had abruptly left Eton and set sail on one of the Roxwaithe ships, bound for America. She'd been so confused at the time, and he'd refused to tell her why. Six months later, they had received word the ship had been lost at sea. None had survived.

With startling clarity, she remembered that day. Her father's face, careworn and concerned, as he'd told her. Her mother's worried eyes. The pain in her chest, frozen at first, until she'd excused herself, blindly making her way to her chamber only to stand in its centre, confusion filling her until she'd happened to glance upon his cricket ball, the one he'd given her the last time she'd seen him, three days before he'd left when he'd refused to tell her why he was leaving, and once she'd returned home she'd thrown it onto her dressing table, angry beyond belief at him, that he was going away, and then, then a great gaping hole had cracked open inside her and she'd slid to the floor, pain and grief and devastation growing inside her until it had encompassed all, it had encompassed everything and it hadn't stopped, it hadn't stopped, it—

It was eleven years ago. The pain had faded, but had never truly left. She'd thought she'd learned to live with it. But now…he was here?

A thunderous scowl on his face, he made a noise of impatience. "I do not have the inclination for this, girl. Tell me why you have come."

His voice crashed over her. That, too, had deepened with age, but it was him. It was *him*.

"It *is* you." Joy filled her, so big it felt her skin couldn't contain it. Throwing herself at him, she enveloped him in a hug.

He stiffened.

Embarrassment coursed through her. What was she thinking? Immediately, she untangled herself from him. "I beg your pardon," she stammered. Always before they'd been exuberant in their affections. They'd always found ways to touch one another, even though that last summer, the one before he'd gone away, she'd begun to feel...more.

Clasping her hands before her, she brought herself to the present. Much had changed, now they were grown and he, apparently, had not died.

Maxim had not died.

A wave of emotion swept her, a mix of relief, joy, incredulity.... It buckled her knees and burned her eyes. He was alive. *Maxim was alive.*

"When did you return? Do your brothers know?" she asked, steadying herself as she swiped at the wetness on her cheeks. "The earl is lately in London, but I'm certain he would return should he know. My father will be so pleased to see, as will my mother. George and Harry will be beside themselves, and Lydia and Michael too, though they were so young when—" She cut herself off, barely able to say the word *died.* "We mourned you, Maxim."

He came closer. He'd grown so tall. When last she'd seen him, barely an inch had separated them, but now he was at least two hands taller. Faint lines fanned from his eyes, the tanned skin shocking in the cold English weather. Wherever he'd been, it had been sunburned.

"I ask again," he said. "Why have you come?"

Confusion drew her brows. "Maxim? Don't you remember me?"

Starting at the blonde hair piled limply on her

head thanks to the rain, he ran his gaze over her. He traced her face, her throat, travelled over her chest, swept her legs. A tingling began within her, gathering low. She was suddenly aware of how her breasts pushed against the fabric of her chemise with every breath, of a pulse between her legs that beat slow, steady….

He raised his gaze to hers. Silence filled the space between them before, succinctly, "No."

It was like a punch to her belly. "It's me. Alexandra."

No reaction.

Oh. Oh, this hurt.

Lifting her chin, she managed, "I am Lady Alexandra Torrence, daughter of your neighbour, the Marquis of Strand. We grew up together."

His expression did not change.

"Your father, the previous earl, and mine were like brothers."

He stared at her. "Previous earl?" he finally asked.

"Yes," she said. "Your father passed away some years ago. Your eldest brother is now earl."

Again, no change in expression. Did he not care his father had died? But what did she know of this new Maxim? Less than an hour ago, she had not known he was alive.

He continued to stare at her. She fought the urge to shift under that flat gaze. "Why are you here?" he repeated, his tone harsh and impatient.

"I was—" Her voice cracked. Cursing her nerves, she cleared her throat. "I am investigating. The villagers spoke of a ghostly presence, lights and wails, and I…." She trailed off. Lord, it made her sound so odd. He'd always teased her about that oddness, and always with affection. She didn't know what this new Maxim would do.

Finally there was expression on his face. She wished it had remained stony. "Ghosts? You have invaded my home for ghosts?"

The disgust in his voice made her cringe. "To be fair, I didn't know you were here. No one did."

Expression still disdainful, he didn't reply.

Irritation pushed aside devastation. How could he not remember *her*? "This is not *your* home."

His brows shot up. "*That* is your argument?"

He sounded so much like *her* Maxim. They'd argued often, and the number of times he'd said those exact words, in that exact tone.... She shook herself. "Yes. It is."

"A fallacy. You argue a fallacy."

"It is not a fallacy. It is objectively true. Waithe Hall is the ancestral seat of the Earls of Roxwaithe. You are not the Earl of Roxwaithe, ergo, it is not your home." Knowing it was childish, she tossed her hair and glared.

Crossing his arms, he scowled. "I know you are somewhere you don't belong."

"So are you," she pointed out.

"This is my family home."

"It's your *brother's*," she said. "You're being deliberately obtuse."

"And you're being obstinate."

"*I'm* being obstinate? Me?" This was such a ridiculous argument, and yet it was familiar. They'd argued like this all the time, and he was reacting exactly as her Maxim would react, and—

Stepping forward, he deliberately loomed over her. "I come into my library to find a trespasser, poking around in *my* things."

"Waithe Hall is shut. Roxwaithe hasn't been here in years. *No one* is supposed to be here. You aren't even supposed to be *alive*. How are you even *feeding* yourself?"

Pinching the bridge of his nose, he shook his head. "Why am I arguing with you? You're a trespasser I don't know."

Rage, such as she'd never experienced before, exploded. How dare he? How dare he pretend not to know her? Her fingers curled into fists and she told herself she could not punch him. She was a lady, and he was a *clodpole*. "Don't be *stupid*."

He stilled, and something flickered in his dark eyes. "You will leave the way you came."

"With pleasure," she snapped. Pushing past him, she stalked from the library, through the entrance hall, and wrenched the door open. Rain pelted her, almost horizontal as the wind howled and lightning crashed across the sky. She plunged into it, anger propelling her even as she was drenched in moments.

She'd not gotten more than two strides before a large hand grabbed her shoulder and hauled her back inside. Maxim slammed the door shut and shook himself, water falling to the marble floor. "Do you have any brains?" he demanded.

"You told me to go. I have no desire to say here with *you*."

"You wouldn't get half a mile before you'd catch your death. You'll stay here."

"It would not be proper," she said stiffly.

He laughed harshly. "Hunting a ghost is not proper, either. You will stay here."

Mutinously, she glared at him. Damnation. She could not even *argue* that point. Belatedly, she realised the rain had plastered his shirt to his body, clinging to hard muscle and broad shoulders.

Mouth abruptly dry, her breath locked in her chest.

He didn't seem to notice her distraction. "Come," he said, holding aloft a lamp he'd magically produced, before turning on his heel to stride down the corridor. Hesitantly, she followed.

They wound through the Hall, climbing the grand stairs and making their way to the family apartments, the corridors she remembered from her—their—childhood. Wrapping her arms about herself, she cursed herself at the soaked fabric. She'd only brought two gowns, and now both were wet.

He halted before a door. "You may stay here," he said, pushing it open.

Passing him, she entered a bedchamber, again with most of the furniture covered. The bed, though, was not, holding a mattress along with pillows and sheets.

Surprise filled her. "Is this where you sleep?"

He placed the lamp on the dresser. "Goodnight."

"Good—?" He was gone before she finished the word.

Wrapping her arms about her torso, she stopped herself from rushing after him. She wanted to assure herself she hadn't imagined him, that he was real, that he was alive...and she needed to get her bag, she had a nightgown and a change of underclothes, and—Maxim was alive.

She collapsed onto the bed. The bed he had slept in, unmade with the sheets rucked to the foot of the bed. A faint scent wound about her, woodsy and indistinct, but she knew it was his, knew it was

Maxim's. A harsh sob broke from her, and another, eleven years of emotion exploding. Sliding from the bed, she pulled herself into a ball, hot forehead against her updrawn knees, her cheeks wet, her chest hurting.

The wind howled, rain pelting the window. They'd all thought him dead. *She'd* thought him dead. Her dearest companion, her best friend. Maxim.

Slowly, her sobs subsided. She couldn't stay here. She couldn't take his bed from him, and she.... She wanted to know. She wanted to know everything. Why was he here? Why hadn't he gone to his brothers? Why was he lurking in Waithe Hall alone? When had he returned?

Did he really not remember her?

Taking a shuddering breath, she wiped at her cheeks. She needed to know and surely he would tell her. Even if he didn't remember her.

Rising to her feet, she squared her shoulders. Well, she would make him remember her...and then she would make him let her hug him.

SILK & SCANDAL
THE SILK SERIES, BOOK 1

by Cassandra Dean

Eight years ago...
Thomas Cartwright and Lady Nicola Fitzgibbons were friends. Over the wall separating their homes, Thomas and Nicola talked of all things – his studies to become a barrister, her frustrations with a lady's limitations.

All things end.
When her diplomat father gains a post in Hong Kong, Nicola must follow. Bored and alone, she falls into scandal. Mired in his studies of the law and aware of the need for circumspection, Thomas feels forced to sever their ties.

But now Lady Nicola is back...and she won't let him ignore her.

ROUGH DIAMOND
THE DIAMOND SERIES, BOOK 1

by Cassandra Dean

Owner of the Diamond Saloon and Theater, Alice Reynolds is astounded when a fancy Englishman offers to buy her saloon. She won't be selling her saloon to anyone, let alone a man with a pretty, empty-headed grin…but then, she reckons that grin just might be a lie, and a man of intelligence and cunning resides beneath.

Rupert Llewellyn has another purpose for offering to buy the pretty widow's saloon—the coal buried deep in land she owns. However, he never banked on her knowing eyes making him weak at the knees, or how his deception would burn upon his soul.

Each determined to outwit the other, they tantalize and tease until passion explodes. But can their desire bridge the lies told and trust broken?

About Cassandra Dean

Cassandra Dean is an award-winning author of historical and fantasy romance. She grew up daydreaming, inventing fantastical worlds and marvelous adventures. Once she learned to read (First phrase – To the Beach. True story), she was never without a book, reading of other people's fantastical worlds and marvelous adventures.

Cassandra is proud to call South Australia her home, where she regularly cheers on her AFL football team and creates her next tale.

Connect with Cassandra

cassandradean.com

facebook.com/AuthorCassandraDean

twitter.com/authorCassDean

instagram.com/authorcassdean

bookbub.com/authors/cassandra-dean

To learn about exclusive content, upcoming releases and giveaways,
join Cassandra's mailing list:

cassandradean.com/extras/subscribe

Printed in Great Britain
by Amazon